WESTERN

Rugged men looking for love...

Training The K-9 Companion
Jill Kemerer

The Cowboy's
Marriage Bargain
Deborah Clack

MILLS & BOON

TRAINING THE K-9 COMPANION
© 2024 by Ripple Effect Press, LLC
Philippine Copyright 2024
Australian Copyright 2024
New Zealand Copyright 2024

First Published 2024
First Australian Paperback Edition 2024
ISBN 978 1 038 91079 0

THE COWBOY'S MARRIAGE BARGAIN
© 2024 by Deborah Clack
Philippine Copyright 2024
Australian Copyright 2024
New Zealand Copyright 2024

First Published 2024
First Australian Paperback Edition 2024
ISBN 978 1 038 91079 0

Published by
Harlequin Mills & Boon
An imprint of Harlequin Enterprises (Australia) Pty Limited
(ABN 47 001 180 918), a subsidiary of HarperCollins
Publishers Australia Pty Limited
(ABN 36 009 913 517)
Level 19, 201 Elizabeth Street
SYDNEY NSW 2000 AUSTRALIA

MIX
Paper | Supporting
responsible forestry
FSC® C001695
FSC
www.fsc.org

Cover art used by arrangement with Harlequin Books S.A.. All rights reserved.

Printed and bound in Australia by McPherson's Printing Group

Training The K-9 Companion

Jill Kemerer

MILLS & BOON

Jill Kemerer writes novels with love, humour and faith. Besides spoiling her mini dachshund and keeping up with her busy kids, Jill reads stacks of books, lives for her morning coffee and gushes over fluffy animals. She resides in Ohio with her husband and two children. Jill loves connecting with readers, so please visit her website, jillkemerer.com, or contact her at PO Box 2802, Whitehouse, OH 43571.

And therefore will the Lord wait,
that he may be gracious unto you, and therefore
will he be exalted, that he may have mercy upon you:
for the Lord is a God of judgment:
blessed are all they that wait for him.
—*Isaiah* 30:18

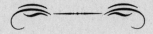

DEDICATION

To everyone taking a leap of faith.
I know all about starting over someplace new.
May the Lord bless you.

CHAPTER ONE

As USUAL, THE restlessness snuck up on him, and, too late, Cade Moulten realized his mistake. Offering to help his mother train a therapy dog was just another attempt to atone for his past.

He couldn't back out now. He wouldn't if he could. Cade had other reasons—good ones—for being here.

"It's not much to look at, is it?" His mother, Christy Moulten, sat in the passenger seat of his truck and stared at the small industrial building with faded gray aluminum siding. Next to it, a matching structure roughly three times its size shared the parking lot. The early June sunshine began to fade as the day wound down.

Cade cut the engine, and his mom bent to pick up her purse. A few months shy of turning sixty-four, his mother hadn't slowed a bit. Her stylish blond bob, subtle makeup and smile lines gave her the appearance of someone who enjoyed life, but she also had a stubborn streak wider than a country mile.

At thirty-five, he'd mellowed to the point of not minding driving her around town whenever her driver's license was suspended—and that was often—nor did he mind living with her in the big house on the ranch. Kept her out of trouble.

Maybe they kept each other out of trouble.

He pocketed his keys. "What's it supposed to look like? It's a vet clinic, not a spa, Ma."

Cade had personally taken a loss on this property by selling it to the new veterinarian and her father for pennies on the dollar. Anything to convince a vet to take a chance on moving to Jewel River. When Dr. Bill Banks, the only veterinarian within two hours of here, retired last fall, it had affected every rancher and pet owner in this swath of Wyoming.

Jewel River needed a veterinarian ASAP.

Cade needed one, too. For his ranch and to be on call when Moulten Stables opened this fall. Ideally, his new horse-boarding venture would have an equine-certified vet, but they were hard to come by in rural Wyoming. Any animal doctor was. How much experience did the new vet have with horses?

"I don't know." Mom's nose crinkled in distaste as she shrugged. "I was hoping she'd have a nice sign and a few potted flowers to make the entrance more inviting. The beat-up siding and chain-link fence surrounding the property leaves a lot to be desired."

"Cut her some slack. The clinic isn't even open for business. She could be waiting for her father to arrive before updating the exterior. He's going to have plenty of renovations in order to turn that old warehouse into a service-dog training center."

"I suppose it doesn't matter. I'm thankful she found us a dog and is helping us train it. When I think of how happy it will make your grandmother and all the other nursing-home residents to have a dog visit them…well, I can't wait to get started. Plus, I miss having a dog around to spoil."

Cade wouldn't argue with that. Trudy Moulten was his only living grandparent, and he'd always been close to his paternal grandmother. She'd blanketed him and his younger brother, Ty, with love, affection and homemade treats as they were growing up and into adulthood. He couldn't count how many times she'd pointed him back to Jesus when he was getting in trouble.

He'd gotten in trouble a lot.

Probably would still be getting into trouble if his days on Wall Street hadn't ended so abruptly.

He stepped out of the truck at the same time his mother did. Their doors shut in unison, and they walked together across old blacktop with the occasional weed popping through.

He wished Nana hadn't broken a hip and become wheelchair bound. Ever since she'd moved into the nursing home last year, her dementia from Alzheimer's had been rapidly progressing. The doctors said she was entering the moderately severe stage. The impractical side of Cade hoped the comfort of having a therapy dog visiting her on a regular basis would slow the progress. The practical side of him knew it wouldn't make much of a difference. The dog would bring her joy, though, and that alone would make these training sessions worthwhile.

Besides, his late father would want him to help. Pete Moulten had been gone for six years now, and Cade missed him every day. The last time they'd been together, Cade had been living the high life in New York City. The memories of Dad's visit would always sting. Words had been said. Feelings hurt. Not long after, his father had died unexpectedly from an aggressive cancer they'd known nothing about. And ever since, Cade had been trying to be a man his father would be proud of, the one he'd raised him to be.

He'd never be that man.

He'd made mistakes. Mistakes no one knew about. Mistakes he didn't want anyone to know about.

Most people around here saw him as a successful rancher and a financial genius who'd climbed the ladder of Wall Street by the age of twenty-eight. None of them knew what a slippery climb it had been. And he hoped they'd never find out.

"What kind of dog do you think she picked out for us?" Mom paused when they reached the front door.

"Hopefully, a golden retriever. They're friendly and easy to be around." He held the door open for her, and she went inside.

"But they shed something terrible. I was thinking more along the lines of a cocker spaniel. Smaller. Less difficult for me to handle."

"I guess we'll find out."

"I guess so," Mom said. "She said to go straight to the back."

A construction zone greeted them, and they made their way through a small waiting room and unfinished reception area to proceed down a hall with several doors on either side. Cade assumed they were examination rooms. At the end of the hall, they went through another door and emerged into a large, open warehouse space. Empty kennels in a variety of sizes were stacked haphazardly on the concrete floor as if they'd recently been unpacked.

And then Cade saw her. Mackenzie Howard—Dr. Mackenzie Howard—the woman he'd talked to on the phone several times last summer in the hopes she'd take a chance and move to their town. Thankfully, she'd left Cheyenne to start her own practice right here in Jewel River.

He hadn't expected Mackenzie to be around his age. Hadn't realized she'd be so tall. So assured. So absolutely stunning.

Why he'd pictured her in her late forties, he couldn't say. Her slightly husky voice perhaps? The woman striding their way had long strawberry blond hair, hooded midnight blue eyes, high cheekbones, thin lips and a row of not-quite-straight white teeth. She was wearing jeans, a gray T-shirt and athletic shoes.

Her style was simple. Unfussy. If she had on any makeup, he couldn't detect it.

"Hi there." She stopped near where they were standing. "You must be Christy. I'm Mackenzie." She held out her hand, and his mom shook it and sandwiched Mackenzie's with her other one.

"It is such a pleasure to meet you," Mom said. "Should I call you Dr. Howard?"

Her throaty chuckle hit Cade in the gut. Gorgeous and unpretentious. Not a good combination if he wanted to avoid trouble. And he did want to avoid trouble. He hadn't dated in a good long while, and he planned on keeping it that way. His ethical lapse at his job in the city had made him question his values. How could he be sure he wouldn't mess up again?

He couldn't. And until he was sure he had integrity, he refused to get close to a woman. It would only end badly.

"Call me Mackenzie."

"Okay." Mom shifted and smiled at him. "This is my son Cade."

"We finally meet." Mackenzie thrust her hand to him.

"Nice to meet you." A prickly feeling simmered at the base of his neck as he shook her hand.

"Yeah," she said with a grin, "I feel like we're old buddies after all the conversations we had last year."

Buddies? She might think they were pals, but his pulse didn't race like this when he was around his friends.

He gave her a controlled smile. "We're glad you're finally here."

"I'm glad to be here. Dad can't wait to join me. Only a few more weeks of traveling and he'll move here for good."

Last September, Cade had tried to convince her to relocate to Jewel River, but she'd insisted on waiting until her father could come, too. As a trainer of service dogs, her dad traveled to teach people with disabilities how to handle their new dogs, and Mackenzie had decided to work temporarily with a large animal veterinarian in Montana to get acquainted with the typical problems ranchers faced.

Personally, Cade was glad she'd brushed up on large animal care. He had a gut feeling the luxury vacation companies he was courting to winter their horses with Moulten Stables would expect him to have a vet available with extensive experience treating horses. Without their business, he might not be able to offer low rates to the locals. One of the reasons he was opening the stables was to provide horses for rent to teens who wanted to join the rodeo team.

"Well, we're thrilled to have you." His mom beamed. A cautionary tingle went down his spine. His mother was a confirmed matchmaker. She'd been trying to get "her boys" married off for years. She'd only stopped badgering Ty after he'd gotten engaged, but Zoey had died from cystic fibrosis before the wedding. That had been almost five years ago. Ty hadn't been the same since.

And that meant their mother focused her matchmaking efforts on Cade.

Christy considered any single woman a potential bride. And by any, he meant *any*. Only a few months ago, his mother had casually tried to set him up on a date with a recently divorced school librarian who was ten years older than him and had four kids. Cade sighed. Mackenzie had no idea what was about to hit her.

"Are you ready to meet your new dog?" Mackenzie's hands were in the prayer position near her chest.

"Yes." Mom's eyes sparkled. Whether it was from the thought of seeing the dog, the idea of him and Mackenzie together, or both, Cade didn't know, nor did he care.

He never should have offered to join her for these training sessions.

Do it for Nana.

He mentally girded himself. *Fine.* It would be worth the discomfort if it meant bringing even a smidgeon of joy to Nana's life.

It wasn't as if he'd had a choice in the matter, anyhow. Two weeks ago, Mom had attempted to park in front of Annie's Bakery. Her car had jumped the curb and ended up partially on the sidewalk. Sheriff Smith had caught her in the act. There went her license for another ninety days.

Cade *had* to drive her here. Ubers and taxis weren't a thing in Jewel River.

Mackenzie disappeared through the door into the clinic area. Cade didn't even peek at his mother. If he saw the gleaming, scheming, wedding-dreaming expression on her face—the one that said she'd found Cade's bride—he would lose his temper and get into it with her right there.

Not happening.

In no time at all, Mackenzie returned with the smallest, fluffiest dog he'd ever seen. She kept a firm hold on its leash as it pranced their way.

His mother gasped, bringing her hands to her mouth. Then she crouched as the little peach fluffball spun in circles before her.

"This is Tulip." Mackenzie smiled.

"Are you sure this is the right one?" Cade squinted at the pint-size ball of fuzz. He wiped his palm down his cheek. "I've seen raccoons three times its size."

His mom rose and shifted to stand next to Mackenzie. They gave him identical glares.

Double trouble.

That right there was a problem. His mom was bad enough. Cade had a feeling Mackenzie was equally formidable.

"Is she a Pomeranian?" His mother turned to Mackenzie.

"Yes, she's three years old. Her former owner was an elderly woman who passed away. Her son couldn't keep the dog, so a local animal shelter took her in. Dad has a number of contacts who call him when they have a dog with potential to be a therapy or service dog."

"Where has she been staying?" Cade asked. "Tulip, right?"

"Yes, Tulip. She's been staying with me. She's a sweetheart. Very in tune with people's moods, and she's surprisingly mellow for a toy breed."

Tulip trotted on tiny legs over to him. Her face was cute. Big brown eyes. He bent and let the dog sniff his hand. She nudged the side of it with her little brown nose, and he chuckled. "You want me to pet you, huh?"

Her tongue stuck out as if to say yes. Her pale peach fur was as soft as it looked. She ate up the attention.

"I've been working with her on basic commands," Mackenzie said. "She's smart. A fast learner. She has a few bad habits, but I think she'll overcome them with time. Tulip, come." Tulip immediately turned and headed toward her. She gave the dog a small treat and patted her head. Mackenzie handed Christy the leash. "Here, I'll let you get to know her."

Within seconds, his mom scooped up Tulip and petted her. The dog twisted to lick her face, and she laughed.

"Actually, Christy, that's one of the behaviors I'm trying to stop. Tulip is not allowed to lick faces." Mackenzie sounded pleasant enough, but Cade recognized the strength in her tone.

"She's just giving me a little kiss." Mom hugged the dog and set her back on the ground.

"When you take her to the nursing home, she can't lick the residents' faces. She needs to be calm, sit nicely and allow them to pet her."

"That's all well and good, but I'll be her owner, her person, her mommy." She gave Mackenzie a pointed look. Cade's eyelid started doing the flickering thing it did whenever she used that tone.

"I can see we have a lot to cover." Mackenzie shrugged pleasantly. "While Tulip is very cute, she isn't a baby or a child. She's a mature dog, and we're going to have expectations for her. You'll work with her at home, and each week I'll give you more instructions. Six weeks should be enough to train her to be a therapy dog. Like I said, she's very smart. My dad is qualified to do the certification testing for her to become a Canine Good Citizen. She's a bright little pup."

"Six weeks, huh?" Mom couldn't take her eyes off Tulip.

"If you work with her at home, yes."

"I suppose you're going to tell me she can't sleep with me." She looked crestfallen.

"Her crate would be best at night. During the day, you'll want to spend plenty of time with her and give her lots of attention and affection. In the meantime, we can go over the basic commands she already knows, and then we can load up your car with her supplies." Mackenzie gave Cade a confused glance. "You're welcome to stay here with us or wait in the reception area. It's up to you."

"What? Oh, no, Mackenzie." Mom shook her head with an amused smile. "Cade is going to be learning everything, too. Since Tulip will be living with both of us, it's best we're on the same page. He volunteered, didn't you?"

At least his mom hadn't pinched his cheeks during her speech. He didn't have a chance to answer because Mackenzie spoke first. "I'm afraid I'm missing something. Are you two sharing the dog? I don't know about her living in two separate homes."

"No, no, nothing like that. Cade and I live together." To his horror, Mom came over to him and wrapped her arm around his waist, then leaned her cheek against his upper arm.

Mackenzie's eyes widened, and her mouth formed an O.

Cade didn't embarrass easily. In fact, not much fazed him. But the flames licking his neck had to be turning his cheeks brick red. This was *not* the first impression he wanted to make with Mackenzie. Did she think he was a mama's boy?

A slew of justifications came to mind.

My dad died, and I'm looking out for my mother. I need to live at the ranch because I'm in charge of it. I'm independently wealthy, not sponging off my mom. Her driver's license was suspended for the seven hundredth time, and I'm making life easier on myself by joining her since I have to drive her anyway.

"We'll both be training Tulip," he said. Why explain anything more? It would serve no purpose. Besides, none of those things were the full truth.

Helping train Tulip was another attempt to be a good guy. But he wasn't. The vain, insecure side of him was still there. He'd been trying to bury it ever since his father passed away.

No sense in dwelling on the past. He just wanted this meet and greet with the dog to be over.

WHILE SHE WAS certain Tulip would thrive with the Moultens, Mackenzie wasn't convinced Christy had what it would take to train Tulip to be a therapy dog. The next six weeks would prove it one way or the other. But that was the least of her worries at the moment. She'd never been the sole veterinarian of a community before, and she wasn't certain she was ready to treat large animals. Small ones? No problem. But emergency surgery on a cow or a horse? Questionable.

She'd done her best to put the past behind her, but the C-section gone wrong on a family's beloved horse during her residency was always there like a rock lodged in her gut. She'd never forget the children's wails or the lawsuit that followed. She'd been cleared of wrongdoing, but the emotional damage remained. All these years later and she still got nervous at the thought of repeating that nightmare.

Mackenzie motioned for Cade to follow her to one of the patient rooms where she'd stored all of Tulip's supplies. It had taken only twenty minutes to show the mother-and-son duo the basic commands to use with Tulip. As much as Mackenzie had enjoyed meeting them both, she was dying to check out every nook and

cranny of the trailer she'd had outfitted to be
her mobile vet clinic, which had arrived only
an hour ago.

Cade—all six muscular and rugged feet of
him—followed closely behind her, throwing
her off slightly. And that in itself was strange.
Yes, like most women, she appreciated a fine-
looking man, but at thirty-two, she didn't see
herself finding *the one*.

Her life wasn't exactly conducive to romance.
In Cheyenne, she and the senior vet had split
the on-call duties. Here? She'd be the only veterinarian for miles, and she anticipated being on
call 24-7. Plus, she wasn't girlie. She liked jeans
and sweats and old T-shirts. Her beauty routine consisted of brushing her hair and swiping
on lip gloss. Occasionally, she'd braid her hair.
Anything more seemed too fancy.

In addition to the no-time factor, she couldn't
seem to shake her skeptical nature. She blamed
her mother for that. How many times had Bonnie Howard disappeared from her life, only to
show up unannounced, claiming she missed
Mackenzie, and then vanish a few weeks later
after Mackenzie had loaned her money that was
never repaid? Too many to count.

It had been three years since she'd seen her mother. She counted it as a blessing.

Her parents had divorced when she was ten, and after a few years of the nomad lifestyle with her mom, Mackenzie had insisted on living with her father full-time. Best decision she'd ever made.

"Here we are." Mackenzie opened the door to the second room on the left. "I packed her crate with treats, toys, food dishes, a therapy-dog vest, harness—you name it. Oh, and here's her doggy booster seat for the car." Mackenzie reached for the crate's handle at the same time Cade did. Their hands touched. She almost dropped the handle.

Yes, it had been too long since she'd been on a date. She'd forgotten what it was like to be attracted to a man. Cade threw her off-balance. And she didn't need anything else disrupting her life at the moment.

"I've got it." His cowboy hat tipped forward, shading his eyes. She'd discretely checked him out earlier when he'd taken off said cowboy hat. He had dark blue eyes and short, tousled dark blond hair. A straight nose, full eyebrows, broad shoulders. His expensive brand of jeans fit him well.

"I thought you'd be older," she blurted out. But then, she tended to say whatever was on her mind.

A grin slowly spread across his face. "I thought you would be, too."

"I get that." She lifted a shoulder in a shrug. "It's my voice. Raspy."

"I like it."

He did? Mackenzie had no idea how to respond, so she regrouped, pointing to the unopened bag of food nearby. "Um, there's her food. One cup a day. No more."

"Got it. Is this it?" He hauled the large bag onto his shoulder as if it weighed no more than a pillow. The crate dangled from his other hand.

"Yes. That should do it. Here, I'll show you how to install the booster seat in your car." She headed to the doorway, taking care not to touch him as she passed by. The faint scent of his cologne added to his masculine appeal.

Until now, she hadn't really thought about Cade Moulten beyond the fact he was the one who'd convinced her to start a new practice here and had sold her and her father this property. But now that they were face-to-face?

She had questions. Ones she wouldn't ask. An internet search would be a better place to start.

Later.

"How much experience do you have with horses?" he asked as they continued down the hallway to the back room.

The question made her uneasy. Had he found out about the incident where she'd lost both the mother and foal? The lawsuit was public record. Her acquittal was, too.

"I've worked with horses. Not a lot. Why?" She glanced back at him.

"I'm in the process of opening a horse-boarding facility on the outskirts of town, and I need to have an experienced vet on call."

She opened the door to the back room for him. The past months had boosted her confidence in treating horses. Eventually, she might even enjoy it. She'd always wanted a horse of her own. Had ridden plenty of her friends' horses as a teen. But until she faced an emergency with a large animal, she couldn't say for sure if she'd be up to the task. Only time would tell.

"I'm pretty much on call for everyone in the surrounding area. I know the basics—I'm licensed to treat large and small animals—but I've been treating mostly pets for the past several years. If you need an expert, I suggest finding someone else."

His jaw seemed to jut out. Stubborn...like his mother. Mackenzie wasn't fooled by Christy's warm, welcoming demeanor. The woman knew how to get her way. Mackenzie admired her for it.

"All set?" Christy, holding Tulip in her arms, beamed and joined them as they continued to the door leading outside. On the blacktop, Mackenzie gave the trailer a longing glance, then followed Cade to his truck.

"I just love our little princess," Christy said. Tulip licked her face again. Mackenzie would have to ignore it for now.

Cade's truck looked top-of-the-line and brand-new. He didn't seem to be hurting for money, so why was he living with his mother?

None of her business.

"This buckles into the seat..." Mackenzie quickly installed the doggy booster seat in Cade's truck and showed him how to attach her collar to it.

"Thank you for everything, Mackenzie." Christy hugged her. "If you need anything, give us a call. I hope to see a lot more of you.

Cade does, too, don't you?" With the back of her hand, she playfully slapped his stomach.

He sighed loudly and gave Mackenzie a tight smile. "We'll let you get settled. If you're not busy tomorrow night, you're welcome to join us at the community center for a Jewel River Legacy Club meeting. It will give you a chance to get to know some of the residents."

"I'd like that."

"It starts at seven."

"Thanks. I'll be there." Mackenzie backed up a few steps and waved to them as they buckled in and drove away.

Good. The meeting would give her the opportunity to get the word out that she was ready to treat large animals. Her trailer was fully equipped to haul to any ranch or farm in the area. As for pets, the clinic's renovations would take a few more weeks before it would be ready to open.

Mackenzie strode between the two buildings where the mobile vet trailer was parked. Working with Dr. Johan up in Montana had been exactly what she'd needed before moving here. She'd gained much-needed experience with cattle and the occasional horse, plus Dr. Johan had helped her order this trailer and all the equipment. She'd driven his mobile vet clinic so often, hauling this one would feel like second nature at this point.

She wasn't sure what the future held, but she knew one thing: whatever troubles she faced would be worth it to live in the same town as her father again. It had been too long since they'd spent time together on a regular basis. She couldn't wait until he moved to Jewel River, too.

Growing up, she'd helped him train and take care of the service dogs. She'd loved the simple dinners with her father. They'd discuss the dogs and their days. She missed her dad more than she cared to admit. That was why she'd taken a leap of faith to move here. Dad had been the one who believed in her enough to encourage her to branch out on her own. And he'd suggested opening the small vet clinic three days a week so she could focus on the mobile vet duties the other two.

He'd also assured her that if working with large animals proved too much for her, she could always focus on pets and hire another vet to round out the practice. It would make life easier for her, but she didn't want to.

It was time to overcome her nerves about treating horses and cattle. It was time to find out what she was really made of.

CHAPTER TWO

DESPITE THE TEMPTATION to eavesdrop on his mom's conversation with Mary Corning, Cade focused on the entrance to the community center. He was surprised Mackenzie hadn't arrived yet. The meeting would be starting soon. He wanted to introduce her to some of the members, partly because he felt responsible for convincing her to move to Jewel River and partly to show he was a respected member of the community and not some man-child dependent on his mother.

"…and I told her no way that was going to be enough dessert for an O'Leary family reunion, but she insisted two dozen cookies and a pan of brownies would suffice…" Mary's voice rose as his mother made sympathetic murmurs. "I mean has she looked at her brother lately? John's only a few inches shy of seven feet tall. The man can eat…"

Cade mentally conceded two dozen cookies and a pan of brownies would not be enough for an O'Leary family reunion. Mary was correct about that.

Where was Mackenzie? Had she already gotten called out to a ranch? Yesterday, while they'd loaded Tulip's supplies in the backseat of his truck, Cade had noticed the trailer parked next to the clinic. It looked new. A mobile vet trailer would be a big improvement over the plastic bins of outdated equipment Doc Banks had kept in his ancient Ford. Cade would have to ask Mackenzie about the trailer's features at some point. It would be a good selling point for the clients he was hoping would board their horses with him. He'd been courting Forestline Adventures for the past couple of months but, so far, hadn't gotten a firm commitment from them.

"Just tell her to order lemon bars from Annie's Bakery and make a sheet cake. It will all work out." Mom flourished her hand as Mary mumbled something Cade didn't make out. "Tulip? Oh, yes, our little sweetie is a delight. Follows me everywhere. And Tulip just loves Cade. Mackenzie couldn't have picked out a better dog for us. I am *so* glad she moved here. And Cade is, too, aren't you, Cade?"

He ignored his mother. The door opened, and Mackenzie, with her hair pulled back in a ponytail and wearing jeans and a T-shirt, slipped inside and headed straight to an empty chair at the table across from the one where he sat. Erica Cambridge took her position in the front to speak to everyone sitting at the tables shoved together to form a U.

"Oh, there's Mackenzie now." His mom's voice lowered as she spoke to Mary. "Isn't she a cutie?"

He braced himself for his mother to try to drag him into the conversation. If Mom publicly asked him if he thought she was "a cutie," he would mentally lose it.

Erica clapped her hands to get everyone's attention. Then Clem Buckley, a retired rancher tougher than a two-dollar steak, led everyone in the Pledge of Allegiance and the Lord's Prayer. Erica then went through old business.

"Angela, where are we at with this year's Shakespeare-in-the-Park film?" She addressed Angela Zane, a good-natured woman and one of the livelier members of Jewel River Legacy Club.

"I'm happy to report that after last summer's smashing success of *Romeo and Juliet: Wyoming*

Style, Joey had a big uptick in people wanting to take part in *A Jewel River Midsummer Night's Dream*. He had to bring in an assistant—little Lindsey Parker, Joe and Abby's youngest. She's the one who sprained her ankle trying to do those hurdles at the track meet last year. Wasn't her fault she couldn't clear them. They were set too tall, if you ask me—"

"Yes, we all know Lindsey." Erica had mastered the art of moving along the prone-to-get-sidetracked members during these meetings. Angela's grandson, Joey, was a junior in high school with a talent for creating and editing videos. Whenever he made one related to a club proposal, it tended to add spice to the meetings. Cade, personally, enjoyed all the special effects. "How is she helping Joey?"

"He put Lindsey in charge of auditions, and she's working with him on plot development. Joey wants to really show off our part of Wyoming and give the story a Jewel River feel."

"I'm sure he does," Erica said. "Will everything be ready by mid-August?"

"Oh, yes." Angela nodded with enthusiasm. "Don't you worry, hon, the film will be ready in time. Just like last year."

"Are the characters falling into piles of cow

patties in this one, too?" Clem asked loudly. A few titters spread throughout the room.

"I'm not sure. I can ask Joey if you'd like." Angela didn't seem to grasp that Clem was being sarcastic. "I do know they're trying to figure out how to add a herd of pronghorns in one of the scenes, and I believe the strange character—Bottom, is it?—his head might be turned into a moose instead of a donkey. Don't you worry, Joey has a *lot* of special effects up his sleeve."

Cade wasn't surprised at all. Maybe the kid would add a rocket to this one. Who knew?

Erica checked her notes. "Let us know if Joey and Lindsey need anything from us. The online fundraiser has been set up to cover the costs of costumes, sets and equipment." She then turned to Marc Young, who headed up one of the committees. "Any updates on the empty build-ings?"

"The former industrial park still has three for sale…" Marc, a local rancher and one of Cade's good friends, had married Erica's sister, Reagan, a few months ago. Fun wedding. Cade had been one of the groomsmen. Reagan owned and operated a thriving gourmet chocolate store in town. Cade should probably stop in there soon for another box of her dark-chocolate covered caramels. His mouth watered just thinking about them.

Marc nodded toward Mackenzie. "Once Dr. Howard gets settled, her clinic and her father's service-dog training center are sure to bring traffic to the area. I think we can anticipate the other buildings getting new occupants in the near future."

"Good point," Erica said. "By the way, everyone, this is our new veterinarian." She turned her attention to Mackenzie and made a rising motion. "Why don't you stand up and tell us about yourself?"

"Hello, I'm Mackenzie Howard. I grew up in South Dakota, got my undergrad at the University of Wyoming—go Cowboys!—and was accepted into the Doctor of Veterinary Medicine program at Texas A&M. I specialized in rural and mixed animals and have been working for a veterinarian clinic in Cheyenne for the past five years."

"Do you have any experience with cattle?" Clem gave Mackenzie a cool stare.

"Yes, sir, I do. In addition to my residency, I spent the past several months working with a large animal vet up in Montana."

"What about in Cheyenne?" Clem made a sucking sound with his teeth. "What did you do there?"

The question didn't seem to fluster her. "I treated pets. Dogs, cats, the occasional wild animal."

"Hmm." Clem shrugged, appearing lukewarm about her credentials. "Takes a good cowboy years to understand the ins and outs of cattle. A couple of months ain't gonna cut it."

"Clem, will you stop grilling her?" Christy glared razor blades his way. "Mackenzie is more than qualified."

"Grilling?" Clem threw his hands up. "What did I say?"

"It's the way you're saying it. It's disrespectful."

"I just want to know if the doc here knows what she's all about."

"She knows what she's all about." An abundance of attitude came through his mother's words. Great, Mom was getting worked up. When her chin bobbed as she spoke, watch out.

"What I don't know, I'll figure out," Mackenzie said. "As a veterinarian, I feel like I learn something new every day. I suppose I always will." She calmly surveyed the rest of the room.

"If any of you have horses or cattle, I can drive out to your property with my fully equipped mobile vet trailer. It's set up and ready for business. My clinic here in town should be ready for pets by the end of the month. It'll be open Mondays, Wednesdays and Fridays to treat cats, dogs and other small animals. I'm in the process of hiring a vet tech, but I still need a part-time receptionist, so if anyone is looking for a job, send them my way."

"What kind of hours are those?" Clem sounded flabbergasted. "You're only working three days a week?"

"They're travel-vet hours." From the way her jaw tightened, Cade guessed Mackenzie's patience was wearing thin. "I often work seven days a week. I'm on call for any emergencies, and I'm leaving Tuesdays and Thursdays free for large-animal care. Like I said, the trailer's ready, so if anyone has cows or horses needing treatment, call me. Oh, I have business cards."

Mackenzie reached down and grabbed the string bag she'd set on the floor. Then she pulled out a small stack of cards and passed them to Johnny Abbot on her right. He took one and passed the stack down.

"We're grateful you're here, Mackenzie,"

Erica said. "Dr. Banks has been gracious enough to help out with emergencies, but it will be a relief to have regular treatment for our cattle and horses again. Winston Ranch will be using your services."

"I'm glad to hear it." Mackenzie nodded. A shadow passed over her face, making Cade wonder if she had regrets about moving here. Had Clem gotten to her? Or was something else going on that he wasn't aware of?

Erica moved on to the next order of business. Mary Corning admitted her lack of progress on putting together a survey on whether to add a pickleball court to Memorial Park.

"I don't know what questions to put on the survey." Mary opened her hands as her shoulders lifted.

"No one here wants to play pickleball," Clem said. "Why can't you ever suggest something practical?"

"Pickleball *is* practical. My niece in Ohio says it's all the rage there right now. I'm sure a lot of people around here would like to get in on the fun."

"Fun?" Clem said. "Riding horses is fun. Going fishing is fun. Waving a paddle around a court that would fit in a dollhouse is not fun.

Why do they call it pickleball, anyhow? Are dills involved?"

"Mary," Erica said loudly to override Clem, "why don't you talk to Janet Reese about setting up an online survey? She's done them before. And we can leave a stack of printouts at the library, too."

"I'll do that." Mary's chin rose. The meeting continued.

Cade updated everyone on his committee's progress on assessing if a workout center in town would be viable. When he finished, he counted the minutes until the meeting ended. As soon as Erica dismissed everyone, he stood, hoping to head off Mackenzie before she left.

"Oh, Mackenzie?" Mom called out so loudly it caused a few people on their way to the door to turn back and look at her. "You should join Cade's committee if you're thinking of becoming a member. You two have so much in common."

"I'm sure she doesn't have time—" Cade stopped in his tracks.

"I don't have time—" Mackenzie, wide-eyed, said.

"Will you stop your matchmaking, woman?" Clem was several feet away from Christy, and it was a good thing. Cade did not want to have to separate those two. He'd also never wanted to disappear as much as he did in this moment. So he responded the way he always did, by making it into a joke.

"Don't worry, Clem." Cade grinned. "I wouldn't be surprised if she was fixing up an online dating app for the singles in Jewel River as we speak."

"I am not—" Mom lifted her fingers in air quotes "—'fixing up an online dating app.' Although now that you mention it, I think it's a fabulous idea. You boys could certainly use it." His mom redirected all her annoyance at Clem, and Cade walked away as Clem scoffed.

"Wouldn't surprise me, you know," Clem said. "Desperate. That's what you are. You're desperate for a wedding."

"I am *not* desperate."

"Instead of worrying about your son's love life," Clem continued, "why don't you take one of those remedial driving courses? Maybe you'd be able to keep your license for more than two weeks at a time and could get yourself some independence."

"Oh, so now I'm desperate *and* dependent? I can drive just fine…" His mother's voice rose.

Cade hurried over to where Mackenzie was stuffing the remaining business cards in her string bag.

"Sorry about things getting a little heated in here. My mom and Clem can be…" He shook his head. He had no words to describe either of them. "Do you want me to introduce you to some of the members?"

She glanced around, and he realized everyone had either left or was on their way out.

"Too late." Her left cheek flashed a dimple, and he couldn't look away from it. She wriggled the bag's strings onto her shoulders. "How's Tulip settling in?"

"Great. For a small thing, she sure has a lot of personality." They both headed to the door. "She made herself right at home. Mom's spoiling her, and she's eating it up."

"Is your mom working with her on the commands we went over?"

"She is and I am, too." He held the door for her and followed her out into the warm night. "Don't worry. My mom loves to spoil kids and pets, but she's no pushover, not even with Tulip."

"That's good to hear."

They stood outside on the sidewalk in awk-

ward silence for a few moments. Several topics came to mind, but he couldn't seem to put
them into words. What was it about her that
tied his tongue into knots?

She pointed to her truck. "Well, I guess I'll
see you next week."

"Yeah." Disappointment settled over him. He
didn't want her to leave. But he couldn't seem
to toss out a charming line to make her stay.

Something was definitely wrong with him.

He rocked back on his heels. "You'll be so
busy getting calls and driving out to ranches,
you might regret our training sessions." That
was what he'd come up with? *Real smooth*.

"I hope so. I need those calls. I have a lot invested in this move." She angled her head. "But
I won't regret helping you and your mother
train Tulip. That little dog is going to brighten
a lot of people's lives."

"Yes, she will."

The glance she gave him had questions in
it…and doubts.

Why would she doubt him? He stiffened. He
wasn't one to brag. Never felt the need to list
all of his accomplishments.

But the look she'd thrown his way? Made
him want to tell her all about the large, profit-

able cattle ranch he owned thirty minutes from town. Not to mention the sprawling property on the outskirts of Jewel River where his high-end horse-boarding facility with state-of-the-art stables, riding paths and acres of fenced pastures would be located. Then there was his portfolio of investments, which included several properties right here in Jewel River.

Mackenzie knew none of it. And she didn't need to know, either. He had nothing to prove to her.

"See you on Monday," she said.

"See ya."

She turned and strolled to her truck. She clearly didn't view him as successful and inde-pendent. More like a guy joined at the hip to his mommy. Or merely one half of the mother-son team training Tulip.

It was probably better that way.

He hadn't forgotten his past. A down-to-earth woman like Mackenzie would be repulsed by his ethical lapse. If she wasn't impressed with him now, she certainly wouldn't be impressed with the old him—the one still lurking deep inside.

If he could wipe that entire time frame from his memory, he would.

The single life was his penance for his mistakes. But at times like this, he wished he could have more.

"Ah, there's my girl." Two days later on Thursday afternoon, Patrick Howard held his arms open inside the entrance of Mackenzie's clinic.

"Dad!" What a great surprise! After rising from the floor, where she'd been checking out the newly installed cabinets, Mackenzie ran to him and laughed as he hugged her. "I thought you were in Texas all week."

"Finished early." He released her and took in the reception area—still a work in progress. "This is it, huh? It's a good space. The right size. I was worried your building would be too small."

"I was, too, but it's bigger than it looks." She still couldn't get over the fact her dad was here. He looked younger than his sixty-two years. He was in good shape—worked out daily in addition to training the service dogs—and he had on a plain black T-shirt, jeans and boots. She hitched her head to the side. "Come on, I'll show you around."

She took him through all the rooms, noting

his comments and suggestions. They ended up in the large back warehouse space.

"I've already had a training session with Christy and Cade. They seem to be a good fit for Tulip."

"Did you tell them your old man taught you everything you know?" His blue eyes twinkled.

"If I didn't, I should have. You really *did* teach me everything I know about dog training."

"You wanted to learn. That's half the battle."

"It looked good on my application to get into the vet program, too."

"It sure didn't hurt." He pointed to the door. "Mind taking a break? I'm itching to check out my building."

"I am, too. I haven't been inside yet. I thought it would be fun to go through it together. Let me grab the keys." She'd been the one to pick up the keys to both buildings from the realtor when she'd arrived in town. It had taken considerable self-control for her to refrain from checking out the large building next to the clinic. Would it be full of junk? Torn up? No matter what shape it was in, her father would find a silver lining somewhere. It was his personality to find the good in things. She, on the other hand, was always preparing herself to be let down.

They emerged into the late-afternoon sunshine. A breeze kept the temperature in the low seventies, perfect in her mind.

"Any calls yet to try out the trailer?" he asked.

"Not yet." Mackenzie was trying not to let it bother her, but she was surprised she hadn't gotten a single call. All last summer, Cade had made it sound as if the veterinarian situation was dire. "I'm sure they'll start calling when they realize I'm open for business. I went to a local meeting Tuesday night to get the word out."

After the meeting, she'd settled on her couch and searched for information about Cade. She'd unearthed an article in a business trade journal about him. He'd graduated from the University of Michigan and immediately had been hired by a global investment bank in New York City. He'd quickly become a star. Been promoted multiple times. The article was from six years ago. She'd found no information since, not even a social-media profile of the man.

Something had happened to bring him back to Jewel River. But what?

"Your phone will be ringing nonstop soon."

Her father studied the exterior as they approached the entrance.

Would it? That Clem guy had been awfully confrontational. Were the ranchers around here skeptical of her skills?

Why would they be? She might be on the younger side, but she had good credentials. And she didn't think her gender was an issue. It hadn't been in the past. Still, she'd be the first to admit, she wasn't as experienced with large animals as they might have been hoping for. It didn't make her a complete novice, though.

Dad unlocked the double glass doors, and they entered a small entryway with another set of double glass doors. "This is a nice feature. The entryway will help keep out the cold."

"Good point." She continued inside, and her dad switched on the lights. "Wow."

"You can say that again. I'm glad the previous owner didn't go through with their plan to convert it into a machine shop. The fact it was a warehouse will make it easier for me to lay out the space."

Mackenzie marveled at how wide-open it was. Small windows near the ceiling were spaced apart every ten feet or so, and at the other end, a tall garage door allowed for a bay. To the right, a hallway led to offices and bathrooms.

"I have a feeling this place is going to need extra insulation and a top-notch furnace." Dad strolled to the middle of the warehouse. "And I haven't solved the problem of where the clients are going to stay while they're here learning how to handle their dogs. Obviously, their accommodations need to be accessible to people with disabilities. Have you had a chance to snoop around town much?"

"No, I haven't. Sorry." She'd been so busy trying out the equipment in the trailer and overseeing the renovations at the clinic that she hadn't ventured out beyond the grocery store and diner. "I can ask Cade for suggestions on Monday."

"Yeah, good plan. Ask him if there's a hotel or old apartments we could fix up for my clients."

"He seems to have the pulse of Jewel River."

"What makes you say that?"

Mackenzie lifted one shoulder, dragging the toe of her canvas sneaker in the dust. Her instincts were usually pretty accurate. "I mean, he sold us this property, and I wouldn't have even considered moving here if it wasn't for him."

"Well, he's a good salesman, I'll give him that."

Mackenzie knew what he was thinking. He'd reserve further comment until he met Cade in person. Her father was a good judge of character. She was curious to find out his take on the man.

Personally, she considered Cade Moulten a little too good to be true.

Too gorgeous. Too involved with the community. Too smart. Too savvy, given his experience in New York finance. Too available to help his mother.

Why was he so generous with his time? Did the guy have a selfish bone in his body? There must be an ulterior motive in there somewhere.

Dad crouched to inspect an electrical outlet. The bundled wires climbed the wall, then edged along the ceiling. "I don't like exposed wires. I'll have to do something about those, too."

"Add it to your list."

"Have you heard from your mother?" Dad straightened to stare at her.

"No." Where had that question come from? "Why?"

"Just wondering. Did you tell her you moved?"

"Why would I do that?"

"I'm sure she'd like to know."

"So she can drive up here and gush about how great I'm doing and then vanish with barely a wave goodbye? No thanks." She hated hearing the bitterness in her tone. She'd been praying to let go of her anger toward her mother, but every time she thought of the woman, her chest tightened and something hard locked around her heart.

"She loves you, Mackenzie."

"She has a funny way of showing it."

"Like I always say, she is who she is."

"And like I always say, it's not my job to care. I don't know why you defend her." She turned away from him, hoping to suppress the adrenaline firing through her veins.

He sighed. "I don't know, either. Maybe I wish you could have known your mom when she was full of energy and ideas. Back when she cared."

"Yeah, well, the full of energy and ideas I remember. Living with her was pure chaos. As for her caring about us? Sorry, you're on your own there."

With sadness in his eyes, he slowly nodded. "You know a good place to eat around here? I'm hungry."

"That I *can* help you with." She grinned.

"You're going to love Dixie B's. Huge portions and down-home cooking."

"Now you're talking."

As Mackenzie led the way out of the building, Cade crowded her mind. He had a close relationship with his mother. Where was his dad? Maybe they'd divorced like her own parents had. Maybe his father had passed away… or was she wrong on both counts? He might be around. She didn't think so, though.

The way Christy acted made Mackenzie think she relied on Cade. Strange, since the woman seemed so independent. The two were together all the time, though. And Christy definitely had matchmaking on her mind.

Mackenzie shivered. She'd hate to break it to the Moultens, but the more Mackenzie was pushed in one direction, the more she dug in her heels to go the other way. Regardless of what Christy hoped for, Mackenzie was not looking for a boyfriend.

Her work already took up most of her life, and something told her getting her practice up and running would take every free minute she had.

She had no time or room in her life for romance. And she planned on keeping it that way.

"I WISH I could bring you with me, Tulip. But it will be a few more weeks before you can meet my nana." Cade petted the dog lounging on his lap as he sat on the sectional in the living room Friday afternoon. It had been a typical day. This morning he'd checked cattle with his ranch manager for a few hours, then he'd gotten cleaned up and dropped off Mom at the nursing home. From there, she had plans with friends to do something or another.

After dropping her off, he'd made the five-minute drive to Moulten Stables to check the construction progress. Everything was on track. So why did he have this nagging worry that something would go wrong?

Tulip let out a contented sigh and snuggled deeper into his lap. She'd blended into their household so quickly it was hard to remember what life had been like without her. He shifted, and her little head rose as if to say, *Don't even think about getting up, mister.*

"I know, I know. It's naptime. When isn't it, though?" He chuckled to himself. He enjoyed the feel of her soft fur. "We'll hang out when I get back."

Every evening, he and his mother had been

taking her on a stroll around the property to get her used to walking loosely beside them. Tulip seemed to love the walks. She'd sniff around the trees and trot beside them with her head held high.

"I really do need to go." Cade picked up Tulip as he stood. Cradling her to his chest, he smiled at her. "Soon, you'll get to come with me and sit on Nana's lap. She loves dogs."

Tulip licked his hand, and he laughed.

A few minutes later, he got into his truck. He texted Ty before starting it up. I'm on my way to Nana's.

His brother's response came right away. Leaving now.

As soon as Cade arrived at the nursing home, he got out of his truck. Ty came over, and Cade pulled him into a half hug, then hitched his thumb toward the entrance. "You ready for this?"

"As ready as I'll ever be." Two years younger than him, Ty always seemed to have the weight of the world on his shoulders. Spontaneous smiles were rare occurrences, and as much as Cade and Mom hoped time would heal his wounds, Ty was as reclusive as he'd been when Zoey passed away.

He missed his brother. Wanted the old Ty back. But he'd take this version of him over the one who wouldn't leave his house. Any progress was better than none. It was one of the reasons he insisted Ty visit their grandmother with him every Friday afternoon. Got him out and about.

"Let's catch up a minute first."

Ty was physically similar to him but on the leaner side. Their personalities were where they differed. Cade was outgoing, where Ty was reserved. After Dad died, Cade had quickly realized he wasn't suited to full-time ranching, so he'd hired an experienced manager to take care of the cattle. Ty, on the other hand, was happiest riding horseback around his ranch every day, preferably alone.

They each had their own land and their own cattle operations thanks to their father's business decisions. After Cade went away to college, Dad had split the massive ranch into two and continued to run half while Ty took over the other part. They'd all agreed if Cade changed his mind about his career, he'd take over their father's portion. If he didn't, Ty would run both. Their father's death had made that decision for Cade. He'd moved back to Wyoming permanently a week after the funeral.

"Do you think she'll recognize us this time?" Ty asked.

"She did last week. I'm hoping these visits will be easier when Tulip can come with us."

"Yeah, she'll like having a dog to pet." Ty swatted away a fly. "Remember Skippy?"

"How could I forget? Droopiest eyes on a hound I've ever seen."

"How's the training going? Mom not so subtly suggested I get to know Mackenzie better, and I told her I would block her number if she mentioned it again."

"Is that how you get her off your back? I wish I could do that. It's a little harder when you live with her."

Ty's eyebrows rose as if to say *don't I know it*. Over the years, Cade had learned there was nothing he could do to prevent his mother's schemes to get daughters-in-law and, eventually, grandkids. He simply threw himself into his work and ignored her.

"How are the stables coming along?"

"Great. They're framing the stalls next week. I reached out to the companies hosting outdoor retreats around the state. Forestline Adventures might be interested in wintering their horses here."

"Are they the ones with all the luxury rentals?"

"Yeah, they organize hunting and fishing trips from first thaw to mid-October. Expensive trips. They need reliable, healthy horses for their clients, and rumor has it they're tired of the hassle of taking care of the horses all winter. I guess they've been struggling to find good help, and they lost two horses to injury and illness last year."

"That's where you come in." Was that a hint of a smile on Ty's face? Oh, to see a full smile again. Cade tried not to be greedy, but his brother meant the world to him. *God, please bring my brother back. He deserves to be happy. Unlike me.*

"Yes. I can board all their current horses and rent them any additional horses they might need in the summer."

"Sounds like a win-win for you both."

"Yeah, but I have a feeling they're going to want a veterinarian on call specifically certified for horses."

Ty let out a snort. "They aren't going to find any of those around here. Near Jackson Hole, maybe."

"Yeah." He hadn't brought up the veterinarian situation to them, but before he could present them with a contract, it would need to be addressed. He'd already waited to begin construction on the stables until Mackenzie and her father had bought his buildings. He'd needed to be certain there would be a vet in the area before moving forward with his plans.

And now he couldn't stop wondering if having a vet was enough.

He needed the right vet.

What was the point in going through the expense of developing the property if he couldn't be certain it would be profitable?

It never stopped you before. You were born taking risks.

And look where it had gotten him.

"If you're worried," Ty said, "why don't you talk to them about it? Now that we have a vet practicing in town, they should be fine."

But that was where his brother was wrong. Ty didn't know how life outside of this small town worked, and Cade did. He understood how the elite thought and lived—he'd been one of them for years.

Companies like Forestline Adventures catered to extremely wealthy business people. Everything had to be the best, including the horses, the stables, the facilities and even the veterinarian treating the horses. All of it wrapped around status.

"I'll figure it out." Cade clapped his hand on Ty's shoulder. "Let's go see Nana."

They strode together to the glass doors leading into the brick one-story building. Red, purple and white flowers waved a cheery greeting. Inside the building, Charlene Parker, one of his mother's best friends, raised her hand in greeting from the reception desk. In her late fifties, she wore scrubs and had a big smile. Her daughter, Janey, had gotten engaged to Lars Denton at Christmas, and Charlene liked to give Cade all the updates on the upcoming wedding, whether he wanted them or not. He wasn't into weddings and all that, but it made her happy to tell him, and it didn't cost him a thing to listen.

"Howdy, boys, Miss Trudy is in good spirits today."

That was a relief. "Thanks, Charlene. How've you been?"

"Good, hon. Janey had a hiccup with the florist. We're trying to figure out the bouquets. Your mother has been my rock. I don't know what I'd do without her."

"If you want to borrow her, give me a holler.

Keep her at your place for a while. A month. Two. More." He always teased about his mother. Charlene ate it up.

"Oh, you!" She waved him off and laughed. "I have to tell you I do agree with her on one thing—it's a crime that you two strapping cowboys are single. If my Janey was still on the market, you can guarantee I'd want her to snatch up one of you boys."

"It's a shame she's taken." Cade grinned. He glanced at Ty. His brother looked positively green. "We'd better get in there."

As they made their way down the hallway, Ty gave him a sideways glance. "That's why I stay home."

"She doesn't mean anything by it." Cade focused on the wreath his mom had hung on Nana's door up ahead.

"Are you sure about that?" Ty sounded a little disgusted and slightly terrified. "No one is *snatching* me up. I'm done with women."

Cade knew better than to argue when Ty was about to launch into one of his *I'm done with women* rants. Next would be a lament about how he'd had the only woman he'd ever loved, and God had taken her from him, and he'd never love again. Cade didn't blame him, but the familiar words did get stale after a while.

Cade stopped at the open door and knocked twice before entering. "Hi, Nana."

Sitting in her wheelchair, she turned and smiled at them. "Cade! Did you bring Ty today?"

"I'm here, Nana." Ty removed his cowboy hat. They took turns bending to hug her, then they each sat in a chair to visit for a while.

The room was nice enough. She didn't have to share it with anyone, and his mom had added plants and some of Nana's favorite pictures from home. His mother also decorated the bulletin board every month with a new theme. At the moment, it had a purple and yellow border and pictures of pansies and kittens on it.

"How are you feeling today?" Cade asked.

"As good as can be." Her cloudy blue eyes brightened. "We had chocolate ice cream and listened to a man play guitar."

Every afternoon, the nursing home had activities for any of the residents who wanted to participate.

"What kind of music?" Ty asked.

"All kinds. I clapped along, but I sure would

have liked to dance. Your grandfather was a fine dancer. He'd twirl me around like I weighed less than a feather."

He and Ty laughed. "You probably did." She'd always been a bitty thing.

"Your mother said there will be a little dog coming soon."

"Yes, her name's Tulip. She has some more training to complete before we can bring her."

Nana clasped her hands to her chest. Her eyes looked suspiciously watery. "I can't wait. I love dogs. It will be so nice to pet one again."

Cade's heart tugged. The woman missed her husband, couldn't dance and was confined to either her bed or the wheelchair. All she really looked forward to was the chance to pet a dog. Maybe if he and Mom worked extra hard with Tulip, they could speed up the process.

He wanted Nana to have something to look forward to. Before it was too late. "We'll bring her as soon as we can."

After twenty minutes, they hugged Nana once more and left.

"That wasn't too bad." Ty strode beside him down the hall.

"Wish every visit went that well." Cade

didn't stop at the reception desk since Charlene wasn't around. They turned the corner and headed out the doors.

"Do you think Tulip will help her?"

"I don't know. If nothing else, it will make her happy. I'd train five dogs if I thought it would slow her dementia, but at the end of the day, there's nothing we can do about it."

They emerged into the sunshine and continued through the parking lot until they reached their trucks.

"I'm sick and tired of losing people I love." Ty balled his hands into fists.

"I know." Cade blew out a frustrated breath. "I'll do what I can with Tulip."

Ty ducked his chin, shaking his head. "It won't matter. Nothing will help."

"I guess all we can do is make the best of the time we have with her."

Ty exhaled loudly. "I'm taking off."

"We could get a pizza. Hang out."

"Another time."

Cade figured Ty would say that, but it made him feel bad just the same. "All right. See you later."

Mackenzie had said Tulip's training shouldn't

take more than six weeks. So why did he feel like he was running out of time? The sooner the dog was ready to visit Nana, the better.

CHAPTER THREE

HAD CADE BROUGHT her to Jewel River under false pretenses?

The following Monday, Mackenzie showed Christy and Cade the commands for Tulip to lie down and stay. They were blessed Tulip was such an eager little dog. Well, that and the fact Mackenzie had already taught her several commands when the dog was living with her. Their session was about to wrap up, and when it did, she needed to pull Cade aside and have a tough conversation with him.

It had been almost a week since the Legacy Club meeting, and she'd gotten exactly zero calls from ranchers or horse owners. No one seemed to be desperate for her services. In fact, no one seemed to want her services at all.

That was not what Cade had told her so many times on the phone.

"I think that should do it for tonight." Mackenzie bent to give Tulip one more treat before petting her fluffy head. "She's a fast learner. In a few weeks, I'll bring in a wheelchair, and we'll train her how to handle being around it."

"Will we be able to take her to the nursing home after that?" The intensity in Cade's eyes confused her. He must really be into training Tulip. Or did he have unrealistic expectations about Tulip helping his grandmother?

"No, she needs to be certified. But we'll go on a field trip first to teach Tulip how to respond to the nurses, residents and all the new scents and sounds she'll be dealing with. I'll clear it with the director."

"Nana is so excited to meet Tulip." Christy squeezed Cade's biceps, then took the leash from him. "It's going to make her day when we bring this little princess in for the first time."

Mackenzie wished her dad could have stayed in town one more day to meet Christy and Cade, but he'd left yesterday afternoon to head back to the training center he worked for. Two more weeks. Then he'd officially be self-employed. Here in Jewel River. She couldn't wait.

"Christy, why don't you practice with Tulip for a bit. I need to discuss something with Cade."

Her eyes grew round as she nodded rapidly.

"Take your time. I'll be fine right here with our girl. No rush. You two get to know each other better."

"Seriously, Ma?" Cade's frustrated eye roll and the way he was shaking his head would have made Mackenzie chuckle if she wasn't so keyed up.

"What?" His mom's innocent protest didn't fool either of them.

"Never mind," he muttered.

Mackenzie led the way through the door to the main clinic. The contractor she'd hired had finished most of the work. The cabinets and counters had been installed in the reception area. All new waterproof flooring had been put in throughout the space. The kennel room and bathrooms were completed, too. The only thing left to finish was installing the equipment in the surgery room. Once that was done, she'd be able to get the final permit, and Jewel River Veterinary Services would be ready to open.

When she entered her office, Mackenzie whirled around to face Cade. He stood in the doorway with a confused look on his face.

"Were you being completely honest with me?" she asked.

His cheeks slackened, then his eyebrows drew together. "About what?"

"About how much this area needs a vet." She crossed her arms over her chest and felt her jaw lock. She tried to relax it and failed.

"Of course, why?" Faint color flushed his cheeks.

"Because I haven't gotten a single call from anyone needing my services."

"Really?" He shifted his weight to one hip and seemed to consider it. "I wonder why."

"Yeah, I wonder why, too." The words flew out with an edge. "Is there something going on I should know about?"

"Not that I'm aware of."

They stood in tense silence.

"You handed out your business cards at the meeting." He seemed to be talking to himself. "Several ranchers attended, so they should have your number. Do you have a website set up?"

The website. She mentally cringed. She'd started putting together a DIY site, but it wasn't finished. She needed to make the website a priority. "Not yet."

"Let me see one of the cards." He held out his hand. She went behind the desk and rummaged through a box of supplies until she found one. Then she straightened and handed it to him. He read it and gave it back. "It's the right number, correct?"

She hadn't thought of that. What if she'd accidentally had them printed with the wrong number? The thought was so horrifying, she didn't even want to look. But she did. And to her relief, her cell number was correct.

"It's the right number."

"Then I'm not sure what to tell you. Unless... I mean...it's summer. Not everyone has a need for a vet right now. That will change in a few months with preg checks. Plus, a lot of people in the surrounding area don't even know you're here. I suppose it will take some time for the word to get out."

She didn't have time. She'd sunk a lot of cash into this venture, and she had living expenses to pay for.

Shaking her head, she tried to think of what could have gone wrong. Maybe she was being impatient. Cade was right. Not many people were aware she'd opened a practice here. And until the clinic opened, they might not know. If she was being honest with herself, the bulk of her income would be from treating pets in the clinic, anyhow.

Cade wasn't the enemy. Why had she automatically blamed him for her problems?

Because you're used to Mom convincing you to help her, then feeling like a fool when you realize she manipulated you for her own reasons. And now you've thrown Cade into the same category. Good job.

"Hey, I know this can feel overwhelming." He bent his head slightly to gaze into her eyes. A flutter rippled across her skin at the kindness in his stare. "It will all fall into place. You've gotten a lot done already. I can't believe how quickly this clinic came together. And the trailer looks amazing. I wouldn't mind taking a tour of it sometime when you get a chance."

"Really?" No one besides her dad had shown the slightest interest in the trailer…or in her. Okay, that wasn't true. Yesterday, a few older women had stopped by her rental house in town to drop off cookies and introduce themselves. They'd been nice. Nosy, but nice.

Cade wasn't the enemy. He'd been on her side from day one.

"Do you want to see the trailer now?" she asked.

A grin spread across his face, and he nodded. "Sure, why not?"

"Come on. I'll give you the tour."

WHY WAS MACKENZIE questioning his integrity? Did she really think so little of him—that he would lie to get her to move here?

Was there a grain of truth in it, though? One of the reasons he'd pushed her to relocate was for his stables. Was he selfish? He wanted her to think he was a stand-up guy.

She clearly didn't.

And deep down he wasn't.

When he'd worked in the city, he'd justified what he'd done for the investment bank. They'd hired him because of his gift for finding more efficient ways to do things. He could locate loopholes where other people wouldn't even think to look. And when he'd been asked to work on one of their special teams, he'd jumped at the chance. Everything had been legal. His bosses and the lawyers they employed—the best in the business—had assured him it was all aboveboard.

But just because something was legal, didn't make it right.

Maybe Mackenzie saw right through him. In some ways, it would be a relief. It would force him to maintain a friendly distance. He'd show up for Tulip's training sessions. Say a brief hello to her if he bumped into her around town. And that was it. It would zap this growing attraction he had for her.

Besides, he was a busy man. Had his hands in a lot of ventures. There was no need for him to feel responsible for Mackenzie's success or lack thereof.

Friendly distance…

They went to the back room, where Mom was practicing commands with Tulip.

"Done already?" Mom asked. "Look, she's a pro at this. Tulip, down." The little dog lay down and rested her chin on her forearms while watching his mom expectantly. "Release. Good girl."

Tulip trotted over and cheerfully accepted her treat.

"I'm going to check out the mobile vet trailer." Cade pointed to the side door. "Mind giving me a few more minutes?"

"Take all the time in the world." His mom beamed. Then she scooped up Tulip and started talking to her in a baby voice. "We'll hang out here, won't we, princess?"

"You ready?" Mackenzie arched her eyebrows at him.

He nodded. They went out the side door and crossed the narrow strip of blacktop between the buildings where she'd parked her trailer. She pulled the key out of her pocket and unlocked the back.

"Here, let me." He pulled up on the handle and swung it open. At the sight of the chute, he whistled. "Wow. This is something."

"Something good, I hope." Mackenzie set one foot on the ledge and hauled herself up. Then she held out her hand. He almost laughed. Didn't really need a boost inside, but he took her hand anyway. Liked the way it felt in his. So much for keeping a friendly distance.

"More than good." The interior had tight quarters. Mackenzie moved along the side of the wall lined with cabinets while he poked around the equipment. "You can do just about everything in here."

"Preg checks, feet trimming, bull testing, mobile X-rays, ultrasounds. I might look into embryos—flushing and freezing—in the future, but I don't have the qualifications yet. I can basically provide health for the whole herd from this trailer."

"It's impressive." He rubbed his thumb and forefinger along his chin. "How do you trim feet? I don't see a belly band."

"Portable hydraulic tilt." She placed her hand

on the chute. "I bought the quietest model I could afford."

"Keeps them from getting spooked."

"Exactly." Mackenzie opened the cabinets and showed him the supplies she stored inside. They chatted about vaccinating, checking bulls and some of the common diseases cattle were prone to get in the summer. Then they returned to the blacktop. Anticipation built as he thought of all the possibilities this trailer could bring to the area.

"I'm opening a horse-boarding facility this fall." He adjusted his cowboy hat.

"Yes, you mentioned it."

He had, hadn't he. "I'm wondering if you'd come out sometime. Check out the stables. They're still being built."

"Why?" Her eyes narrowed.

"Do you like horses? I mean, are you a rider?"

"I do like riding. Haven't been on a horse in a decade, though." She closed the trailer's back door and locked it.

"A decade? Why so long?"

"Veterinary school was pretty intense. I had no time, and I never owned a horse, either."

"You rode friends' horses."

She nodded.

"And after you graduated?" He watched her closely, enjoying how open her expressions were. She was honest. Easy to read. Except... a cloud passed over her eyes before she met his gaze.

"It wasn't on my radar. I was busy establishing myself in Cheyenne. I was on call a lot. Didn't leave much time for long horseback rides."

Cade straightened slightly. There was more to it. Her hesitation told him so. He'd always been able to read people and situations. He used this to his advantage more often than not.

"And now?" he asked.

"I don't anticipate having much time for long rides on horseback here, either." She rested her hand on the side of the trailer. "I'll still be on call."

"If you did have time, would you want to ride?" Why was he pressing this?

It probably had something to do with those hooded eyes and her no-nonsense demeanor. It had been ages since he'd been interested in a woman. And no matter how hard he tried to tell his brain he wasn't interested in her, it wasn't listening.

Her eyelashes fluttered, then she stared at

her feet. A beat passed. Two. She met his gaze again, and this time she looked vulnerable.

"Yeah, I would." Her voice was soft, softer than he thought possible coming from her. "I've always wanted my own horse. Silly, I suppose. I don't have time to take care of one, and I'd hate to own a horse and neglect it."

"I can't imagine you neglecting an animal." He spoke the truth. She'd devoted her entire life to animal care.

"Yeah, well, a cat or a dog is one thing. But a horse? They need more than I can give at the moment. It's probably why I'm single and can't imagine a husband or kids in my life, either. I can only fit in so much, you know?"

The words were so unexpected, he blinked. The masculine side of him responded to the challenge. Sure, she might not be able to fit *other* guys into her life. But she could fit Cade in. If she really wanted to.

Did he want her to?

No. Friendly distance, remember?

"Of course, my logic doesn't add up until I get some clients here." The wry way the corner of her lips lifted brought on a twinge of guilt.

He wanted her to have those clients. Wanted her to succeed. After all, he was the one who'd convinced her to move here. He was the one who'd spelled out how much they needed a vet.

Not ten minutes ago, she'd basically accused him of lying to her. The last time he'd been called out like that had been in New York City, by his father. Only back then, Dad had been right.

Mackenzie was wrong. He hadn't lied to her. Jewel River did need a veterinarian.

"I tell you what." He hooked a thumb in his pocket. "Why don't you and I drive out to a few of the ranches. Bring your trailer. I'll introduce you, and you can show them what you're all about."

Her expression told him she wasn't keen on the plan. What about him bothered her so much? No one else around here seemed to have an issue with him. In fact, he could have a date any night of the week if he wanted one—but he didn't want one.

He stared at the trailer. "They'll check out your equipment, talk to you in person and see for themselves you know what you're doing."

"I suppose." Her lips tugged down as if she was nauseous.

"Okay, it's not your thing. That's fine." He brought his hands near his chest and stepped back. "I just think it would help if ranchers could see for themselves all you can do for their herds."

"Why are you offering?" Her eyelids formed slits.

"Because you're needed here. For months, I searched for a vet, and now that you've arrived, our animals will get the care they deserve. The sooner you're established, the better off everyone will be." He gave her a lazy grin. "Plus, I need you to be on call for my stables. But you already knew that."

She let out a half snort, half laugh. "You may have mentioned it a time or two."

"So? What do you say?"

"I've got nothing to lose at this point." She shrugged. "Let's do it."

Victory coursed through his veins, and it wasn't lost on him that this type of victory came with a fair amount of trouble.

He had no business spending time with Mackenzie. Not when he was attracted to her. Not when she presented a challenge his personality couldn't seem to turn down. And not when he had zero intention of letting her know the truth about the lines he'd crossed in New York.

He'd introduce her to the local ranchers, and then his duty would be done. But something told him it wouldn't be that easy. Life never was.

CHAPTER FOUR

"YOU DON'T WASTE TIME, do you?" Two days later, Mackenzie finished hooking the trailer to the hitch on her truck, double-checked that it was secure and took a step back. Sunshine beamed down, and the temperature was sure to reach into the high eighties later. Cade stood on the other side of the hitch but, to his credit, didn't try to help. He merely watched her with a twinkle in his eyes.

"I don't. The best time is now, in my opinion." He crooked a finger toward the hitch. "By the way, you're good at that."

"Yeah, well, I've had a lot of practice over the past months." She mentally reviewed that she did indeed have everything needed for their trip to Triple B Ranch. The trailer was fully stocked, and earlier, she'd tossed a few bottles of water and snacks in the backpack she carried instead of a purse. "Are you riding with me? Or do you want me to follow you?"

"We can ride together." He promptly opened the passenger door to her truck and made himself comfortable.

There went her hope of calming her nerves by rehearsing her spiel during the ride. Small talk with Cade wasn't the scenario she'd hoped for, but she couldn't say she was surprised, either. It wouldn't make sense for them to drive separately on a long trip like this.

She climbed into the driver's seat. When Cade had called her yesterday to tell her he'd arranged for her to meet Marvin Blythe at Triple B Ranch this morning, she'd been taken aback. He didn't mess around when it came to fulfilling his word. While she was grateful he'd arranged the visit, she resented it a little, too.

It would be nice if the ranchers contacted her instead of her having to rely on Cade for an introduction. Oh, well. She didn't have many other options at the moment. Besides, this would give her a chance to start off on the right foot with Mr. Blythe. She hoped he'd call her for more than just emergencies, though. Ideally, she'd take an active role in the health of his herd by coming out on a regular basis for vaccines and checkups.

She started the truck and glanced at Cade. "You'll have to tell me where to go."

"I can do that." His grin caught her off guard. The man was too handsome. "Go to Center Street and take a left. The ranch is close to the county line, so it will take a while to get there. And if you have time in the next week or two, I'd like for you to come out to my place. I've told Micky, my ranch manager, to set some time aside to discuss a plan for our cattle with you."

"Really?" She wasn't surprised Cade would want her services, but it still made her happy. "Tell him I'll come over first thing tomorrow morning."

"I'll text him now."

Mackenzie didn't speak until she'd checked the rearview to verify the trailer was still connected. Once they were on Center Street, she began to relax. The blue sky was full of puffy clouds, and soon they were surrounded by rolling prairie.

"I could get used to this." Cade leaned back with an air of satisfaction.

"Used to what?"

"Having someone else drive for a change."

"Really?" She sent a sideways glance his way. He looked as appealing as ever. His large frame fit well in the truck. Gave his long legs ample room to stretch. The cowboy hat and boots had already won her over. She wished they hadn't.

There was something about a cowboy.

"I'm my mother's chauffer," he said.

"I noticed you're with your mom a lot."

He shifted, arching his brows, but the shimmer in his eyes assured her he wasn't offended. "There's a reason for that. She's…um…how do I put it?" He brought his index finger to his lips. "A terrible driver."

Mackenzie laughed. It wasn't what she'd expected to hear.

"If she's not speeding, she's driving up on the sidewalk in an effort to park, hitting traffic cones or making her own rules about traffic lights. Honestly, I feel safer—and the entire community does, too—when her license gets suspended."

"Christy? A bad driver?" Mackenzie shook her head. "I don't believe it."

"That's because you haven't seen it. Just wait. In two months, she'll be allowed to drive again, and then…well…you've been warned."

"I think you're being melodramatic." She

barely noticed the grazing cattle in the distance. The conversation was too much fun.

"I'm being proactive. Honestly, if there was an award for good citizenship in Jewel River, I would win it every year simply for keeping Mom off the streets."

"Um, that phrase didn't come out right." She flashed him an exaggerated grimace.

"Oh!" He chuckled. "Let me rephrase that. For driving Mom around."

"A good citizenship award, huh? You should take it up with the Legacy Club."

"You know, that's a good idea. I might." Cade pointed to the right. "You're going to turn up ahead."

Mackenzie made the turn, and her heart lightened at the sight of the bluish-purple mountains in the distance. "This is beautiful. So empty and wide-open. Have you always lived here, aside from college and…" She didn't mention New York. Didn't want him thinking she'd been stalking him online.

"I grew up here. Moved to Michigan for college. Then New York City after graduation." The words tumbled out quickly, and she got the impression he didn't want to talk about it. Normally, he wasn't one to rush his speech. "After my dad died, I moved back. Can't imagine living anywhere else."

His father *had* passed away. How sad. "How did he die?"

"Cancer. It was aggressive. He'd barely been diagnosed, and he was gone."

"I'm sorry. That must have been hard."

"It was. It's been six years. I still miss him. Mom and Ty do, too."

"Ty is your brother?"

"Yep. He has his own ranch nearby."

"I see. So, in addition to running a cattle ranch, you're opening a horse-boarding facility."

"That's right."

"Then how do you have time to drive out here with me today?" She hoped she didn't sound judgmental or mean, but really, how did he have the time?

"I don't have the patience to manage the ranch on a daily basis. Micky and the ranch hands take care of it. Soon, I'll hire someone to manage Moulten Stables, too. I do keep track of my investment properties and still manage an investment portfolio. I'm never bored."

"Still? Is that what you did in New York City?"

"Not exactly. I started out as a trader in securities finance."

"Started? After that, what did you do?"

"Whatever my employers asked me to do." He turned away to stare out his window, and Mackenzie got the impression the topic was closed.

She couldn't resist asking one more question. "Do you miss it?"

"The job?" He shifted to face her again. "Parts of it. My mind is always on the fast-track. Even now. The accelerated aspect of Wall Street—the split-second decisions—I thrived on that. And I liked living in the city. It's busy. I never had to slow down."

"Didn't you ever want to slow down?" She could relate. Somewhat. She might not have lived in the big city, but her job forced her to be ready for anything at any time.

"Back then, no. Even now, I struggle with it. But I'm trying to learn how to slow down. Not sure I'll ever master it. What about you? You're busy, too. Does it ever bother you?"

"That's a tough question." She thought back over the past decade. "I think it's normal for me at this point. I've been on a time crunch since I graduated from high school. I was always working toward a goal, though, so it didn't bother me."

"Does it now?"

"No. This is what I want. This is what I signed up for. Long, odd hours come with the job."

"That's fair." He nodded more to himself than to her. "Your ideal day—one with no work, no meetings, no errands or appointments—how would you spend it?"

Innocent enough question, but why did it feel so intimate? She tapped her thumbs on the steering wheel. The scenario spread out before her. It should be easy to answer. But her mind was a complete blank.

"I have no idea." She gave him her best *sorry* expression. "What would yours look like?"

"Come on, there must be something you'd want to do if you had time on your hands."

The first thing that flashed through her mind was a memory of riding a horse with her friend Tawny in high school. She could still feel the sun on her face, the breeze blowing through her hair and the relaxing sway of the horse under the saddle.

"I'd probably borrow a horse and go riding. Pack a lunch. Soak in the nature around me." Once the idea formed, she realized she wanted to make it happen—when things were more settled. "What about you?"

"You miss riding horses." He wore a smug smile, and it didn't bother her one bit. "I can help with that, you know."

"I know," she said in an exaggerated manner. "You're building a barn for stables. Opening a horse-boarding facility. You need me to be on call. Trust me, I got the message."

"Good." They rode in easy silence for several miles. Mackenzie kept waiting for him to tell her what he'd do if he had a day off from everything. But he didn't add to the conversation. He made no effort to speak at all.

"You're avoiding my question," she said.

"What question is that?"

"Free time. An entire day. What would you do with it?"

"I'm not much for free time."

They were similar there. Beyond errands and chores, she had few hobbies. Few? Scratch that. None. Did reading veterinary journals count? Her dad was always trying to get her to have a social life.

"I'd probably round up my buddies for some outdoor fun."

"What if you *had* to spend the day alone?"

He cringed. "I thought this imaginary day was supposed to be something I looked forward to? It's starting to feel like a punishment."

"You don't like being by yourself?"

"I didn't say that. And if you're thinking I live with my mother because I'm scared of being alone, you're wrong."

"Why do you live with her?"

"Convenience. It's home. If she could keep her license for more than a month, maybe things would be different. I don't know. I don't like to worry about her."

This guy is actually sweet. Before she could overthink the unexpected tenderness his words brought on, Cade instructed her to turn again, and before long, the truck was kicking up dust down the long drive of Triple B Ranch. Mackenzie parked near the outbuildings and joined Cade as they strolled toward the largest pole barn.

"His office is this way." Cade had barely finished speaking when a burly older gentleman came out of the barn and strode toward them. Everything about him screamed rancher. The hat, the boots, the jeans, the vest, even the mustache.

"Good to see you, Marv." Cade shook the

man's hand. "Thanks for agreeing to meet us. This is Mackenzie Howard, the vet I told you about."

"Doc." He shook her hand, but there was a wariness in his expression that gave her pause.

"This is quite the operation you're running, Mr. Blythe."

"Call me, Marv. Everyone does." His chest puffed up. "I raise a lot of cattle. Keeps me on my toes."

She figured she could start by feeling him out on his preferences for their nutritional balance. "May I ask what you're feeding them?"

"What do you think I'm feeding them?" He gave her a disapproving look. "It's summer. They're grazing."

"Of course. I just thought you might want to discuss their nutritional needs."

"I know their nutritional needs. I've been running this ranch for over fifty years."

She was handling this all wrong. And it was extra embarrassing with Cade standing there witnessing it.

"Why don't I show you my mobile vet trailer? Then you can see what I have to offer your cattle and horses. Oh, and pets. I'm guessing you have some herding dogs about."

"That I do." He seemed to calm down at the mention of dogs. "Sometimes I think I've got more dogs than cattle. The missus can't say no to a puppy."

"My father can't either." She chuckled. "He loves dogs. Trains them to be service dogs—that's his job."

"Really?" Marv began walking toward the back of the trailer. "We have two basset hounds, an Australian shepherd, three mini dachshunds—they are spunky little things—a yellow Lab, a black Lab and a Chihuahua. The Chihuahua does not like me. Loves the missus, though. I call it the rat. Then my wife gets mad and chews me out." Grinning, he shook his head as if it couldn't be helped.

For the next half hour, Mackenzie showed him her equipment and explained the general health checks she offered, all while emphasizing the importance of herd health. He asked her about her experience and tried to trip her up with a few scenarios, but she explained how she would handle the situations, and he seemed to accept that she was qualified.

After she locked the trailer, she shook his hand once more. "Thanks again, Marv. Give me a call with any questions or if you need me to come out for anything. I'd be happy to give the dogs their checkups while I'm here, too."

He rubbed his chin, tilting his head to the side. "That might be a good idea. With Doc Banks retiring, it's been a struggle to get them up-to-date on their shots."

"I understand," she said. "Before I come out next time, we can figure out what shots the dogs need, and I'll do a wellness check on them, too."

"Sounds good."

After saying goodbye, Mackenzie and Cade got back into her truck and began the long ride home.

Even with her gaze on the road, she could feel Cade watching her. What was he thinking?

"That went well," he said.

"It could have gone better." She wished she could have worked out a schedule with Marv to come out regularly to check the cattle. All in due time, she supposed.

"Why do you say that?"

"He wasn't exactly enthusiastic about having me come out to care for the cattle."

"He'll call you."

"Maybe."

"When you told him you'd look at the dogs,

his demeanor changed. I give it less than two months, and you'll be on a regular schedule with the dogs *and* the cattle."

"I hope you're right." She sighed. "By the way, I finished the website. I stayed up late last night adding pictures and content."

"That's great. Now everyone will know you're available to service the area."

"But will anyone actually want my services?"

"They won't have a choice." He grinned. "You're all they've got."

"Yeah, well, I'm used to being a consolation prize." As soon as the words left her mouth, she wanted to draw them back in. Cade didn't say anything, but the look in his eyes told her he was puzzling through the words to make sense of them.

Whether he did or not didn't really matter. He was right. In time, she'd gain the trust of the local ranchers. She'd make sure of it.

WHY WOULD MACKENZIE believe she was a consolation prize? The following evening, Cade was still contemplating what she'd said on the ride home yesterday. Why was she on his mind so much? He shouldn't be thinking about her at all.

With long strides, he headed down the final stretch of path that led from the outbuildings to the rear of the ranch house. After letting himself through the back door of the garage, he washed his hands in the mudroom. Voices carried. Female voices.

His mother must have invited friends over. Charlene? Mary? He forced his feet forward, plastered on a smile and hoped to say just a few words before making a quick escape.

"Thank you so much for coming over, Mackenzie."

Mackenzie? Cade halted. Why was she here?

"Tulip seems fine now," Mom said. "I don't know what got into her earlier. You're staying for supper, of course."

"Oh, um, I'd better not."

Cade held his breath. On the one hand, he wanted Mackenzie to leave. Needed some distance between them. The woman had already taken up too many of his thoughts. On the other hand, he wanted to know more about her. Craved being around her.

Either way, hiding was stupid.

He forced his feet forward through the large kitchen into the open living room. Hardwood floors had been installed throughout the house, and his mother had picked out large area rugs to *make the rooms cozier*—her words, not his. Vaulted ceilings soared above wooden beams. A stacked-stone fireplace climbed one wall. Large windows overlooked the covered front porch and yard.

Mackenzie sat kitty-corner to his mother on the massive gray sectional. Tulip was sleeping on Mackenzie's lap.

"Hey, there." Cade took a seat at the other end of the sectional.

"You're home early." Mom's wide smile amplified the sparkles of delight in her eyes. "I was just telling Mackenzie she needs to have supper with us."

Mackenzie's cheeks grew rosy.

"That's a great idea." Why had he said that? Probably because every time he caught sight of her pretty face and dark blue eyes, he wanted to prolong their time together. He turned to his mom. "Am I grilling tonight?"

"Chicken and shrimp kebabs. They're on skewers in the fridge." Mom turned back to Mackenzie. "I always make extra in case Ty stops by. Have you met my youngest son?"

He frowned. Mom wasn't trying to push Ty and Mackenzie together, was she? He didn't like that thought. Ty was still grieving. And Mackenzie was—

"I haven't," she said. "But I'm hoping to stop by his ranch soon. I understand it borders yours."

"It does. Used to be all one big ranch, but Pete wanted both boys to have their own cattle. Ty's about your age, I'm guessing. Thirty-three."

"I'm thirty-two." Mackenzie absentmindedly petted Tulip, who let out a contented sigh, licked her tiny lips and settled more deeply on her lap.

"Right. I thought so. Anyway, the two of you have a lot in common."

Cade bolted to his feet. He fought the temptation to pace. Instead, he gave his mother a tight smile. "Should I get the grill started?"

"Yes, please. Potatoes are baking in the oven." She addressed Mackenzie. "Are you okay with baked potatoes?"

"I love them."

"I do, too. I fried some bacon for breakfast and chopped up the leftovers. We'll have loaded potatoes tonight. Now, what was I saying?"

Cade didn't want to listen to his mother rave about Ty to Mackenzie. Couldn't the woman see those two would be all wrong for each other?

He needed to intervene. "Mackenzie, I have some questions about training Tulip. Would you want to join me while I grill the food?"

"Sure. I can do that." She lifted Tulip off her lap. The dog stretched out each hind leg on the couch, then worked her way over to Christy and settled on her lap to finish her nap.

He led the way to the kitchen, took out the wrapped trays of kabobs from the fridge and carried them to the sliding door to the back deck, where they kept the grill. The house had been built on a hill. A walkout basement below the deck was finished with extra bedrooms for guests. The deck ran the length of the home, and it boasted views of the huge backyard that trailed off into a forest.

Two deer—young does from the looks of it—grazed near the woods.

"This is beautiful." She headed straight to the deck rail and leaned her forearms on it. She smiled as she took in the view. "So peaceful."

"It is." He opened the cover and fired the grill. Then he joined Mackenzie and looked out over the lawn, too.

"What did you want to ask me?"

He'd forgotten about that. "Um, her vest. Should I put it on her when I bring her to the construction site in the morning?"

"Not unless you're actively working with her."

"Okay."

What now?

"Did you grow up here?" she asked.

"I did." He straightened, pointing to the far right corner of the yard. "Ty and I used to have a fort in the woods. It was an old hunting blind my dad set up for us. There's a trail to it over there. We'd stuff our pockets full of granola bars and race each other. The games we would play." He shook his head as the fond memories flooded him. "The fort became a pirate ship, a castle, even a penthouse in the city. We hammered out the rules, fought like feral cats and had a great time."

"Is it still there?"

"No, Dad tore it down after Ty got his driver's license. We'd given up on it years before. Got too cool and too busy for our games."

"A fort sounds like fun. So does having a brother—except for the feral-cat-fighting part."

He chuckled. The sun glinted off her long hair. "No siblings, huh?"

"Nope. Just me."

"You grew up in South Dakota."

"You remembered." She shifted to give him a smile. "Yes, we lived in Rapid City. Dad worked at the company he's about to retire from, and Mom had odd jobs. I didn't have a fort or playhouse, but I got to go to the training center to help him take care of the dogs all the time, and that more than made up for it."

"Is that why you went into veterinary care?"

"It's part of it. I hate seeing anything suffer. Even when I was young, Dad took in rescue animals temporarily to help get them adjusted. I became well acquainted with the typical injuries—physical and emotional—they had."

"Where is your mom now?"

"I have no idea." Her gaze slid away.

Her clipped tone alerted him to change the subject. "When do you think Tulip will be able to visit the nursing home? Nana is really looking forward to meeting her."

Her face cleared. "The earliest? Three weeks. We need to get her used to the wheelchair and have the training session at the nursing home. It wouldn't be fair to Tulip to throw her in a situation without teaching her how to deal with all the sounds, smells and obstacles."

"I see your point."

"She also needs to be able to ignore a pill on the floor when you say 'leave it.' And she needs practice meeting other dogs and other people when out and about. In order to get certified, she needs to be able to do *all* the commands, and she hasn't learned them all."

"Do you think she'll be able to pass the test when the time comes?"

Straightening her arms so the tips of her fingers touched the rail, she nodded. "Yes, I do. But don't rush it. Don't rush her. She's lost her owner, lived with me for a while and now she's settling in to another home. It's a lot to deal with in a short time."

"She's happy here."

"I know. And I want her to stay happy here. We need to think of her needs, too."

Mackenzie was right. He'd been so caught up in wanting to help Nana that he'd overlooked Tulip's needs. The dog did everything they asked of her and more. Sure, she was smart and trainable, but she was also their pet.

Why was he in such a rush, anyhow? Yes, Nana was getting worse, but there wasn't any indication she'd pass away in the immediate future.

God, I can't seem to slow down. I'm never satis-

fied with what's in front of me. I always have to do more, be better. And for what?

If he didn't get a grip on his restlessness, he might push Tulip too hard. And then Nana wouldn't get to enjoy the dog. The training schedule they were on would have to be good enough. He'd follow Mackenzie's lead. She was the expert, after all.

CHAPTER FIVE

MACKENZIE COULDN'T BELIEVE how much had changed in a few short weeks. Today was the grand opening of Jewel River Veterinary Service, and she'd already given two cats and three dogs routine checkups and shots. She'd also cleaned an infected scrape on a schnauzer. The poor dog had tangled with a wild animal over the weekend. Several locals had stopped in for the free cookies and coffee, and they'd left with coupons for 20 percent off their first visit.

She hoped all of them would use the coupons. While today had been bustling, Wednesday and Friday only had half the appointments filled.

"Mind if I take my lunch?" Greta Dell, the receptionist in her early twenties she'd hired, stood and stretched her back.

"Go ahead." Mackenzie smiled at the pretty woman with springy curls and big brown eyes.

Greta had been a good hire. She loved animals and had a sunny nature. All morning, she'd made the pet owners comfortable. Sure, she could be chatty, but Mackenzie figured it was better for business than if she was curt. "I'll stay up front until you're finished."

After today, she'd lock the clinic for the lunch hour, but since this was the open house, Mackenzie was keeping it open for anyone to drop in and check out the facilities. She had too much nervous energy to eat, anyhow.

"Greta, will you tell Emily she can take her lunch, too?" Mackenzie asked. Emily Fulton had two years of experience as a vet tech. She didn't have to be told what to do, and she had a nurturing touch with the animals. Another good hire.

"I'm happy to, Dr. Howard." Greta snatched a tote from under the desk and headed down the hall to where the small break room was located. Mackenzie had insisted on outfitting the room with a sink, microwave, refrigerator, coffeemaker and small table that seated four. Her staff would need the quiet spot to recharge.

She gave Greta's office chair a longing glance. She'd been on her feet since seven this morning, and although it was only one, tiredness seeped into her bones.

The front door opened, and all thoughts of sitting fled. She pasted on her brightest smile as she waited for the newcomers to round the corner into view. To her surprise, Christy, Cade and Tulip, wearing her therapy-dog vest, arrived.

"We just had to stop by and say hi." Christy handed the leash to Cade and hurried around the counter to give Mackenzie a hug. Then she stepped back, keeping her hands at Mackenzie's shoulders, and beamed. "You did it. This place looks amazing, and I've heard you were busy all morning."

She blinked, overwhelmed at the warm welcome and the fact people were actually talking about the clinic. "Yes, we've had a full morning. I have a few more appointments this afternoon, too."

Tulip sat quietly next to Cade, and Mackenzie came out from behind the counter to greet them. She bent to pet the little dog. "Well, hello there, Tulip. Look at you sitting so nicely. I'm honored you came all this way to check out the new clinic. You look spiffy in your vest."

The dog's tail wagged as she remained seated,

and Cade took a treat out of his pocket to give to her. She gobbled it up. Mackenzie laughed, stroking her fur. Then she straightened and found herself looking directly into Cade's shimmering eyes.

"Congratulations," he said with a light drawl. "This place looks great."

"Thank you. It's nice of you to come check it out." Their support meant more to her than either would ever know. They were the only two friends she had in Jewel River at this point.

"We brought a clinic-warming present, too, Mackenzie." Christy's face glowed with excitement.

"You didn't have to do that." What in the world had they brought?

"It's outside. Two planters with flowers. Cade set them on either side of the door, but feel free to move them wherever you want."

"Oh, that's so thoughtful." She hadn't considered adding flowers to the front entrance. Wasn't much into decorating. "Thank you."

"You're welcome."

"I told Mom to check with you first, so don't feel like you have to keep them if they aren't your thing," Cade said. Did she detect a touch of concern in his gaze?

"They *are* my thing. I just never thought to buy them. I appreciate it. Truly."

Christy shot him a smug smile. They'd obviously argued over it. Imagine that. Arguing over giving her a gift. There was a first time for everything.

"Have you gotten any more use out of the trailer?" Cade kept an eye on Tulip as Christy retreated to the counter and selected one of the pamphlets Mackenzie kept for clients.

"Actually, yes. Erica and Dalton Cambridge had me come out last Wednesday. I'll be going to Winston Ranch regularly to check the cattle and vaccinate them." She was thrilled. Having the largest ranch in several counties on her herd-health plan boosted her confidence.

"Did I hear Winston Ranch?" Christy called over her shoulder. "Did you see their event center? It's ideal for wedding receptions."

"Ignore her." Cade shook his head.

"Your brother set up an appointment for me to come out to his ranch on Thursday."

"I'm not surprised. By the way, I like this look on you." He moved his finger up and down to indicate her outfit—jeans, orthopedic sneakers and a lab coat. She'd braided her hair to keep it out of her way.

Heat shot up her neck. Was he poking fun? As usual, she wore no makeup. The most generous thing she could say about her uniform was that the lab coat gave her an air of authority. She wore it to protect her clothes from all of the animal hair and secretions she dealt with on a daily basis.

"You look like a doctor in it." He grinned.

"Good, because I am a doctor in it." Bantering with him was easy.

The door opened again, and to her surprise, her dad appeared. He approached with his arms wide and lifted her off her feet in a hug.

"You did it, Mackenzie." He set her down and took the place in. "I'm proud of you."

"Thanks, Dad." Her heart filled with pride. She'd been positive he wouldn't be able to make it back to Jewel River until Wednesday—yet, here he was. "Dad, this is Christy and Cade Moulten."

Both mother and son stood behind her. Christy had picked up Tulip.

"Hi, I'm Patrick Howard. We finally meet." He shook Cade's hand first, then turned to Christy. "Nice to meet you, too."

"What a lovely surprise for your daughter." Christy gave Patrick the attentiveness she showed everyone. "Are you in town for good? Cade's been telling me about the training center you're opening."

"I am." Her dad shoved his hands in his pockets as he rocked back on his heels. "I'm itching to get started with the renovations."

"Where will you be staying?" Christy asked.

"I'm renting a small house around the corner."

"The one on Adams Street?"

"That's the one."

Cade hitched his head to the side for Mackenzie to join him. They moved to the corner of the waiting area.

"Do you want me to set up another visit with one of the more rural ranchers?"

Yes, she wanted to meet the other ranchers, but no, she didn't want to have to rely on Cade to do it. And that was stupid. She couldn't let her ego get in the way of her business. Their morning at Triple B Ranch had gone well. Cade had stayed in the background and let her handle Marv. The drive there and back had calmed her nerves, too, as they'd chatted and gotten to know each other.

What could she possibly have against this guy?

Nothing. All Cade had done for her since their very first phone call was offer her opportunities.

"I've been to most of the local ranches," she said. "There are still several I'd like to see eventually. But for now, I'm good."

Her cell phone rang, and she answered it without checking the caller.

As soon as she heard "Hello, darling," Mackenzie felt the blood drain from her face. Her knees went wobbly. With a sharp whoosh, she exhaled and willed herself to stand tall. She would not let this call ruin her grand opening.

Her mother had found her.

It wasn't as if she was in hiding, but Mackenzie hadn't expected to hear from her. Especially not today, of all days.

"Why are you calling?" Her voice sounded sharp to her ears. *Calm down. It's just a phone call.*

"To congratulate you on your big day, of course."

She hated the burst of hope spouting at her mother's words. Hated that she still craved her approval. Hated that a part of her still needed her mom's approval.

"How did you find out about it?" The words were clipped. Tone? Ice-cold. She didn't know how else to handle this woman who had caused her so much pain.

"A mother keeps tabs on these things." A nervous undercurrent rode under the role of *proud mom* she was trying to convey. It was on the tip of Mackenzie's tongue to say she only kept tabs when she wanted something.

"I'm kind of busy here." She shifted her weight to one hip.

"I'm sure you are. We can catch up later, Bumblebee."

"Don't call me that." Her lungs seemed to be clenching. If she held the phone any tighter, she'd crush it.

"Fine, *Mackenzie*." Her mother laughed as if it was all a big joke. Maybe it was. Maybe acting like a mother was all one big joke to the woman.

"I've got to go." Mackenzie readied to end the call.

"I'll call you later."

"Don't bother."

"It's important."

Mackenzie clenched her jaw, glanced up at the ceiling and counted to three. "Fine. I'll be done at five thirty."

"I'll call you then."

Mackenzie ended the call, closed her eyes and mentally prayed. *God, please let her forget to call. Distract her. Anything. I can't go through this again.*

FASCINATED, CADE WATCHED as Mackenzie talked on the phone. He'd never seen this side of her—tense, upset. Who was calling to bother her so much? An ex-boyfriend?

When the call ended, Mackenzie seemed to morph back to her normal self. Cade wanted to put his arm around her, to comfort her, but it wouldn't be appropriate. "Are you all right?"

She turned to him, and he'd never seen eyes so full of suppressed hurts. She tried to hide them, but they were there, making him wonder what had caused her so much pain. "I'm fine."

Patrick and Christy stepped forward to join them. Tulip sniffed a mint someone had dropped.

"Leave it," Christy said sharply. Tulip ignored the mint and headed to Mackenzie, then sat at her feet, looking up at her. Mom gave her a treat. Cade was impressed the dog left the mint. The take-it and leave-it commands had been last week's training focus. He and his mom had been working hard with her, and it was clearly paying off.

"Did *you* tell Mom about the grand opening?" Mackenzie opened her hands as she spoke to her father.

"No, I didn't." Patrick shrugged, maintaining eye contact with her. "I thought about telling her, but after our conversation a few weeks ago, I decided not to. Why? Was that her?"

"Yes, it was her. If you didn't tell her, how did she know I moved and that my grand opening is today?" She rubbed her forearms.

Tulip began to whine softly and nuzzled her leg. She bent and picked up the dog, holding her close to her chest. Tulip lifted her little head to try to lick Mackenzie's chin, but she stopped her with a "No lick."

If Cade had any doubts about Tulip bringing comfort to someone in pain, they'd been silenced. The pup had a knack for knowing when someone needed emotional support.

"Maybe your mother saw your website?" Christy's sympathetic tone rang loud and clear. That was one thing about his mom, she was good at making people feel better in rough situations. "I checked it out, and I loved it."

Mackenzie's face cleared, and she nodded. "I'm sure you're right. I wasn't expecting her to call. I wish I'd had a warning."

Patrick had the look of a parent ready to lecture, so Cade tugged on Mackenzie's sleeve. "Let's talk a minute."

Her eyes narrowed with doubts, but she allowed him to lead her out of the waiting area, down the hall to the back room where Tulip's training sessions were held.

Once the door closed behind them, he turned to face her and searched her eyes.

"Is there anything I can do?" he asked. "You're upset."

"I'm not upset." Did she even know she was lying? "I'm... I was surprised. That's all."

"I don't know what you need, but..." He wasn't sure what to say. All he knew was that the unflappable Mackenzie had gotten a shock, and he hated seeing her like this. "I'm here if you need me."

She tilted her head slightly and studied him through questioning eyes.

"Most of my life's together, Cade. I tell myself it's together, but then she barges back into my life and... I feel it threaten to come apart." She shook her head, cuddling Tulip closer. "I appreciate your support. I do. And if there was anything that you could help with, I'd tell you. But this is a heart thing."

A heart thing.

He had one of those, too.

"I pray, but I'm so angry and bitter about my mother, I don't seem to make any progress."

He wanted to find out what her mom did to hurt her, but he couldn't. Asking a question like that would mean opening himself to questions she might ask him. Ones he wouldn't answer.

He doubted he had the capacity to emotionally deal with them beyond what he'd already done.

Her mother had obviously made mistakes. He'd made his share of them, too.

"Don't let it ruin your day. The clinic opening has been a success. Hold on to that."

She glanced at him and stroked Tulip's fur. "Thanks."

"Why don't you go to the break room for a few minutes? Get a cup of coffee or something and relax? Mom and I will man the front desk until you're feeling yourself again."

"That's nice of you, but—"

"Ten minutes, Mackenzie. Take a break."

He pinpointed the exact moment she stopped fighting it.

"Maybe you're right." She set Tulip on the

ground and handed Cade the leash. "If someone comes in, though, come and get me."

"I will." Good. She'd agreed to take a few minutes for herself. As she led the way, it hit him how much moving here and opening this practice meant to her. She had high expectations for herself. He did for himself, too. And it seemed both of them had prioritized their careers over their personal lives.

He knew why he had. But why had Mackenzie?

Another question he wasn't willing to ask. They were better off leaving all those questions unanswered and sticking with their priorities—their careers.

At five thirty, Mackenzie opened the door to her house and strode directly to her bedroom to change. All afternoon, she'd put the impending phone call out of her mind to greet visitors and treat her four-legged patients. But when she, Greta and Emily cleaned the clinic after closing at five, her mother's call was all she could think about. She was going to have to make it clear to Bonnie Howard that she wasn't welcome in Jewel River. At least her mom hadn't shown up here with no warning the way she'd done in the past.

Maybe her mom would forget about calling her.

Mackenzie's phone rang.

Of course not.

She popped in her wireless earphones, took a deep breath and answered the call. "Yes?"

"Hello to you, too." Her mother's laugh sounded forced. "It's been a long time since we've caught up."

Not long enough in Mackenzie's opinion.

Straightening, she decided to play along. It wouldn't kill her to be civil. She dropped the combative tone and attempted to loosen her tight muscles by stretching her neck side to side. "Okay, you go first. Where have you been living?"

"Santa Fe."

"What are you doing there?" Mackenzie hoped her mother had a job, but from past experience, she couldn't assume she was currently employed.

"I'm—I was—the creative assistant for a gallery. Handmade jewelry. Gorgeous pieces."

Was? Just as she'd feared.

"You're not working there anymore?" Mackenzie was too keyed up to sit down. Instead, she hustled to the kitchen and opened the refrigerator. Nothing. She should have stopped by Dixie B's for takeout before coming home. Or casually popped over to the Moultens' place. Christy seemed the type to have supper planned every night. The kebabs Cade had grilled had been delicious.

As if she'd ever just drop in on them. Wasn't going to happen, not with her feelings moving in the direction of liking Cade a little too much. He'd been supportive earlier. Perceptive. He'd known the exact thing to say to make her feel better. The break he'd insisted she take had helped her get back to a better frame of mind.

A girl could rely on a guy like him in a time of crisis.

Her mother coughed. "Um, technically, no."

What did that mean? "And not technically?"

"Well…" The sounds of traffic came through the phone. "The economy took a downturn, and Sherelle had to make some tough choices."

In other words, she'd been fired.

"I'm sorry to hear that." Mackenzie was sorry. Because now it meant Bonnie Howard would become her problem.

"I have options."

Sure, she did. Most likely her mother had one option—coming to Jewel River. Mackenzie was merely her mother's fallback—her last line of hope when life fell apart. Too bad it fell apart so regularly.

"You're not coming here." Mackenzie couldn't deal with the emotional pain it would bring. Not this time. These extended visits always started out okay, but then she'd get lured into believing Mom actually wanted to spend time with her. She'd fool herself into thinking her mother really, truly cared. And she'd end up empty and sad after her mother left—on to a new life, big adventures, exciting people.

"Who said anything about coming there?" Her bright voice told Mackenzie that was exactly what she'd been thinking.

"I know you. You find me when you have nowhere else to go."

"That's not fair, Bumblebee."

"I told you not to call me that." She looked up at the ceiling and ground her teeth together. "Dad doesn't need you mooching off him, either. There aren't any creative jobs in this area. You'd be bored in eleven days. Tops."

"Your father...he's there?"

She brought her palm to her forehead. Why had she let that piece of info slip out?

"Yes, and he's busy. He doesn't need any distractions right now."

"I see." Gone was the sunny, hopeful tone her mom had carefully curated over the years. "I'm not a distraction."

"Yes, you are."

"I wouldn't be mooching—"

"It's all you ever do."

"You think I take advantage of you?" Her pained tone would not make Mackenzie feel guilty.

"Yes. That's exactly what I think." It was a relief to spell it out.

"And here I thought we could have a good catch-up session."

"We are." A good catch-up session? Mackenzie could barely handle talking on the phone with her. To have her show up here would be unbearable. She hated that she had to be so blunt, but she'd been hurt too many times.

"I meant in person," Mom said. "It would be nice to spend some quality time together."

Exactly as she'd feared. Mom did plan on coming there. Her emotions skipped the offended phase and went straight to sad. Her throat felt scratchy as she held back the bad memories.

"It's not quality time when it always ends the same way," Mackenzie said quietly. This conversation would be easier if she could get rid of the hurt little girl inside her and channel the angry adult instead, the way she usually did when dealing with her mother. But anger eluded her.

"What are you talking about?"

"Don't act like you don't know." Mackenzie left the kitchen and stood by the front window to stare at her lawn. "It's all hugs and catching up until you get restless. Then the real reason you're spending time with me reveals itself. Money. It never takes long for you to latch on to a new scheme in a new city, and I'm the one who has to fund it."

"That's not true."

It wasn't true? She let out an incredulous laugh. *That's better.* She was no longer on the verge of tears.

"Buffalo, New York," Mackenzie said. "The radio station assistant position. Two thousand dollars to help with the move and rent. You promised you'd pay me back."

"You said there was no hurry."

Pressure began to build in her temples. "Ashville, North Carolina. You were excited about being a tour guide for the brewery, or was it a winery? I can't remember. Fifteen hundred dollars, again, for the move and rent. You still haven't paid me back."

"If you didn't mean there wasn't a hurry, you shouldn't have said it."

Mackenzie cupped her hands behind her neck and stretched her elbows to the sides. The tightness in her upper back eased slightly. This woman pushed her buttons and didn't even know she was doing it.

"New Orleans. Bakery assistant. You raved about making king cakes and beignets. I gave you three thousand dollars. To get you started. First and last month's rent. That money's long gone."

"New Orleans is an expensive place to live," she said softly.

"What do you really want from me, Mom?" She was tired of this game. Had promised herself she'd never get suckered into it again. Yet, here they were, having this conversation.

"I miss you. I saw online that the clinic was opening, and I figured I'd tell you how proud I am of you."

The words simultaneously touched her and repelled her. She used to think her mother could do no wrong.

Mackenzie liked to think of herself as a forgiving person, as someone who didn't expect perfection. But her mother had crossed too many lines. All the lines, really.

The woman had let her down every single time she'd shown up unannounced to *catch up* and *spend quality time together.* It always ended the same. With Mackenzie's hard-earned money driving away and a false hope that this time would be different.

It never was.

"Thank you." Mackenzie put no feeling behind the words. She couldn't. Her mom didn't only ask for money and take it and run, she also went silent for months—sometimes years—and barely responded to Mackenzie's calls or texts.

Bonnie Howard's words held no meaning for her anymore.

It was too bad. If they had a normal relationship—a real one—it would have been nice to have a good chat with her mom, to share the ins and outs of the grand opening. Feel the love of a mother. It had been a long, exciting day. But what would be the point? Mom reached out when she needed something, and as soon as she got it, forgot Mackenzie existed. It was just the way life worked with her.

"Give it a week or two," her mother said. "You'll change your mind. I want to see your new place. We can buy rugs or curtains or whatever you need. Spend some time together."

"I don't need rugs or curtains." She did, but the last person she'd go shopping with was her mother. Christy would be a much better choice.

"It wouldn't be for long. A few days. A week, tops."

The nerve of this woman! Hadn't she heard a word Mackenzie said? The fact her mother thought she could stay with her after all the pain she'd put her through was mind boggling.

"I said no."

Neither spoke for a while. This whole routine was too predictable.

"I guess having your mom camp out on your couch is too much for you." The teasing lilt boiled Mackenzie's blood.

"Save your guilt trip. It won't work on me."

"I don't know what I did, but I hope I can make it up to you soon."

She didn't know what she did? And what did

she mean by soon? Mackenzie squeezed her eyes shut, trying not to react.

"I'm busy. I have ranches to visit and pets to treat."

"I know you do." Her tone reverted to the optimistic one Mackenzie recognized all too well. Her plans were clearly in motion, leaving Mackenzie no choice in the matter. "We'll find time to hang out. I can work around your schedule."

She was too tired to argue. She'd said all she'd planned on saying. There was no way she'd play along with her mother's weird games. If the woman thought Mackenzie was okay with her staying with her and would fit her into her schedule, she was dead wrong.

She'd been through this one too many times. She'd given all she could give. This time her mother was on her own.

CHAPTER SIX

"I'M IMPRESSED WITH how quickly Tulip mastered the release and place commands. It's obvious you've been working with her." Mackenzie was crouching to pet Tulip in the back room of the clinic the following Monday evening. Cade hadn't seen her since the previous week's training session, and he wanted to ask about her mother and if she'd been out to any more ranches. But not with his mom next to him.

He also wanted to draw her into his arms. Ask her how her day was and listen to everything on her mind. To say she'd been dominating his thoughts was an understatement.

Instead, he glanced at his mother. She gave him a proud smile.

"We're motivated," Mom said. "Trudy's memory is slipping a little more each day. We really want her to be able to enjoy Tulip before things get too bad."

It was the first time his mother had mentioned any concerns about how quickly Nana's mental state was declining. She should know. She visited her almost every day. Cade hadn't wanted to face the fact Nana had been having more bad days than good lately. Last Wednesday, when he'd stopped by, she'd been fine. But Friday's visit with Ty had been a bust—she'd barely been able to keep her eyes open.

A heavy sadness weighed on his chest. What if they trained Tulip, and it ended up being for nothing? He'd seen the late-stage dementia patients in the nursing home enough to know that many of them had almost no awareness of what went on around them.

He and Mom should have trained a dog months ago. Before Nana's Alzheimer's had worsened. Seeing his vibrant grandmother diminished and confused always punched him in the gut. He missed the caring woman he'd taken for granted for far too long.

"I understand," Mackenzie said, rising. "Tulip's training is coming along fine. No need to worry. She'll be ready soon. I asked Dad to observe our session tonight. He should be here in a few minutes."

"Rumor around town is that your clinic is a

smashing success," Mom said. "Everyone's relieved to have you taking care of their pets."

"Thank you. It's been chaotic getting everything ready. I, for one, am glad the appointments filled up so quickly after the grand opening. The flowers at the entrance really make it welcoming, too. Thank you again for bringing them over."

"You've already thanked me ten times," Mom said cheerily. "We couldn't be happier to have you here, Mackenzie."

Cade almost raised his eyebrows at her use of the word *we*, but he didn't. He *was* happy to have her here. Even if it made him uncomfortable at times.

Mackenzie was transparent. What you saw was what you got. Cade, on the other hand, hid himself behind a socially acceptable exterior. And lately, he'd been tempted to let down his guard. Allow Mackenzie to catch a glimpse of the real him, the one he'd been trying to hide since New York. He had a feeling she'd already glimpsed it, but if she hadn't? She'd hate that side of him as much as he did. He'd just have to keep it under wraps.

"Let's see how she adapts to the wheelchair." Mackenzie pointed her thumb over her shoulder in the direction of the door. "I'll bring it in. If she barks at it, use the quiet command. A lot of dogs feel threatened by strange objects. We have several strategies to help them overcome their fears."

Mackenzie hustled away, and Cade turned to his mom. "Is Nana getting worse?"

Her expression fell. "Yes. It might be temporary. Her immune system could be fighting something or maybe she's tired, but she's been out of it lately. Has she been okay when you've dropped by?"

"For the most part. I haven't been getting over there as often as I should. I'll drop by to see her tomorrow."

"Here we are." Mackenzie pushed a wheelchair through the door. Tulip immediately began barking at it.

"Quiet," Mom said to the dog. She stopped barking, but then she started again.

"She feels insecure around it. That's normal," Mackenzie said. "I'll move it out of sight, and when she's calm, let's try the place command."

"In the bed over there?" Mom pointed to the dog bed placed off to the side.

"Yes, it was her bed when she lived with me, so she's familiar with it."

Cade watched as his mother nodded and gave her the command. Tulip followed Christy to the small bed and got into it. His mother praised her and gave her a treat.

"Good job." Mackenzie watched the process from where she stood in front of the wheelchair. "Now have her lie down."

"Lie down." Mom used the hand signal. Tulip obeyed and got another treat.

"Nice work, Christy." Mackenzie watched to make sure Tulip stayed put. "I'm going to have you stand a few feet away from her. I'll slowly move the chair your way. Considering the fact she initially barked at it, I'm expecting her to get antsy, maybe even circle around as I bring the chair close to her. If that happens, your job is to remind her to lie down. Are you ready?"

His mom nodded. Cade's gut tightened. What if Tulip didn't get used to the wheelchair? Nana would never get a chance to enjoy the dog. This low-grade tension constantly made him feel like time was running out.

Mackenzie slowly pushed the wheelchair to the side of the room. Then she brought it over near Christy, and Tulip began to shake. As she wheeled it near Tulip, the dog got up to pace around the bed and never took her eyes off the wheelchair.

"Lie down." Mom's voice wavered.

"Speak normally, Christy. Stay relaxed. She gets her cues from you." Mackenzie then turned the wheelchair and walked it past Cade around the room and right back to the bed. Tulip began to shake, but this time, she didn't get up, nor did she bark.

Patrick arrived and stood by the door watching them. Cade nodded to him in greeting.

Mackenzie took a few more laps, brought the wheelchair to the edge of the bed, wheeled it back and handed it to Cade. "I'm going to have you push it around for a few minutes."

It was on the tip of his tongue to ask why, but he simply took the handles. "Where to?"

"Anywhere you'd like, but make sure you get it close to Tulip. We want her to accept it as a normal, non-threatening object in her life." Mackenzie must have noticed her father. She waved to him. "We're getting her used to the wheelchair."

"I see." Patrick's eyes crinkled in good humor.

Cade didn't know how he felt about being watched by her father, but he began to push the wheelchair anyway. He stopped it close to the bed and moved it around the room. Mackenzie held her phone to video Tulip.

"Keep going, Cade," Patrick said. "Make a smaller circle with it, get it close to her several times."

He felt kind of foolish, but he continued to move the wheelchair back and forth and up to Tulip.

"There. You see?" Mackenzie pressed the button on the phone and pointed to the dog. "She's decided—for the moment anyway—that it's nothing to get worked up about. See how she's ignoring it? Keep going, Cade."

He kept pushing the chair, but he could tell Mackenzie was right. Tulip rested her chin on her front paws as she lay in the bed. She kept an eye on the chair, but she was no longer shaking.

"Okay, that's enough. You can stop pushing the wheelchair. Christy, you can free Tulip from the place command." Mackenzie slipped her phone into her back pocket as Mom told Tulip to release, then lavished the dog with praise and treats. Mackenzie grinned. "Ten minutes. That's all it took."

Patrick moved farther into the room. "Let's see how she does with a stranger approaching.

Christy, have her walk to the center of the room with you. Then tell her to sit."

His mom obeyed, and Tulip obliged.

"I'm going to come over and shake your hand. If she moves out of her sit command, remind her to sit and give her the physical cue, okay?"

"Sure thing." His mom's cheeks were rosy, but she commanded Tulip to the center of the room and had her sit. Thankfully, the dog walked loosely on the leash next to her, the way they'd been insisting on their evening walks.

Patrick approached Christy and extended his hand. "How are you doing today?"

Mom shook it, and they chatted for a few seconds while Tulip sat calmly beside her.

"Nice," Patrick said. He crouched to pet the dog. "Hi there, Tulip." Then he straightened. "She's doing well. Next week, she might revert to barking at the wheelchair, but this was good progress."

Cade didn't want to wait another week for her to encounter the wheelchair. "What if we took the wheelchair home with us? Worked with her on it for a while each day?"

Mackenzie tilted her chin as if trying on the

idea and slowly nodded. She glanced at her dad, who waited for her decision.

"I don't see a problem with it," she said. "What do you think, Dad?"

"I'm all for it."

"Ten minutes at a time. That should be enough." A frown line grew above her nose. "If she gets to a point where she's not responding to it at all, would you want to teach her to walk beside the wheelchair, too?"

"Yes," Cade and Christy said in unison.

Mackenzie met her father's gaze, and they both chuckled.

"Good," Mackenzie said. "Here, let us show you what to do."

With a leash in her hand, Mackenzie sat in the wheelchair and explained how to hold it for the dog to be far enough away from the chair. "You want her to go at your pace, and you want her to learn how to avoid the wheels. Being walked by someone in a wheelchair isn't something I anticipate her needing to do, but it will help protect her when she's at the nursing home."

"Anything that will keep our princess safe," Christy said. "Right, Cade?"

He nodded. For once, he agreed with his mother.

"Yes," he said. "Mackenzie, how much longer will we have to wait?"

"For what?"

"For her to get certified?" He'd been trying not to push the dog. Trying to think of her as just their pet. But she *was* training to be a therapy dog, and he longed for his grandmother to enjoy her. "I want Nana to meet her."

"Dad, I'll let you take this one."

"She's almost there," Patrick said. "Work with her this week. Be relaxed, praise her and give her treats when she succeeds. Get her out around other people. Make her sit at your feet while you talk to them and do the same if they have a dog."

"Do you think she'll be ready for a test run at the nursing home next week?" Mackenzie asked.

"I do."

"I'll call them and see if we can bring her there for training. Are you both available on Tuesday afternoon?"

He and his mom nodded.

Cade's spirits lifted. Finally.

"Good," Mackenzie said. "That's settled."

She began chatting with his mom, and Patrick approached him. "I looked into the building you mentioned to Mackenzie."

Cade racked his brain, and then he remembered. "Oh, right. For the people to stay at when they get their dogs."

"Yes." He nodded. "It's a little too off the beaten path. You wouldn't happen to know any real estate agents who could help me out, would you?"

Cade rattled off the names he trusted. "The property across the street from here might be an option."

"What do you mean?"

"You could build something to accommodate them."

"Wouldn't it be expensive?"

"Probably. But it's worth looking into."

"I appreciate it." Patrick clapped him on the shoulder. "You've helped both me and Mackenzie more than you know."

Guilt crept over him. *You think I'm a good person, but I'm not.*

He didn't deserve Patrick's thanks. Or his daughter. And he'd better not forget it.

"Who is this?" As soon as Mackenzie entered her dad's building the next day at noon, she spotted the German shepherd. The past couple of weeks had been a rollercoaster—tough, exciting, fantastic and predictable—all at the same time. The full days at the clinic had her missing coming home to Tulip. She'd been seriously considering getting a dog of her own, but she wasn't home much. She had no time for pets. No time for a boyfriend. Not even for a guy like Cade.

Why her spirits plunged at the thought, she didn't want to evaluate. Everything was going well. She should be happy.

Dad grinned. "Meet Charger."

"Where did you get him? And when?" She approached the dog and let him sniff her closed hand before petting him. His tail wagged as his big eyes looked up at her with affection. "He's a sweetie. And from the looks of it, already on his way to being well-behaved."

"Leslie called this morning, and when she explained his situation, I drove out there straight away. He's full of energy, but a smart dog like him needs a job to do. He'll be easy to train, despite his bad habits." Dad had a soft spot for energetic large dogs who proved too much for their owners. Like her, though, he'd opted not to own one since he wasn't home much. But now he would be. Dad ruffled the dog's head. "He turns one in October."

"A puppy."

"Moldable. I'm hoping he'll be able to help settle the dogs we train here. They do better when they have a good role model around."

"Where has Charger been living?" Mackenzie continued to pet him. He ate up the attention.

"A young couple bought him as a puppy, but they brought home a newborn last week and can't meet his needs."

"That's sad." She rubbed behind his ears.

"It's better that they realize it now." Dad tilted his head and watched her. "You're doing a good job training Tulip. You settling in at the clinic okay?"

"Thanks. She's been easy to train. And yes, the clinic is booked out for the next couple of weeks. It's amazing how much business even a small town has when it comes to pets."

"I'm sure people in the surrounding towns are making appointments, too."

"True. Now, I just need the mobile vet services to take off. The ranchers I've met around Jewel River seem to be on board with my animal husbandry plan for their cattle. Hopefully, the ranchers in the surrounding area will reach out, too."

"They will." He pointed to the door. "Have you eaten lunch?"

"No. I came straight over when I saw your truck."

"Let's get burgers at Dixie B's."

"Yes."

Ten minutes later, after dropping off Charger and crating him at her father's house, Mackenzie and her dad sat opposite each other in a booth at Dixie B's. The forest green walls held framed pictures of wildlife. The place was hopping for a Tuesday. They both ordered burgers, fries and sodas, then settled in to catch up.

"Have you hired a contractor?" she asked, smiling at the waitress when their drinks arrived.

"Ed McCaffrey is number one on my list if he can fit me in."

"Yeah, I liked him, too. I wish he'd had time for the clinic. The contractor I hired did a good job, but the finish work wasn't the greatest. I touched up some of it myself."

"If you need me to help with anything, say the word."

"I will."

"Have you heard from your mother again?"

"I talked to her the night of the grand opening. Since then? No." She left it at that. "When do you plan on opening the training center?"

"It depends on how quickly the renovations can be finished. Plus, I need a place for the clients to stay. Last night, Cade mentioned the possibility of having something built."

"That might work." A prick jabbed her conscience. Cade had helped her time and again since she moved to town. All he'd ever asked of her was to come out and see his stables. And she hadn't made the time.

She liked being with Cade. He made it all feel easy, and she wasn't an easy person. "By the way, we're set for the training session at the nursing home next Tuesday. Want to join us?"

"Of course I do. Tulip's almost ready. I have a good feeling about that little dog." He grinned. "Have you made any friends yet?"

Cade. Christy. "Some."

"And your free time? Are you relaxing?"

"Yep." It was mostly true. After supper each night, she'd been reading up on the latest recommendations for equine care in case she was thrown into a situation she hadn't handled before.

She still hadn't gotten any emergency calls. Her nerves kept climbing with worry that she'd encounter a problem she couldn't handle. What if she lost a cow or horse due to inexperience? What if it soured the community against her?

The thought had kept her up a night or two.

"Are you *really* taking time for yourself?" His gaze probed her.

They'd had this conversation off and on throughout the years. He worried she was all work and no play.

So what if she was? She liked work. Didn't have much desire to play.

"I watched a show on television last night."

His deadpan stare made her squirm. "Let me guess. A reality show about a veterinarian."

"It's still a show. It counts." Heat rose to her cheeks.

Sighing, he gave his head a slight shake. "There's more to life. Watch one of those romantic movies or get coffee with a friend. Make a life—a real life—here, Mackenzie."

She wanted to tell him she had a real life, but it wasn't true. While she got along well with her employees, she couldn't share with Greta and Emily everything going on in her life, nor did she want to. They were gossip machines.

"Have you been to church?" he asked. Their food arrived. It looked and smelled delicious.

"Not yet. I was waiting for you to get here."

"Okay, then, Sunday we'll go together. I'm sure there are plenty of nice people your age here. Get to know them."

What he was really telling her was to get a life. For the first time in years, she could admit to herself that he was right. The thought of having to put herself out there made her squirm, though. Dad made it all sound easy. But for a girl like her? There was nothing easy about it.

Maybe the first step could be taking Cade up on his offer to tour his stables.

The next time he asked her to stop by, she would.

But what if he didn't?

Then she'd stop by on her own. There was more to life than work. At least, that was what she'd been told.

She liked Cade. But what if getting close to him was a mistake?

THE FOLLOWING AFTERNOON, Cade finished his to-do list at the makeshift office on the construction site of the stables and climbed into his truck. He'd reached out to Forestline Adventures again and left a message with their receptionist. He'd called five other companies on his list, too, but none of them were as large or had as many horses as Forestline. With the Fourth of July the day after tomorrow, Cade didn't expect to hear back from any of them until next week at the earliest.

He could have waited to call them, but sometimes people surprised him and were more available during holiday weeks. This didn't happen to be one of those times.

After starting the truck, he cranked the air conditioning. Everything that needed to be done to open Moulten Stables was falling into place. Next on his hot list was to start looking for a manager to hire. Someone with an impeccable record, superior experience in taking care of horses and the credentials to back it all up.

And integrity. The person he hired had to have integrity.

Yeah, like you?

He was trying. Every day for six years, he'd been trying to have integrity.

No matter how hard you try, you'll never have it. You're fooling everyone, but you can't fool yourself.

Grinding his teeth together, he shook away the thoughts. The manager he hired would also have to be okay with living in a small town. Cade drove away and cast a glance toward the huge old house across the road. He'd purchased it last year. It had been sitting empty for months. Everything in it was outdated, but it had good bones. He figured its proximity to the stables made it valuable. Maybe he could throw in free rent to a manager to sweeten the deal.

Ty might be able to suggest someone. Despite being reclusive, his brother had a knack for knowing these things.

The short drive to the nursing home went by in a flash. Part of him dreaded going there. He wished Nana was back at her home, baking cookies and giving him a big old hug. They used to sit at her kitchen table, and she'd ask him and Ty about life and school. He'd tell her everything was fine. But after three or four cookies, he'd open up and confess what was really on his mind.

Right now, what was on his mind was Mackenzie. He tried to push her out of his thoughts, but there she was.

Lately he'd been feeling off. Not queasy or ill—just not himself. Instead of constantly thinking about opening Moulten Stables or studying the stocks he'd invested in or coming up with a new improvement for the ranch, his mind had been glued to one thing—Mackenzie.

She didn't mince words. He got the impression she wasn't one to reveal much, although she'd revealed quite a bit to him over the past month. Her patience awed him. Her attention to detail did, too. As did her unpretentious manner.

He wanted to spend more time with her.

If only he could get Nana's advice. He could use it—and a cookie or two—at the moment. He wasn't fool enough to think that in her current state she'd be able to smooth out his troubles the way she used to, but he still liked being with her. Missed her unconditional love.

A parking spot at the far end of the lot caught his eye, and he backed the truck into it.

Out in the fresh air, he pocketed his keys and pulled back his shoulders. Enough thinking about Mackenzie.

Which Nana was he going to get today? The one who remembered him and was happy to see him? The one with blank eyes and no energy? Or the one lost in the past who didn't recognize him?

Did it matter? He'd handle whatever version was presented, even though the latter two broke his heart.

"Hey there, Cade," Charlene said as he approached her desk. "Miss Trudy is in her room."

"How is she today?"

Charlene winced. "She's tired. But she'll be happy to see you. You always brighten her day."

His spirits sank knowing it was going to be one of those visits where she didn't speak much, and he simply held her hand. He liked when she had color in her cheeks and was sitting in her wheelchair. On good days, she'd know who he was. He'd tell her what was going on around town, and the updates made her smile.

If Charlene's expression told him anything, today would not be that day.

"Thanks for the head's up." He strode down the hall. Besides the disinfectant smell and moans coming from one of the rooms, the place was decent enough.

Her door was open. He still knocked on it before entering. "Hi, Nana."

As he'd feared, she was not in her wheelchair but sitting in the raised hospital bed. She stared out the window with a blank expression, but she turned her head. Her eyes opened wider. "Pete?"

Cade's heart pinched. This wasn't the first time she'd mistaken him for his father. It always

hurt, mainly because he wished it was true—
that his father was still alive. He'd do about
anything to see his dad again. "No, Nana, it's
me, Cade."

Her eyelashes fluttered, and her cloudy blue
eyes floundered trying to place him.

"Pete's son." He approached her and covered
her hand with his.

"Oh, yes." She nodded, but he could tell she
was simply going along with him and didn't
know who he was. He pulled the chair over
to the bed, sat down and took her hand in his
again.

"How are you doing today?" he asked.

"I'm pretty good." She gave him a smile.
"Did you know Aunt Jo came over yesterday?"

"Aunt Jo? Really?" He raised his eyebrows
and kept his tone even. Nana had claimed many
times that Aunt Jo had visited her, but Aunt Jo
had passed away thirty years ago.

Cade and his mom had learned from the doctors and staff that it was best to stay calm and
go along with any delusions. Dementia and Alzheimer's patients couldn't help the changes in
their brain and just wanted to feel understood.
It would do no good to argue with her.

"Yes, she brought the necklace she promised

me." She fingered the neckline of her shirt. The necklace with the cross pendant was there. Nana had worn it every day Cade could remember.

"It's pretty, Nana. Aunt Jo must really love you."

"Oh, she does." She stared at him then, her eyes shining. "She's worried about you, Pete."

His chest grew tight. He always felt uncomfortable when she was like this.

"Next time you see her, tell her there's nothing to worry about." He tried to change the subject. "What did you have for lunch?"

Nana tightened her grip on his hand and implored him with her eyes. "I'm worried, too. Christy's good for you. You should ask that girl to marry you. She can't help it her mama didn't know how to be a parent. Be patient with her, and she'll learn to trust you."

This was new. When Nana's mind retreated to the past, she never mentioned his mother, and Christy and Trudy had been close. Close enough that Cade knew his mom considered Trudy Moulten more of a mother than her own estranged parent.

"I will."

"Good." Nana relaxed back into the pillow

with a sigh of contentment and let go of his hand. "Is Dolly okay?"

"Yeah, Dolly's great." Who was Dolly again?

"That dog misses me. Tell your daddy to give her extra attention until I can come home. The doctors should be letting me out any day now. You cuddle Dolly, too, okay?"

"I will." Cade wasn't going to be able to take much more of this. He was already getting choked up, and he'd only been here for a few minutes. "You'll get to see another dog soon. Tulip. She's a Pomeranian. You'll like her. She's tiny, like a little peach puffball."

"Tulip?" She frowned. "I don't remember a dog with that name."

"She's new. You haven't seen her yet."

Her face cleared. "Oh, good. I thought I'd forgotten. I've always liked small dogs."

"She's growing on me." In fact, Cade wished the little dog was here with them now. She'd sit on his lap and lick his hand and make him feel like he could handle his grandmother thinking he was his father and sharing things from the past he didn't know what to do with.

"Little dogs need to sit on your lap, you know," Nana said. "Don't push her away.

You're used to big dogs, but the small ones need your affection."

"I know. I'm learning."

"Good." She closed her eyes, and he took that as his sign to leave.

Then he bent over and kissed her forehead. "Goodbye, Nana. I'll see you in a few days."

"Goodbye, Pete. Don't forget what I said. Christy's good for you."

"Okay."

He left the room. All the way down the hall, he fought a sense of disorientation. It was true that he and Ty resembled their father. He'd have to ask Ty if Nana ever confused him with their dad, too.

"How was she?" Charlene bustled toward him.

"About as good as could be expected."

"I'm sorry, hon." She looked two seconds away from giving him a hug. He couldn't handle one at the moment. Might break the dam of tears he was holding back. "Your mom's been showing us pictures of Tulip, and Mackenzie called to bring her out next Tuesday afternoon. We can't wait to see her. It's so nice of you to offer to bring the little pup when you come visit."

"Anything for Nana." He didn't feel nice. He felt sad. Sad that Nana was here thinking about Dolly, a dog long dead, and giving him dating advice about his own mother.

"We have several seniors who could really use a pick-me-up, too. I think getting to interact with Tulip would make their days brighter."

He hadn't thought about bringing Tulip around to other people in the nursing home. "Yeah, that's what Mom said, too."

"When the time comes, I'll take you to the patients who could use a little pick-me-up." Charlene's expression changed from hopeful to understanding. "Showing the dog to the other seniors might bring you some peace, too, hon." She rubbed his upper arm in compassion.

"I'll think about it." He gave her a tight smile. How would bringing the dog to other elderly people bring *him* peace? All it would do was remind him they'd once been strong, and now they were stuck in a nursing home. At the moment, this entire place depressed him. "Thanks, Charlene. I'm going to take off."

He strode down the hall, through the door and out into the sunshine. The sadness slowly lessened, only to be replaced with questions. Questions he'd never really considered.

He'd always assumed his mom and dad had fallen madly in love, gotten married and lived happily ever after. Sure, he knew the stories they'd told him about Christy arriving in town when she was in high school. About Pete stopping in at the discount clothing store where she worked even though he didn't need any clothes. They'd been opposites—Dad was calm and reserved; Mom was bubbly and outgoing.

But Cade had never considered there'd been any hiccups along the way to their engagement and marriage. Had never really thought of his parents as real people at all. They'd just been Pete and Christy. At one point, though, they'd been individuals with their own problems, their own dreams.

He climbed into the truck and started it. His phone rang.

"Hello?"

"Are you free tomorrow morning?" The voice was female. He didn't recognize it.

"Who's calling?"

"Paris Grove. I'm passing through Jewel

River tomorrow, and my father wants me to stop by your new stables."

Paris Grove. Michael Grove's daughter. The CEO of Forestline Adventures was sending his daughter to check out the operation? Why wouldn't he come himself?

"I'll be at the stables in the morning," he said. He wasn't missing this opportunity. "Do you need the address? The property is close to town, but the town itself is off the beaten path."

"Text it to me. I'll find it. I hope it's as good as you told my dad. I plan on taking pictures during the tour."

"Take all the pictures you want." The stables were coming along as scheduled, but he wished she would have called a few weeks from now. Actually, he wished her father would have called. Giving Paris the tour wouldn't be the same as convincing Michael to board their horses with him.

Regardless, this meeting needed to go well. He'd make sure the construction zone was as clean as possible. Highlight all the features that would be added by summer's end. If this was his shot at landing their business, he'd make the most of it.

And if it took his mind off of everything

else, all the better. He'd been thinking about Mackenzie too much, worrying about Nana too much. He needed to get his head back where it belonged—on his business.

CHAPTER SEVEN

CADE COULDN'T HELP wishing he'd be giving Mackenzie the tour of the property this morning instead of Paris. The horse barn, though not finished, was coming along nicely. He'd worked with a designer to select materials to give the finished space a rustic, timeless—and expensive—feel. At the moment, the stalls were roughed in, and the windows and exterior doors had been installed. If Paris would have waited two more weeks to visit, she could have seen the lantern-inspired sconces with textured glass above the door of each stall, along with the special floors he'd picked out, the hooks, the benches—all of it.

In its current shape, the place was unlikely to impress her.

Last night, he'd researched Paris's role with the company. She was the marketing manager, described herself as an aesthetics specialist—

whatever that meant—and brand guru. He was under the impression if she didn't think his facility worthy of being photographed, she'd tell her father to use a different boarder.

Cade wanted their business.

He slowly took in the construction site, looking for anything that needed to be cleaned or put away before Paris arrived. The sweet scent of wood shavings filled the air. Nail guns *pop, popped* at the other end of the long barn. A sports drink lay on its side next to an overturned bucket to his left. He picked up both and took them to the crew's trailer.

Once that was finished, he mentally reviewed all of the selling points he'd finalized yesterday. Then he checked his phone—she'd be arriving any minute—took a deep breath and prayed.

Lord, I need this meeting to go well. I've done everything possible to make this property the best it can be. I've spared no expense. Please, let her see what it could be, not what it is.

He strode around the barn, then stopped to look over the grounds. Fencing was being installed at the back of the property to create pastures for the horses. The outdoor arena had been cleared, but it would be a few more weeks before the materials for it would be delivered.

Would Forestline be able to make a decision based on the current shape of the property?

The sound of tires on gravel made him turn. Paris must have arrived. He went back through the barn's large sliding wooden doors, then across the barn aisle and out the opposite set of sliding wooden doors. A large, black SUV came to a stop in front of him.

Showtime. Cade plastered on a confident smile and waited. The passenger door opened, and out stepped a woman in her late twenties who could have graced the cover of any magazine. Thick, wavy black hair bounced past her shoulders and stopped midway down her back. Oversized sunglasses hid her eyes, and dark red lipstick punctuated her heart-shaped lips. Her fitted sheath dress hugged her curves. Dangerously high heels made Cade blink.

The woman knew she'd be touring a construction zone, right?

She whipped out her phone and began snapping pictures. Before he could greet her, she began filming and talking into the phone. "I'm getting the when-you-want-to-escape-it-all vibe. Blue skies. Trees along the back of the property. Pasture for miles. Nothing—and I mean nothing—to do except ignore it all…"

Cade wasn't sure what to do in this situation. Did he interrupt her and introduce himself? Wait for her to finish whatever she was filming? This wasn't one of those live videos on social media, was it?

The choice was made for him when she touched her screen to end the video, slipped it into her small designer purse, shifted her sunglasses to rest on the top of her head and strolled toward him with a wide smile.

"Hello." Her big brown eyes sparkled as she extended her hand. "Paris Grove. You must be Cade Moulten."

In that instant, his nerves disappeared. He knew exactly what to do, what to say and how to handle this woman. Hers was a world he'd mastered during his time in New York.

"Miss Grove. It's a pleasure." Giving her a playful smile, he shook her hand. "I hope your drive was uneventful. Are you hungry? Thirsty?"

"Paris, please," she said. "Yes, uneventful is exactly how I'd describe it. You're on the edge of civilization out here, aren't you? As for your other question, no, thank you. Gerald and I already ate." She looked back over her shoulder and waved to the driver. "Gerald takes me everywhere. He's used to my detours and she-nanigans. Best driver in the world."

"Gerald is welcome to join us, or he can stretch his legs around the property."

"He needs a break from me, but that's sweet of you." She shifted her weight and studied him. "You're not what I was expecting."

"Oh, yeah?" He had a good idea what she'd expected. Either a wealthy businessman or a no-nonsense cowboy. He was neither and he was both.

"Yeah, I figured with your Wall Street background, you were playing out a childhood Western fantasy here."

"Sorry, no childhood fantasies involved. I grew up in Jewel River."

"I see." Her eyes twinkled. "Was the city too big for you?"

"Nah," he said with a grin. "My dad died. I came home to take over the ranch."

"My research didn't turn up any of that." She hooked her arm in his, and together they faced the stables. "Hope you don't mind. I need a steady arm to lean on in these heels."

"You don't strike me as the type to need any help at all. You know what you're doing."

"Flatterer." She laughed. "But you can't

blame a girl for wanting an excuse to lean on a strong cowboy."

He chuckled, but it was all for show. He had nothing to worry about from Paris Grove. Yes, she was a flirt, but there would never be anything between them. She wasn't his type. Even if she was, his life was here, and she'd be off on a new adventure within twenty-four hours.

Lately, all he could think about was strawberry blond hair and hooded blue eyes.

Over the next hour, he showed Paris the unfinished barn and gave her an overview of the pastures and grounds. As they strolled back to his makeshift office, he described the services the boarding facility would offer. Inside, he pulled out a comfortable chair for her to sit on. He'd brought four of them in last night, in case more people—namely, her father—showed up with her. They both sat, and he directed her attention to the table where his laptop was set up.

Paris pushed her chair back and to the side, then crossed one leg over the other. He angled his chair to face her better. Then he went through the digital renderings of the finished stables, pastures, riding paths and outdoor arena.

"Who's going to run this place?" she asked. "You?"

"No. I'll be hiring a manager."

"Anyone in mind?"

"I just started the process. I'm looking for an expert with horses. I have high standards."

"That will make our customers happy."

"I know."

"Who else will have access to the stables?"

"We'll have other people boarding their horses here."

"That could be a liability."

He narrowed his eyes slightly, then forced himself to appear open and relaxed. "How so?"

"We provide highly trained, expensive horses to our clients. I'm not sure we want anyone off the street around our investments during the off-season."

He hadn't considered that aspect. The building was one long barn at the moment.

"Your horses will be treated like the prizes they are. No one but my staff will be allowed to take care of them, feed them, ride them or even approach them. Their safety, health and well-being are my primary concern."

"We'll keep that in mind." She opened the folder he'd given her with all the information about Moulten Stables. "When did you say this place would be ready?"

"By September. You can board all of your horses here this winter. Say the word."

"We'll think about it." A knowing smile lifted her lips, then she took out her phone again. "Mind if we get a picture together?"

He hated having his picture taken. Refused to sign up for any social media accounts. But this was business, and it was obvious social media was Paris's wheelhouse.

"Sure."

They smooshed together, and she raised the phone and clicked a few selfies. Then he walked her back to the SUV, where Gerald was waiting, shook her hand and said goodbye.

They drove away. Paris was probably any other guy's dream girl, but he still would have rather spent the morning with Mackenzie.

His old world—although he'd moved easily within it—had never fulfilled him. And the people he used to spend time with thrived on a busier, louder, more competitive life than he had the stomach for.

So why was he still chasing it?

I'm not. I just want to provide a service to my community, and I need the big clients to fund it.

Did he though? He had a high net worth.

Yes, I need them. Why was he second-guessing himself?

He wanted to find Mackenzie and tell her how the meeting had gone. Tulip's next training session was too far off to wait. He could drive over to the clinic. But she was busy.

Maybe he should ask Ty his take on the issue of the stables being one building. He could pick his brain about hiring a manager, too.

What time was it? Lunch time at the clinic. A quick call wouldn't hurt.

He pressed Mackenzie's number.

"Hey, Cade. What's up?"

"Just checking in." He wanted to thump his forehead at how lame that sounded.

"How's Tulip doing with the wheelchair? Or have you had a chance to work with her?"

"Mom and I tag-teamed with it last night. Tulip trembled at first but eventually settled down."

"I'm glad."

A long pause ensued.

"Charlene Parker mentioned you set up the training session at the nursing home." Why was he talking about this when he really wanted to tell her about the stables and the meeting?

"Yes, the staff is very accommodating. They

seem excited at the prospect of having a therapy dog come around."

"Yeah." He didn't know what he was hoping to accomplish. All he knew was he liked hearing her voice. "Are you going to the Fourth of July festival tomorrow?"

He always enjoyed walking around the booths and food trucks. American flags lined the sidewalks up and down Center Street. The street would be blocked off, with a stage set up at one end for various entertainment throughout the day. Fireworks were scheduled at night, too.

"I don't know. I probably should go. The clinic will be closed, and I don't plan on visiting any ranches unless they have an emergency."

"Why don't you come over to the stables in the morning?"

"You don't give up, do you?" Her teasing tone made his heart skip a beat.

"I don't."

"Okay. You wore me down. What time should I come by?"

"How about nine? I'll stop by Annie's Bakery and get us doughnuts and coffee first."

"Deal. But only if you pick me up a couple of her crullers."

"They're delicious."

"Don't I know it."

"And after, we can go to the festival together."

"Like a date?" she sounded skeptical.

"Sure. Like a date." His heart started pounding. Now he'd gone and done it. He'd crossed his own invisible line—and asked her on a date. It wasn't panic making his pulse race, though. It was excitement.

"I'VE GOT A pregnant mare acting funny."

The words stopped Mackenzie cold that evening. Marc Young was on the line. The day had been long. Rather than being tired, though, she'd been keyed up at the prospect of hanging out with Cade tomorrow morning at his stables and going to the festival with him after.

A date. Only a slightly less terrifying thought than this phone call.

"When is your mare due?" She focused on the problem at hand. A pregnant mare acting funny wasn't just a problem—it was her biggest fear.

"In about six weeks." Horses had long gestational periods—ten to eleven months. Since foals gained almost all of their weight toward the end of the pregnancy, Mackenzie hoped the mare wasn't going into premature labor.

"Describe how she's acting." She listened as Marc described Miss Lightning's symptoms. "I'll bring my trailer out right away. What's your address?"

After they ended the call, she typed the address into her phone and grabbed her keys. The drive to the clinic took all of two minutes, and once she'd connected the trailer, she headed out of town to his ranch.

Memories of losing the horse and foal all those years ago crowded her mind. What if this was a similar situation? What if she had to perform surgery and she lost the mother and foal again? It was no secret Marc's mom ran the bakery in town, and his wife owned the gourmet chocolate shop. Mackenzie couldn't afford to mess this up. Couldn't get a bad reputation this early in the game. More than anything, though, she needed to get it right for the horse's sake.

God, I'm scared. It's not like I haven't worked with horses. Dr. Johan insisted I take the lead on several calls. But what if something goes wrong? What if I make the wrong choice? Please, help me!

She wished Tulip was here. Wished she

could pet the little ball of fluff. The dog always calmed her nerves.

She went down the line of everything she knew about horse health in the final months of pregnancy. No clear diagnosis came to mind based on what Marc had told her. She'd have to wait to see for herself.

When she arrived at his ranch, he waved her to the stables. She wasted no time parking and grabbing her supplies. Marc explained the situation in more detail as she zipped up her lightweight coveralls.

"She's in the paddock over here." Marc unlocked the gate, waited for her to enter, followed her inside and closed it once more.

The pretty mahogany quarter horse had a white diamond on her forehead, and her forelegs, mane and tail were black. She raised her head as they approached. She had a listless air about her.

"Hey there, Miss Lightning." Mackenzie used her soothing voice as she slowly approached the mare. The horse looked to be a healthy weight. She took her temperature, listened to her lungs and performed an overall health check.

The stethoscope hung around her neck as she continued to study Miss Lightning. The weather hadn't been scorching hot, nor did there seem to be any infection or typical problem a pregnant mare might face.

What was she missing?

"She hasn't been eating fescue?" she asked.

"No, she hasn't."

"Is she up-to-date on her vaccines?"

"I'm not sure. Dr. Banks came out regularly until he retired..." Marc rubbed the back of his neck.

"I understand."

"I have her records. I can get them."

"That would be a big help." As Marc loped away, Mackenzie stroked the horse's neck, murmuring sweet nothings to her.

Then she examined her front legs and hooves—and immediately recognized what was wrong. Marc strode back with a folder in his hand.

"When was the last time her hooves were trimmed?"

"It hasn't been too long...wait...when did I have it done?" His eyes grew round as he nodded. "Of course. It's been a good six months. I could kick myself. I'm always on top of everything, but we had her shoes taken off in the winter since we weren't riding her. Normally, Doctor Banks would remind me about her hooves."

"It's okay. I can take care of it now. She's still far enough away from her due date that it shouldn't cause a problem, and it will make her more comfortable as the foal grows bigger."

They discussed the particulars, and Mackenzie backed the trailer up to the paddock. She'd known the extra expense of the portable hydraulic lift would be worth it. This little mama would be as comfortable as Mackenzie could make her while she took care of those hooves.

When it was over, Marc took the horse back into the paddock while Mackenzie removed her suit and locked the trailer.

Three women and two toddler girls strode their way across the lawn.

"Mackenzie, have you met my wife, Reagan?" Marc walked back to her as the ladies arrived.

"No, but I hear you make the best chocolates around."

"That's very kind." Reagan had a quiet air about her. "What's your favorite? I'll make you a batch. We appreciate you coming out to help Miss Lightning."

"I'm happy to do it. But I'm not turning down sweets. I love chocolate-covered pretzels."

"Dark or milk chocolate?"

"Milk."

"Done." Reagan beamed and turned to the middle-aged woman Mackenzie had chatted with several times at the bakery. "This is Anne, Marc's mom, and Brooke, his sister. And these two little sweeties are Alice and Megan."

"Oh! They're identical." What adorable little girls. Both had dark curls, big blue eyes and chubby cheeks.

"Is Miss Lightning going to be okay?" Brooke couldn't hide the worry in her eyes.

"She'll be fine. Her hooves needed trimming. If she still seems off over the next couple of days, call me. I'll come out and check on her."

"What a relief." Brooke's face cleared, then scrunched in disgust when she checked on the twins. "Alice, put down that worm!"

Mackenzie stuck around for a few minutes before saying goodbye. Later, as she drove back to town, she said a silent prayer. *God, thank You for giving me the wisdom to know what was wrong with Miss Lightning. Thank You for reminding me You're with me at all times. I can depend on You.*

She hadn't panicked. She'd been fine. And spending time chatting with Marc's family had made her feel welcome and appreciated. Maybe Dad was on to something about making a life here. And now that Cade had asked her out on an actual date, maybe it wouldn't be as hard as she thought.

What if he wanted to get serious, though?

She gripped the steering wheel. One date did not automatically lead to wedding bells. She'd keep it casual. As much as she liked Cade's company, she wasn't sure she was capable of getting close to him. He might only be asking her to tour the stables for his own reasons. She couldn't count on keeping his interest long-term. But, for once, she wished she could. A guy like Cade didn't come around all that often.

CHAPTER EIGHT

EXCITEMENT ADDED A spring to his step the next morning, and it wasn't anticipation of the Fourth of July fireworks that night. Cade strode down the main aisle of the stables with a box of doughnuts in one hand and a cardboard caddy holding two iced coffees in the other. Tulip kept her nose to the ground as she trotted ahead of him. Mackenzie would be arriving in fifteen minutes. He was eager to find out what she thought of his property.

Yesterday afternoon, Cade had driven to Ty's house and asked him if he could think of anyone qualified to manage Moulten Stables. After discussing the options, Ty had snapped his fingers and announced, "Trent Lloyd."

Trent had graduated from high school with Ty and moved away for college. Ty talked to him occasionally and believed he'd graduated with an equine degree in Alabama. After Cade left Ty's, he called and left a message for Trent. If he wasn't the right person for the job, he'd have to post the position online and hope for the best.

Discussing Moulten Stables with Ty had helped Cade lighten up about offering perfection to Forestline Adventures. He didn't need to beg any company to board their horses with him. He was offering a high-end service that had few true competitors. Yes, there were plenty of horse-boarding operations around the state, but none had the facilities and attention to detail his would.

Tulip sniffed her way to the makeshift office, and Cade set the doughnuts and coffees on the table. Then he bent to pet the dog.

"You're going to visit the nursing home next week." He used his baby-talk voice and chuckled as her little tongue panted in a smile. "You've almost got it down on how to avoid the wheelchair. Pretty soon, you'll be coming with me and Mom every time we visit Nana. You'll like that, won't you?"

He stopped petting her, and she pranced in place until he picked her up. Cuddling her to his chest, he kept stroking her fur.

"Charlene is going to love you. I guarantee she'll keep a box of treats for you at her station."

Tulip let out a yip, and he laughed, setting her on the ground. "I hear you. I like treats, too."

"Knock, knock." Mackenzie stood in the doorway.

Cade sucked in a breath and held it. Talk about a treat. What was it about her that stirred his emotions? Her hair hung over her shoulder in a long braid, and she wore a short-sleeved blouse with shorts and sandals. She was as beautiful as a meadow full of spring flowers.

Mackenzie approached and, smiling, picked up the dog. "Hello, sweet Tulip."

He took one of the coffees and waited for her to set the dog down before he handed it to her.

"Thank you. So this is it, huh?" Her eyes sparkled, and he wanted to reach out and touch her hand, but he held back. Wasn't his place. Her gaze fell beyond him. "Ooh, are those the doughnuts you promised?"

"Yes, help yourself."

"Don't mind if I do." She set her coffee on the table, then flipped open the lid of the box and took her time selecting one. She ended up with a cruller. No shock there. "Is it okay if I sit?"

"Go ahead." Cade reached past her to grab a chocolate-covered doughnut as she took a seat. He sat in the chair next to her, angling his to see her better. His doughnut went down in three bites.

"I didn't realize you had so much property." Mackenzie took a sip of her iced coffee.

"Twenty acres." He began to relax, remembering when he'd first bought the land not long after Dad passed away. Even then, he'd figured it would be a good investment. It had taken a few years for him to know what to do with it, and now his plan was almost in place.

"Why horses?" She took another bite of her doughnut, and he briefly considered snagging a second one for himself. Yeah, why not? He took a cruller out of the box.

"I was talking to a buddy from my days on Wall Street, and he told me he'd rented a cabin up in the Big Horn Mountains for a week. Apparently, his group went big-game hunting. They rode horses, went trout fishing and raved about how great it was to get away from it all."

"Sounds like an active vacation."

"Yeah, well, they had a chef on-site, a housekeeper and plenty of downtime." He chuckled. "And when I say cabin, I mean massive log home with all the amenities."

She brushed crumbs from her hands. "My kind of cabin."

"Luxury has its perks." He nodded to her iced coffee. "Want to walk and talk?"

"Sure. By the way, everyone's talking about the tour you gave Paris." She picked up her coffee and stood, batting her eyelashes at him. "Greta got all the updates from our clients, including the Instagram picture of you two together that I'm told went viral. I have to say, she's as stunning as they all said."

"She's not my type."

"She's every guy's type."

"Not mine."

"Okay, then what is your type?"

"Not her."

They made their way to the doorway leading to the rest of the stables.

"Did the meeting go well?" she asked. "Did she give you any indication their company wants to board their horses with you?"

"It went well. She didn't make any promises, but none of her concerns were deal-breakers, either. I wish the place was finished. Then she could have seen for herself the final product."

"Eh, that's just cosmetics. I'm sure she saw beyond the construction zone. You have a lot to offer them."

"I hope you're right, but I don't know. Cosmetics tend to seal the deal." He shrugged. "I'm letting Tulip off-leash here if that's okay. All work and no play..."

"I approve."

Cade waited for Mackenzie to exit the office, and Tulip darted ahead of them. "Anyway, back to my buddy. I started thinking about the horses and who took care of them during the off-season. I did some research into the types of luxury vacation services people like him use and found out they board their horses during the winter. After I talked to a few of the managers, I realized the disadvantage they have by boarding the horses themselves."

"You saw a need, and you're filling it." Mackenzie matched his easy strides.

"Exactly." He stopped when they reached the main aisle.

"I'm surprised." She looked up at him, the cup dangling from her hand. "I was sure you were going to tell me how much you love horses."

He frowned. Should he have answered differently? "I do love horses."

"But?"

"But I'm a businessman. I make decisions based on profitability."

"I see." She turned away to check on Tulip. The dog moseyed into one of the recently built stalls.

Did she have a problem with him making money? Or was he reading into things? Getting defensive because of his past?

"From what I see, this should be profitable. What's going on there?" She pointed to the caution tape he'd extended last night from one stall across the aisle to the opposite stall. Paris's comment had him toying with ideas—one of which was to divide the barn in half. That way the locals' horses would be separate from his other clients' horses. But was it really necessary?

"It came to my attention that the companies trusting me with their expensive, well-trained horses might not want the general public mingling with them."

"What do you mean?"

Tulip came out of the stall with her head high and joined them. They resumed their stroll.

"I'm offering stalls at a discount for locals to board their horses here. I also plan on keeping a handful of horses on-site to rent to the high-school kids who want to join the rodeo team but don't have the funds to buy one of their own. Ty and I talked about it last night, and he's going to help me start buying suitable horses."

"Won't that cut into your profits?" she asked with a teasing smile.

"No. Actually, it's the reason I'm going after the luxury market. If I can take care of their horses, it will bring in enough income to fund the entire operation and allow me to offer low prices to the teens."

"Hmm." With a soft smile, she paused near the caution tape. "I can't figure you out."

"What do you mean?" He got an uneasy feeling. Like when his dad had visited him in New York. Was Mackenzie about to call him out on something? But what?

"I don't know. On the one hand, you're a successful rancher and businessman. On the other hand, you seem to have time to help everyone. And then there's this." She extended her arm to the barn. "It's just... I don't get you."

"Get me? What is there to get?"

She used her iced coffee to point to the caution tape. "You're like that tape. One side is catering to wealthy people, and the other is helping the community."

"Is that bad?"

"Of course not." She shook her head. "I'm just not sure where you fit. Are you in the middle? On one side? Or the other?"

A reply in his defense leaped to his tongue, but he swallowed it.

She'd hit on something. He'd been trying to figure out how and where he fit, too. He'd been trying for years. And as far as the community, he'd always been a part of it. As much as he wanted to tell her he didn't fit in with the wealthy clients, it would be a lie. He couldn't deny he was still drawn to their world, and their opinion of him mattered.

But then again, he had acquaintances from his time in the city, but he wasn't close to any of them. That, too, had to mean something. He wasn't sure what. He hadn't embraced being a cowboy, either. He still wanted his investments. Still constantly searched for his next venture.

He chalked it up to his restless nature. But maybe it was more.

Today wasn't the time to think about it. Today was for hanging out with Mackenzie.

"Come on. I'll show you the rest of the property."

For the next hour, Cade gave her a thorough

tour. He answered her questions about the materials he'd selected and showed her the same digital rendering he'd shown Paris depicting the stalls, the tack room, the bathrooms and the common area.

"Cade?" she asked as they finished walking along one of the new riding paths.

"Yes?"

"Why are you showing me all this?"

Because I want to. Why else would he show her around? He enjoyed having her here. Liked telling her about his plans. The fact that she was interested in what he had to say filled a neglected part of him—a lonely side of him.

"I thought you'd like to see it."

"You're not going to try to talk me into becoming the full-time vet for this place, are you?" Her tone was light, but it held an edge of truth.

Ahh…he'd forgotten about that. How, in a few short weeks, had he gone from wanting an equine-certified vet to merely enjoying her company?

"No," he said, forcing a grin, "but if you want to get certified in equine care, I wouldn't complain."

"You never give up, do you?" Her eyes sparkled as she grinned. "You do know it takes six years of experience, usually with a residency, to qualify for certification, don't you?"

No, he did not know that. "I take it that means you're not interested in going that route."

"Correct." She headed to where the arena had been cleared. The sun gleamed on her braid, and he couldn't help admiring everything about her.

"You'll still be on call for my horses, right?"

"Of course. You can count on me."

As he took in her profile, it hit him that he could count on her and not just for vet services. He'd seen her in action. Had faith in her abilities as a veterinarian. But he also liked being in her company. He found himself wanting to tell her things he didn't feel comfortable sharing with other people.

By the time they finished discussing the outdoor arena, Tulip was panting from the climbing temperatures. Mackenzie gazed off to the edge of his property.

"I should probably get her out of the sun," Cade said. "Is your dad coming to the festival? I should have told you to bring him."

"Nope. I told him about it, but he said he wants to work with Charger, the German shepherd he recently adopted. By the way, he's been talking with contractors about getting the training center renovated."

"That's good news. I'm sure he's excited to get started."

"Yes, he is." Mackenzie wiped the back of her neck. "Whew. It's getting hot."

"Let's head back. It's time to have some fun." Cade picked up Tulip as they made their way back to the stables.

"What kind of fun are we talking about?" she asked.

"We're talking shaved ices, fresh-cut french fries, live music and kids waving American flags. If Mary Corning is involved, there will be a kettle-corn booth set up in the park."

"I love kettle corn."

"I do, too. Oh, and fireworks."

"Can't have the Fourth of July without those."

"Right?"

"Okay, cowboy. I'm ready. Let's get patriotic."

Cade grinned. He liked the sound of that. "I have to drop off Tulip and pick up Mom. Want to join me?"

"Will she read too much into it if I'm with

you?" Mackenzie's worried expression cracked him up.

"Absolutely." He nodded. "She reads too much into everything if it involves me or my brother being around a woman."

"Maybe it's time for me to live a little dangerously."

"You're really living on the wild side."

"Tell me about it."

They looked at each other and smiled. Why did he have the feeling *he* was the one living dangerously? And why was his heart pounding *yes, yes, yes*?

"I GUESS WE aren't living dangerously after all." Mackenzie finished setting up the crate and small dog bed in her living room fifteen minutes later. Christy had called Cade as they were heading to their trucks at his stables. Apparently, one of her friends had picked her up for the festival. Instead of driving all the way to his ranch, Mackenzie had suggested letting Tulip stay at her house while they walked around town. The dog was used to being there.

"What should I use for a water bowl?" Cade called from the kitchen on the other side of the hallway that ran down the center of the one-story home.

"I have bowls for her. I'll get them." She fluffed the bed, and Tulip hopped onto it, then circled around twice before curling up for a nap. Mackenzie gently petted her before heading to the kitchen.

She brushed past Cade, all too aware of the fresh scent of his cologne. The dog bowls were stacked in a lower cupboard. She filled one with water and made her way to the back of the house, where her laundry room was located. She always kept cat food and dog food on hand in case someone found a stray or an injured animal and needed her to keep it for the night.

Back in the kitchen, she set the bowl with the dog food next to the water bowl, then looked around to see if she was missing anything for little Tulip. She didn't think so.

"Are you ready?" she asked.

"I am. Let me say goodbye to Tulip first." He went into the living room, crouched next to the dog bed, murmured something Mackenzie couldn't make out and petted her. The dog licked her lips and closed her eyes again. "I think this morning tired her out."

"I think you're right."

When they got to the driveway, Cade motioned to keep going. "You're close to town. It's
always hard to find a parking spot since Center
Street gets blocked off. Why don't we walk?"

"Sounds good to me."

They fell in step next to each other on the
sidewalk.

"Have you heard from your mother since she
called?" Cade asked.

"We talked the night of the grand opening,
but we haven't spoken since." It was a relief.
For over a week now, she'd been half expecting her mother to pull into her driveway. The
more time that passed, the more she loosened
up. If Mom hadn't shown up by now, there was
a good chance she wouldn't at all.

"The conversation didn't go well?" He continued at a pace she had no problem matching.

"She threatened to come visit."

"Threatened?" He chuckled, glanced her way
and sobered. "Oh, you're serious."

"Dead serious. I used to enjoy her visits. I'd
get so excited to find her on my doorstep."

"What happened to change it?"

What happened? Mackenzie had finally opened
her eyes to reality, that was what happened.

"She's good at pretending she's here to see

me, but there's always another reason—a selfish one—for an impromptu visit. That's what
she does. She lulls you into thinking she cares,
and you help her. Then she takes off without
a warning. You don't see or hear from her for
months, even years."

"I didn't realize…"

Although he sounded like he could possibly understand, she doubted he did. Look at
his family—his mom was everything Mackenzie's mom wasn't. Christy was generous and
thoughtful. Her gift for the clinic's opening
still touched Mackenzie's heart. The tall black
planters with red geraniums, white petunias and
green ivy made the entrance to the clinic so
much more inviting than anything Mackenzie
would have come up with on her own. And this
from someone she'd barely known at the time.

Her mother, on the other hand, wouldn't
think to bring a gift to celebrate her grand
opening. Mackenzie couldn't remember the last
time her mom had called to wish her a happy
birthday or had sent her a Christmas gift. She
didn't need or expect gifts, but she did want her
mother to at least care about her.

Maybe that was what hurt. Knowing her own
mother didn't really love her. Every word the

woman spoke was meaningless. Empty. Bonnie might insist on spending time together when she showed up, but it wasn't out of love. She always had an ulterior motive.

"Do you think she'll actually come to Jewel River?" Cade asked.

"I hope not." Mackenzie kept her gaze ahead. "I have no idea, though. If she does, I don't know how long she'd stay. A week? A month? Who knows? She's not bunking with me."

She glanced his way and wished she hadn't. Cade was handsome on a whole different level. And she was a no-frills, busy, single woman in her thirties.

Friends. They were friends.

On a date.

Did that make them more than friends?

Could she handle being more? Could he?

It wasn't only the time issue—all of the after-hours emergencies and being on call she anticipated dealing with soon. Cade was respected and well-liked and involved with the community. She wasn't used to having a social life, and she wasn't sure she wanted one. But, out of everyone she'd met over the past several years, she felt the most comfortable with Cade.

And what about last night? She'd enjoyed talking to Reagan, Marc and Brooke.

Stop worrying about the future. Just enjoy today.

They turned the corner and soon joined the crowds on Center Street, where the smells of barbecue, popcorn and funnel cakes mingled in the air. Country music blared through speakers mounted on a makeshift stage. Everywhere she looked, people of all ages were enjoying themselves. Some were in line at the food trucks. Others ambled around the craft booths. Laughing teens weaved their way through the crowd.

"I had no idea it would be this busy." She slowed to get her bearings.

"Cade!" A trio of women headed their way. Mackenzie recognized all three—Erica, Reagan and Brooke. Another woman—a curvy blonde—ran up to Brooke and hugged her.

"Hello, ladies." Cade had a spark of mischief in his eyes. "What food truck should we start with?"

"Mackenzie, I didn't see you there." Erica came right up to Mackenzie and hugged her. Then she stepped back and glanced at the other women. "You've met Reagan and Brooke, right?"

"Yes, we met last night." Mackenzie turned to Reagan. "How is Miss Lightning?"

"Great. She's acting like herself again. I'm so glad you were around to help. Marc is relieved. He's mad at himself for missing the signs."

"What happened to Miss Lightning?" Cade asked.

"I trimmed her hooves." Mackenzie shrugged as if it was nothing. Because it wasn't a big deal. She'd feared the worst and been blessed with an easy fix.

Brooke stepped forward with her friend. "Mackenzie, this is my best friend, Gracie French. I keep trying to convince her to move back here, but she won't listen." Brooke grinned, clearly teasing.

Gracie elbowed Brooke's side. "You never know. Stranger things have happened."

"Let's make it happen," Brooke said. "I miss you. It's always better when you're around."

"We'd better scoot," Erica said with an apologetic smile. "Dalton and Marc have their hands full with the kids over at the cotton-candy booth." She reached over and gave Mackenzie's arm a light squeeze. "It was great running into you. We need to get together soon. Hang out. Have a coffee at Annie's Bakery or something."

The thoughtful gesture went straight to Mackenzie's heart. The people of Jewel River made her feel right at home. All those times she'd told herself she didn't have time for friendships or relationships—had she been lying to herself?

Maybe she'd always had time for friends but hadn't made it a priority. Surely, she could fit in a coffee date with Erica or any of the women she'd recently met. They all seemed down-to-earth and fun.

If she could make time for a friend or two, she could probably make time for a boyfriend as well. What if time wasn't the issue at all?

"Oh, boy." Cade took Mackenzie by the arm. "Quick, let's go to the barbecue truck."

"Why?" She forced herself to hurry as he broke into a light jog.

"My mother, Mary Corning and Charlene Parker are up ahead buying candles. They haven't spotted us yet. We still have time to escape."

She had to hustle to keep up with him. "Why are we running?"

He gave her a sideways glance and didn't slow a bit. "Are you prepared for questions—and I mean terrible questions—from them?"

"How terrible?" Slightly out of breath, she scrunched her nose.

"The worst. It will start with them cooing over you."

Cooing? "As in a dove?"

"Yes." He stopped next to a table with condiments and napkins. Tugged her beside him to hide behind the line of people waiting for barbecue pulled pork. Then he craned his neck this way and that before staring directly into her eyes. "After the cooing, the questions will begin. It will seem innocent, but trust me, it's not."

He altered his tone to sound like his mother. "How are you settling in? Did you know we have a book club on Thursdays? Oh, Cade, you should bring her to book club. I have a novel for you, Mackenzie. It's a romance. Love at first sight. You'll adore it. Do you ever think about getting married? I've always thought a summer wedding is the way to go. The Winston is the best venue. And Dorothy Bell does the most beautiful flower arrangements."

Mackenzie couldn't contain her laughter any longer, and she guffawed. A few people in line turned at the noise. Sheepishly, she covered her mouth but continued to giggle softly.

"You laugh, but it gets worse." His eyes had a panicked gleam, and he looked over her head and groaned. "I knew we should have hidden behind the building. They spotted us."

Mackenzie turned as Christy, Mary and Charlene pushed through the crowd to stand in front of them. The three women were all smiles.

"I didn't expect to see you two here," Christy said, her grin wider than the Grand Canyon, as she gave Mackenzie a hug. Two hugs in one day. Huh. "Cade, that was so thoughtful of you to bring her to the festival. I was going to suggest it, but I got busy and forgot."

"Yes, it's sure good to see you kids getting out and about." Mary nodded. "This'll give you a chance to get to know each other better. I say a little barbecue, an ice cream cone and a blanket at the fireworks is a real good way to spend your time."

Mackenzie didn't dare look at Cade. She was afraid she'd burst out laughing again.

"Now, Mackenzie, are you settling in okay, hon?" Charlene had a concerned look. "You know we have a book club, right?"

A book club? She'd thought Cade had been kidding.

"That's a great idea!" Christy piped up, nodding rapidly. "Cade, you should bring Mackenzie to the book club. That way she won't feel awkward." Christy turned her attention back to her. "I know it's uncomfortable walking into a room where you don't know anyone."

"Do you still have the book from April, Christy?" Charlene steepled her fingers. "That was a goodie."

Christy brightened. "Why yes, I do, Char. Mackenzie, I think you'll like this one. It's a reunion romance. There's a secret baby involved, but don't let that throw you off."

Mackenzie found herself speechless. How had Cade known?

"Cade, honey," Charlene said, reaching out to pat his arm. "I'll make sure Janey sends you an invitation to the wedding that says *plus one* on it. That way you can bring Mackenzie with you."

"Perfect," Christy said, nodding.

"That is really thoughtful of you, Charlene." Cade stared at something beyond the women and pointed. "Hey? Is that Clem? I'll wave him over."

The women's smiles vanished, and they shared a long, serious look. His mother was the first to speak. "We'll let you two get on with your day." She leaned in toward Mackenzie.

"Be sure to go to the booth at the end. Laura is having a buy-one-get-one sale on her candles."

"We'll do that."

"Oh, good, he's almost here." Cade's tone was innocent. "I don't want you ladies to miss him."

"No, no. We'll find him later." The women scurried away.

Mary called over her shoulder, "Go get yourselves some kettle corn, kids."

"We will!" Cade yelled.

Mackenzie scanned the people in the area. "I don't see Clem."

"That's because he's not there." Cade grinned. "You can thank me later."

She shook her head as she chuckled. "You're terrible."

"Am I? I think you meant to say I'm your hero." He grabbed her hand and herded her around a young couple pushing a stroller. "I saved you from the next phase of questions. You were about to get bombarded with the do-you-like-kids question. That would be followed up with 'How soon do you see yourself with a family?' Trust me, I did the right thing."

Mackenzie's mood soared like the red, white

and blue balloons bobbing in clusters up and down the street. Cade was fun to be with. It didn't escape her notice that he hadn't let go of her hand, either. If he wanted to get his mother and her friends off his back about them as a couple, he had a weird way of showing it.

Maybe he didn't want them off his back. He was the one who'd said this was a date, right?

Why, though? Why would handsome, successful, popular Cade Moulten be interested in her?

Stop it! This was her day off, and she was going to enjoy it. Even if it meant holding Cade's hand. Especially if it meant holding Cade's hand.

For the next couple of hours, they made their way through every craft booth. They bought lunch and snacks and shaved ices. Everywhere they went, people stopped to talk to Cade. He introduced her to them, and he took special care to point out to the ranchers that she was the new veterinarian.

They were on their way back to Mackenzie's house to check on Tulip when Mackenzie came to a halt on the sidewalk. Couldn't move if she tried.

Her mother was walking straight toward them. And Dad was with her.

Mackenzie swallowed the bitter taste in her mouth.

"What's wrong?" Cade frowned down at her.

Squaring her shoulders, she widened her stance and kept her gaze on her parents.

"My mother's in town."

"She is?" He followed her gaze. "Is she the one with your dad?"

"Yes."

As soon as they neared, her mom threw her arms around Mackenzie. She stood there like a statue until her mother stepped back.

Cade greeted her father, who introduced her to Bonnie. After they exchanged pleasantries, no one seemed to know what else to say.

"What are you doing here?" Mackenzie didn't want to sound so mean, but really? On today of all days, her mom had to show up?

"I told you I missed you." Mom had her pretending-to-care face on. Too bad it was a mask. Easily slipped on and off.

Mackenzie faced her dad. "What are you doing together?"

"Just thought we'd see what the festival was

all about." His eyes were full of understanding, yet Mackenzie didn't think he understood at all.

"Don't worry. I'm not staying with you." Her mother's tone was getting under her skin. "Patrick said I can stay with him."

She circled her fingers over her temples. Why was this happening? Why now? Why here?

"How long will you be in town?" She tried—really tried—to sound pleasant.

"Oh, I don't know." Mom shrugged happily.

"Not long." Dad crinkled his nose.

No one spoke. The sounds of laughter and music in the distance made the silence more pronounced.

"We have to go check on Tulip." Mackenzie jerked her thumb to the right.

"Go, go." Mom waved the backs of her fingers in a fluttery manner. "We'll catch up soon."

She didn't respond. Just marched away. Cade said goodbye to them and hurried to join her.

It had been a near-perfect day. She should have known her mother would ruin it.

The woman ruined everything.

"DO YOU WANT to talk about it?" Cade kept a

brisk pace next to Mackenzie as they turned the corner of her street.

"No."

The only time he'd seen Mackenzie like this—pale, tense, jittery with anger—had been when her mom called during the grand opening.

"Your parents seem to get along, huh?"

"Not really." She flicked him a glance. "They don't have much contact with each other."

"Hmm." Her house was up ahead. American flags waved from the neighboring porches, and most of the lawns had yellow patches from the lack of rain.

"What?"

"Why is she staying with him?" He found it strange. Were her parents reconnecting or something?

"Because I point-blank told her she couldn't stay with me."

He kept his mouth shut until they climbed her porch steps. She opened the door, and he held it for her to go inside. She zoomed straight to Tulip, who must have heard them and was waiting in the hallway, wagging her tail.

"Were you a good girl?" Mackenzie gathered

the pup in her arms and petted her. "Did you have a nice nap?"

They went through the kitchen and out to the backyard. Cade stayed behind. In no time at all, Mackenzie and Tulip were back inside. She carried the dog to the living room and sat on the couch. Cade crammed next to her. On her lap, Tulip nudged her hand. Mackenzie's rigid stance slowly melted as she caressed the dog's fur.

Cade wanted to comfort her, too, but he wasn't sure how. Her mother had seemed nice enough. Pleasant, anyway. Looks could be deceiving, though.

"My mother is what I guess you'd call a free spirit." She kept her gaze on Tulip's fur. Her throat worked as she swallowed. "I don't know what she's looking for, but it's not me."

"She found you here, though."

A brittle laugh erupted from her. "Yes, she always finds me. But only when she's desperate and needs something."

"Like what?"

"A place to stay until she can cook up her next adventure and get the money—from me—to fund it."

Oh. He grimaced. That didn't sound good.

"The sad thing, though, is if things were different, I'd love for her to stay with me more often. I actually like hearing her figure out her next job and where she'll move. I never minded giving her money to help her get started."

"But?" He took her hand in his, and she didn't pull it away.

"But that's all I am to her. A couch to crash on. A wallet to borrow from. Then she's out the door and out of my life."

Indignation began to spread in his chest.

"She's dishonest. She pretends to be someone she's not. And it hurts, Cade. After last time, I told myself I wasn't falling for her act again. I can't. I won't."

He wrapped his arms around her, with Tulip between them, and held her. She softened in his embrace, and he wanted to tell her he'd never let anyone hurt her again. But how could he?

She was the first to pull back. "I don't expect you to understand. Your family is close and loving."

Yeah, they were. But that didn't mean he couldn't understand the whole pretending-to-be-someone-you're-not situation.

Hadn't he done the same thing?

Wasn't he still doing the same thing?

"Hopefully," Mackenzie said, "she'll get restless and move on quickly."

Restless.

He knew all about getting restless, too. A sour taste bloomed in his mouth.

"I can't trust her, and I'm tired of trying." Mackenzie looked so vulnerable. He wanted to kiss her and make her forget about her pain.

But he didn't. He couldn't.

Mackenzie didn't deserve to be hurt. She thought he was someone he wasn't. Thought he was respectable—a stand-up guy.

He'd gotten his hands dirty. And nothing he could say or do would ever change it. He wouldn't burden her with the details.

Burden her? Come on. Don't lie to yourself. You hide it because you're embarrassed. Ashamed.

"I'm not in the mood to go back to the festival," Mackenzie said. "I hope you don't mind."

"I understand. We can still watch the fireworks from your backyard."

"Really?" Her eyes lit up with hope.

"Yeah." He put his arm around her shoulders and drew her closer to lean on him. He kissed the side of her head. "We'll stay right here."

And after tonight, he needed to do a better job of keeping his distance. She'd been hurt enough. Getting close would only add to her pain.

CHAPTER NINE

WORKING WITH TULIP at the clinic was one thing. Working with her at the nursing home was another. Would the dog get nervous and forget her training?

Cade squashed his worries as he held open the door to the nursing home for his mother the following Tuesday afternoon. Wearing her therapy-dog vest, Tulip walked beside Christy with slack in her leash the way Mackenzie expected. The dog rarely strained at the leash anymore on their nightly walks, and she no longer viewed the wheelchair as a threat, either.

Up ahead, Mackenzie chatted with Charlene, and when she spotted them, she excused herself and strolled their way. His mother stopped in front of Mackenzie. Tulip sat at Mom's feet. Cade joined them, keeping his eye on the dog, but she seemed content where she was, smiling up at Mackenzie.

Maybe this session would go better than he feared.

He didn't know why he was worried. This was a practice run—a training session. It wouldn't count against Tulip if she struggled, failed to obey commands or barked like she had last week with the wheelchair.

Cade just wanted her to pass her test. Wanted Nana to enjoy the dog—while she still could.

After the fireworks, he'd tried hard to put Mackenzie out of his mind, but she was wedged in there. Keeping a friendly distance? Forget it. He'd texted her every day about her mom (she'd been avoiding her), the ranches she was visiting (none since the Fourth), how Charger was settling in (great) and if she wanted the romance novel his mom recommended (a hard pass on that one).

Over the weekend, Ty had told him about a few horses for sale, and Cade had taken one look at the black Morgan horse named Licorice and had known she would be perfect for Mackenzie. He and Ty had contacted the owner and driven out there on Sunday to inspect the beauty. Cade had purchased Licorice, and Ty had bought the other horse for sale.

Since Mackenzie didn't have time to take care

of her own horse, Cade figured he'd provide one for her. Licorice would stay on his ranch until the new facility opened. Then he'd have his staff take care of her along with the other horses. Mackenzie could stop by Moulten Stables and ride her whenever her heart desired. No strings attached.

He'd been thinking a lot about her heart and its desires lately. Thinking about his own, too.

Ty was picking up both horses and bringing Licorice to his ranch tomorrow morning. It was perfect timing, since Cade had spent an hour with Trent Lloyd on the phone about the manager position, and Trent would also be arriving tomorrow to check out the stables and interview for the job. His credentials were impressive, and the fact he'd grown up around here made him the ideal candidate. But Cade really wanted to see him interact with Licorice.

"Where's Patrick?" Mom asked Mackenzie as she looked around the reception area.

"He'll be here."

"Is your mother coming, too?"

Cade should have warned his mom not to bring up her mother.

"I have no idea." She didn't seem upset.

"Oh, before we get started, I have something

for you." Christy dug around in her large purse, then pulled out a paperback. Her smile could only be described as triumphant. "The book I mentioned. Book club isn't for two more weeks, and I can get you a copy of this month's selection if you want to join us."

A frown line appeared as Mackenzie studied the cover of a woman holding a baby. "I don't know. This isn't really my thing." She tried to hand it back to his mother, but Mom just shook her head and pushed the book back to Mackenzie.

"You'll love it. Trust me. Keep it."

Patrick entered the building and headed straight to them. He was alone. Probably for the best.

"I'm going to be observing and taking notes, so ignore me." Patrick nodded in greeting to them as he pulled out a clipboard.

"Let's begin." Mackenzie addressed his mom. "Christy, why don't you give Charlene your purse? Cade, would you go down to the end of that hall and set up a trail of treats like we did at the clinic last week?"

He didn't have to be told twice. The reception area was the central hub of the nursing home, and three wings branched off from it.

One led to the dining hall and activities center. The other two housed the residents. Both of those wings ended in circular common areas surrounded by windows.

Cade headed down the closest hall and placed treats a few feet apart on the floor at the end. Then he straightened and gazed out the windows. Birdfeeders and benches had been installed in the fenced-in back lawn. The view was peaceful. He'd have to bring Nana down here on one of her good days.

He returned to the reception desk. Several staff members were oohing and ahhing over Tulip, and she smiled at them with her tongue out as she continued to sit quietly by his mom's side. A rush of pride filled his chest.

The dog—their dog—was behaving the way they'd trained her.

When the meet and greet ended, Mackenzie asked Charlene and one of the nurse's aides if it would be possible to bring a few residents down the hall past Tulip.

"Sure thing, hon." Charlene grinned. "They're about done with their afternoon snack."

Mackenzie instructed him and his mother on how they should handle Tulip. Soon, a man in a wheelchair emerged from the activities room and wheeled himself down the hall toward them. Tulip stayed calm. Then an aide helped a woman with her walker.

Cade tensed as he watched the dog. How would she handle this? Two people *and* a walker. Tulip looked up at Christy, and she simply smiled and reminded her to sit, praising her for obeying as they approached. After they passed by, Mom gave Tulip a treat.

Another woman with a walker approached.

"Hi, Dolores," Mom said to the woman. "What activity did you do today?"

"Heh?" Dolores Jones squinted.

"Activity," Mom said loudly. "What did you do today?"

"I didn't want to color, so I didn't."

"Maybe next time."

Dolores noticed Tulip. "What's that?"

"It's my dog, Tulip. She's going to be coming around to visit soon. She's in training."

Her face softened, and she wiggled her fingers to Tulip. "Hey there, puppy."

Tulip wagged her tail but didn't move.

After a steady line of residents trickled past from the activities center to their rooms, Mackenzie and Patrick agreed it would be a good time to move to the end of the hall, where Cade had placed the treats.

"Cade, why don't you take the lead on this?" Mom handed him the leash.

"Okay." He didn't want to take the lead. Not with half the staff watching and Mackenzie's dad taking notes. But he'd pull up his big-boy pants and do it.

"Remember what to do?" Mackenzie asked.

"I tell her to leave it, and I lead her past each treat." They'd practiced this for a few weeks. They'd started by giving her an even better treat each time she ignored one on the floor, and they'd worked up to rewarding her with a special chew bone if she left all the treats with only one command.

"Right. Go on and move to the back. I'll tell you when to start." As soon as he and Tulip were ready, she gave them the go-ahead.

"Leave it." He walked Tulip past the treats. She didn't even sniff them.

"Okay, now weave your way back."

He did, and again, she ignored all the little treats on the floor. When they finished, he crouched and ruffled her fur. "Good job. You did amazing."

Cade handed her a small chew bone.

"What do you think, Dad?" Mackenzie tilted her head to Patrick. "Anything else you want to see?"

"Not today. She's done well." Patrick motioned for Christy and Cade to come closer. "If you want to practice her meeting other dogs, we can set up a time with Charger. I've been working with him, and he's learned to stay calm and not run over to other dogs or their owners."

"Yes, we'll do that," Christy said. "We've taken her to town a few times, and she's done a pretty good job of ignoring the other dogs…"

Cade kept an eye on Tulip, still munching on her treat, and sidled up next to Mackenzie. "Do you think there's any way I could take Tulip to meet Nana right now?"

"Normally, I would say yes. But Tulip has dealt with a lot of new things today, and I don't want to overwhelm her." Her deep blue eyes were bright. "It's not that I don't think Tulip is ready."

"I understand." He did. Kind of. "I'm going to pop down there and say hi."

"I'll come with you."

While he liked the thought of Mackenzie with him, he didn't want her to be freaked out if Nana thought he was his father or said something else that was weird. "Nana isn't always with it. Sometimes she thinks I'm someone else."

"Don't worry about it." She patted his arm. "I understand."

"Ma, we're going to say hi to Nana for a minute." He handed her Tulip's leash.

"Okay, Cade." Mom smiled. "I'll stay here with our princess until you're done."

CADE'S GRANDMOTHER HAD been sleeping, but the tenderness in the way he held the woman's hand as she slept had tugged at Mackenzie's heart. She understood at a deeper level why he and Christy were so adamant about getting Tulip certified.

They wanted to bring a little joy into his grandmother's life. Who could argue with that?

Standing next to her father in the nursing home's parking lot, Mackenzie waved goodbye to Cade, Christy and Tulip. Then she turned to her dad. "I'm taking off, too."

Normally, she would ask him to have supper with her, but with her mom still around, Mackenzie couldn't stomach it.

"Wait," he said.

She paused next to her truck.

"The three of us need to talk."

The three of us? They hadn't been a trio for two decades. Why start now?

"No, thank you."

He leveled her with a stern look. "She won't be in town for long."

"Good." With her chin high, she kept a firm grip on her backpack.

"I think you two need to clear the air."

"There's no air to clear. She has her life. I have mine. I don't wish her ill, Dad. I'm tired of being hurt."

He sighed. "Have supper with us."

"Tonight?" She may have sounded a touch too horrified.

He nodded.

"I can't." She could, but she didn't want to. Needed time to prepare first. However, Dad wouldn't let up until she agreed.

"How about tomorrow?" he asked.

How about never? She closed her eyes, found her bearings and nodded. "Fine."

"Come over after work." He gave her a hug. She barely returned it.

"Want me to bring anything?"

"Nope. Just yourself."

They said their goodbyes, and she sat in her

truck without starting it. She needed someone to talk to. And the only person she wanted to talk to was Cade.

Without giving herself a chance to change her mind, she called him.

"What's up?"

"I know you're with your mom and you have Tulip, but is there any way we could talk?"

"Just a sec." Muffled voices left her no idea what was being said. "I'll swing by your place in a few minutes."

"Okay." Her heart lightened. He ended the call without responding, and she didn't care. Was he bringing his mom and the dog? She, personally, would love to have Tulip there, but she didn't really want Christy to hear their conversation. She simply wanted to talk to Cade alone.

As soon as she got home, she brushed her hair and threw on some clean shorts and a short-sleeved shirt. A knock on the front door kicked up her nerves a notch, and she half jogged to open it.

Cade stood there with Tulip in his arms. Other than that, he was alone. A smile spread across his face. The way he looked at her made her feel feminine. Pretty. Special.

"What's going on?" He brushed past her. Whatever cologne he wore should be outlawed. It smelled that good.

"Thanks for coming over." She peered outside before closing the door. "Where's your mom?"

"I dropped her off at her friend's house, and Ty's going over there to take her home. I thought you might want Tulip here."

"I do." She took the dog from him and hugged her. "You're the best, you know that, girl?"

Her tail wagged swiftly. Mackenzie set her down, and she went straight to the kitchen, where her empty dog dishes still sat on the mat. The dog looked back as if she'd been betrayed. "I'm sorry, Tulip. I'll get you some food and water."

After filling the bowls, Mackenzie joined Cade again. "Are you hungry?"

"I'm always hungry." He'd taken off his cowboy hat and was running his fingers through his hair.

"Pizza?"

"Cowboy John's?"

"Of course." She might have only lived here a month, but it hadn't taken long to figure out

Cowboy John's pizza was delicious. She placed the order and directed Cade to the living room, where she got comfortable on the couch as he lowered his frame onto the oversized chair kitty-corner to her. Tulip trotted over and put her little front paws up on the edge of the cushion near Mackenzie.

"You want up?" She lifted the dog and waited while she settled on her lap.

"What's going on?" He gave her his full attention, and she got lost in his concerned blue eyes.

"Dad insists I join him and my mother for supper tomorrow." She absentmindedly stroked Tulip's fur. Tulip, in turn, licked the back of her other hand.

"Are they getting back together or something?"

"Eww." She grimaced. "I hope not. I don't think so. They didn't have the best marriage to begin with. I'm guessing your parents did."

He shrugged. "They loved each other. But they argued, too. Dad was steady, and Mom's... well... Mom."

"I wish I knew what to do. My whole life, I've followed a checklist. Get good grades. Apply to colleges. Gain enough experience to get into the vet program. Graduate. Find a job. Open my own practice. With my career, I know what to do. But with my mother? I don't."

She'd never admitted any of that, not even to herself.

"What do you think you should do?" He leaned forward, resting one forearm on the arm of the chair.

Hard question. The Bible said to forgive. But what did that look like? Was Mackenzie obligated to help her mother every time she showed up? Was she supposed to wave and smile as Mom drove away with Mackenzie's hard-earned cash and another chunk of her heart?

"I don't know," she admitted. "I guess I should lower my expectations. Give her what she wants."

"Why would you do that?"

She shrugged. "The pastor's always talking about forgiveness."

"Forgiveness is one thing. I must have missed the section of the Bible where it says to become a doormat."

She snorted in surprise.

Cade stacked one ankle on his opposite knee

and leaned back. "I think you can forgive someone without compromising your values."

"Can you? I don't know. I resent every cent I've given her. I must be a scrooge."

"A scrooge? You? Never." His kind smile wriggled under her skin in the best way.

"How would it work?" She kind of got his point, but she couldn't quite grasp the concept. It was as delicate as a spider web in her mind.

"I don't know. For starters, you could set some rules."

Rules. She was good at those. *Rule number one—don't shut me out of your life until you need something from me.*

"My mom would tell you to pray about it." His eyes twinkled. "That's what she tells me."

"Would you tell me the same?"

"Yeah, I would." He squirmed, clearly uncomfortable with where the conversation was heading. He'd been the one to bring it up, though. "But I'm a hypocrite."

"Why? Don't you pray?"

"I pray about a lot of things." His gaze skewered her, and she wondered why he seemed so intense. "But there are things outside of my control. Things I can't change. You live and you learn."

"Like what?" She wanted to know more. She'd told him about her awkward relationship with her mother. Cade tended to keep his personal stuff to himself. "You keep a lot inside, don't you?"

He stiffened. "Why do you say that?"

"I don't know." The air conditioner kicked on, filling the room with a buzzing sound. "You haven't shared much with me. I mean, I feel close to you, but…there's a lot I don't know. I'm not sure how to describe it."

"What do you want to know?"

"Who was the last girl you dated?"

"Phoebe Armstrong. A paralegal in Casper."

"Why didn't it last?"

"Distance. And I wasn't that into her."

"Have you ever been in love? A serious relationship?"

"I thought I was." He sat back, tapping his fingers on his thighs. "I dated Gia for almost a year. She worked for an art dealer in New York."

Her heart shriveled as he talked. Gia. The name alone sounded classy. And she'd worked in the art world—in the big city.

The relationship was over, so why did this bother her? *Because you want him for yourself.*

"Why did it end?" She braced herself for him to tell her about his broken heart.

He hesitated before answering. Gia must have hurt him really badly.

"She wanted to move in together. For years, I'd been getting further from God, and when she gave me an ultimatum, it kind of hit me. What was I doing? Who was I? What were my values? I broke up with her. The following week, my dad visited for a few days."

"Did he give you a pep talk?" she said brightly.

"I guess you could say that." His expression grew sad.

"You must miss him a lot, don't you?"

He swallowed, nodding.

A knock on the door startled her. The pizza. Cade stood, holding his palm out. "Stay there. I'll get it."

Soon, the aroma of mozzarella and pepperoni wafted to her. She nudged Tulip off her lap and joined Cade in the kitchen. While he opened the refrigerator for sodas, she pulled plates out of the cupboard. They returned with their hands full to the living room and dug into their slices.

"I've told you about my dating past, so it's

only fair you tell me yours." He watched her in between bites. "How many hearts did you break?"

"Me?" She sputtered as her soda went down the wrong tube. She thumped her chest. "None."

"Yeah, right. There had to have been a college romance."

"I mean, I dated here and there." And cut things off quickly with each guy.

"You didn't find the one, huh?"

"Nope." She hadn't given any of the guys much of a chance, either. "I was pretty focused. The minute they got in the way of homework, I ended things."

"Really?" He drew the word out. "They must not have been very exciting."

"I'm not looking for exciting."

"What are you looking for?"

You. Heat climbed her neck. She kept her attention on her half-eaten slice. "I don't have much to offer a man at this point. My time is limited."

"That's not what I asked." His eyes shimmered with something that made her pulse quicken. Dangerous. This conversation was loaded with explosives.

"I don't know, Cade." She shouldn't have said his name. It felt too intimate. "I'm not really looking for anything."

"My mom would say that's when you're most likely to find it. But I don't listen to my mom about stuff like that. She reads too many romance novels."

"What are *you* looking for?"

The shimmer vanished. "I've got all I need."

She couldn't argue with that. He was successful, well liked, had a great family—

"Actually, that's a lie." He set his empty plate on the end table and joined her on the couch. Tulip looked up from the corner cushion where she was napping, then she closed her eyes again.

What was he doing? Her heart began to pound. Mackenzie set her plate on the coffee table.

"I'm not looking for anything, but if I was," Cade shifted to face her and ran the back of his finger down the hair framing her face, "I'd be partial to strawberry blond hair and deep blue eyes."

Her mouth went dry, and all she could do was blink.

"I'd also be way too interested in a mobile

vet trailer if she had one, and I wouldn't mind running with her to hide from my mom and her matchmaking buddies during a festival."

Mackenzie didn't know much about flirting, and she didn't have much experience with whatever was happening to her pulse. But one thing she did know was if Cade kissed her, she'd have no objections.

He must have read her mind. His hand slid behind her neck, and he leaned closer. Pressed his lips to hers. And she let out a soft sigh. Then he held her closer, and she wrapped her arms around his neck. His embrace was the support she didn't know she needed. His kiss was the connection she'd been missing.

She'd never realized how alone she'd been all these years. Never knew she could be necessary to someone. But the way his mouth pressed to hers spilled secrets she'd never anticipated. He really liked her. As she kissed him back, she reveled in new sensations, throwing her fears and doubts aside.

When he drew away, his eyes crinkled in the corners, and she could see the little boy he'd been.

"I've wanted to do that for a while."

"Oh, yeah?" Why did she feel so out of breath?

He nodded, taking her hand and raising the back of it to his lips. "Yeah."

He continued to sit next to her as they talked about everything and nothing for the next couple of hours. Finally, he stood and helped her to her feet. He slid his hands around her lower back, staring into her eyes. "Thank you. This was the best night I've had in a long time."

"Same here." She wanted to lean into his strong chest, and so she did. He held her tightly, and she savored his strength and warmth.

"Call me tomorrow after supper with your parents. Let me know how it goes."

Her parents. Right. She stepped back, giving him a weak smile. "I will."

He kissed her again before gathering his hat, picking up Tulip and heading out the front door. He paused on the first porch step and looked back at her. She waved. He hitched his chin toward her and left.

As soon as she shut the door, anxiety and excitement kicked in. She really liked Cade, but she didn't want to be this close to him. To fall in love was too scary. Too unpredictable.

She padded back to the living room.

You're flirting with the danger zone.

Yeah, she was, and she didn't know how to stop it. And she wasn't sure she could if she tried.

CHAPTER TEN

CADE HAD BEEN fighting an uneasy feeling all day. He didn't know why, either. Trent's flight had been delayed, but he'd be arriving within the hour for the interview. Licorice seemed to be settling in fine. Ty had dropped off the horse bright and early. They'd put her in a paddock adjacent to the horse pasture. One by one, the horses kept stopping near their shared fence line to check her out. So far, Licorice had been the most taken with Tulip. The dog kept running over to the fence, and Licorice would drop her head to sniff her. It was cute. Best buds already.

Cade would have to mention it to Mackenzie later. She'd be proud to know that Tulip was helping the horse get settled. *Wait*. He smacked his forehead. He couldn't tell her about it. The horse was a surprise. A thank-you gift. Once Tulip passed her Canine Good Citizen test,

Cade planned on bringing Mackenzie out to give her Licorice.

Maybe the uneasiness had something to do with last night's unbelievable kiss.

He called Tulip's name, and she instantly left the horse to race to Cade's side. He chuckled. "You're getting good at that. Come on. It's time to get spoiled by Mom."

As they made their way to the house, he studied the ranch. Everything appeared to be in order. Potted flowers brightened the back deck. The house itself showed no signs of wear and tear. He and Tulip entered through the sliding doors off the deck, and he yelled that he was back. Mom stood in the kitchen with Tulip's vest in her hand.

"Just let me grab the treats. I'm working with her on meeting other dogs today. Angie's bringing Duke, and Mary's borrowing her son's beagle. We're going to walk up and down the sidewalks, then treat ourselves to lunch from Dixie B's and a box of candy from R. Mayer Chocolates."

"Sounds good, Ma." He washed his hands as she flitted here and there gathering Tulip's things. If she was this bad fussing over a dog, he could only imagine how she would be with a grandchild.

Grandchild?

That thought froze him into a statue. He hadn't thought much about kids, but after last night's kiss, he could see himself holding a baby girl with blue eyes.

Whoa, there. You're getting ahead of yourself.

No one had said anything about kids or marriage or…love.

He bowed his head. *Lord, I'm flirting with disaster, aren't I?*

"Ready?" Mom held Tulip under one arm, with her leash in hand and humongous purse over her shoulder.

"Yep."

Out in the driveway, he held the truck door open for her and helped her get settled. Then he strapped Tulip in her doggy seat and began the drive to town.

"I think it's great you're hiring Trent." Mom watched the scenery go by. "I always liked him. He and Ty had a lot in common when they were young."

"I haven't decided if I'm hiring him or not. We'll see how the interview goes and if he even wants the job."

"Why wouldn't he want it?" Her indignant tone made him smile. "It's home. Caring for horses."

He wouldn't argue. She was probably right.

An unfamiliar urge kicked in—the urge to ask his mother for advice. About Mackenzie. Would she take it the wrong way? Start bombarding him with truth bombs he didn't want to hear? Did he even know what he wanted to ask? The last thing he needed was for his mother to start mentally planning a wedding. Not that she didn't on a daily basis, anyhow, but still.

"Can I ask you something?" He gave her a sideways glance. Her forehead wrinkled with curiosity.

"Go ahead."

"How did you know you were in love with Dad?" He winced. Why had those words spilled out of his mouth? That wasn't what he wanted to ask.

"I was in love with him long before I was ready to admit it." She stared out the front window with a soft smile on her lips. "Pete was patient. He knew I had a lot going on."

"Like what?"

"Relationships weren't my strong suit. My

mother and I never saw eye to eye, and I don't think I had any idea what real love looked like."

He'd never met his maternal grandmother. "What did your mom do?"

"It wasn't so much what she did. It was more that I couldn't live up to her expectations. And she kind of checked out of our family when I was small. She was there physically, and that was about it. I didn't really have a mother, and it affected me."

Sympathy made him want to comfort her, but he kept his hands on the wheel.

"I don't think I really got the strength to consider marrying Pete until Trudy and I spent time together. She was so patient and kind. She'd ask about my day. Your nana was genuinely interested in me, my job and my life."

"Sounds like you fell in love with her," he teased.

"In a way, I did. She helped me see there were better mothers, that I could be one like her. I don't pretend to say I've been as good of a mom as she was, but she's my role model. My friend, too. Your dad could have given up on me—he almost did at one point—but he didn't. I never deserved him, and I'm grateful every day that he was mine. I can't imagine what my life would have been like without him and you boys."

"You deserved him. And you're a great mom. The best." The words were gruff, and he cleared his throat. All these emotions had been sneaking up on him as she spoke. "I take you for granted, and I'm sorry."

When she didn't reply, he flicked her a glance and realized she was stealthily wiping away tears.

Great. He'd made her cry.

"Thank you. I appreciate it." She squeezed his arm. "And you don't take me for granted. You're a good son. You drive me everywhere. Never complain about it. I'm blessed."

He cleared his throat, then steered the conversation to discuss everything Tulip needed to practice before her test, and before long, Cade was dropping Mom and Tulip off on Center Street. He waved to Angie and Mary, then made the short drive to the construction site to meet with Trent. His phone rang as he parked.

"Cade speaking."

"I have a few questions." Michael Grove's deep voice sounded annoyed. "Paris showed me the pictures of your barns and grounds and explained what you were offering."

Finally. The owner of Forestline Adventures must be seriously considering using Moulten Stables if he was calling him personally. Cade got out of the truck and ambled toward his makeshift office as Michael asked about how many horses they could reasonably house over the winter, the type of exercise they'd receive, their security system and liability policy. Cade answered everything with ease.

As Cade entered the office, Michael mentioned the one subject he'd been dreading. "I'm assuming you'll have an equine-certified veterinarian on call."

"I'll have a qualified vet on call." He kept his tone neutral.

"Qualified? That's not what I said."

"I can send you the link to Dr. Howard's website. She has a state-of-the-art mobile vet trailer, and she's within five minutes of the stables."

"If I'm trusting you with my horses, I have to have the best. I'll be paying top dollar, and you know it."

This wasn't about money. Cade understood the game all too well. It was about status, bragging rights, luxury.

"You'll have the best." But was it true?

"I'll think about it."

They ended the call, and Cade pocketed his phone. The veterinarian issue would work itself out. If it didn't, he'd be stuck with an expensive, top-of-the-line barn with no horses to fill it.

MACKENZIE COULDN'T IMAGINE a more awkward meal if she tried. She sliced off a chunk of baked chicken and chewed it slowly so she wouldn't have to contribute to the conversation.

Mom had been overcompensating since the minute Mackenzie arrived, gushing over her outfit—it was a basic navy T-shirt and shorts, nothing special—and how great the clinic was and how she'd love to see her house.

Dad kept giving Mackenzie concerned glances. She wanted to roll her eyes and tell them both to stop it, but she didn't. She'd play along. Eat the chicken and her salad. Pretend everything was fine.

It wasn't fine. It hadn't been fine since she was a little girl.

"Your clinic seems to be doing well." Her mother's eyes pleaded with her—for what, Mackenzie didn't know—as Mom buttered a roll.

"It is." She stabbed a bite of lettuce and cucumber onto her fork.

"Why don't you tell me about it?" Mom asked her.

Mackenzie finished chewing before responding. "I treat mostly dogs and cats. Last week, someone brought in an injured raccoon."

"Oh, that sounds exciting." Mom nodded brightly. "And have you gotten over your fear of horses?"

Irritation gripped her fingers into claws. "I'm not afraid of horses. I've never been afraid of horses."

"Oh, well, I just thought the surgery with the horse that died affected you." With her eyes downcast, her mother fiddled with the napkin in her lap.

"I'm fine." She shoveled a piece of chicken in her mouth before she said something she regretted. What was Dad's point in hosting this meal? What did her parents hope to accomplish?

The sounds of silverware scraping on plates filled the otherwise silent room. Charger lay on his dog bed with his head resting on his crossed front paws.

"He's come a long way." Mackenzie gestured to the dog.

"Yes, we've been spending a lot of time together." Dad gave the German shepherd an affectionate smile. "He's much better behaved than when I first picked him up. Our evening runs have been helping him burn off some of his energy."

"Have you made a decision about what contractor to use for the center?" she asked.

"Ed McCaffrey. I'll have to wait until September for him to start, but I think it will be worth it. After years of working full-time, I could use a break."

"I'm enjoying my break." Mom's smile didn't reach her eyes. "I'd enjoy it even more if I could catch up with you, Mackenzie. I haven't even seen your house."

She debated how to respond. Last night, Cade had made a good point about rules and not being a doormat. Did her mother even know why Mackenzie felt the way she did? They hadn't discussed it. There hadn't been any opportunity to talk about it. If her mom hadn't ghosted her, maybe.

"I don't feel safe spending time with you, Mom." There, she said it. She set her fork down and hoped her heart wouldn't beat right out of her chest.

"Safe?" Mom let out an incredulous laugh. "What are you talking about? I would never hurt you."

"You do hurt me. Every time we do this—" she waved her hands "—whatever this is. I fool myself into thinking you miss me, and you don't."

"How can you say that? I *do* miss you. I wouldn't have come to Jewel River for any other reason."

"That's not true. You're here because you want something from me. Not because you miss me. Not because you want to spend time with me. I don't know—maybe you actually believe the words you tell me. I don't. Not anymore."

"I see." Mom tucked her chin and blinked rapidly. Was she crying?

"Let's not say things we'll regret." Dad stared at Mackenzie, then glanced at Mom.

"The only thing I regret is not saying these things years ago." She hiked her chin. "I think it's time to get it all out there."

"Careful." Her father leveled a stern look her way. She ignored it.

"Mom, I find it incredibly painful when you show up, include me in your plans to start over with a new job in a new town, then borrow money from me and go silent. I wanted—expected—to hear how your new job was going. I wanted to know if you'd gotten settled into your apartment okay, if you'd made any friends. But you wouldn't respond to my texts beyond saying everything was fine. And within a few weeks, you no longer responded at all."

"I was busy." Her eyes grew round. "I didn't want to bother you."

"Bother me? No. Hearing from you wouldn't bother me. It's what people who are close to each other do. They support each other. I wanted to be emotionally supportive."

"But you are. You're always supportive."

"Only when you allow it. It's always on your terms, Mom." Her throat tightened with emotion. She didn't dare look at her father. Didn't need to see the censure and disappointment sure to be in his eyes. "Every time you arrive, I get my hopes up. I enjoy being with you. I even like helping you get a plan together. Then you take my money and run. It makes me feel used. Rejected."

She wished Tulip was on her lap. She didn't know what to do with her hands, so she clasped them tightly, rubbing her thumbs over each other. Her mother's face was pinched and pale.

Dad appeared ready to throw in his two cents on the issue.

And all Mackenzie wanted to do was leave.

"Your mother loves you."

"No offense, Dad, but I don't think you understand the situation." She hadn't told him about all the money she'd given to her mom over the years. Hadn't told him much about their relationship at all.

"Do I understand the situation?" he asked her mother.

"Neither of you has any idea what my life is like." Color bloomed in her mother's cheeks. Her voice grew shrill. "You're both over here making your dreams come true. Opening a service-dog training center—what you always wanted. And you—" she pointed to Mackenzie "—a veterinary clinic. Again, your lifelong dream. I don't have one of those. I'm almost sixty, and I don't know what to do with my life. I can't hold on to jobs for long. I don't even know if I want to anymore."

Mom pushed her chair back to stand.

"No one is leaving this table." Dad had his firm voice on. "We're hashing this out. Right now."

"What do you think is going to happen,

Dad?" Mackenzie sighed, tired of the drama. "Why is it so important to you that we all get along?"

"It just is," he mumbled.

"Fine." She pushed her plate away. "Mom, if you'd like to have me in your life, you're going to have to make an effort with me. No more showing up on my doorstep without any warning. You can make plans ahead of time and stay in a hotel. I'd like to hear what you're doing, but I will not be giving you any money to do it. And please don't think we'll be diving into your fantasy of what you think our relationship should look like. We're not going to be besties anytime soon."

Both her mom and her dad stared at her with matching stunned expressions.

Mom licked her lips, pressing them together. "You make it sound like I have some sinister plan. It's not like that."

"Then what is it like? Help me understand."

Her shoulders sank like a balloon deflating. "I start a new job, and I think *This is it. This time I've found it.* Then I give it a go, and it falls apart. I don't know why. It just does. And it's all so tiring. I don't expect you'd understand because you're like your father. Steady. Smart. Committed. And I'm not."

Her mother had never admitted any flaws or vulnerability in the past.

"You have other qualities, Bonnie." Kindness emanated from her father. "You're always too hard on yourself."

Too hard on herself? The woman wasn't hard enough on herself, in Mackenzie's opinion. She got a free pass for all her bad behavior.

Her mother's lower lip wobbled, but she nodded. Then she glanced at Mackenzie. "I do want to be part of your life."

Mackenzie wanted to believe her, but she couldn't. It would take time for Mom to earn her trust.

"What you said is fair," Mom said, sniffing. "We'll try it your way. It's not as if my way ever works."

Sympathy gripped her, and she tried to push it away. This was how it started. She'd feel bad for her mom, take her in, help her get on her feet and…end up getting burned.

One meal together would not solve their problems.

But maybe it was a start.

CHAPTER ELEVEN

CADE HELD HIS breath the following Tuesday as he and his mother waited for the verdict in the back room of the clinic. Patrick had just finished guiding Mom and Tulip through each step of the Canine Good Citizen test, but he still hadn't looked up from his clipboard. Tulip had excelled at most of the tasks: She'd sat quietly while Patrick came up and greeted Mom. She'd allowed Patrick to pet her. Then he'd checked her ears, teeth and nails before instructing Christy to walk her from cone to cone as he observed that the tension in the leash stayed loose.

Although it was their day off, Emily and Greta had stopped by to help with the test. They'd entered the back room of the clinic and wandered around while Christy walked Tulip. The dog had ignored them as she should.

Afterward, Patrick observed Mom giving

Tulip basic commands like sit, down and stay. Cade had gotten a little nervous when Mackenzie brought in Charger, but while Tulip had perked up, she continued to sit near Mom's feet until Patrick had the dogs walk past each other. Later, when Patrick purposely knocked over a bin to see how Tulip would react to a commotion, the dog barely noticed.

The only unknown element at this point was how Tulip had responded to two minutes alone with Patrick. He'd explained that she needed to stay calm with him and not bark or whine while Cade and Christy were out of the room.

"Good news." Patrick looked up from the clipboard with a grin. "She passed with flying colors. Congratulations. Tulip is now a certified Canine Good Citizen."

Mom scooped up the dog. "Did you hear that? You're such a good girl. You passed your test!"

Cade hugged his mom with Tulip between them. Finally. Everything was falling into place. After last week's interview, he'd formally offered Trent Lloyd the position of managing Moulten Stables. Trent would be moving next month into the old house across the road from the property. And Cade was this close to convincing Forestline Adventures to board their horses with him. The cherry on top was Tulip passing her test.

Mackenzie came over to congratulate them, and he gave her a big hug.

"Can we take her to see Nana?" Cade asked her. They'd been spending time together every day. Hugging her and holding her hand had become second nature at this point. He was falling in love with her, and there didn't seem to be any brakes he could press to stop it.

She beamed. "I don't see why not. You've cleared it with the nursing home, and she did well there last week. Just make sure she's wearing her therapy-dog vest."

"I can't believe she passed," Christy said. "We need to celebrate. Why don't you all come out and have supper at our place? We'll grill burgers on the back deck."

"I'm sorry, Christy," Patrick said. "But I told Bonnie I'd help her with something tonight."

"She's welcome to join us."

"That's kind of you, but I have to pass on this one. Excuse me, I'd better get Charger from Greta. Congratulations, again." He strode toward the door.

"What about you, Mackenzie?" Mom had

a gleam in her eye, and for once, Cade didn't mind it.

"Sure, why not?"

"Wonderful!" Christy turned to Cade. "We'll have to stop at the supermarket on the way home. We'll get the burgers, buns and some chips and dip."

"Actually, I really want to take Tulip to see Nana first." He'd waited six weeks. He didn't want to wait another minute.

"She'll see her tomorrow, Cade." His mom's expression fell.

Mackenzie gave Cade a thoughtful glance. "Actually, Christy, why don't you ride with me? We'll head to the supermarket while Cade takes Tulip to the nursing home."

"Really?" Mom sounded like she'd won a million dollars. "Okay. I like this plan. It will give us a chance to get to know each other better."

Mom handed him Tulip's leash. "Thanks. I'll see you two in a little while."

Ten minutes later, he and Tulip strolled down the hall of the nursing home to the reception desk.

"Guess who passed her test?" He grinned at Charlene. Her mouth formed an O, and she began to clap. Then she rounded the counter and crouched to pet Tulip.

"You did it, huh? Who's the good girl? You're going to be the queen of this place in no time."

Tulip ate up the attention.

"By the way, I made sure Janey added the *plus one* to your wedding invitation."

"Thanks." He grinned. "We're heading to Nana's."

"Have fun." Charlene gave him and the dog a little wave.

Excitement built as he neared the room. He knocked and entered. The shades were drawn, but the light was on. Nana, in bed, turned her head as he came inside.

"Pete?"

His spirits crashed. "No, Nana, it's me, Cade."

"Come here."

He obeyed.

"I've been thinking about it, and you're being too hard on Cade." She must not have gotten the memo that *he* was Cade. "You raised a fine man, Pete. He knows right from wrong."

A prickly sensation spread over his skin. What was she talking about?

"This business in New York isn't worth

getting all worked up over." She clutched his hand tightly.

New York? Had Dad told Nana about their fight that weekend? Had he given her *all* the details? Bile rose in his throat.

"Okay," he said. Should he leave? He didn't think he could handle whatever else she planned on sharing.

"He's a good boy." Nana rested her head against the pillows, patting his hand. "Cade's not doing anything wrong."

That was what she thought. Cade bowed his head and saw Tulip waiting patiently at his feet. Tulip. The whole reason he was here.

His heart wasn't in it anymore. But as he stared at the training vest and the little dog who'd done everything he and his mother had asked, he knew he'd better follow through.

He picked up Tulip and brought her close to Nana's hand.

"I brought the dog I told you about."

"Dolly?" She brightened.

"No, Tulip. The Pomeranian."

"Oh, she's cute." Nana's face lit up as she smiled. She reached for the dog. "Can I pet her?"

"You sure can." He let Tulip sniff her hand a moment.

"She's soft." Nana looked so happy as she petted the dog. "Hi there, doggy."

"Do you want her on your lap?" he asked.

"Yes."

She petted Tulip for several minutes without speaking. The dog seemed to love it.

"Thanks for bringing Dolly out, Pete."

"You're welcome." His heart was wrung, and tears formed behind his eyes. He tried to keep his composure.

"If it makes you feel better, I'm praying for Cade."

"I've got to take off." If she said another word, he'd choke on his emotions. He carefully took the dog in his arms, kissed Nana on the cheek, said goodbye and walked out of the room. He power walked down the hall, waved to Charlene without stopping and headed outside.

Out in the warm sunshine, he sucked in a breath and raised his gaze to the sky.

All this time, he'd thought that no one had known about his falling out with Dad. But he'd been wrong.

Nana had known. Nana knew.

And worse, she'd given him the benefit of the

doubt. For years, Nana had thought the best of him, and he didn't deserve it.

The triumphant feeling he'd been anticipating from having Tulip visit her was nowhere to be found. He strode to the truck and strapped Tulip into her doggy seat. As he drove home, all he could think was that he couldn't keep living a lie.

He had to tell Mackenzie the truth about his job in New York City.

And once he did, he'd walk away from her, like he should have done from the beginning.

CADE WAS BEING unusually quiet. Mackenzie glanced his way as she stood to gather plates. The burgers had been delicious, and spending time with Christy had given her a new appreciation for the woman. She'd asked Mackenzie thoughtful questions and had been genuinely interested in her responses. Cade and Christy were more alike than Mackenzie realized.

Last week, when Mackenzie had filled him in on the supper with her parents, he'd told her he was impressed that she'd been honest about her feelings. She was impressed with herself, too. Usually, all her pain festered inside. Since then, her mother hadn't reached out to Mackenzie.

No surprise there. When had her mother ever played by anyone's rules but her own?

At least she had Cade to look forward to every evening when he stopped by. The way he listened, the way he hugged her, the way he kissed her—he made her feel important.

"Why are you so quiet?" Christy frowned at Cade. The sun dipped lower in the sky, casting shadows on the back lawn below the deck.

"Am I?"

Mackenzie exchanged a glance with Christy. *Yes*.

"Must have been all the excitement." His lips tightened into a not-quite smile. "Mackenzie, would you like to take a walk?"

"Sure. Let me clear some of these plates first."

"Oh, no." Christy shooed her away. "I'll take care of this. You two go."

"Ready?" Cade stood and hitched his head toward the stairs.

"Sure."

Neither spoke until they were halfway down the lane that led to the outbuildings.

"I take it the visit with your grandmother earlier didn't go well?" she asked. There was something off about him, and over the past couple of weeks, she'd gotten to know him pretty well. Enough to care about him. Deeply.

"Nana loved petting Tulip." The words sounded strangled.

"I'm not surprised." She breathed in the air, heavy with summer, and tried to come up with why he was acting weird. Nope. Nothing.

When they reached the horse stables, they continued down the aisle until they came to a stack of hay bales at the end, where another set of doors were open.

"Mackenzie, I need to tell you something." He gestured for her to sit on the hay bales. A sense of impending disaster filled her body, so she remained standing. He shifted his attention to his cowboy boots. "I haven't been honest with you."

Her muscles locked as her brain started spitting out endless scenarios. Was he seeing someone? Had he been married? Was he still married? Did he have kids she didn't know about?

"I'm not who anyone thinks I am." He stared off through the open doors to the pastures beyond. She didn't say a word. Just stood there with her arms by her side, watching him.

He'd murdered someone. Sold drugs. Buried a body in the woods near his old fort.

"Back when I was in New York, I worked for a global investment bank. I moved up the ranks quickly, and they asked me to join a special team that was working on new financial products for investors. I knew I'd be great at it because of the way my brain is wired. At the time, I was caught up in the Wall Street culture, competing against everyone else to get ahead."

No kids? No dead bodies? What did banking have to do with anything?

"I, and the rest of our team, worked with a few of the best coders in the world, and together we created the products our bosses wanted. I won't—and legally can't, due to nondisclosure agreements—get into the details, but everything we created was basically just a new way to charge fees."

"Fees? What's wrong with that?" She was missing something, wasn't she?

"Almost every time these investments are touched, it generates a fee—if not multiple fees—and they're hidden from the customer."

"Is that illegal?"

"Technically, no. Not the way we were doing it. Fees are supposed to be transparent to clients. But we found loopholes. Although the lawyers and my supervisors assured me everything was legal, I knew it was wrong. We were making the fees virtually untraceable. The company made more money from these products than anyone could have imagined. I was a hero. The entire team was. And in exchange for praise, bonuses and promotions, I ignored my conscience."

Mackenzie frowned as she realized how torn up Cade was about this.

"It all came to a head when my dad visited. I wanted to impress him. Took him to the best restaurants. We ran into people from my company, who told Dad what a great job I was doing. Not long before my father left, he looked around my expensive apartment and asked me what I did, exactly, to earn all my money. I knew that tone, and I got defensive."

She knew all about getting defensive. Every interaction with her mother made her bristle.

He stared off into the distance. "I gave him the sugarcoated version. Then he stared at me hard and said, 'Lie to yourself, but don't lie to me.' It was like he knew how many ethical lines I'd crossed. I don't think I even realized how many I'd crossed until that moment. I got mad. We argued. And I was fuming when he looked me in the eye and said, 'Don't lose sight of what's important in all your wheeling and dealing. It ain't money, son.'"

Her heart hurt for him, disappointing his father like that.

"A few weeks later, I stood next to Mom for his funeral."

"I'm sorry, Cade." She didn't know what else to say. Her muscles tensed as she waited for him to spell out the real problem. Whatever else he was about to confess would likely shock her.

"I am, too." His eyes held something wild as he looked anywhere but at her. "Now you know why I haven't gotten serious with anyone."

Wait. That was it?

"Not really."

"The unethical side of me is still there, still a part of me. I can't get rid of the restlessness that drives me. I'm always looking for loopholes. Constantly searching for my next venture. I tried to be like my dad—content with ranching—and I couldn't do it. Every morning, I'm analyzing stocks and investments. Then I'm on the phone with a real estate agent about upcoming auctions on properties. Next thing I know, I'm stopping in at the construction zone of the stables. My mind comes up with fifteen different businesses to start every single day. I can't turn off this part of me. I can't turn any of it off!"

Mackenzie took a step backward. She would have preferred to step forward, to put her hand on his arm and reassure him. But she didn't. Couldn't.

"Why are you telling me this?" She rubbed her forearms.

"Because you deserve to know."

"Why?"

"You just do."

"There's more to it. Why are you telling *me* this?"

He met her gaze. "I'm not good enough for you. You think I'm a decent guy, but I'm not. The real me is a mess. I'm sorry. I'm sorry I wasn't honest with you."

And there it was. The real reason for his confession. To drive her away. To end their relationship. Tears sprang up, and she struggled with her emotions.

In this moment, she could finally acknowledge the truth. She'd fallen in love with him. And it wasn't enough. Her love would never be enough for him.

She'd had enough experience with her mother

to understand that. Either Cade would push her away because deep down he didn't care about her, or if she did matter to him, he'd convince himself pushing her away was the noble thing to do.

She let out a heavy sigh. Now what?

Should she leave? Accept the fact he'd made up his mind?

No, she wouldn't let him push her away without fighting for him.

"Don't I get a say in this?" Her palms grew moist.

"You don't understand." He strode out of the stables to the nearby fence, where horses were grazing. Mackenzie joined him there.

"Cade." She touched his arm.

"Do you see that beautiful Morgan horse grazing? It's the small black one." He pointed to where two horses flicked their tails. "I bought her for you. To keep at my stables so you can come over and ride her whenever you want. Don't worry about taking care of her. My crew will do that."

"What?" Too stunned to respond, she tried to process what he was saying. "I don't want a pony from you, Cade. I'm not a five-year-old girl."

"It's not a pony. It's a—"

"I know what it is. It's a guilt offering. And a poor substitute for what I really want."

"What do you really want?" His eyes glistened with pain. Regrets mounted in them.

"I want you. I care about you. Your past is what it is. Do you think I'm perfect?"

"Yeah, I do."

"I'm not. I caused the death of a pregnant mare *and* her foal during my residency. The family sued me. For the record, I was acquitted." She couldn't believe she was telling him this without getting emotional. "I kept it from you." She shrugged. "Now you know I have things in my past I'm not proud of, either."

"I'm sure you did the best you could. It wasn't your fault."

"And I'm sure you were young and ambitious and wanted to please your supervisors."

"It's not the same."

"I know it isn't. But you recognized you weren't living the way you should, and you changed."

"Only because my dad died."

"You would have quit your job even if your dad had lived. You'd already been making changes. You broke up with Gia, right?"

"See?" He pushed his hands off the fence and shifted to face her. "You think I'm someone I'm not. I wouldn't have quit. I liked being a big shot."

"You would have," she said quietly. "God got through to you."

"By punishing me! My dad's gone."

"Like that's your fault? *You* caused him to get cancer?"

"No, but—"

"What exactly are you beating yourself up over? What do you have to prove? And who are you trying to prove it to?"

"I'm just being honest. Showing you the real me. The way I should have done from day one."

"Fine." She threw her hands up. "You're a terrible person. Is that what you want to hear? I've been around you. I know you're restless. I know you need your hands stoking eight different fires. None of it matters to me. I don't want some perfect guy. I want you, not Mr. Wonderful!"

All the energy drained from him, and his eyes were sad as he shook his head. "You don't get it."

"I get it. You're the one who doesn't get it. I see more than you know. And you see more about me than most people do. Do you care that

I have no hobbies? No. And I'm sure it hasn't escaped your notice, I'm a loner. I get panicky anytime someone wants me to join a group, and I've basically cut my mother out of my life. I'm not perfect, Cade, and you accept me anyhow."

He opened his mouth, but she held her hand up.

"Keep your horse," she said and tightened her jaw. "You know where to find me if you can get it through your dumb head that I'm not interested in perfect. I just want someone who isn't afraid to be real."

It was her turn to pivot. She marched all the way to her truck, started it up and drove away.

She wasn't going to sit around waiting for him to figure out she was worth fighting for. She'd done that for years with her mother. She was going home and getting on with her life. Alone.

CHAPTER TWELVE

THAT HAD BEEN a disaster. Cade waited until Mackenzie's truck faded from view, then he marched to the house.

"Where's Mackenzie?" his mom asked. He didn't answer. He went straight to his bedroom and shut the door.

Soft footfalls warned him his mother was incoming. *Knock, knock.*

He wanted to yell, "Go away!" the way he'd done countless times as a kid, but he was all grown up now, and his mom didn't deserve that.

"What happened?" Mom asked on the other side of the door. "Can I crack the door open for Tulip to go in there?"

"Yeah." The door opened, and Tulip raced inside. He picked her up and set her next to him on the bed. She scrambled onto his lap, licking his hand. Mom didn't close the door, just watched him from the doorway with a worried expression.

"Cade…"

Grr… He might as well get it all off his chest with his mother, too. Seemed he was in a confessional mood. "Just come in."

She glided through the doorway and sat on the edge of the bed next to him.

"Mackenzie left, and she's not coming back."

"Ever?"

He shrugged. "I don't know. It's not likely."

"What did you say to her? Why did she leave?"

"I told her the truth about me." He turned to face her, and the questions crossing her face brought an emptiness to his stomach. He should have told her this years ago. Would have saved him the pain of carrying around all this guilt. "Dad knew my job in New York wasn't anything to be proud of. He saw the truth within five seconds of arriving in the city."

"New York?" Worry lines tightened around her lips. "What does your father have to do with Mackenzie?"

"Everything." He kept a hand on Tulip and shook his head. "Nothing. I don't know anymore. Everyone around here—including you—

thinks I had this great job in New York and that I gave up a lucrative spot on Wall Street to manage the ranch here, but they don't know the truth."

He proceeded to tell her everything he'd told Mackenzie. When he finished, he hung his head and waited for her to lecture him on how disappointed in him she was.

"What do you want me to say?" she asked. "You're a grown man. You made mistakes. You learned from them."

That was it?

Her response wasn't good enough. He deserved a tongue-lashing.

"I didn't learn from them, Ma. I covered them up. Let everyone around here think I'm someone I'm not."

"Oh, please." She gave him a skeptical look and waved as if he was being silly. There was nothing silly about this. "Someone you're not? We're all smarter than that, Cade. We know who you are. Don't think you're such a master at manipulation you could fool an entire town into thinking you're anyone other than who you really are."

He opened his mouth to argue, but she beat him to it.

"After your dad returned from visiting you that weekend, he told me and Nana his concerns. He worried you were on a path that would lead you away from your faith and your values. The three of us prayed for you. And a few days later, Pete went to the doctor, and… well…your city job became the least of our worries."

"But you never said anything." She'd known? All this time? Here he'd thought he'd been keeping this big secret.

"There was nothing to say." Her eyes were bright with kindness. "You moved home, and I could see you doing the right thing. You handled the ranch the way your dad always did. Then you hired Micky. I knew I didn't need to fret. Our prayers for you had been answered. The only thing I worried about was you finding someone to share your life with."

"I didn't see marriage in my future."

"Even now? After meeting Mackenzie?"

His heart finally crashed. He'd pushed her away. She'd been right to be angry about the horse. What had he been thinking giving it to her tonight? After his stupid speech? Had it been to ease his guilt over telling her the truth?

Mom rose. "She's good for you, Cade. Don't let her get away."

Cade stopped breathing as her words registered. *Don't let her get away. She's good for you.* It was practically the same thing Nana had said when she'd thought he was his father.

"And don't try to live up to an unrealistic idea of your dad, either. That man was wonderful, but he was far from perfect." She made it to the door before turning back to him. "Open your Bible and pray. God knows what you need."

It wouldn't do any good. He was too messed up.

The damage had been done, and he didn't know how to fix it.

WHAT AN OBSTINATE, irritating, stubborn man. Why had she fallen in love with him?

Nothing could be simple—no, it always had to be hard with her. She hadn't even wanted to fall in love.

Mackenzie pulled into her driveway and groaned at the sight of her mom's old forest green minivan parked on the street.

What was her mother doing on her porch? Like she needed this on top of everything else.

She parked, got out and slammed the door as

hard as she could. Stomped like a child all the way to her mom. "What are you doing here?"

"I came to say goodbye." Mom wasn't wearing her fake-happy smile for once. Her demeanor was surprisingly subdued.

"Where are you going?" Mackenzie expected to be pleased at the announcement, but sorrow and regrets weighed on her chest.

"Does it matter?"

She selected her words carefully before responding. Yesterday, it probably wouldn't have mattered. But today, it did. "Yeah, Mom, it does. Want to come inside?"

"Sure."

After unlocking the door, she held it open for her mother.

"Nice place."

"Thanks." She closed the door. "Want a quick tour?"

"I'd like that."

Mackenzie showed her around, tucking away each compliment, and steered her to the living room. "Have a seat. Can I get you something to drink?"

"No, I'm fine." She found a spot on the couch. "I want you to know I've been thinking about what you said at supper last week."

Anxiety kicked in. She wasn't sure she wanted to hear her mother's thoughts on her outburst.

Mom fiddled with the hem of her shirt. "I never really put two and two together on how you felt whenever I would leave. Hearing you spell it out was painful. I've been trying to justify my actions—I've had pretend conversations with you for days. It sounds crazy, I know."

Mackenzie knew all about pretend conversations. She had them often.

"But over the past couple of days, it kind of hit me." Mom lifted one shoulder in a sad shrug. "You're right."

She was right? Her mother had never said those words before.

"You're so much like your father." A whisper of a smile lifted her lips. "You're both kind, compassionate. You sacrifice to make other people's lives better. And I'm not like that."

"What are you talking about?"

She gave her head a slight shake. "I don't expect you to understand, Mackenzie. I guess, in some ways, you and your father have always been my last resort."

Ouch. The bottom dropped out of her heart. Of all the cruel things to say.

"And it's because I didn't want to have to rely

on you. You've both got your lives together. I doubt you'll ever know what it's like to be down to your last dollar. I make lousy decisions. Can't keep a job for more than a year. Can't save fifty dollars without spending it a week later."

Mackenzie wanted to say something to make her mom feel better, but she didn't have the words.

"Every time I borrowed money from you, I'd leave with the best intentions. I'd tell myself this time was different. That I'd pay you back quickly, and we'd stay in touch, and you'd be proud of me. And a couple of months later, I'd be stressed out, barely keeping it together. I'd want to call you, but I wouldn't. It was too demoralizing to have you know I'd made another mistake. Couldn't be the failure you and I both knew I was."

"You're not a failure, Mom," she said quietly. Compassion stole over her. "I wish you would have called and texted. I could have given you a pep talk. We could have laughed and cried together. I needed you, too."

"Why would you need me? I have nothing to offer." Her eyes filled with tears, and it took everything in Mackenzie to stay seated and not to go hug her.

"I needed *you*, not anything you have." She was getting emotional, and she hated crying. She turned her head away until she could continue. "Do you know how much I used to love when you showed up at my apartment? I loved hanging out with you. Making a game plan for your next job. I loved all of it. But then you'd leave, and you wouldn't talk to me...that was hard, Mom. I had to build a shell over my heart where you were concerned."

"I'm sorry, Mackenzie. I've made a mess of everything. I can't change what I did."

"No, you can't, but maybe we can do things differently from now on."

The hope in her eyes was almost unbearable. Was Mackenzie right to be doing this? Or would she get burned again?

If there was anything Cade had taught her, it was to be honest and to hope for the best instead of keeping everything inside and expecting the worst.

Ironic, considering he'd destroyed her heart tonight.

"Mom, I meant what I said at Dad's. I'm not lending you any more money."

She nodded. "I understand. It's for the best."

"And I need some warning when you're coming to town for a visit."

"I can do that."

"But if you're not going to communicate with me, it doesn't matter. I don't want to be your last resort."

"You're still willing to give me a chance?" Mom asked.

"Yeah. I am. But with rules in place."

"I have a rule, too." She rose, holding out her hands. Mackenzie held her breath. What rule? "Never change who you are. I'm so proud of you, I could cry. You've made something for yourself with your clinic. You're living your dream."

"Thank you, Mom." She did something she couldn't have imagined a day ago. She wrapped her arms around Bonnie Howard and gave her a long, heartfelt hug. "Want to fill me in on your plans?"

"I'd love to. But first, can I take you up on the offer of something to drink?"

"Sure." They went to the kitchen, where Mackenzie took out two sodas and handed one to her mother.

"I found a night job for a hotel in Casper. I think it will be a good fit."

"Where are you going to stay?" The familiar worries rose up about if her mom could handle the job, but as she looked at her mother, she realized she needed to be part of the solution instead of the problem.

Her mother was a grown woman, capable of making it on her own. Mackenzie didn't need to worry about her.

"I'm not sure, yet. I'll find a cheap place until the right apartment comes along."

They talked for half an hour before her mother rose to leave.

"You're going to be fine." She smiled at her mom.

"I know I will. And you will be, too."

They hugged goodbye, and her mother left.

Mackenzie wanted to call Cade to tell him about this unexpected conversation with her mother, but she couldn't. She wouldn't.

She'd spent too much of her life wanting to be important to her mom. She wasn't wasting a single minute doing the same with Cade. Either he needed her too much to let her go, or whatever they had was over.

And something told her, it was over.

CHAPTER THIRTEEN

THE FOLLOWING MORNING, Cade slumped in a chair with Tulip on his lap in his office at the construction site. He'd already met with Micky for their daily ranch meeting. One of Mom's friends had picked her up this morning for some activity they'd planned weeks ago, and he couldn't be more relieved. The last thing he needed was another pep talk/lecture from her.

All he could think about was last night. Mackenzie's pretty face. The words she'd said. *I'm not interested in perfect. I just want someone who isn't afraid to be real.* He alternated between soaring hope and the depressing reality that he wasn't worthy of her love.

He'd prayed last night. Opened the Bible the way Mom had instructed. And he'd been drawn to Isaiah 30:18. The passage basically said the Lord, a God of judgment, will wait in order to give you grace and have mercy on you in order that He may be exalted.

The passage had dropped him to his knees in repentance. Cade deserved punishment, not grace or mercy. He'd asked the Lord for forgiveness for helping the bank he'd worked for cheat people out of their hard-earned money. He'd repented for the words he'd said to his father and for all the ways he'd failed in the years since. Most of all, he asked for forgiveness for trying to hide it all. Hours later, he'd fallen into an uneasy sleep.

"I've been trying to earn it, haven't I, Tulip?" Cade petted the dog. She lifted her head and, panting, smiled at him. Sounds of nail guns and the whir of an air compressor didn't seem to bother her. "I've been going to church my entire life. I've heard the gospel again and again. How could I have missed it so completely?"

The Lord, in His great mercy, had saved Cade from his sins. There was no earning forgiveness. It was free. By grace alone.

His cell phone rang, and he swiped it off the desk and answered.

"Haven't heard from you in a week." Michael Grove sounded annoyed. "Have you addressed Paris's concerns? And where are you at with the veterinarian?"

"What concerns are we talking about?" Usually, he'd be excited to get this call. It meant he was one step closer to sealing the deal. But today, he couldn't bring himself to care about landing Forestline Adventures for the stables.

"The barn. Access. Any bum off the street being around our horses."

Cade kept his temper in check. He'd dropped any thought of dividing the barn after the Fourth of July. Didn't see the point in it. "They aren't bums. They're locals."

"Locals." His tone hit Cade the wrong way.

"Yes. Mostly teenagers on the rodeo team. This is a small town. We all know each other. Besides, I recently hired Trent Lloyd to manage the stables. He has a degree in equine science from Auburn University and has been working for the past ten years at a Thoroughbred farm near Lexington, Kentucky."

"And what does that have to do with access?"

"He grew up in Jewel River. He'll know if someone shouldn't be there."

"How? He's been across the country for years."

Cade tightened his jaw, wanting to chuck the

phone across the room. "The people he doesn't know, he'll meet quickly."

"I see." The sound of papers shuffling in the background had Cade raising his gaze to the ceiling. His frustration mounted to dangerous levels. Tulip licked the back of his hand, and his stress immediately lessened. He mindlessly stroked her fur.

The dog was right. There was no reason to get worked up over a call. In fact, there was no reason to get worked up about the stables at all. If Michael didn't want to board his horses, Cade would find someone else. And if no one else wanted his facilities, he had enough money to keep it going for a long time without any outside help.

"What's going on with the veterinarian situation?" Michael asked.

"It's handled. I told you that Mackenzie Howard opened her practice over a month ago. She has her license to treat large and small animals. Her mobile vet trailer is impressive. She can handle any emergency within minutes."

"But she's not certified in equine care."

"No, she isn't. I trust her with my horses, though. She's honest. Her heart is one hundred percent focused on whatever animal she's treating. Your horses couldn't be in better hands."

He meant every word. And he wondered why he'd ever thought her credentials wouldn't be enough.

You were still caught up in that world.

Yeah, he had been. Was he still?

No. He wasn't. Last night, God had finally gotten through to him.

He had absolutely nothing to prove. To anyone. Including Michael Grove.

"I checked the link you sent me and did some research." The man's blustery tone didn't affect Cade one way or the other. "Are you aware she lost a mare and foal and was sued by the owners?"

"Yes, I'm aware." Usually, this would be the point in the conversation where his mind would scramble to offer the man an alternative. But there was no reason to. "She was acquitted. It happened during her residency. I stand by what I said. There's no one I'd trust more with my horses than her."

"Hmm." Michael switched topics and asked about the outdoor arena. A few minutes later, they ended the call.

Cade held Tulip under one arm as he stood.

"You and I are going to find Mackenzie. Right now. Because I was dumb, Tulip. I was so stupid. I can't live without her. She's the best thing that's ever happened to me. I can't believe she didn't slap me upside my head last night." Tulip wiggled in his arms as she wagged her tail.

Where should he start? Wednesday—she'd be at the clinic.

"Let's go. Maybe your cuteness will help soften her up. I can't live without her. And I don't care if I have to beg, I'm going to win her back."

Tulip let out a yip and panted up at him.

"That's the spirit."

IF SHE HAD a job where she could call in sick, she would have stayed home today.

Mackenzie had barely slept last night. Every time she told herself it was over between her and Cade, she'd second-guess herself. Should she fight for him? Try to convince him he wasn't a lost cause?

Why? So he could reject her again? No thanks.

Felt too much like texting and calling her mom only to be ignored.

She checked the GPS again to make sure she

didn't miss her turn. Marvin Blythe from Triple B Ranch had talked to Greta this morning about doing wellness checks on all his dogs. Since two of her morning appointments had cancelled, Mackenzie had taken the phone from Greta and told him she'd come out now. Even with the drive, she'd be back in time for her afternoon appointments.

Unfortunately, all this driving was giving her time to think.

And she didn't want to think.

All her thoughts magnetized to Cade. He was the first guy she'd opened her heart to, and he was the only one she could picture having a future with.

Even her old excuse about not having time for a relationship no longer held up. He understood and supported her work. Didn't expect her to be available every minute. They'd found pockets of time to be together last week. Time wasn't the problem.

If he'd just get over his past...

Yeah, like she'd done?

Maybe. After talking with her mother last night, Mackenzie really did think it would be different from now on. She understood the woman better. She'd never realized her mom felt inferior to her and Dad. Her silence made more sense. It didn't excuse her behavior, but at least she'd acknowledged she'd been wrong. And the ground rules they'd set moving forward gave Mackenzie hope that they'd be able to have a relationship of some sort.

What she really wanted was a relationship with Cade.

But not if he wouldn't fight for her.

Pressing the accelerator, she sighed.

She was exhausted, and it wasn't just physical. She was tired of doubting herself. Tired of being alone. Tired of feeling unimportant.

Finally, the driveway with a big sign overhead spelling out Triple B Ranch appeared, and she turned onto it.

Mackenzie didn't get a chance to park. Marvin ran toward her, waving wildly. She rolled down her window.

"Good, you made it." His jeans, plaid button-down shirt and cowboy boots were dusty and smeared with dirt. His face pinched with concern. "See that driveway? Stop at the third barn. I've got a cow with bloat."

Mackenzie's heart started racing. A bad case of bloat could kill a cow in as little as fifteen minutes. "On my way."

She drove past the barns and parked. Her mind raced with questions. If the bloat wasn't bad, an anti-gas foam might do the trick. But if it was bad? She'd assisted Dr. Johan, but this would be her first time treating it on her own.

She wished Cade was here. He'd boost her confidence and ease her fears because that was what he did. He was that kind of man. One she could rely on.

But he wasn't here. And all she could think of was the horse she'd lost. All that blood. The dead foal slipping out. The owner's ashen face. The kids racing across the lawn, when they should have been kept inside.

All the crying. All the blood.

All her fault.

God, I need You. I'm scared. I can't lose this cow. Don't let me lose this animal. Not this time.

With shaking fingers, she climbed out of the truck and unlocked the trailer. Then she zipped her coveralls over her outfit. Grabbed her supplies and hurried to the barn. Marv was waiting for her in the bay.

"Where is she?" Mackenzie matched his pace as he led her through the barn to the outside corral where he'd put the cow.

"Over there." He pointed, not missing a stride.

"Looks like I got here at the right time." The black cow was almost as wide as she was tall. A bad case of bloat. Just as she'd feared. "Poor girl."

"I'll get her into the chute."

Marv expertly moved the cow into the chute, and Mackenzie checked the animal for signs of other illnesses. No snot or mucus. She listened to its lungs. They sounded clear. The cow's slightly elevated temperature didn't concern her.

Once she'd made it through the examination, her anxiety dissipated, replaced with confidence. She knew how to handle this.

"She doesn't seem to be suffering from an illness like pneumonia. She's got a pretty severe case of bloat, though. I need to get the air out. Are you familiar with a trocar?"

"Yes, ma'am. I've had several cows need them over the years."

"It's our best option at the moment. With your permission, I'll insert one now."

"You've got my permission."

With the supplies ready, she mentally reviewed what Dr. Johan had taught her. She'd watched him insert one only a few months ago. She took out the long, hollow needle and the tool to insert it. After making a small incision in the cow's hide, she poked it through the muscle and rumen wall and began screwing it into place. Marv used his body to keep the cow's haunches steady. The man was an old pro at dealing with sick cattle.

The pitiful moo from the animal tugged at her heart. "I know, sweetheart. Doesn't feel good getting poked. I promise you, though, this will make you feel a whole lot better than you do now."

The sound of gas escaping was music to her and Marv's ears.

"Boy, the air is coming out fast, isn't it?" Marv rounded the chute as Mackenzie went to the front to pet the cow's head.

"She should be feeling a lot of relief. I'll come back in a week or so to take out the trocar."

"I've taken them out before." He patted the cow's side, and then he let her out of the chute. She ran off to the other side of the corral.

"I'd feel better if I came out to have a look at her myself."

Marv gave her a firm nod, took off his hat and wiped his brow with a handkerchief. "I'm mighty obliged. She probably gorged herself in the new pasture. Good growth in there this year."

"Wouldn't surprise me." Mackenzie looked around. "Now, what do you say we take care of your dogs?"

They stopped at her truck so she could take off her coveralls. "I'll drive the trailer up to your garage. It will make it easier. Hop inside."

By the time they reached the house, where the dogs were waiting, she knew how many head of cattle Marv was raising, how he rotated pastures, the supplemental feed he gave the herd in the winter and more.

She got out and followed him through the open garage into the house. Three miniature dachshunds raced to him as soon as he opened the door. The other dogs, minus the Chihuahua, followed with their tales wagging.

"See what I mean?" Jim chuckled, pointing to the Chihuahua his wife held to her chest. "The rat does not like me."

"Gigi is not a rat." The woman shook her head and stepped forward to introduce herself. "I'm Pat, by the way. I'm assuming the cow's okay?"

"She sure is." Marv beamed. "Mackenzie inserted a trocar like an old pro. I'm glad you worked us into your schedule today, or I would have lost that cow."

"God's timing couldn't have been better." She bent to let the dogs sniff her hands. They were all cute. The bassett hounds had plopped on the floor.

"I've lost three cows to bloat over the years. Nothing worse than watching their lungs get compressed to the point they can't breathe." He picked up one of the wiener dogs and cuddled it close. Even dogs who weren't trained as therapy dogs helped make people feel better. Pets were such a blessing.

For the next forty-five minutes, she checked each dog in her trailer. When she was finished, both Marv and Pat acted like she was part of the family. Pat even sent half of a chocolate Bundt cake home with her, and she didn't try very hard to dissuade the woman.

As she climbed into her truck to leave, the couple waved, calling, "Come back anytime."

Before starting the truck, she took a moment to savor what had just happened. She'd known how to handle the emergency. God had given her the experience and the knowledge to save the cow's life.

There was no better feeling in the world.

And if she could handle saving a cow with bloat, maybe she could handle trying to talk some sense into Cade. God had brought them together for a reason. She wasn't going to give him up without a fight.

CHAPTER FOURTEEN

"SHE'LL BE BACK this afternoon."

"What time?" Cade held Tulip's leash at the front desk of the clinic.

Greta gave him an apologetic shrug. "I'm not sure. Her next appointment is at half past two, so before then."

Stupid Marv. Having her drive all the way out there for his hundred dogs. Cade wanted to kick the base of the counter, but instead, he gave Greta a tight smile. "I'll stop in later. Would you let me know if she gets back early?"

"Of course, I will. Knowing you're around will put her in a better mood. Those dark circles under her eyes concerned me this morning. Like purple crescent moons, you know? I didn't say a thing because, really, how do you tell your boss she looks haggard? But—"

"I've got to go." He didn't wait for Greta to

finish her thought, just urged Tulip to hurry through the waiting room to the door.

Outside, he blew out a frustrated breath. Now what? He couldn't beg Mackenzie for a second chance if she wasn't here.

He wasn't driving all the way back to the ranch.

He was tired of lurking around the unfinished stables.

Ty would be riding around his ranch this time of day, so there was no point heading there.

Cade stared at Tulip. "How about we try Nana again?"

Ten minutes later, he strolled into the nursing home with Tulip in her therapy-dog vest.

"Why, Cade, I didn't expect to see you today." Charlene beamed. "You've got twenty minutes before we bring her down to the cafeteria."

"Thanks. How is she doing?" It didn't really matter how she was. He wanted to sit by her side and hold her hand even if she was sleeping. He'd listen to anything she had to say even if she mistakenly thought he was his father.

He loved her, and he wanted to spend as much time with her while he still could.

"Trudy is having a good day." She nodded brightly. "Go on. See for yourself." Then she bent, talking to Tulip. "And how is our sweetheart doing? Look at you with your spiffy vest. When you're done in there, you come back here for a special treat from your aunt Charlene."

If he wasn't so keyed up, he would have enjoyed the encounter. But his nerves were sizzling hotter than bacon in a cast-iron skillet. He headed down the hall. Pulled back his shoulders. Knocked on Nana's door and entered.

"Cade!" Nana beamed from where she sat in her wheelchair. "Where's Ty?"

"He's working cattle." He bent to pick up Tulip. "I brought you a surprise."

She covered her mouth with her hands as tears filled her eyes. "A puppy!"

"This is Tulip, the dog we told you about. I brought her over yesterday, but I don't know if you remember."

"You did? I must have been sleeping." She held out both arms, and he set Tulip on her lap. With her tongue lolling, the dog stared at Nana. She gently stroked her fur, exclaiming how soft she was. Tulip did exactly what she was supposed to do—sat calmly and enjoyed the experience.

"Tulip passed her test yesterday. She's all clear to come visit you." He sat in the chair next to her. "We've been training her for over a month. She did really well."

"She's such a dear little puppy." Nana scratched behind Tulip's ears. "And so calm."

"Like Dolly?" he asked.

"Dolly." She jerked her attention to him. "Oh, that's a sweet memory. She was my baby before I had your father. She lived five more years after we brought Pete home."

"What kind of dog was she?"

"I don't know. A mutt. I loved her so." Nana's hand rhythmically petted Tulip. "Thank you for bringing this doggy to visit. Will you bring her again?"

"I will. I can bring her every time I come here if you'd like."

"Yes, I'd love that."

"Nana?"

"Hmm?"

"I think I'm in love."

Her eyes danced with happiness. "What do you mean you think you're in love? Don't you know?"

7"Then what's the matter?"

"I've done some things I'm not proud of, and I think she could do better than me."

Nana gave him an understanding smile. "I've done things I'm not proud of, too. We all have. I'm sure your girl has, too. Why don't you let her decide?"

"I told her about it."

"And she broke it off with you?"

"No, I thought it would be best if we went our separate ways, but I was wrong."

"You're scared." Her tender smile was making him squirm. "It's okay. Love is scary."

Tulip let out a contented sigh and closed her eyes.

"I'm going to let you in on a little secret." She wiggled her finger for him to lean in. He did. "Your daddy was terrified of declaring his feelings to your mother."

Dad? Never. The man had always been as calm and collected as could be.

She chuckled. "I finally had to have a talk with him. I was afraid he'd let her get away." She sat back, affectionately petting Tulip. "You Moulten boys can handle just about anything. But love? Whoo-ee. That's scary for you. But when you do give your heart to the right girl, well, you give it all to her. I should know. Your grandpa was the same with me."

His fears vanished. "So you're saying this is a genetic thing?"

"I don't know about that, but it does run in the family."

His chest lightened. A knock on the door made them both turn to see who it was. One of the nurse's aides stood there. "It's time to head to the cafeteria for lunch, Trudy. Oh, I see you have visitors. What a delightful little dog."

"Her name is Tulip," Nana said. "My grandson brought her to visit. Aren't I blessed?"

"You sure are."

Cade stood and plucked Tulip off Nana's lap. Then he set the dog on the floor and held her leash. He kissed Nana's cheek. "I'll be back in a few days. Mom will bring Tulip over tomorrow. I love you."

"I love you, too." She waved. "Don't let your girl get away."

"I won't."

On the way out, he stopped to let Charlene give Tulip a treat and to hear the latest on Janey's wedding plans. Then he drove to Reagan's store and bought every milk-chocolate-covered pretzel she had in stock. With a tender smile, Reagan wrapped pink ribbon around the box and told him he'd made a good choice. She'd thrown in a fresh batch of chocolate-covered strawberries, too.

Next on his list? The supermarket. He bought out the flower department, which wasn't saying much, but still. The only ones he'd left in the store were the potted flowers.

With the backseat of his truck full of bouquets, he drove to the veterinary clinic and sat in his truck to wait until Mackenzie got back.

Nana was right. The Moulten boys might be scared of love, but when they gave their hearts to the right girls, they gave them their all.

His heart was Mackenzie's. And he wanted her to have it, whether he deserved her or not.

MACKENZIE'S ELATION OVER saving the cow fizzled as she neared Jewel River. Yawns kept creeping up on her, and she could barely keep her eyes open. What she needed was a nap. And the rest of the afternoon off so she could figure out what to do about Cade.

She was going to fight for him—no question about it—but she needed a strategy. She needed one soon because she couldn't take sitting with this uncertainty over their future for long.

Closure. She wanted closure.

But she wanted the *right* closure. Not the one where he doubled down on dumb and acted like he was saving her from a fate worse than death by cutting himself out of her life.

The parking lot to the clinic was up ahead. She pulled into it and parked. Only when she got out of the truck did she realize Cade was there. In fact, he was walking toward her with Tulip trotting by his side and his arms full of... flowers?

Hope rose so sharply, it stole her breath.

"Come on, let's go inside." He hitched his chin toward the entrance. She scrambled forward, unlocking and opening the clinic's door—they locked it for lunch—then waited for him and Tulip to go inside before following him in.

Greta and Emily must have gone out to eat because the place was empty. He strode straight to her office and dumped everything onto her desk.

"Do you have a bed here for Tulip?" he asked.

"I do." She opened the closet, took it out and set it on the floor.

"Come," he said to Tulip. She hopped onto

the bed, and he had her lie down. She did and promptly fell asleep.

"I've been an idiot." Cade turned to Mackenzie with a gleam in his eyes. "I should have listened to you last night. For years, I've convinced myself I was a terrible person."

"You're not."

"I am," he said, shrugging. "But I'm also saved. Forgiven. And I'm thankful for second chances."

She didn't know what to do with her hands or what to say. He closed the gap between them and took her hands in his. That was better. A sense of calm covered her.

"I want you to know I did not buy the horse for you as some kind of guilt offering. I bought Licorice because I knew you'd love her. I wanted you to have a horse of your own that you could ride at any time. And I knew you didn't want to buy one because you don't have a schedule that would allow you to take care of it. So I will take care of her—well, my staff will. That's all. No strings attached. No guilt involved."

"I believe you." She stared into his eyes and pushed all her doubts and fears aside. Whatever he was going to say next? She was open to it.

She couldn't spend another minute doubting his intentions. She'd done it for all those years with her mom, but Cade was different.

"Good, because it's true." He took a breath. "I love you, Mackenzie. I knew you were special the minute I saw you the night Mom and I arrived to meet Tulip."

He thought she was special?

"You're brilliant. Blunt. Beautiful. You're better than me, and I hope you won't let that stop you from giving me a chance." He let go of one of her hands to cup her cheek. "I couldn't even make it twenty-four hours without you. This morning when I woke up, it took everything inside me not to pick up the phone and call you."

She swallowed as joy brought tears to her eyes.

"I know you said you don't have time for a relationship, but I'm flexible. I also know your job is important. It's important to me, too, knowing how much the ranchers and pet owners around here need your expertise. So maybe you could find a way to fit me into your life."

With watery eyes, she nodded, smiling. "I'll fit you in."

"You will?" His eyes shimmered with love, appreciation and maybe even awe.

"I will. I love you, too. I think you're amazing. I think God made you restless for a reason. You help so many people."

"Not really."

She edged closer to him and looked up into his eyes. "You do. You knew this town needed a vet, and you convinced me to move here. You sold the buildings to me and Dad at a steep discount. You trained a therapy dog to make your grandmother happy."

"It was Mom's idea."

"So? You did it with her. You head a committee for a club that exists solely to improve Jewel River. And soon you'll be offering horse boarding at a discount to the community because you want life to be better for them."

"I'm still trying to make a profit on Moulten Stables."

"It's okay to make a profit. And I almost forgot to mention your mother. You drive her everywhere. To keep her safe."

"Trust me. Everyone's safer when she's off the road."

Mackenzie couldn't help but grin. "I love you, Cade. I haven't dated anyone in a long,

long time, so forgive me if I'm rusty. I wasn't all that good at it to begin with."

"It's not something you're good or bad at." His face was close to hers. "We'll figure it out as we go along."

"Okay, I like that. But listen, I don't want you thinking you need to be perfect. If you're not being honest with me by being yourself, we have a problem. I don't want perfect. I want you." She poked her finger into his chest.

"In that case, I'm happy to tell you that I'm far from perfect. No need to worry about that." One corner of his mouth rose in a smile. "Can I kiss you now?"

"I thought you'd never ask."

As soon as his lips claimed hers, fireworks burst over her heart. Never in her wildest dreams did she think she'd end up with this cowboy. He'd always seemed a little too good to be true.

The reality?

He was even better than she'd imagined. And he was all hers.

CHAPTER FIFTEEN

LATER THAT NIGHT, Cade carried a sleepy Tulip in one arm as he held Mackenzie's hand. They ascended the porch steps to his house. Ty's truck was parked in the drive, and from the delicious smells wafting from the back deck, he guessed Ty and Mom were grilling steaks. Cade had asked his brother to stop over. He and Mackenzie wanted to be together to share the good news that they were dating.

They'd already stopped by Patrick's house. Her father had grilled Cade along the lines of *why do you think you're good enough for my daughter?* (he knew he wasn't) and *if you hurt her, you'll have me and Charger to answer to* (no thanks). By the end of the visit, Patrick had given Cade an aggressive half hug with a clap on the back and told them he was happy for them.

"How do you think she'll react?" Mackenzie chewed on the corner of her lower lip.

"Imagine a shaken champagne bottle being uncorked." He gave her hand a squeeze. "That's a mere fraction of the happiness my mom will display."

"Are you sure? What if she doesn't think I'm the right person for you?"

"She already loves you." They reached the door. "Remember the Fourth of July? She would have gladly planned our wedding right there next to the ketchup and mustard stand."

"I don't know. I'm nervous."

"Don't be." He stopped on the welcome mat and turned to face her. "She's been waiting for me to have a serious girlfriend for years."

Her eyebrows rose as if she wanted to believe him but couldn't quite bring herself to.

Cade opened the door. "We're here."

He set Tulip down—the dog went straight to her bed—then led Mackenzie through the living room and kitchen to the dining area. Mom and Ty were out on the deck, and Mom held a spatula in the air as she talked. Ty looked like he was on the receiving end of a lecture.

The glass door slid open easily. Cade waited for Mackenzie to walk through. "It smells great out here."

Ty widened his eyes at him as if to say *finally*.

"Mackenzie!" Spatula still in hand, Mom threw her arms around her and hugged her tightly. "I'm so glad you can join us for supper." She looked at Cade and beyond him. "Where's Tulip?"

"Sleeping inside. That dog is tired."

"Oh, yeah?"

"I took her to see Nana, and she loved her."

"She was having a good day?" Mom's forehead wrinkled in concern. "I hate when I miss visiting her. But I promised the girls I'd help box donation items for the church rummage sale."

"You're at the nursing home every day, Ma," Cade said. "It's fine. And, yes, Nana was having a good day. You would have been proud of Tulip. She did everything right."

Mom clasped the spatula to her chest. "I'm so glad."

Ty grunted. "I need the spatula."

She thrust it his way.

"Before we eat, we have something to tell you." Cade glanced over at Mackenzie and wrapped his arm around her shoulders.

His mother's eyes grew as round as a full moon. "*We* have something to tell?" Her voice grew squeaky at the end.

"Yes," he said. "We're dating."

"Praise God!" Mom lifted her face to the sky and clapped her hands together. Was she about to cry? Then she opened her arms wide. Cade prepared himself for her hug, but she pushed past him to embrace Mackenzie.

Cade shot Ty a look, and Ty laughed. Loudly.

"See how you rank, bro?" Ty pointed the spatula to Mackenzie and back to Cade. "Get used to it."

He shook his head.

"I'm so glad you're taking a chance on my son. Now you come over anytime, okay, hon? Any. Time. I mean it. You can have supper with us every night if you'd like. Oh, and I have another book for you. You know what? I'll give you this month's, too. You can never have too much romance, now, can you?"

"Um, no?" Mackenzie had a shell-shocked look about her. Cade grinned. She was more than capable of handling Christy Moulten on her own. He'd give her time to adjust.

"That's right," Mom said. "And have you been over to Winston Ranch?"

"I have."

"Good." Mom nodded rapidly. "Then you've seen the Winston—the new event center perfect for weddings. I'll call Erica and have her give you a tour."

"We aren't engaged, Ma." Cade rolled his eyes.

"I know that." She had on her exasperated tone. "I'm just saying it wouldn't hurt to give it a look."

Ty's shoulders were shaking with laughter.

"This is the best day!" She actually hopped in place. "We need to celebrate!"

Cade took Mackenzie's hand and tugged her close to his side. "If you haven't noticed by now, Mom is big on celebrating."

"Life can be hard." Christy's chin soared. "We need to celebrate all the good times while we have them."

"I can't argue with that." He kissed Mackenzie's temple and dropped her hand. "Don't I get a hug, Mom?"

"Oh! I forgot!" She bustled to him and gave him a long embrace. "You did good, son."

"Thank you." They shared a loving look. "For everything."

She patted his cheek and turned to Ty. "Where are we at on this food?"

"Five more minutes. I'm not eating raw meat."

"Good. I'll fix us up some sparkling lemonade." She hurried inside the house.

Ty handed Cade the spatula. What was with everyone passing around the spatula? "What do you want me to do with this?"

"Hold it while I congratulate your girlfriend," Ty said.

"Oh, okay."

Ty hugged Mackenzie. "You've got a good one here."

"I know." She grinned.

"And he knows he's blessed to have you."

"Thank you."

"Now give me back my spatula."

Cade tossed it to him, and he caught it.

"Here we are." His mom appeared with a tray. She set it on the patio table and handed each of them a sparkling lemonade. "To Cade and Mackenzie. May you fall more in love each day. Cheers!"

"Cheers!"

As he clinked glasses with Mackenzie, he mouthed *I love you*.

She blushed.

"I saw that." Mom waggled her finger between them. She picked up two books from the tray. "Here you go, Mackenzie. This top one features quadruplet toddlers. I'm not trying to give you ideas. But I am going to call

Erica right now to book you and Cade a tour of the Winston."

Cade opened his mouth to argue, then thought better of it.

As far as he was concerned, his mom was right. The sooner he could spend the rest of his life with Mackenzie, the better.

EPILOGUE

Sᴇᴘᴛᴇᴍʙᴇʀ's Jᴇᴡᴇʟ Rɪᴠᴇʀ Lᴇɢᴀᴄʏ Cʟᴜʙ meeting was getting lively, and he hadn't even made his big announcement yet.

Cade caressed Mackenzie's hand as she sat next to him. Normally, he came to these meetings solo, but she'd agreed to join him tonight. That way they could tell everyone their big news. Currently, Erica stood at the podium navigating old business, and it was going about as well as could be expected.

"We need to talk about last month's Shakespeare-in-the-Park film," Erica said, smiling at Angela Zane. "Angela, Joey and Lindsey did a phenomenal job. The production was top-notch."

"Are you going to mention the raccoon disaster, or do I have to?" Clem interrupted.

Cade personally thought the raccoons *had* been a problem. Apparently, Lindsey had forgotten to tell Joey she'd brought the trio of raccoons featured in the film to the actual festival. Someone's kid had opened the cage, and during the movie's finale, they'd scattered onto the lawn, where everyone was sitting on blankets.

"Lindsey admitted her mistake," Erica said calmly. "She should have had a lock on the cage. Plus, she realized she'd made the wrong decision by not discussing her plan with Joey."

"Rabies!" Clem yelled. His arms were locked under his chest. "Someone could have gotten rabies!"

"They're clean raccoons, Clem," Angela said brightly. "None of them have rabies."

"None that you know of." He glared at her.

Mackenzie rose. "I checked each raccoon before filming began, and they were all healthy. No rabies. Linda Roth domesticated them from birth and has them up to date with their shots."

Clem made a sucking sound with his teeth and raised his gaze to the ceiling in disgust.

"Those little animals added a lot of excitement." Angela waved one hand in dismissal. "No one was expecting the film to come to life, so to speak."

Cade glanced at Mackenzie. She appeared to be suppressing laughter. He leaned in and whispered, "You laugh now, but that night when everyone was worried about rabies and calling you for guidance, you weren't laughing."

"True."

"Anyway," Erica said loudly, "besides the raccoon incident, the film was a success."

"The kettle corn is always a hit, Erica," Mary Corning said. "When are we going to make it a permanent feature in the park?"

Erica's face pinched as she held on to her smile. "We can't. It's a health-code issue. Remember? But if we can continue relying on your crew to run it, we'll make sure there's kettle corn at all our major events."

The meeting continued, and nervous energy built inside Cade. When Erica asked if anyone had anything to add, he started to rise.

But his mom beat him to it.

What was she doing? Was she going to steal their thunder? Cade clenched his jaw. She'd better not.

"I could use some help," Christy said, standing on the other side of Mackenzie. "I've decided to move to town soon. If any of you know anyone who is putting up their house for sale or even for rent, let me know. I need to be within walking distance of the nursing home and the supermarket."

Cade sat there as stunned as could be. Why hadn't she mentioned moving to him?

"Did you know about this?" Mackenzie frowned.

"No."

"You're moving to town, huh?" Clem leaned forward, searing Christy with his gaze.

"Yes, and I don't need any of your snide remarks."

"Point taken." He gave her a nod. "I tell you what. I'll teach you how to drive. I mean it. We'll go over all the things that you're doing wrong. Then you won't keep getting your license suspended, and you'll be able to get yourself around."

With his eyes wide, Cade leaned over to catch his mom's reaction. To his shock, she didn't explode. She simply nodded with her lips in a thin line.

"Thank you, Clem. I'll keep that in mind." She looked around the table. "Like I said, I'm actively house-hunting, so text or call me if you know a place going on the market."

"We'll do that," Erica said with a smile. "Anyone else have news?"

Cade stood. "Uh, yes. I do. We do. Over the weekend, Mackenzie agreed to marry me. I'm a blessed man."

Cheers and hollers erupted around the table. When they died down, he continued. "And Moulten Stables is officially open. I have four horses to rent for anyone who'd like to ride. They're suitable for the rodeo team if you've got some high-schoolers interested. The rates are low, so give me a call."

He sat again, and Mackenzie grinned at him, squeezing his hand.

His new stables were almost full. Forestline Adventures had signed a contract to board all their horses with him this winter. The horses would be arriving by the middle of next month. Trent Lloyd had moved into the old house across the road from Moulten Stables, and he was as obsessed with horses as Mom was with weddings. Trent was turning out to be a great manager.

Best of all, Cade had the prettiest, smartest, most incredible woman by his side. Every night, they had supper together if Mackenzie wasn't out on a call. He couldn't wait to make her his wife.

The meeting adjourned, and several members stopped by to congratulate them. When everyone started clearing out, Cade found his mother.

"Why didn't you say anything to me about moving? I hope our engagement didn't bring this on."

"It didn't." Mom gave him a tender smile. "It's been on my mind for a while. I'm too far away from town. I want to be closer to my friends. Now that I have Tulip, I'm ready for my next adventure. She's a good companion."

That she was. He'd gotten in the habit of taking Tulip around to some of the other nursing home residents after visiting Nana. They all loved the dog. Some of them cried every time they petted her. It moved him, knowing how one little Pomeranian could positively impact so many lives.

Mackenzie stood next to him. "Are you going to let Clem help you with driving?"

"I might." Mom shrugged. "What have I got to lose at this point? My license?"

They all laughed.

"Come on," Cade said. "Let's get out of here."

The three of them walked outside. Clem was waiting on the sidewalk. "Christy, can I have a word?"

"Sure, Clem." Mom went over to talk to him.

Cade took the opportunity to put his arm around Mackenzie's shoulders. "I love you, you know."

"I know." She gave him a sideways grin. "Not as much as you love my mobile vet trailer."

"I do love it. All those gadgets. Makes a guy like me want to touch them all."

"What's mine is yours."

He spun her to face him. "And I'm all yours. Forever."

"You'd better be."

"You might regret those words."

"A lifetime with you? I'll never regret it."

Neither would he. He'd found the love of his life, and he'd never let her go. His heart was hers. Forever.

★ ★ ★ ★ ★

The Cowboy's
Marriage Bargain
Deborah Clack

MILLS & BOON

Award-winning author **Deborah Clack** is a native Texan who believes in the power of fiction, the lost art of lip-synching and that chocolate should be eaten without nuts. A high school AP history teacher for ten years, Deborah earned a master's degree in education and was awarded Teacher of the Year for Arts in Education. Now she creates stories of her own filled with endearing characters and hard-fought romances. She would love to connect with you at deborahclack.com.

For the mountains shall depart, and the hills be removed; but my kindness shall not depart from thee.
—*Isaiah* 54:10

DEDICATION

For anyone with the last name Clack, Long, Hardt,
Jordan, Longoria, Alley and Patton who has
walked with me on the road to publication.
We did it! I'm so grateful to call you my family.

ACKNOWLEDGMENTS

Thank you to Sami Abrams, Lynn Blackburn,
Laura Chen, Kelly Jo Fernandez, David Friedli,
Lynne Gentry, Debb Hackett, Sarah Hepola,
Kerry Johnson, Bethany Kaczmarek,
Sherrinda Ketchersid, Kay Learned,
Allyson West Lewis, Shelli Littleton, Julie Marx,
Rebekah Millet, DiAnn Mills, Ann Neumann,
Tina Radcliffe, Kelly Scott, Stacy Simmons,
Becky Wade, Becca Whitham, and Ann Vande Zande.
Each of you played monumental roles in gently
pushing (some of you shoving) me out of the nest.

Thank you to my father and legal consultant,
Bruce Long, and my mother-in-law
and medical consultant, Debby Clack.
All mistakes in the manuscript are mine,
but you still have to keep me around.

Melissa Endlich, working with you is a gift to me.

Tamela Hancock Murray,
thank you for your steadfast encouragement.

Lance, I love you. T and M,
you are the best cheerleaders on the planet.

Thank you, Lord. To Your glory.
Every word, always, to Your glory.

CHAPTER ONE

CHASE CROSS KNEW better than to tell a woman she looked like a wet dog. Especially the annoyingly precise and beautiful accountant for Four Cross Ranch, the sprawling acreage he owned with his siblings outside of Elk Run, Wyoming.

He leaned his shoulder on the doorjamb to the lodge as Lexi Gardner hurried through the spring rain. She pounded up the stairs to the spacious wraparound covered porch, hugging a three-ring binder to her chest.

The black binder never meant good news. Instead, Chase knew as certainly as he knew the cows would calve soon that she was going to start today's meeting with, "We have a problem."

She skidded to a stop in front of him, cold air puffing out of her mouth. Her enticing floral perfume wafted into his space. "Are you going to stand in my way, or may I please come inside before I catch pneumonia?"

Her attitude set his teeth on edge, but not as much as her words.

She'd stood in his way for the last two years, shutting down his dreams for the family property. From the first time they clashed over budget issues, he had wondered if instead of trying to create a nonprofit on the ranch, he should just reenlist in the army. The United States military had less red tape than the infuriating Miss Lexi Gardner.

"Good morning to you, too," he murmured as he tipped his cowboy hat and shifted for her to enter.

It was unfortunate that his golden retriever liked her. Duke welcomed her with a wagging tail and wide smile, then escorted her inside.

Walking down the hall, pride washed over Chase as he took in what his family had built. Rustic rugs covered the wide-planked wood floors. Paintings of the Old West adorned the walls. Cozy bedrooms awaited guests.

Now if they could get Four Cross Hope, the nonprofit for veterans, up and running, he could feel like he was making a difference in the world again.

Though Wyoming was the least populated state in America, it ranked the ninth largest in square miles. The vast land was the perfect place for veterans to find peace, quiet and open space. Skirting the edge of a national forest with Elk Mountain in the backdrop, the property included acres of rolling prairie that beckoned to those in need of healing.

Today was the day Lexi would tell him that he and his siblings could finally move forward with the nonprofit's long-term plan. The anticipation tasted sweet.

Though Lexi walked next to him, she stared at the ground, her face drawn as if she carried a heavy burden.

His chest tightened.

It always bothered him when he cared about her well-being. He couldn't seem to help himself. Being concerned for her was as automatic to him as being annoyed with her.

"Everything okay?" he asked.

Her head shot up, locks of damp sandy blond hair sticking to her round cheeks. Confusion filled her deep brown eyes, almost as if she'd forgotten he was there. She nodded once. "Yes. Fine."

He stopped at the entrance to the back half

of the lodge, a vast space that included a great room with oversized leather chairs and a chambray-covered couch facing a stone fireplace. Nearby sat a long, sturdy dining table next to an open kitchen where guests could mix and mingle while meals were prepared. He loved this room and couldn't wait for it to be filled with people. But first he had to get through this meeting.

"That's about the fifteenth 'fine' I've heard from you this month," he said.

"Then I must be fine." She wiped the wet strands of hair off her cheeks and stepped past him.

This was one of the reasons he wouldn't marry again. Ask a woman a question, and you never got a straight answer. Clearly, she wasn't fine. And hadn't been fine in several months. But every time he tried to ask her about it, she shut him down.

As he crossed the room, his eyes skittered across the black-and-white photographs framed on the wall. His gaze stopped on the same picture it always did.

A woman on skis, face determined, flying midair over a mogul.

Laura. His wife. His gorgeous, unassuming, adventurous and deceased wife.

No. He would never marry again. He wouldn't survive if he lost someone else.

Chase wrapped a hand around the back of his neck, hung his head and took a deep breath to shake off the heavy feeling. Still imagining his wife's smile, he walked to the sideboard and poured himself a cup of coffee into a black mug with the Four Cross Ranch logo.

A familiar slap on his back jerked him out of the moment, causing the hot drink to slosh onto his shirt.

He righted himself, then glared at his twin, the man who was his opposite in every way except the image that stared back at him in the mirror. "Watch it, Hunter."

Never one to use a lot of words, Hunter lifted his chin in greeting.

Chase grabbed a napkin and wiped the coffee off his plaid flannel shirt. It was what his wife used to refer to as his rancher uniform. Jeans, thermal undershirt, flannel long-sleeved shirt and boots. Always boots. Just like the army, only now with a cowboy flair.

Lexi placed stapled packets of papers in front of five of the dark leather chairs that stood sentry around the massive oak table. Bold capital letters at the top of the cover page announced the current financial report.

Running cattle on the ranch side of the property was good, honest work, it just didn't fulfill his desire to help others since he left the military. But his retirement checks couldn't pay for his dreams on their own. He needed the green light from Lexi to use ranch funds toward the nonprofit.

Lexi straightened papers at exact right angles to each corresponding chair, then looked up. "Has anyone heard from Ryder?"

Hunter shook his head once. No surprise that Hunter hadn't talked to their little brother.

"My guess is he's still on the bull riding circuit, but will be home when the calves come," said Chase.

She scrunched her nose, something he only admitted to himself he thought was cute. "Maybe I need to schedule a meeting when he's in town to give him an update."

"He handed his proxy to me when he left." Along with a whole host of problems. Chase poured a cup of coffee for Lexi, this mug a pale pink with the ranch logo. "He doesn't get to have feelings about how it's going here if he doesn't care enough to stay."

"Still, he's your brother," she said in a quiet voice.

Steam from the coffee rose out of the cup and disappeared into the air. Just like Ryder seemed to do after each short visit. Chase grabbed three sugar packets. "He is our little brother." He ripped the packages open and poured the sugar, watching the granules dissolve like late winter snow. "I love him. But he's still not here."

She cleared her throat. "Will Cora be attending?"

The thought of his brave little sister made him shake his head. They all had a hand in raising Cora after their parents died. Raised by wolves, she claimed. Then a wolf almost claimed her. "I don't think she's going to set foot on the ranch unless someone is birthing a baby."

"Well, she is the most highly sought-after midwife in town," Lexi said.

Smiling proudly at the thought, he poured creamer into the cup. "She's fearless."

Chase pulled a peppermint out of his pocket, unwrapped it and dropped it into the coffee.

He walked the pink mug across the room and handed it to Lexi.

A flash of surprise crossed her face.

Why she was surprised, he'd never know. He always made her a coffee the way she liked it if he was around. Even started carrying peppermints in his pockets. This time, however, her face seemed conflicted.

"Thank you," she said quietly.

He narrowed his eyes at her, and her gaze darted away. The last time he'd handed her a cup, she asked him if he'd laced it with poison. Today she merely thanked him? Something was definitely wrong.

"Not sharing your coffee with me?" his twin asked.

"We shared a womb. Does that mean I'm required to bring you coffee the rest of our lives?"

A smile tipped at the corner of his mouth. "As I recall, I kicked you out of that womb," Hunter muttered as he fixed his own cup of joe.

"Didn't you already have a cup down at the chow hall?" The ranch employed a cook who fed the ranch hands three squares a day in a building on-site. She'd declared Mondays Breakfast Burrito Day, and he knew his brother wouldn't miss it.

"I'm not the one who can't hold my coffee," Hunter murmured.

Chase would have defended himself, but then he looked at Lexi. She'd put her coffee down and was wringing her hands, a show of nerves from the normally confident woman. He might not agree with many of the things she said, and she might raise the hackles on his neck during most of their interactions, but he didn't like to see her in distress. He cared for her.

Kind of. Mostly. In an employer-and-employee way. Or possibly as a friend, on the rare occasion they got along.

She sat down, opened her copy of the financial report and tucked the first page behind the staple. But seconds later, she returned the cover sheet to the top.

The more stressed-out she seemed, the more something in his gut burned.

He caught Hunter's attention and sent a silent message to his twin. Hunter studied Lexi, then flicked his eyes back to him. He agreed. Something was off.

Both men dropped into their chairs and faced Lexi. She glanced at Hunter, then at him, her eyes holding a touch of fear.

Chase leaned forward. "You going to tell us what's going on, Lexi, or do we need to guess?"

LEXI GARDNER PUSHED a piece of damp hair behind her ear, wishing she had something she could use to tie her hair back. She probably looked like a wet dog after running through the rain. Fortunately, her trusty old Civic had gotten her safely from her small rental house off Main Street all the way out to the country. Soon, she'd have to bargain with the town mechanic for a set of new brakes. A task for another day.

She clasped her hands around her warm mug and inhaled the peppermint aroma, hoping it would calm her nerves. Maybe if she spilled her coffee on the financial report, it would erase the dismal results.

Finally, she said, "We have a problem."

Hunter grunted.

Chase glared.

The twins resembled two cars of the same model, only wired differently under the hood. Both ruggedly handsome, they had brute mountain man appeal, six foot two inches of height and a daring look behind their hazel eyes, the weight of the family ranch on their shoulders. But Hunter believed everything would work out fine, whereas Chase wanted all the details nailed down and pursued accordingly.

Still, the two were close. And as hard as it was to wrangle the four Cross siblings together to talk about the financials of the ranch, she found herself envious of their family. In spite of their parents' deaths, they still had each other.

All Lexi had was two ex-fiancés, an estranged mother and a high stakes last will and testament left by her grandmother.

At least Duke liked her, which probably infuriated Chase. She ran a hand over the dog's golden coat for courage.

Refocusing on the twins, she went on. "When you all decided to use the lodge to start a nonprofit, you laid out specific financial goals."

"Yes." Chase nodded, his tone already impatient. "We didn't want to take on a huge loan. Profits from the newly added ranch revenue streams would fund the adjustments we needed to convert the lodge for guests, as well as fund the following year's goals. We've been over this and we're on target for the year. Which is why we made modifications to the lodge and have our first veteran and his wife arriving next week."

Internally, she cringed. With dozens of freelance accounting jobs in three of the surrounding counties, giving tough news to a client wasn't new to her. But she had a soft spot for Four Cross Ranch, even if Chase Cross came with the territory.

"We *were* on target. The money the ranch invested in the development of the lodge worked in the beginning."

"But…" His word weighed heavy.

She looked him in the eye. No matter how much he grated on her last nerve, she owed it to him to give the information straight. That was her job. "We didn't hit our goals the last quarter. Any of them."

Chase rested his elbows on his knees and ran his hands through his short brown hair but said nothing.

"We had no way of predicting the early freeze last fall." The freeze killed the natural vegetation, which meant they used their hay inventory earlier than planned. When the price of feed skyrocketed, every rancher in the area was busting their budget to get their cattle fed.

"I'm so tired of the success or failure of our ranch being dependent on the weather," Chase muttered.

She softened her tone. "The biggest period

of risk, we all agreed, was this first year leading to the lodge opening. There was no way to
predict the rise of construction costs, old pipes
rotting and that we'd lose a crop of hay. The
loss of revenue from the significant head of sick
cattle was the final straw."

"It's like the ten plagues of Egypt," Chase
said. "Only instead of frogs and locusts, it's the
ten plagues, rancher's edition."

She hated it when he did that.

He tended to joke through tough situations.
It put everyone around him at ease. But watching him closely over the last two years, pain
sometimes laced those jokes, and she could see
it etched now in the creases that lined his eyes.

The temptation to say something comfort-
ing rose in her throat but stopped abruptly. The
truth clogged any words that wanted to come
out.

After laying out the financials for the men,
she sat back. "I'm sorry. But we have to cancel the nonprofit's next growth phase. Instead
of housing veterans and building more cabins,
we need to concentrate on paying the bills for
the ranch. We are one mistake or bad weather
incident away from the entire operation going

under. We have to stabilize things first if we're going to move forward in any way."

Hunter nodded, shifting his gaze out the window.

Chase speared her with a death glare. "You want us to completely let go of the nonprofit?"

"We can't do it, Chase. I know you're slated for the builder to start early next year to expand Four Cross Hope, but Four Cross Ranch can't afford it. You could barely pay the ranch hands as it was. And my professional suggestion is to use the converted lodge for paying guests instead. For profit." Cold seeped into her bones despite her jeans, thermal shirt and secondhand puffer vest. Maybe buying used clothes didn't always translate to warmth. Handing out bad news to clients didn't, either.

Chase made a fist, set it on the table and leaned toward her. "That's unacceptable, Lexi. It's not just about the couple arriving next week. I already have soldiers planning to come here to recover when they return from deployment. Additional military families, desperate for support, are waiting in the wings."

Heat hit her face. She hated being the numbers person when he talked about his passion to help veterans. It was one thing to offer a local artist free accounting services in exchange for her work on the beautiful antler chandelier in the room. This was something completely different. "We don't have the financial capacity to take it on."

"What about the tax benefits that come with having the nonprofit on the property? All of that was laid out in the plan." A hint of uncertainty underlined his tone. "Or the other arms of the ranch that were supposed to support the cause."

"Yes." She took a sip from her mug, but the conversation embittered the taste of the coffee. "In theory, the farming and ranching was going to support the dining options. Activities like horseback riding and the Little Wranglers program would fund the staffing for guided tours and massage appointments. The list of how we use our existing resources is quite impressive. And yes—in theory, the nonprofit status would have benefited us financially."

His eyes seared into hers, and she almost couldn't continue.

"But if we can't make a significant profit from the ranch," she whispered, "we can't fund the nonprofit side."

"Well... I've already started," Hunter declared.

Dread crawled up her spine. Slowly, she turned to him. In a controlled voice, she asked, "What does that mean?"

Lexi only advised the family on how best to use their money. She had no control over what the members spent daily.

"I bought two pups," he said unrepentantly.

Chase had the audacity to shake his head and chuckle.

"How much did you—"

Hunter held up a hand, the calluses of hard work in her view. "I purchased them with my own dime. I'm going to train them as therapy dogs whether we use them for the veterans and the nonprofit business or not." He pushed to stand. "And all due respect, I need to get back to work now."

"I'm sorry," she said with regret.

"No reason to be. You're just doing your job." He nodded, gave a chin lift to his twin and left the room.

Rain pelted against the windows, and for a few seconds, Chase stared at her in silence.

He leaned back in his chair and cocked his head. "What aren't you saying?"

Sitting ramrod straight, she shifted her focus

to the stapled sheets. "I think it would be best if we went over the information in the report."

"I don't want to look at the report. I want you to say the words."

A defensive streak ran up her spine. "I don't know why I prepare for meetings with you guys. Half of you don't show, and the other half, I suspect, use my reports as animal feed."

"If we did, it would certainly save us some money."

She must have looked shocked because Chase's expression filled with remorse, and he shook his head.

"I'm sorry, Lexi. That was uncalled for." He scrubbed a hand down his face and stood. "I'm just frustrated."

His vulnerability stopped her hurt feelings in their tracks. Instead, all she could feel was sympathy.

She was squelching his dream.

Even if they didn't see eye to eye on most things, his passion for military veterans was noble. Honorable.

Which is why for months, she'd been considering the unfathomable.

After pacing the room twice, he approached her and crossed his arms over his chest. "Give me some good news. How do we get back on track?"

She wished he understood how desperately she wanted to fix this problem and how far she was willing to go to help him. But she worried that he might think she was ridiculous if she made the suggestion that'd been rattling around in her head the last few months. Even if the solution she offered would solve significant problems for both of them, he might throw her out on her head anyway.

She tapped two fingers rapidly on the table. "There's one bank who might consider giving us a loan."

He covered her hand with his, stopping the noise and movement, then pulled back. "You know we don't want to go in that direction. Plus, my guess is you're going to tell me we probably won't qualify."

She offered him a wry smile. "You always were the smart one."

"I'm not the smart one. Cora's the smart one," he said about the sister he adored. "I'm the nice one."

"Cora's the astute one." She pointed to him. "You're the mean one."

"Only to you." She scoffed at him, but he continued. "To others, I'm not mean. I'm clever."

"Oh, please. Now you're the delusional one. Ryder is clever," she said. "You're the responsible sibling."

"I am." He splayed his hands on his lean hips and blew out a heavy sigh. "I'm the responsible sibling. So how do we get out of this?"

Her stomach clenched in a way she knew she couldn't ignore. She chose her words carefully. "For the next year, finances will be tight. No matter how badly you want to, or how much it could help others, you can't give out free rooms to the nonprofit. If we leave the lodge open, we have to let go of the nonprofit and instead fill every inch with paying customers."

He growled. "That's not a solution, Lexi. That's leaving war-torn veterans and their families in the lurch."

Acid rose from her stomach up her throat. She didn't know if she would be able to say the words.

"Well..." The word croaked out, and she paused to swallow. "There is one thing."

He opened his arms wide. "Anything. I'll do anything to get the nonprofit fully functional."

Sweat broke out across her forehead. "This

might—" her heart pounded "—sound unexpected. A little…um, illogical. All things considered."

"What is it, Lexi?" he asked with impatience.

She looked straight into his hazel eyes and said, "You could marry me."

CHAPTER TWO

EVERY NERVE ENDING in Chase's body came to attention. He hadn't felt this way since being close range to enemy fire on the battlefield. Dropping his voice low, he enunciated each word. "What did you just say?"

Lexi's eyes widened, and her face paled.

He wasn't sure he'd ever seen the color go out of her rosy cheeks, but he couldn't concern himself with that right now.

"I, um—" She cleared her throat. "I know it sounds weird—"

"Repeat the words, please, Lexi. I need to make sure I heard you correctly."

She shook her head. "Of course you would make me repeat it. Nothing's ever easy with you."

Ignoring her jab, he crossed his arms over his chest and waited.

She huffed out a breath and stared him directly in the eyes. "I said that you could marry me."

The air in the room was completely still. The rain even seemed to silence.

Closing her eyes, she continued quickly. "As a solution to the financial issues with Four Cross Ranch and to get Four Cross Hope funded. You could marry me."

He felt as if she'd lobbed a grenade and it was coming at him in slow motion.

"Explain," he grunted.

Her eyes shot open, this time with a familiar fire behind them. "My grandmother left me a trust. A significant amount of money. I'll be granted access to the entire fund on my thirty-fifth birthday with one condition."

Everything in him blanched. "You're a trust fund baby?"

"What?" She reared back, her tone shocked. "No."

He hated people who had things handed to them easy. There was something disingenuous about it. "Sounds like you're about to become an heiress on your thirty-fifth birthday."

She rested her elbows on the table and leaned her face on her hands. "I'm *not* an heiress. And I may not get the money, according to my grand-mother's wishes."

The picture of a frail, elderly woman in hos-pice popped up in his memory. Deep-veined hands and a raspy breath. But her eyes had held the same fire as her granddaughter's. "Is this the grandmother I met? Louella Chadwick?"

"Yes."

The woman was as eccentric as she was kind and wise. Chase thought she said outrageous things just to make him laugh. He'd enjoyed his time with her.

The side of his mouth hitched up. "She was a trip."

"I believe you told me you knew I was re-lated to her because she said nonsensical things like me."

Amused, he grinned. "Sounds like something I would say."

"She liked you," she said.

He shook his head. "That doesn't make sense. You and I fought the entire visit over a stupid tray of hospital food. I still can't believe you let her eat that stuff."

"It's what she ordered. I was just glad she had an appetite."

The reminder of the elderly woman's last days

hung heavy between them. So did whatever was pushing Lexi to propose to him. He wanted to see the spark back in her eyes. Experience the bolt of lightning she could be. "What made your grandmother change her mind about me?"

Lexi's eyes flashed.

Good. He wanted to see more of that.

"I told her you were more than just your pretty face," she said dryly.

He cocked his head, ready to give her a hard time right back. "You think my face is pretty?"

"No. I lied so she would feel better."

"A worthy cause."

Lexi sighed. "She said she liked how you challenged me."

If her grandmother only knew how much the reverse was true. He gentled his voice. "I'm sorry you lost her."

"I had only just found her again." Her eyes glistened. "I didn't even get a chance to ask her what I really wanted to know."

Chase didn't know the whole story.

When Lexi showed up in town two years ago, she stuck like glue to her grandmother for the final six weeks of her life. By the time he'd met Ms. Chadwick, she was only days from her last breath. And with Lexi new in town, she was in need of a friend. Elk Run might be Chase's hometown, but he had recently moved back and felt a little unsure himself. He might have needed a friend as well.

But just days after her grandmother's funeral, Lexi put up an impenetrable wall. Maybe it was the grief that overtook her. He understood all too well the things grief could destroy.

All he knew now was that they'd been fighting ever since.

Lexi stood and walked to the windows. She rubbed her arms as if trying to warm herself.

He needed to steer them back to their original conversation. "You mentioned there was a condition to getting access to the trust."

Her eyes were aimed at the window but appeared unfocused. She mumbled something he couldn't understand.

He stepped closer to her. "What did you say?"

She looked at him. "I have to be married on my thirty-fifth birthday in order to access the funds."

Realization hit him square in the chest. "And you think we should get married?"

"I don't—" She rubbed her forehead. "I *don't* think we should get married. No one who knows us thinks we should get married."

That sounded about right. Everyone who knew them had seen them spar at one point or another. Sometimes for fun. Sometimes for not-so-fun. "Then why did you ask?"

"I didn't ask," she said, her voice raised and her face red. "I added up the numbers. I'm an accountant. It's what I do."

"What does that mean exactly?"

"This entire situation is an equation." She paced like a caged animal alongside the table. "There are only a few ways to solve it. I offered you one possible solution to your problem. Marry me, and the money from the trust can help every aspect of Four Cross Ranch."

"Why in the world would you offer up this option? You must have other prospects." People who didn't cringe when they saw her walking toward them. Men who actually wanted to spend the rest of their lives with her.

She stood straighter and lifted her chin. "I'd rather not discuss that right now, if that's all right with you."

"No." He scoffed and ran a hand through his hair. An anger he didn't quite understand began to simmer just under the surface. "It's not all right with me. I don't want to get married again, Lexi. I've said that to you before. Why in the world would you pick me?"

Without moving a muscle in her body, she stared at him, but said nothing.

He swung his arms out in the direction his brother had gone earlier. "Hunter. You could have asked Hunter. Since he only mutters a few words at a time, you'd have less chance of disagreeing with everything that comes out of his mouth."

"Hunter has a girl in town who's sweet on him. They've had dinner a few times over the years. I'm not going to step on someone else's territory."

Confusion almost knocked him sideways. "Hunter has a girlfriend?"

"If you looked up from your work every now and then, you might have noticed he isn't always at dinner."

Chase stared through the window across the field as if he could see Hunter's social life. "Hunter's seeing someone?"

She sighed and walked to the table. "I don't think it's serious, but I get the impression she would like it to be more."

"Who is it?"

"If you think I'm going to subject an innocent woman to a Chase Cross interrogation, you've got another think coming." She pointed her index finger to the ground. "And I don't care if you are twins. Hunter gets to have a separate life from you if he wants to."

Her words struck a chord. "I'm fairly certain I know that better than anyone else, seeing as how he left the military long before I did." They'd been twenty-six years old at the time, both living their dream of serving their country. After their parents had died in a car wreck, Hunter's insistence that he return home to take care of their younger siblings, then teenagers, still plagued Chase with guilt.

"What about Ryder?" he asked, even though he could guess the answer before the words left this mouth.

She hitched a hand on her hip, and he knew before she said a word that he deserved the attitude she was about to throw at him. "Are you going to try to farm me out to all of your relatives? Besides, I've only met Ryder a few times and he seems a little young for me."

Ryder was a little young for anyone right now. Chase hoped he'd grow up before a bull took him down and he had no future left to live.

She shoved the financial report across the

table. "Did you not catch what I'm saying? I'm offering you the money to save the ranch and set up your nonprofit. You won't have to worry about funding anymore."

It was time to get to the heart of this conversation before he came across like a complete jerk.

He took a breath and said more gently, "I apologize, Lexi. But in my defense, this entire conversation feels like a stealth attack."

"Attack?"

"You had to know it was going to catch me off guard."

Leaning over the table, she swept the stapled packets into a pile in front of her. "I apologize for that." She looked at him, her deep brown eyes holding a hint of burden. "I didn't know how to approach the subject. There's not really a manual for this kind of thing."

"How long until your thirty-fifth birthday?"

She took a deep breath and blew it out slowly. "One month," she said softly.

The marriage grenade she'd hurled at the beginning of the conversation spun head over tail toward him. He caught it, pin intact. But if he made one wrong move, it would explode, taking him and his ranch with it. He was wrong.

Nothing about getting this money would be easy for Lexi. And he didn't think he was going to be able to help her.

He would have to watch his ranch implode right along with her untouched trust fund.

LEXI SAW IT in Chase's chiseled face the moment she told him she only had one month until her thirty-fifth birthday.

The defeat of her cause.

The rain picked up again outside, rivulets of water sliding down the tall windows of the great room.

She couldn't let the conversation end. Not until he understood her. "Chase, will you please hear me out?" She held her arm out to one of the leather chairs around the table. "Please. Sit down and give me a few minutes of your time."

After nodding, he folded his military-grade body into the seat across from her, the huge oak table and a massive chunk of tension between them. He crossed his arms over his broad chest for the third time in this conversation. But at least his glare was no longer burning a hole in her resolve. Small victories.

She lifted the stack of papers, neatly placed

them on the table and folded her hands on top of the pile.

"I know this sounds ridiculous."

"Illogical," he said.

"Illogical." She cleared her throat. "But it could also be a strategic move to get us both what we want." Thinking about how that might sound to him, she cringed. "Sorry. That's not what I mean. This went more smoothly when I said it to the mirror."

"You practiced in the mirror?"

"Of course I did. This isn't easy," she said, trying to force the insecurity out of her voice.

His face softened, and he leaned across the table and put his hand over hers. "I'm sorry. I'll be quiet."

She raised one eyebrow. Neither of them ever kept their mouth shut if there was an opportunity to give the other one a hard time.

He squeezed her hand and leaned back in his chair with a chagrined look on his face. "Quieter. I'll stay quieter."

"I don't think that's a word, but thanks."

"Lexi, one month out from your birthday, why are you just now looking for a husband?"

She desperately wanted to avoid telling him the embarrassing truth, so she'd start with simple answers and see where that led. "I've known about the trust for a while. I knew it wasn't—" she paused "—probable for me to fulfill the requirements."

His stare remained steady, except for one glint of sympathy. At least she hoped it was sympathy.

"For every trust, there's a trustee. A designated person who verifies the requirements of the trust and dispenses the assets when those requirements are met." He nodded. "The trustee called a few months ago. He was surprised to hear I wasn't married. Shocked, actually."

She ran her thumb over the bottom of her bare ring finger. Not as shocked as she was.

"What happens to the money if you don't get married?" he asked.

"That's just it. For years, it was my understanding that in the event that I wasn't married, the money would simply go to a designated charity. My fail-safe was that if I didn't get married by the allotted time, it wouldn't feel like a total loss. The funds would still go to good use."

"But the phone call changed things." He said it as a statement, not a question.

"Yes. He called to inform me that the trust stipulated that if I didn't fulfill the requirements, the money would go to a second cousin who served some jail time for embezzlement. But in general—" she bored her eyes into his "—he's known for blowing through money as quickly as possible and doing questionable things to get more."

Chase swiped his coffee mug off the table, got up and stomped over to the carafe.

"Isn't that your second cup?" she asked. "You'll be on a tear all day if you have them so close together."

"I'm already on a tear," he said as he poured.

She thumbed the edge of the papers while she waited for the last bit of the conversation to settle. Chase's top always blew when presented with new information, but he was usually quick to adjust if she just waited him out. She only wished that she'd known he'd need more than a month to adjust to her proposal.

He turned around, leaned his hips against the sideboard and crossed his legs at the ankles. Then he zeroed in on her. "Your second cousin doesn't sound like an upstanding citizen. Are you safe?"

Unexpected warmth hit her belly. He always had a protective side to him. Over the last two years, she found herself wishing he would aim it at her more often. "Yes. I'm safe."

"Does he know about the trust?"

"No."

"Well," he exhaled, "there's one less thing to worry about."

"Thank you," she said quietly.

His eyes shot to hers. "Lexi, no matter what has been said between us over the years, I care about you."

"I know. It's why I thought of you." She shrugged and gave him a small smile, one that offered peace. "We might not get along—"

"That's putting it lightly."

"—but I think we have a mutual respect for each other."

He stilled, then nodded.

His agreement gave her the courage to continue. "I've spent the last two years getting to know you and your siblings. People in town think the world of what you've each done to hold your family together. Everyone talks of the strong Cross legacy."

Chase held his head a little higher.

"I know I showed up in your life not long ago. Your family has stories thick with generations of love and loss that I'm not privy to.

And you don't often mention your years in the military. But your love for this ranch is written all over you. And when you talk about your vision for veterans who could find restoration on your family's acreage, it's…" She paused to tamp down emotion and beat back the tears. "It's inspiring," she whispered.

Chase said nothing, but his breathing sped up.

"I know it's not conventional. But if you married me, this money could do some powerful things. Otherwise, it's lost forever. My second cousin is sure to squander it in record time."

"You're talking about marriage," he whispered across the room.

"I know."

"There's something I don't get about all of this, and I'm not sure if I'm allowed to ask."

"I think since I suggested that we bind ourselves together for the rest of our lives, you're entitled to a question or two."

He smiled at her for the first time since she arrived this morning. It was a smile she wouldn't mind seeing the rest of her life, even if she annoyed him so much that he didn't show it often. A smile that spoke of tough living, perseverance and victory on the other side of hard times. A smile that never came easy, but when earned, could stop her in her tracks.

"You said you've known about the trust for a while," he said.

"Yes."

"You're telling me that there's been no candidate to marry you in almost thirty-five years?"

Although Lexi had expected the question, his comment cut into a wound she knew would never heal. "Sometimes a loving marriage just isn't God's plan for everyone."

Confusion crossed his face.

"Before my father died, he taught me about sacrificial love. The key word being sacrifice. God loved us sacrificially. I know you believe that, which is another reason I think we can do this. We both have faith in God, even though it didn't come easy over the years. It might be a sacrifice to actually get married, but it won't be without blessings. If only for the veterans."

He set his cup down and pushed to his feet with an intimidating force. "Lexi, I cannot take away the opportunity for you to marry for real love. That is out of the question."

Panic surged through her body. She was going to have to tell him more, and her heart thundered in warning. She stood up. "I'm not ever going to get married."

He shook his head and took steps around the table to her. "You can let your thirty-fifth birthday pass, let go of the money and wait for the love of your life."

Red spots dotted her vision. He couldn't know the pain he was digging up from her past. "I am. Not. Going. To get married. Ever. You've stated clearly that you wouldn't marry again." Her voice rose, and she didn't care what it said about her desperate state. "Why can't we make this a partnership? Why can't we come together to do something significant for others in need? Why can't we do something honorable with the money?"

Matching her intensity, he said, "Because it's incredibly dishonoring to you."

She threw her arms out wide. "What? Why? I'm walking into this with my eyes wide open."

"I know that. And I want to understand why you're willing to do this. Why you're willing to throw away a chance at marrying for love. Unless—" His eyes crinkled with his smile and his tone changed. "Are you in love with me?"

Years of pent-up frustration bubbled through her veins and came out in ironic laughter. She threw a pen at him, and it bounced off his shoulder. "Are you for real?" She grabbed her stomach and bent at the waist. The pain from the laughter was almost as bad as the pain from the situation at hand.

Lips twitching, he had the decency to look part amused and part guilty. "Okay. So you're *not* in love with me."

Her love life was like a pressure cooker with no valve, heating toward an explosion on her thirty-fifth birthday. But she couldn't get anyone to love her.

And now she couldn't give the money away to save her life.

His noble streak stretched a mile wide. Why couldn't it just shrink this one time?

Her laughter turned to exasperation. "What is wrong with you?"

"I'm asking myself the same thing about you," he shot back.

"If I knew what was wrong with me, I'd—" She stopped. No. No way was she going to tell Chase the deepest pain in her heart. No way would she tell him that if she knew what was wrong with her, she'd fix it so someone would actually want to marry her because of who she was.

But there was no way around the ugly truth of how she got that wound.

She turned to the windows again and stepped close, ignoring the sad reflection that stared back at her. "I've been engaged twice. Called off weddings. Twice," she said to the glass. It was easier than looking at him, though she heard the small grunt in response.

"Lexi," he said, his voice filled with sympathy.

She closed her eyes, as if that would make the next words easier. "My first fiancé cheated on me with my maid of honor a month before the wedding. My best friend since childhood." The horrid memory of walking in on them kissing flashed through her mind.

He cleared his throat, but remained silent.

"My second fiancé," she said, opening her eyes and turning to look at him, needing him to understand, "sought me out and pursued me because of my grandmother's trust. My mother was part of the matchmaking. I overheard them talking at the rehearsal dinner and I cancelled my wedding the night before the ceremony."

His next response was a growl.

"It's okay. I left town before she could track me down and tell me what percentage of the trust she was going to get for making the match," she went on, even though it wasn't okay. It was, in fact, very not okay. Two years later, the betrayal still pierced her heart, and pain laced the few conversations she'd had with her mother.

Chase placed his hand on her arm, and she stared at it. "I wish I could fix this for you," he said, his voice gentle. "But I can't do that. I don't want to get married again."

She knew. The death of his wife was too hard on him. She just thought maybe he would view this differently.

"And even if I did," he continued, "I can't marry you for your money. It's just not right."

"Thank you for your consideration of me, Chase." Before he could interrupt her or she could lose her nerve, she continued. "You're a man of integrity through and through. It would have been an honor to marry you. No matter the circumstances."

His only reaction was a slight gape of his mouth.

She shrugged and offered what she hoped was a gracious smile to cover whatever thing was passing between them.

This conversation was a disaster.

Lexi had told herself she at least had to try.

She'd tried. Now she'd disappear from Four Cross Ranch until after her birthday. Maybe forever. She could find Four Cross Ranch another accountant.

He squeezed her arm. "I'll find another way to help the ranch."

"Chase, I just don't know what other options you have."

"If the heifers are doing all right in the morning, I'll head into town. My family has been in these parts for generations. That has to be good for something at the local bank."

Her stomach clenched. She knew he didn't want to have to go down that road.

As he walked out of the room, she realized she shouldn't have chosen someone so honorable to ask to marry her.

She should have called her ex-fiancé.

The one she'd left at the altar because she found out his ulterior motives. The one she knew would definitely marry her for her money.

Yes. She should have contacted Vance Miller.

Chase could go to the bank. But her accounting experience told her that unless he wanted to put the ranch up as collateral, he would get turned down. And with all the problems they'd had in the last year, she wouldn't advise taking that route. They could lose their family's land.

In the meantime, she'd contact a lawyer about the trust. Maybe there was a loophole.

A loophole would solve everything. Everything except the tug in her heart that wished she didn't have to do life alone, that wished Chase had said yes, even if they couldn't always get along.

CHAPTER THREE

CHASE HAD LIVED a life full of land mines and cow patties, but the situation Lexi had thrown at him yesterday felt more tenuous than either of those.

"What crawled in your cowboy hat?" Chase's twin asked from the passenger seat of the ranch's white F-150 pickup truck.

Chase started the engine. "Nothing."

Clouds dotted the sky. The light grey puffs wouldn't commit to a storm, but they also wouldn't go away and let the sunshine stream over the land.

Hunter picked up the travel mug from the cup holder and stared into the clear, plastic lid. "Have you had two cups of coffee today?"

Shaking his head, Chase headed in the direction of town. It irked him that both his brother and Lexi knew him well enough to know he couldn't handle his coffee. Soldiers and cowboys should be able to drink black tar if they wanted to. "I haven't had two cups of coffee."

"You're in a worse mood now than you were when the cattle crossed the property line last week, and I didn't think that was possible," said Hunter.

Chase didn't think it was possible either until Lexi left him with a parting shot yesterday that could have cleared all the animals out of the barn. After blowing out a long breath, he looked at his brother. "Lexi needs someone to marry her."

Hunter stared out the windshield but said nothing. It was his way. The man had incredible restraint and patience. He could wait out any situation. Chase might as well tell him everything.

After explaining Lexi's ludicrous solution to the problem, he concluded with, "Which is more absurd than the early freeze we had last September."

"Except that freeze actually happened," Hunter said in a sage-like tone.

Chase did a double take. "What's that supposed to mean?"

Hunter shrugged. "I'm just saying the freeze happened."

At the next country road stop sign, Chase

threw the car in Park and turned to look at his twin. "Are you implying I should actually consider this? Have you noticed how Lexi and I can't get along for more than five minutes? That's a real problem when you're picking a spouse."

Hunter stared back, his entire body exuding a calm that only ratcheted up Chase's frustration. Of course Hunter said nothing. Silence was Hunter's stealth weapon.

Chase put the car back into Drive, hit the gas and scrubbed a hand over his face. His brother had worn him down quicker than usual, but at this point, Chase would welcome someone else's perspective on the situation. "I didn't sleep last night."

His brother grunted.

"Because I keep thinking about how else she might try to solve this problem. Who else is she willing to marry?" He slammed the palm of his hand on the steering wheel. "She is willing to *marry* someone she doesn't love to get this money."

Another grunt.

"You're right. It's not about the money for her," Chase said on a sigh. "The thought of that cash being squandered away would make anyone sick. I don't even know her cousin and it's a little hard to swallow. And she has a point. That money could be used for good."

Entrance gates to neighboring ranches whizzed by every few miles. Still nothing from his copilot.

Chase pointed his finger to the windshield. "I'll tell you what she needs to do with that money is buy herself a new car. She drives a Civic, no doubt for the good gas mileage, but she has no business trying to maneuver that thing during a Wyoming winter. It's not safe."

Another idea hit Chase. "Maybe it's leftover grief for her grandmother," he said. "Grief does funny things to a person."

They knew this firsthand. The memory of a fistfight between Hunter and their younger brother ran through his mind. He knew not to bring up the subject. The only thing Hunter was more tight-lipped about than a woman he might be interested in was what happened between him and Ryder.

Hunter grunted, but this time he added words. "Why is it, do you think, that she didn't ask me to marry her?"

Something unpleasant bristled up Chase's spine at the thought of his brother marrying

Lexi. Something he planned to ignore. "She didn't ask me to marry her. She *told* me I could if I wanted to. There's a big difference."

"Sounds the same to me," Hunter muttered.

The speed limit decreased as they approached town. Chase's thoughts slowed down as well, and he replayed his conversation with Lexi.

"You know what?" he said. "Let's talk about why she didn't bring the subject up with you. Anything special you want to share with me about your social life?"

"Not that I can think of."

Chase approached the one stoplight in town and signaled his turn onto Main Street. He raised his eyebrows. "Anything about a certain woman in town you've been seeing?"

"Nope." Hunter grinned. "Doesn't sound like anything I want to share."

"Come on, Hunter."

"Sheila." He nodded at Elk Run's Diner up ahead.

"Sheila the waitress?"

He shrugged. "I eat dinner there sometimes. She's nice to me. We go out once in a while."

The men might be opposites, but Chase couldn't picture his twin with Sheila even if she was kind and had a good smile. "Are you interested in her?"

Another shrug. "I like the time I spend with her."

"What does that mean?"

Hunter knocked on the window as they passed the diner. "It means that if we're supposed to be together, it'll all work out."

Angling into a parking space in front of the bank, Chase shook his head. "I cannot wait for the day a woman walks into your life and turns you inside out."

"Kind of like you right about now?"

"You've got to be kidding me." Chase stretched his arm to the back seat and grabbed the manila file folder with the ranch's financials and loan proposition. "Lexi isn't turning my life inside out."

Hunter looked toward the building's glass double doors. "Then why are we going to the bank?"

"I have to find another way to make up for the lost funds at the ranch."

Hunter shook his head as if Chase was missing something. "You're an idiot."

Chase dropped the file folder between them.

"Why am I an idiot? For wanting a woman to marry someone for love?"

"Why do you think she asked you?"

Running a hand through his hair, he said, "She said it was because I have integrity. Something about it being an honor to marry me no matter the circumstances."

That finally got a reaction out of his stoic twin. Hunter's eyes grew round. He didn't say anything, of course, but Chase felt like this time was different. As if the words Lexi said had shocked his brother, something Chase had only seen a few times in their lives.

"Plus, I think my dog likes her better than me," Chase muttered.

"Understandable."

He shook his head. "Could you try to be a little more helpful?"

Just then, the Stimpsons strolled down the sidewalk past the truck, their heads together. Mrs. Stimpson laughed at something her husband said to her. When Mr. Stimpson caught sight of the Cross Boys, as the older man called them, he waved.

Chase gave him a thumbs-up to acknowledge the town's most senior and most beloved couple.

What would it be like, just strolling down

the street for a lifetime with the woman you love, making her laugh? Once upon a time, he thought he'd get to do that.

Chase had sworn off that kind of life. His anger spewed sideways to Lexi because she'd brought the entire subject up again. A subject he'd declared closed after his wife died.

"What's your biggest concern, Chase?" Hunter asked.

He rubbed his forehead. "What if she marries someone dishonorable to get access to the money? Someone who doesn't treat her right." Or who didn't appreciate her mad money-saving skills. Or who didn't buy her a safe car to drive. What if she married someone who didn't treasure her?

Hunter's eyes flashed, then he blinked as if to mask the reaction. After years of knowing each other's thoughts before they were spoken, Chase felt annoyed that his twin was so cryptic during this important conversation. "The ranch going under." Hunter counted off the points on his hand. "The money being squandered. Marrying again when you don't want that. Or marrying someone you claim you can't stand. None of those are at the top of your list?"

"No," Chase said, offended, as he angled his

body toward his brother. He rested his left forearm on the top of the steering wheel. "I read an article the other day about mail-order brides. I feel sure she can track down a mail-order groom if she were so inclined. That kind of recklessness is much worse than her asking me to marry her."

"You said she didn't ask you."

"She didn't." Chase got out of the truck. "Let's go." He slammed the door and beat Hunter to the sidewalk.

"Interesting that her focus is protecting the ranch, something you're passionate about. And you're intent on protecting her to the point that you're at the bank for a loan. Something you said you would only do as a last resort."

Chase grumbled. There was nothing interesting about any of that. Except the part where he couldn't deny that the words were true.

"You're overthinking this." Hunter opened the tall glass door to First Bank of Elk Run and held it while Chase stomped through.

Chase checked in with a teller, plopped into a worn burgundy leather chair and lowered his voice. "It feels like we're not having the same conversation. Are you even listening to me?"

Hunter raised an eyebrow. "A kind, Christian woman who isn't hard to look at has offered to save the ranch and secure the nonprofit through a partnership that just happens to be sealed with a marriage certificate, but requires absolutely nothing of you. What am I missing?"

He threw his hands up. "I'm not marrying this woman for her money."

"I think the thing you don't understand is that she's not asking you to." He paused. "She's just trying to help."

This time, Chase was the silent one. Was it that simple?

"You guys already fight like an old married couple anyway."

Chase's entire body jolted, and he stared in the wise eyes of the man who knew him better than anyone. Even better than his mother when she was alive.

A picture of his wife, Laura, flashed in his mind. He lowered his voice. "I'm not up for getting married again. You know that."

"I do. I also know that people change their minds."

Across the lobby, a toddler started crying. Chase could not agree more with the kid.

But he couldn't process the warmth that spread through him at the news that he and

Lexi already acted like a married couple. Or the visual he had of them walking down the sidewalk. Just like the Stimpsons. He scratched at the left side of his chest, trying to get rid of whatever was happening in his heart.

Chase huffed out a short breath. The army taught him to do his research and plan for all contingencies. "Fine. I'll keep this appointment and get more information about a loan. But saying yes to her is still a possibility."

Hunter studied the mother trying to console her young boy. "Or, you could bypass what is bound to be a rejection by the bank and just go tell Lexi you'll marry her."

"The family would lose their minds," he muttered. Not just his siblings. The ranch hands, too. They were a tight-knit group at Four Cross Ranch.

The little boy toddled over and stood next to Hunter, gnawing on a fist. Tears stained his cheeks, but he was calm, mesmerized by the cowboy in front of him. Hunter pulled the Stetson off his head and placed it on the child, who then giggled. "Or maybe Four Cross Ranch just falls in love with her."

"Exactly." Chase sat back, stretched his legs out and crossed his arms over his chest. When

Hunter's words registered, he sat up so quickly, he had to right his hat. "Wait. What? No. I mean, yes. Everyone will like her."

"Everyone will love her." Hunter waved at the kid, but said to Chase, "We still meeting with the banker?"

"Absolutely."

His brother shook his head once. "You really are an idiot."

WALKING INTO THE BARN, Lexi didn't think she'd ever get used to the smell of horse manure. Really, any manure for that matter. She would take the aroma of her freshly sharpened pencils and office supplies any day of the week.

But there was something pure and honest about the earthy smells of the ranch. Every time she left her house in town and had to go on the property, she was struck by the way the country stripped life down to a beauty that couldn't be duplicated anywhere else. She could breathe here. And she so very much wished Four Cross Ranch could share their space with deserving veterans and their families someday.

But today the only thing she could smell was her discomfort. All the way to the ranch, the knots in her stomach tried to convince her that avoiding Chase would be preferable. But she couldn't avoid him forever. Best to get over seeing him again with something simple.

"I'm an idiot," she murmured to herself.

She walked down the middle of the red horse barn, glancing in each stall for Chase. A grunt sounded from the end of the row.

"Hello?" she called.

Chase stood tall, his mouth tight with a grimace, and rubbed his shoulder. "What?" he barked. When he caught sight of Lexi, he blanched. "Sorry."

Though clearly in pain, the cowboy looked good.

She shouldn't be thinking of him that way. Even if the army-green Four Cross monogrammed shirt set off his well-defined arms and currently blazing hazel eyes. Eyes that held a touch of pain.

A foreign feeling came over her. Was that concern? For Chase? "Are you okay?"

"I'm fine." He bristled. "Do you need something?"

Her fleeting concern for him flew out the barn window. Along with it, her discomfort.

Frayed nerves around Chase? No, thank you. Concern for whatever was bothering him? She would prefer not. But sparring with Chase? This she could do. This was normal.

"As a matter of fact, I do," she said with a little sass. "I need a lot of things, actually. I need the price of gas to go down. And I need someone to create a universal charger for electronics regardless of the device or brand."

He leaned against the handle of the broom. "Apparently, you also need a husband."

His words hit her in the gut, but she pushed through. "You're aiming below the belt today. Have you had two cups of coffee?"

He closed his eyes and shook his head gruffly. "Sorry. Again." After he blew out a long breath, he looked at her. "I got sent to the barn."

"Hunter put you in the corner for your bad attitude?"

"Something like that. This morning hasn't gone exactly like I had hoped."

"You're going to kill your rotator cuff if you muck stalls all day."

He said nothing, but the muscles in his jaw ticked.

"I'm here because I need your signature on a check for the company who fixed the pipes underneath the chow hall."

"Why didn't you ask Hunter?"

"He's doing fence repair and that would require a horse ride."

"What's wrong with a horse ride?"

"Nothing." Except she'd never been on a horse. "Can you please just sign the check?"

"Can't you just give the company the card?"

"It saves us three percent in fees to write a check instead of using a credit or debit card. Sign this, and I promise I will leave you to your crankiness."

He nodded, pulling off one of his work gloves. "You are on brand, Lexi Gardner. Well done."

"On brand?" she asked as she passed the check and ballpoint pen across the stall gate.

"Consistent. Like you're a brand sold at stores." He held the check against his muscled thigh and waved the pen in a circle with his explanation. "You're always doing things to save the ranch money. Your brand should be Gardner's Savings."

"Gardner's Savings? That's the best marketing slogan you can come up with?" Giving him the side-eye, she said, "Keep your day job."

Bowing his head, he signed the check, then returned both items back to Lexi. But not without his hand skimming hers. Her eyes shot to his. She snatched the items away, sure that her face was flushed red from the heat she could feel rising up her neck.

What was wrong with her?

He pulled his glove back on and gave her a small smile. "Now I'm going to ask you a serious question."

Her stomach clenched, and she held each muscle in her body still, wary of what was coming.

He placed his hand on the rail and studied her. "Are you doing okay? Really?"

"Yes, fine. Why do you ask?"

"There's that 'fine' again. Which we figured out clearly wasn't true yesterday when you explained your situation to me."

She bit her bottom lip.

"You asked me to marry you yesterday, but you won't make eye contact with me today. What's that about?"

The more she thought about Chase's reaction to her proposal, the more mortification settled into her bones. Her dating history read like a bad TV show. The latest rejection by Chase the crushing series finale.

And it felt final.

She wouldn't get married. Ever. For love or for logic.

She swallowed, straightened her spine and said with confidence, "Well, today, I'm just the ranch's accountant, Chase."

"An accountant who has gone out of her way for her client in spite of an awkward conversation yesterday with one of the owners." He nodded to the check she had personally hand-delivered to his ranch for his signature.

Lexi didn't know why she gave Four Cross Ranch perks. Something felt natural about being on this land and helping this family. She didn't mind completing basic supply orders or contracting work for them.

He gentled his voice. "I'm just checking on you."

What was she supposed to do with his regard for her? It almost sounded like he cared when he'd asked if she was okay.

His mouth curved just slightly, and his eyes looked like he knew something she didn't. "You're so uncomfortable standing there, I think you're considering paying a courier to bring the next check over to be signed even though it would cost you money to do it."

Her lips twitched while she tried to hold back a smile.

"Aha!" He pointed at her. "I'm right."

A horse in the next stall huffed in agreement.

"I appreciate your concern for me, really I do, but I made a phone call that might lead to a solution to my…problem."

Chase narrowed his eyes at her. "What kind of a solution?"

She swallowed, trying to figure out why she was still standing in the barn. "I asked my lawyer to look into the trust and see if he can find any loopholes."

After a beat, he cleared his throat. "Did he have any initial impressions?"

"Actually, he wasn't optimistic. He'll do some research and reach out to a buddy of his who deals with this sort of thing. He's sympathetic, but not optimistic." She sighed and offered a resigned smile. "Then *he* asked me to marry him."

Irritation radiated off Chase. "What?" he growled in a low voice.

"Calm down. He's sixty-three years old. A few years from retirement." A playful smile lifted her lips. "Plus, I think his wife would object to our union."

He pointed at her. "Don't do that to me."

"What?"

"Give me a heart attack."

"What are you so angry about, anyway?"

Chase's golden retriever sauntered into the barn, walking purposefully as if he was mayor of the ranch animals and was here to check on his constituents. When he caught sight of Lexi, his tail wagged double-time and he took off running toward her. She knelt and gave Duke a body rub while she looked at Chase. "I've let you off the hook. This isn't your problem to solve."

"I'm glad you contacted your lawyer. Even if he isn't optimistic." He paused, cocked his head. "Fess up. What did you trade him for his services?"

She shrugged, pleased he would ask. "He had a few questions about his tax return. I spent some time untangling the language for him."

"Lexi's Low-Cost Living," he murmured.

"Seriously?" She stood up. Duke stared at her, his tongue hanging out of his mouth as he panted. "Surely you can come up with something better than that."

His gaze turned concerned. "I hope the lawyer has some good news for you."

There it was again. His protective streak. It felt better than she wanted to admit. But she couldn't lean into that feeling. It was temporary and would only bring her disappointment. "Me, too. It doesn't look good. But me, too."

He opened the stall gate and walked through. When he latched it closed, he glanced at her. He shifted his feet and looked as uncomfortable as she'd felt when she'd arrived this morning. "I think I owe you an apology."

"Yes. You owe me an apology for your appalling marketing slogans. And I accept."

He stared at her, and his jaw muscles clenched. "I'm not sure I've handled this situation well. It seems to bring out the worst in me."

"More than usual?" She hoped giving him a hard time would convince him he was off the hook.

But he shook his head. "You know what I mean."

"I know what you mean." She quieted her voice. "But these aren't normal circumstances. You get all kinds of grace."

He pulled his hat off his head, ran a hand through his hair and studied his Stetson. When he looked up, his stare bored into her, and something worked behind his eyes. "Lexi, what you said yesterday…well, I feel the same way. You're a woman of integrity, too."

Her mouth parted, but no words came out. She didn't know what to say or where this was going, but every nerve ending was on full alert, skittering across her skin as if in warning.

Then his face turned suddenly vulnerable in a way she'd never seen before, as he said, "It would be an honor to marry you."

Her heart hammered. She could feel her chest rising and falling with quickened breaths. It's not that she thought she was going to pass out, but she felt light-headed. Like the world had just tilted a little bit, and somehow she was still standing. Duke rubbed up against her leg as if to steady her, but she could hardly feel the contact.

Chase stepped toward her. "Lexi? You okay?"

She wasn't sure his close proximity helped her inability to move. She shook her head. Laughter laced with disbelief escaped her mouth. "Sorry. I, um. Yes. I—did you just agree to marry me?"

"I believe I did." He twirled his hat once in his hands. "That is, if the offer still stands."

"The offer still stands," she whispered, barely able to speak.

"But I don't think we should do anything rash. I think we should wait until closer to your birthday in case the situation changes." A seriousness crossed his face. "If at any time, Lexi, you want to change your mind, it's okay with me. Do you think that sounds reasonable?"

"I do," she said. "And if at any time, Chase, you want to change your mind, it's also okay. Do you think that sounds reasonable?"

He nodded once. "I do."

In an unusual silence rarely found in a barn, they stared at each other. She took in his features, searching his face for anything that might have looked like doubt or regret. But all she found was confidence and strength. She didn't know what he saw when he looked at her, but she hoped he found evidence of her belief in him and all that he would be able to do with the nonprofit.

The safe haven for veterans would grow and thrive now. And she was so grateful to put the trust money toward something important and significant.

Just then, a bird flew down from the rafters and startled her, breaking the moment between them.

"Well," she said as she tucked a strand of hair behind her ear, "I, um… I need to get going. I've got to change a tire."

He looked out the front of the barn, then back to her. "What happened?"

"Oh, it's just a flat tire." She glanced at her watch and grimaced in disappointment. She was supposed to make a delivery to the retirement home and then have dinner with the Stimpsons. "I'm afraid I'm going to have to miss my other appointments today."

"Let's go take a look at your tire," he said.

"Oh." She tried to wave him off. "It's okay. I don't want to interrupt your day. I'll figure something out."

"Lexi." He grabbed the hand she was waving and stopped her movement completely. "It's all right. I'll go check it out, and if I need to drive you, then I'll make time to take you where you need to go."

She could feel her brow furrow. "Why would you do that?"

"Because that's what fiancés do," he said, full of logic and void of emotion.

And with that, he took her hand and led her out of the barn as Duke trotted beside them.

CHAPTER FOUR

"I'M NOT SURE about this," Lexi murmured as the wind blew through her thin red sweater. She wrapped her arms around herself and held on tight.

Clouds covered the sun. Pulling her sweater snug, she was thankful she at least wore jeans. Sometimes, she dressed up to go to Bright Horizons Retirement Community. But today she felt the need to be comfortable. As if the soft fabrics would help her relax during the awkward conversation she wanted to have with Mr. and Mrs. Stimpson.

But what in the world was she going to do with Chase?

The cowboy popped his head up over the trunk of her car. "Are you not sure about my ability to change a flat tire?"

She wasn't sure about having a fiancé. She'd had two and it didn't go well. But this was different, she tried to remind herself. This was just a business transaction.

She didn't need a knight in shining armor riding to her rescue. She was doing just fine on her own, thank you very much.

If only Chase wasn't treating it like he had some kind of duty to perform along with the title, maybe she could calm down.

He raised his eyebrows at her as if waiting for a response.

"I'm not sure I should accept your help. We don't get along. This could be the longest afternoon of our lives."

"Well—" he slammed the trunk "—you don't have a spare, so you're stuck with me. Let's just see if we can get along for more than five minutes."

"And what happens if we can get along for more than five minutes?"

Walking to her, he brushed his dusty hands together. "Then we'll see if we can get along for ten minutes."

Slowly, a smile broke over her face. "Ten minutes would be a record for us. Are you sure we should go in five-minute increments?"

"If we need to set smaller goals we can. But I'll let you handle the numbers part of the process."

"Now you're speaking my language." She

smiled, nodding. "That seals the deal. Let's go make each other miserable and see who balks first."

Droplets of rain hit Chase's broad shoulders, but he didn't flinch. She wasn't sure anything could make this man flinch. Other than maybe marrying her, but he was even going to do that.

"Do you even know how to change a tire?" he asked.

"No. But I can follow directions. How hard can it be?"

"Is that how you tackle everything in your life?"

"Sure, if it has instructions."

She'd love an instruction manual on love. Maybe someday she'd have the courage to ask God to explain why she wasn't marriageable material. Gruffly, she shook her head. She had to stop thinking about this kind of thing.

She called the tow truck and tucked the keys on her driver's-side tire. "I can't believe it's so late," she murmured, then turned her focus to Chase. "Are you sure about this?"

"My truck was made in this century. I can take you anywhere you want to go."

"My car was made in this century." She

added quietly so he wouldn't hear, "Just not this decade."

His shoulders shook and his next words were said with amusement. "Where can I take you, Lexi?"

"I'm delivering cookies and fresh flowers to Bright Horizons."

Surprise showed in his eyes.

"Don't worry," she said. "I made the cookies from scratch, and I have a deal with the florist."

He cocked his head. "You have a deal with the florist?"

"I buy the flowers that are close to dying at cost." She hitched her thumb to point to the box in the back seat. "I have a slew of vases I got from the granddaughter of a resident at the retirement home. She used them for her wedding, but didn't need twenty vases afterward. Every so often, the florist calls to let me know she has flowers, and I throw them in these vases and take them up to the home."

"You do this all on your own?"

She felt her cheeks heating. "Everyone deserves fresh flowers."

He rubbed a spot over his heart. "Yeah," he murmured, his eyes a thousand miles away.

Then he looked at her. "Let's get you and your flowers loaded up in my truck."

When he opened the back door and grabbed the box of floral arrangements, he paused. "What's the rest of this?"

"Casserole dish carriers. I'm also taking a meal to Mr. and Mrs. Stimpson."

After she grabbed the two insulated carriers and reusable grocery bag full of side dishes, they headed to his truck.

He held the box between his body and the truck, opened the back door to the cab and nodded to her to put her things in first. After placing the box on the back seat, he slammed the door and then opened the front passenger side for her. "How do you know the Stimpsons?"

"They were good friends with my grandmother when she lived at the home." Once she was securely inside, he closed the door and went around to his side. Her heart squeezed at his chivalry. Her stomach flipped once. Before he got into the truck, she growled to herself about her new reactions to his kindness and interest in her. Someone needed to remind her body that even though he was now her fiancé, it usually cringed at the first sign of Chase Cross.

"Is this a way to save on gas money?" he asked. "If so, it might be taking Gardner Economics to an extreme."

Her mouth hitched to a small smile, even if she didn't want it to. "Gardner Economics?"

"Yeah. That's my favorite so far. It's not just a marketing slogan. It's an entire way of life."

It was her favorite, too. There was something charming about his brainstorming slogans for her approach to living. But she tamped down the flattery.

He turned the engine on and put the truck in Reverse. "I just saw the Stimpsons in town today." Placing his hand on the back of her headrest, he looked over his shoulder while he backed out, then righted himself and pulled onto the highway.

"What were you doing in town?"

She looked at his profile, his strong jaw working the muscles. "Hunter and I went to the bank to discuss getting a loan," he finally said.

She sat up straight and turned to him, all senses on alert. "What did they say?"

He shook his head once. "They shut me down pretty fast."

"You should've asked me for help. I have all the property financials ready to go."

He threw a smile her way but kept his eyes on the road. "I know. I've kept every last report you've written for the ranch over the last two years."

He kept them? With all the bickering between them over the numbers, she didn't realize he actually valued the work she did for the ranch. She reached over and squeezed his forearm. "I'm sorry they couldn't help, Chase."

The air in the cab changed, almost softened the space between them.

"You really mean that, don't you."

"I do." She released his arm, leaned back in her seat and looked out the window, not seeing anything but his vision for the property. "I believe in everything about Four Cross Ranch. In an odd way, it tethered me to Wyoming when I first moved here, and it won't seem to let go."

With a gentle tone that almost implied he cared, he asked, "Why did you move here, Lexi?"

Ranch land floated by outside the window, green grass dotting the plains with promises of a colorful spring.

"Denver might be a city, but at times it can feel like a small town. After I broke off my second engagement, I needed to get away from everyone and everything. A fresh start." She bit her lip, urging the tears that threatened to fall to go back to where they came from.

Gripping the wheel, his knuckles whitened. "Why Wyoming?"

"My grandmother lived here in Elk Run, and I had some questions for her." She blew out a breath and shook her head. "Why would she leave me a trust with the condition of marriage? Did she realize what kind of strain that would put on me? What that might do to any new relationship I had?" Her voice got louder, the passion behind her questions unleashed. "How was I supposed to go on a first date with someone without feeling unbelievable pressure?"

Chase looked at her, turned his head back to the road, then did an immediate double take, something dawning in his eyes. But he remained silent.

"I had only met her twice in my whole life up to that point. Once I'd arrived in Wyoming, I tried to get my new life started all while dealing with the aftermath of a canceled wedding and an angry mother who was estranged from the woman I was trying to get to know. But before I could get any answers, my grandmother passed away."

The last few miles of the ride, the road rumbled under the tires of his truck as if trying to fill the awkward silence. When he parked the car in the Bright Horizons lot, he turned his body toward her, his face marred with conflict. "I want to ask you something."

She clasped her hands and looked down. "Okay."

"Why is understanding the trust so important to you?"

With one breath, she looked directly into his searching hazel eyes.

"I followed the rules." Her voice was firm. "I went to church. I dated nice men. I made wise choices in those relationships. And look where it got me. Two failed engagements."

His face softening, he stared at her.

Embarrassment crawled up her neck and she felt like it was going to choke her. Why did she blurt all that out to Chase? That was between her and God.

"I had…" she shook her head "…still have questions for my grandmother because it just felt so confusing. Why did she include the marriage condition? What was that going to accomplish? If she wanted to give the money to me, why couldn't she trust me with it as a single woman? Had she thought about the ramifications of the contingency?"

"I don't know."

"I'm sorry," she said quietly. "I didn't mean to get into all of that. I'll just get my things unloaded and you can go."

"Don't be ridiculous. I'll stay and give you a ride home."

"That's okay. I'm having dinner with the Stimpsons." She undid her seat belt. "I was hoping to see if they knew anything about the trust. Maybe get some answers."

Chase looked at the building, tapped his thumb on the steering wheel three times, then aimed his eyes back to her. "Then let's go get you some answers."

FOR THE SECOND time that day, Chase rubbed the spot over his heart. What was that? Tightness? His irritation at the woman in front of him?

If the military taught him anything, it was that rules were important. Sometimes your life or others' lives depended on following well-planned rules. But rules about finding love? That was a stretch, even for him.

Why was it so important to him that she understand she deserved love regardless of a cheating fiancé, confusing trust funds and rules that didn't work the way she thought they would?

In the Bright Horizons community room, he watched as she placed vases filled with colorful flowers on several tables. One woman clutched her hand to her chest in surprise at the sight of the unexpected gift. Lexi meandered through the residents, offering affectionate touches on shoulders, laughing with a few, kneeling on one knee to talk softly to another.

The answer to his question revealed itself. Because Lexi was generous. Kind. Beautiful, if you liked the way her brown eyes lit up when she saw you. Those were just a few reasons it was important to him that she understood she deserved love in her life.

When she finished her floral deliveries, she approached him, and the smile lighting up her face knocked him in the gut. "That was fun," she said.

"It was fun to watch," he murmured, unable to tear his eyes from hers.

A blush hit her cheeks, and she pushed a piece of hair behind her ear. "The Stimpsons are meeting me in their apartment. It's in the independent living wing on the other side of the building."

"Lead the way."

"Chase, I, um…" She looked away and grimaced. Then she said to him, "I would rather not mention to the Stimpsons that we're engaged. Things just feel a little too complicated to tackle that today."

He tipped his hat to her. "I understand."

As they walked, she explained the layout of the facility and how it housed seniors at different stages of life. He remembered her grandmother had moved inside the main building to a lovely room when hospice was needed.

An Easter wreath with a wooden rabbit holding a sign that read "Some bunny loves you" decorated the Stimpsons' door. Mrs. Stimpson answered their knock wearing a sweater adorned with a basket of pastel eggs. Mr. Stimpson stood behind her in a long-sleeved pastel plaid shirt. They wore matching warm smiles aimed at Lexi, then they both were surprised when they caught sight of Chase.

Is that what happened when married couples grew old together? Matching outfits and facial expressions? Chase nodded his greeting to the senior couple.

"Mr. and Mrs. Stimpson, have you met Chase Cross? My car has a flat tire, and he gave me a lift to Bright Horizons."

Mr. Stimpson offered his hand and gave Chase a hearty shake. His wife placed her palm on Chase's cheek. "Of course we know Chase. I changed his diaper plenty of times in the church nursery."

The couple led them into their apartment, then to the dining room. Lexi leaned over and whispered, "I thought you were born a cranky old man."

"I was. They must be thinking of Hunter."

She giggled, and he shook his head. What was he going to do with this woman?

Mrs. Stimpson set out an extra place setting and transferred the food to serving dishes while Mr. Stimpson filled everyone's drink orders.

After they gave thanks to the Lord for the food and fellowship, they filled their plates with Lexi's chicken and rice casserole, bacon-wrapped green beans, and tossed green salad.

"Mr. Stimpson, I don't know how well you know the Cross family," Lexi said while she passed the rolls, "but Chase is a decorated military hero just like you. Twenty years in, four deployments, more honors than anyone can count."

Chase had grabbed the basket but now froze. No one talked about his military service anymore. His parents died when he was twenty-six. Eight years later, he lost his wife. After that, no one noticed his honors or awards, which was fine with him. His siblings had their own lives and challenges. Chase quietly served his last few years and then retired. The focus of the family then switched to creating the nonprofit for veterans. As it should.

Lexi's words of praise felt like a stealth attack that came from his past. Her mention of his service in an overtly proud way gave him pause. Encouraged him even. Which just wasn't something he was used to feeling.

Dinner continued, and for the next twenty minutes Lexi surprised him with her passionate description of the ranch's nonprofit. Mr. Stimpson shared several stories about military buddies who had both struggled and thrived. Between Lexi's enthusiasm, and the veteran's support of the nonprofit, Chase's motivation to get everything up and running was at an all-time high.

"I remember when you and your brother enlisted." Mr. Stimpson dished out a second helping of casserole on his plate. "I'm sure that made your parents proud."

Something unpleasant lodged in Chase's throat. "Thank you, sir. But they probably would have been more proud of Hunter for returning home to take care of our siblings." Would he ever let go of the guilt?

Under the table, Lexi's soft hand slid into his, and he stared from their connection to the sincerity in her eyes. "You were both heroes in your own right," she whispered. She leaned into him a little, their shoulders touched, and she smiled. It was a smile that told him she meant every word.

An unfamiliar warmth spread through his chest. Like something in his insides was thawing after a long winter. Before he could understand what it meant, she squeezed his hand and let go.

Mrs. Stimpson's gaze popped between Chase and Lexi, a glint of mischief in her features. "And how do you two know each other?"

"She's the accountant for Four Cross Ranch."

The woman's eyes glittered. "And what do you think of our Lexi?"

He shifted his weight in the hard wooden chair and felt the heat of the small chandelier lights. It was as if the quaint dining area had morphed into an interrogation room. "I think Lexi can save money in her sleep."

Mrs. Stimpson nodded as if for him to continue. "If she could make two plus two equal five for her clients, she would."

Mrs. Stimpson lifted an eyebrow, and Chase broke out in a sweat. He wondered if local law enforcement knew about her interrogation skills. If not, they needed to think seriously about employing her.

He rubbed his palms against the tops of his thighs. "What I mean is—" he looked at Lexi and saw a hint of vulnerability in her eyes "—she would do anything she could to help the ranch."

She blinked.

"Anything," he said quietly to her. "And that means a lot to me."

The silence stretched for a few seconds before Mr. Stimpson cleared his throat. He smiled at Lexi. "She certainly is a talented accountant. But everyone around here knows her for her generous heart."

Lexi ducked her head and a blush pinked her cheeks.

"We met her through her grandmother Louella Chadwick. God rest her soul," Mr. Stimpson said with affection.

Chase chuckled. "I got to meet her before she passed. She was quite a pistol."

Lexi placed both palms flat on the table. "Speaking of my gran—" she cleared her throat "—I was wondering if I could ask you two a few questions about her."

"Of course." Concern crossed Mrs. Stimpson's face. "Is everything okay?"

"Yes." Lexi glanced around the table. "If we're all finished eating dinner, maybe we could talk over dessert?"

Mrs. Stimpson shooed everyone to the living room and scurried off to the kitchen. She returned with a plate of homemade cookies and a stack of napkins. "Lexi, you made my favorite. White chocolate chip without the nuts." She turned to Chase. "Nuts are just nature's way to ruin chocolate."

With her tone as serious as if she were discussing the end-time, he bit back a laugh and nodded. "Yes, ma'am."

She then smiled at him and said, "And we eat our cookies on the couch without a plate. Because I don't have much time left on this earth, and I'm not going to spend it worrying about crumbs. I did that in my twenties, thirties and forties, and I'm not sure it did a whole lot of good for anyone."

While everyone chuckled, Chase wondered

if he was going to look back on his life and wonder if he should have approached it differently. His eyes shot to Lexi, and something in his gut stirred.

The Stimpsons settled onto the love seat, Chase and Lexi on chairs that flanked the fireplace.

Instead of holding a cookie, Lexi tightly clasped her hands in her lap. "This might be a bit awkward, but I know you were close with Gran."

"She cheated at bridge," Mr. Stimpson interjected.

"Hush, George," his wife admonished with a stern look.

But Chase couldn't contain his laughter, which earned him the same stern look.

Lexi smiled. "That sounds just like her."

"Go on, sweetie," Mrs. Stimpson encouraged.

"Did she happen to mention anything about a trust fund she left for me?"

Mrs. Stimpson looked at her husband, and he shook his head. "That doesn't sound familiar," she said.

Lexi twisted her fingers one way and then the other. Chase wanted to place his hand on hers to soothe her nerves. "I know so little about her. We only had those last six weeks of her life together, and I feel like I lost her without really understanding who she was. Did she ever mention anything about marriage or falling in love or money?"

"What's this all about, Lexi?" Mr. Stimpson asked gently.

Watching Lexi struggle, knowing what it meant to her to find answers, filled Chase with discomfort. And the protective side of him wanted to take over the conversation. But why did it feel like he had something at stake in this discussion as well?

Lexi took what looked like a weighted breath. "My grandmother left me a sizable trust fund to be accessed on my thirty-fifth birthday. With one condition. I have to be married."

Mrs. Stimpson's eyes grew round.

Lexi quickly added, "I'm not focused on the money. Even though I've known about the trust and her marriage requirement most of my adult life, I've set myself up to live without it."

Chase watched as she explained about the second cousin who served time for embezzlement. His stomach clenched as she muddled through an explanation of why she wasn't married and how hard it was to find a spouse. And thick guilt hit him head-on when he realized he'd made her this uncomfortable with his recent lines of questioning.

In that moment, her reality hit him like a stampede of livestock. The pressure she felt from her circumstances was underlined with a heartbreaking layer of shame. She'd lived under the weight of a burden she didn't ask for and felt embarrassed by the ridiculous marriage requirement. But she also felt shame because she couldn't find a husband to solve the problem. As if it were a reflection on her.

He didn't like it one bit.

Lexi stood, walked to the window, sighed, then turned back to them. "I just want to know why she would do that. Did she have issues with money or security? Was there a love she lost because of a financial issue?"

At her last question, Mrs. Stimpson's demeanor changed. She pursed her lips and glanced at her husband.

Lexi returned to her seat, leaned forward and rested her elbows on her knees. Her eyes locked onto Mrs. Stimpson, imploring her for an answer. "Did I do something wrong, that she thought she needed to word the trust fund requirements this way? It feels—" her voice became thick, and Chase could hardly stand to watch "—like I'm being punished for something I have no idea I did wrong."

"Now you listen to me, young lady." The elderly woman took Lexi's hands in hers, a fierce look in her eyes. "This has nothing to do with you."

Tears lined the rims of Lexi's eyes, and Mrs. Stimpson continued. "Your grandmother was a fine, upstanding woman. But she was imperfect, like the rest of us. From what she shared with me, her relationship with your mom tested her. She never quite knew how to deal with her daughter-in-law."

"My mother never let me see my grandmother," Lexi whispered.

"I know. And that was one of your grandmother's biggest losses. You need to know that."

Lexi's face filled with a cross between relief and confusion.

"Your grandmother didn't want to speak ill of your mom. But she shared some details with me over the years. Things changed with your mom after your father died. Grief does funny things to people. I don't know what kind of woman your mom was before the accident, but she got it in her head that she needed that money. Your mother did everything she could over the years to get her hands on your grandmother's money. She even tried to declare her unfit."

Lexi gasped, and Chase couldn't handle it any longer. He rose from his chair and stepped behind Lexi, placing a hand on her shoulder.

"Though Louella never talked about the specifics of a trust, she always wanted her money secured tightly, away from your mother." Mrs. Stimpson gentled her voice. "And I think she was a little old-fashioned. She probably wanted you to find someone who could be by your side. And our generation got married earlier in life."

It was so subtle that Chase almost missed it. But everything in Lexi slumped just slightly, almost as if in defeat.

Mrs. Stimpson cupped Lexi's face. "I think if your grandmother knew the pressure she put on you with this trust, she would feel terribly. She loved you. She told me those last few weeks with you were the best of her life. And if she could come back from the grave and change the circumstances of that trust, I believe she would."

Tears streamed down Lexi's cheeks, and Chase felt useless. He squeezed her shoulder.

After somber goodbyes and promises to enjoy a more cheerful dinner another time, Chase and Lexi left. A heavy quiet descended on the car during the drive home. Chase's brain reeled with confusing thoughts. His heart felt even more baffled.

He thought he knew the woman seated next to him. But as they rolled through town under the starlit skies, he realized he'd made more incorrect assumptions about her than he could count.

When they arrived at her house, he walked her to the porch. "Do you need help getting your car back to you?"

She dug through her purse. "No. Thank you, though. The tire shop towed it and said they would get to it tomorrow. They're only a few blocks away, so I'll walk over and get it when they're done."

He felt the edge of his lips tip. "And what will you barter in return for their services?"

"Sometimes I pay people like a normal person."

"Come on," he chided. "Fess up. What is it this time?"

She chuckled, and something tight in his

chest released at the sound. "I may have promised to help them unravel their budget issues."

"You are something else, Lexi Gardner." He stared at her sparkling eyes, and everything around them stilled.

She shifted, almost a little bashful, the porch light reflecting off her silky hair. "Thank you for taking me to Bright Horizons."

"It looks like we got along for more than just five-minute increments," he said.

She laughed softly, the smooth sound hanging in the air. "I think that means I need to come out to the ranch and see how it works."

"Why would you do that?"

"Because I'm going to live there and be your wife."

Struck silent, Chase just stood there. The word *wife* played over and over again in his head. He knew he'd agreed to marry her, but somehow talking about it this way made it more real.

She cocked her head to the side. "Will you show me, Chase? Will you show me what my life will be like in a month?"

All he could do was what any good cowboy would do. He tipped his hat and said, "Yes, ma'am."

Warmth hit Chase's chest as he walked to his truck. He could get used to this Lexi.

But as he drove away, he wondered if he wanted to get used to this Lexi.

CHAPTER FIVE

"I'M SORRY, MAN," Hunter said through Chase's phone the next evening. "I hate to do this to you. I know Lexi's on her way."

Chase rubbed the back of his neck. "It's okay. It's calving season. If she can't understand what it's like on a cattle ranch during calving season, then we're in trouble."

"She'll understand." Chase thought he could hear a smile behind Hunter's words and decided not to acknowledge it. He wasn't in the mood to be ribbed by his twin tonight.

She had to understand calving season for him the way he had to understand tax season for her. How unfortunate those happened around the same time of year.

Disappointment hung in the air as he looked out over the acreage of Four Cross Ranch. In spite of Wyoming's gorgeous scenery, tonight's sunset seemed dull.

He was hoping to show her the more impressive sides of the ranch on her first visit out as his fiancée. Which irked him because why would he want to impress her? She'd been out here many times before today.

Chase hit the end button for the call and scrolled through his contacts to find Lexi's number. At some point, he supposed he'd have to move her to the Favorites list on his phone. If Hunter had told Chase last week that this week he'd be thinking of moving Lexi Gardner to his Favorites list, he'd have socked him in the arm.

She answered on the first ring.

"Lectured anyone today on the importance of receipt organization?" he asked.

"I may or may not have casually mentioned it to three clients," she said with humor in her voice.

He smiled. "Attagirl." Then he sighed and said, "I hate to do this to you, but I can't greet you at the gate. I'm heading down to the grey barn. We've got a first-time heifer that doesn't understand it's her job to feed her calf. I've got to lend a hand. We should probably cancel the tour and do it another day. I don't know how long this is going to take, and the sun's fading."

"Oh." Chase could hear disappointment in

her voice. "Oh, right. Absolutely. I'm sorry. Things at work took a turn and time got away from me."

He lowered his voice. "It's okay, Lexi. Another time."

A long pause filled the call. She cleared her throat. "Is there anything I can do to help?"

He smiled. "I wish you had something to trade this momma to convince her to feed her baby. But I'm not sure if Gardner Economics applies to cattle."

She was still laughing when they disconnected.

Still, he dragged a bad attitude with him into the barn. That spot in his chest ached and it felt a little bit like he was going to miss seeing her, so he did his best to ignore the feeling.

Thirty minutes later, he was grateful no one was around to see him. He found himself shoved to the ground by the momma cow. Grabbing his hat off the floor, he pushed to his feet. Thankfully, the calf had started to nurse. He stroked the momma's back. "Let's be glad you didn't need to be put in the head chute," he said to her. Restraining cattle wasn't Chase's favorite thing, but sometimes it was the only way to get the job done.

"Chase?" a voice whispered from outside the pen. "Are you okay?"

He glanced up and found Lexi, wide-eyed and fidgeting. She looked like a hen who didn't know where to go. Except in her jeans and puffy-sleeved green top, she looked cuter than a hen. "I'm okay now that this heifer is allowing her calf to feed. Are you okay?"

She bit her lip, then released it. "I heard a scuffle back here and thought you might be hurt."

He took off his hat and wiped his brow with the back of his hand. "This is her first calf, and she didn't care for nursing. We had a little chat about it, and I helped her see the error of her ways."

She glanced at the halter the momma had thrown off, and back to him. A smile broke out over her face, but she tried to hide it with a hand. "You're covered in hay."

Hitching a grin, he said, "It may look like I lost the battle, but I won the war." He glanced down at the calf, thankful she had stopped bawling.

"Will the cow know what to do from now on?"

"Sometimes they need a few more bouts

of encouragement." He shifted slightly and the heifer gave him a stern look. Calmly, he soothed, "You've got this, momma. You don't need me anymore." At the sight of the heifer nursing, relief hit him. They would be okay.

He sauntered toward Lexi, wiping hay off his staff shirt along the way.

With a face full of wonder, she said, "I can't believe you bring life into the world."

He shook his head. "My sister Cora's the one who has the superhero midwife powers. I just watch while the cows do what they were born to do. If they need help every now and then, we're available."

"I haven't seen Cora around lately. Does she usually help with calving season?"

While dusting off his jeans, he didn't make eye contact. "She won't set foot on the ranch side of the property."

"Seems like there's a story there."

"There is," he said somberly, shifting his focus back to her. "It's hers to tell. But fair to say that ranch life wasn't good to her."

He was surprised Lexi didn't know what happened to his sister. But maybe she'd been shielded from the rumors.

"I guess Ryder is a no-show for calving season, too?" she asked quietly.

All Chase could do was clench his teeth and nod. If Ryder were here to help, Chase could focus more on the nonprofit.

His rodeo brother was an enigma to him. A riddle he would never solve. But no matter his youngest brother's actions, Chase knew there was a good man in there.

He gave a chin lift to the basket in her hand. "What do you have there?"

Pink hit her cheeks, and she curled a strand of her pretty blond hair around her ear. "Dinner. I couldn't think of a way I could help you with the cows, so I brought dinner."

"That was thoughtful. Thank you."

"It's just a sandwich, chips and carrot sticks."

His shoulders shook with a chuckle. "Carrot sticks?"

"Yes." She spoke with authority. "Everyone needs their vegetables."

He leaned over the edge of the stall railing and lifted the red-and-white-checkered cloth napkin covering the food. "You got dessert in there, too?"

She playfully slapped his hand away. "Only if you eat all your carrots."

He pulled back and laughed.

She looked around the barn and let out a sigh that sounded like contentment. "I like seeing this side of your life."

"I'll always help with the ranch when I can. It's in my blood."

She studied him. "But the nonprofit is your oxygen."

"Yes," he whispered, emotion getting caught in his throat.

"Today's introduction to ranch life got cut short, but at some point, I'd also like to see your plans for the nonprofit," she said.

"You've seen the budget." He pulled hay off his hat. "You already know what I want to do."

"Yes. But I know you have more ideas swirling around in your head about how you want to use your land." She grinned. "Numbers can't show you everything."

He balked. "Don't let your colleagues hear you say that, or you'll get kicked out of Math Club."

She swung the basket back and forth. "I know you mentioned your first guests were coming soon. You're going to eat the cost yourself, aren't you."

"Maybe," he hedged.

"I'd love to help get everything ready. Maybe I could walk the land and see the nonprofit through your eyes and really get a feel for what you need. Will you show it to me?"

How she'd gone from being his biggest critic to his biggest cheerleader, he didn't know.

Maybe he hadn't been fair in his past assessment of her. She wasn't critical of him or his ideas. She just wanted solid foundational funding. She didn't wish for the nonprofit to fail. Which was starting to make him *her* biggest cheerleader.

"Well—" he shifted his hat to his head "—I'd love to do that. But not on foot. That's going to require a horse ride."

"Oh." She stepped back, shaking her head a few times. "Oh, that's okay. No worries."

"It's not a problem."

She looked everywhere but him. "Oh, I don't want to take up any of the ranch's extra time or resources."

He cocked his head and studied her reaction. "Lexi," he said, quiet but firm. She snapped her eyes to his. "What's going on?"

The calf let out a gentle moo behind them, but Chase kept his focus on Lexi.

She pulled on the hem of her shirt. "I kind of...don't exactly...know how to ride a horse."

The words hit him, and a slow grin broke out over his face.

Chase had a new goal in life. One that would take precedence above everything else.

He was going to get Lexi up on a horse.

FOUR DAYS LATER, a horse in the stall next to Lexi whinnied.

"What am I doing?" Lexi whispered to the horse. She wasn't sure if she was more nervous about riding, or about spending more time with Chase. Whatever the case, here she was about to hop on a twelve-hundred-pound animal.

She stared at the beautiful light chestnut horse named Mildred, who Chase assured her was as calm as her name. He'd reverently brushed a hand down her side and said she was the most loving animal on the ranch.

Chase had headed to the tack room and left Lexi with the quarter horse. Having been in Wyoming two years, she knew enough to wear jeans and boots. But my word, she felt out of her element. Even though somehow, the ranch brought her peace like it always did.

She wished that peace would line up with

her feelings about its owner. In a bizarre turn of events, she seemed to be enjoying him. She'd spent pockets of time over the last few days learning the ropes of the ranch while bringing small items to the lodge for the upcoming guests.

The horse stepped closer.

"Feelings aren't a part of a business proposal, old girl." Lexi ran her palm over Mildred's neck.

The horse adjusted her tongue around the bit in her mouth.

"You really pulled the short stick on names, didn't you? Mildred. That's not how I would describe you."

Chase chuckled from behind her, hoisting a saddle on the wooden rail. "Don't knock the name. It helps first-timers feel comfortable."

He brought the sixteen-hand horse out of her stall, murmuring soft words to her as he led her into the open air of the paddock. After he tied off Mildred's rope, he fetched the saddle.

While he worked, she studied him.

Chase had so many dimensions to him, she'd stopped counting a long time ago. She found the role of sensitive cowboy more attractive than she wanted to admit.

He pulled at the saddle buckle under Mildred's belly and made adjustments. The creak and smell of the leather grounded her to the heartbeat of the ranch.

"So, what's behind her name?"

"Mildred means gentle strength." He ran a hand down her leg. Mildred's shiny light brown coat turned to a stunning black just above the knee in a beautiful contrast that matched her mane and tail. "Which is perfect for her because she really is the most intuitively gentle animal on the ranch. She's going to follow my lead, just like she will with the kids who visit the lodge."

"And her strength?"

He stood to his full height, impressive in his jeans, boots and Western shirt that tugged subtly at his arms and broad chest. "Millie's also the most protective animal on this ranch. She'd never let anything harm you."

Chase seared his eyes into Lexi's, and she knew, even though he didn't say the words himself, that he also would never let anything harm her.

Suddenly, the death of his wife hit her from a different angle. It wasn't just that he'd lost his wife. It was that he lost her to something he couldn't protect her from.

No wonder the soldier didn't want to get married again. Laura's death had wrapped its tentacles around Chase's most vulnerable point and squeezed.

Lexi took a breath and released as much tension out of her muscles as she could. The best way she knew how to show Chase that he could relax and enjoy himself was for her to lead the way. "Okay, cowboy." She cocked a smile at him. "Let's get me in this saddle, and you show me your land."

His lips twitched. "Yes, ma'am."

She walked up to the horse, which brought her closer to Chase. He smelled of earth, and maybe a little bit of hope.

"Left hand on the saddle horn. Put your left foot in the stirrup, push up and swing the other one on over."

Lexi followed the directions and when she hiked her foot into the stirrup and whipped her opposite leg around the saddle, she was surprised at how natural it felt.

"Mildred is the perfect size for you," he murmured while he adjusted the stirrups. After handing her the reins, he said, "Wait until you see Harvey."

"Harvey? Where do you guys get these names?"

Chase jogged back and then led his horse out of the barn.

Lexi felt her eyes widen at the sight of the black Friesian. "Whoa. Harvey's huge."

"About three hundred more pounds than Mildred." He guided Harvey toward Lexi. After mounting, he leaned over and released Mildred's rope from the fence.

As Chase took the lead, Mildred fell in line behind him. The movement of the horse underneath Lexi felt clunky, but not scary. She loosened her grip on the saddle horn.

"Mildred and Harvey." She chuckled, and Chase looked back at her. "They sound like an old married couple. Mildred and Harvey."

Chase patted Harvey on his neck. "Don't listen to her, buddy. She doesn't know."

"I don't know what?"

"Harvey means battleworthy."

Mildred. Gentle strength. Harvey. Battleworthy.

With acres of grass crunching under the horses' hooves, the sun lowering in the sky and a light breeze swirling around them, a soft

peace fell over Lexi. Gentle strength and battleworthy felt about right.

AN HOUR LATER, they sat on their horses at the
tree line on the back edge of the property, looking out over the land that would someday be
the playing ground for Four Cross Hope. Guests
would stay at the lodge for now, but he had
plans for expansion.

"How do you feel on that horse?" he asked.
"Because it looks like it comes naturally to
you."

"Pretty good, actually. Mildred makes this
easy."

"So, I showed you where the individual
tiny cabins will be built. But look across this
meadow." Chase pointed to Hunter in the distance working with a small dog. Beside them,
Duke stood alert as if he were supervising the
entire lesson. "That's where the play and thera-
peutic area will be."

Lexi looked around, the complete picture becoming clear. "That's perfect because the trails
will lead here."

"Yeah," Chase said, leaning his weight into
his hands at his saddle horn. A simple word, but
laced with pride.

"Chase, this is so well planned. Each of the ten houses has a private trail that leads to and from the community areas. Every path points to the chow hall and recreation spots, but there's enough open land that if someone didn't want to get pigeonholed anywhere, they could just breathe in the space."

She swallowed, unsure if she should say what she was thinking, then gentled her voice. "You laid the main features out between the trails like the runs on a ski slope." She paused. "It's like you brought a piece of Laura here."

Slowly, he turned to look at her. He cleared his throat, but didn't say anything. Instead, he took her hand in his, squeezed and looked back across the property.

He didn't let go of her hand, and the moment filled with warmth.

Closing her eyes, she took a long breath in and allowed the exhale to take its time on the way out.

But Mildred shifted her footing and jerked her head up once, yanking Lexi's attention to the horse. Lexi tore her hand from Chase's and grabbed the reins at the ready. Up until now, Mildred had done nothing out of the ordinary. The horse just followed in step with Chase.

"Whoa, girl," Chase soothed, and leaned over to run a hand down her horse's neck. Mildred shook her head back and forth as if she were shaking off a bad thought, then she lowered her head and stomped on the grass.

From afar, Hunter waved.

Lexi lifted her hand in response. "Hunter's going to train the therapy dogs himself?"

"He worked with a K-9 unit in the military, so that's the goal. But his service was so long ago, he's got to go through certification, and that takes resources. In the meantime, I've got a buddy I know who owns a training facility for service dogs. I'm hoping to consult with him."

"Have you thought about equine therapy?"

He nodded. "Another goal. We've got the land out here to make that happen. I've done some general research, but it would take more manpower and funding."

"You never know. You might find a therapist with a horse that needs boarding and make some kind of a deal."

A grin slowly spread across his face, and he cocked an eyebrow at her.

Her shoulders shook with her giggle. "Don't say it. I know. Gardner Economics."

He nodded, the grin still intact.

"But it works," she insisted, sitting taller in her saddle.

"And what did you trade for your new, fancy boots?"

Heat hit her face. She didn't think he'd noticed her shiny new Western boots. "Well..." The wind pulled at a lock of hair, and she tucked it behind her ear. The lock came loose a second later. "If you must know," she said defensively, "I paid full price for these boots."

His gaze shot from her boots to her eyes. "You paid full price?" he asked quietly.

"If I'm going to be living on the ranch, I thought quality was important," she said just as quietly.

The long-term implications fell between them. Lexi's heart sped up. Maybe Chase's thoughts weren't going in the same direction hers seemed to be galloping.

But his face softened, something so beautiful, it made her heart shift. He leaned toward her and pushed the errant strand of hair behind her ear. "You made a good choice," he said, his voice low and gravelly.

Lexi didn't know what to think about the thick emotion he held in his voice.

But Mildred jerked her head again. This time adding an anxiety-riddled whinny to her movement.

Chase reached for Mildred's bridle, but Harvey reared up on his back legs.

With no time to think or digest what was happening, Lexi gripped the saddle horn. Panic hit her with the next jerk of the horse when Lexi realized she had dropped the reins.

Mildred backed up, her front feet pushing against the hard ground in a way that lowered Lexi forward in the saddle, then jerked her up over and over again. The horse twisted and bumped against Harvey, pushing the other horse forward. The startled Harvey thrust his head up and down in protest and stomped his front legs several times.

"Snake," Chase growled loudly, trying to gain control of his bucking horse. Harvey stopped trying to throw Chase, but pounded his hooves to the ground in his disapproval.

Snake.

Fear slapped her in the face. Every muscle in her body clenched tighter to her horse.

Chase turned his animal away from Lexi, took him several feet in the opposite direction, threw his leg over the saddle and slid off. He hit his horse on the rump, sending him across the pasture on a run.

The sound of Duke barking grew closer, but Lexi couldn't process what that meant as Mildred started to buck in small jumps that lifted Lexi out of the saddle. On one of the downward motions, Lexi's left ankle got caught at an odd angle in the stirrup, and her knee twisted. Pain shot down her leg and made it difficult for her to maintain her tenuous grip on the saddle horn.

"Hang on, Lexi." Chase tried to grab Mildred's bridle, but it slipped from his hands. "Come on, old girl. It's okay," he grunted while shifting between the horse and the snake.

After vaulting over a log to get to them, Duke skidded to a halt five feet from the snake.

Chase's face tightened. "Duke, back up," he said gruffly, finally able to get his hands on the bridle.

The dog snapped furiously at the snake. The reptile rose taller and hissed a ferocious reply.

"Chase," Lexi breathed out, squinching her eyes at the pain in her knee.

"I've got you," Chase soothed.

Lexi was unsure if he was talking to her or

the horse, but his words seemed to calm both of them.

Duke and the snake continued to duel. The snake slithered back a foot, but kept its eyes on Duke and let out an eerie hiss. He'd launch forward six inches, only for Duke to snarl, and in turn he'd slink backward.

Mildred stomped her front hooves, but her overall demeanor calmed down enough for Chase to lead her several feet away from the canine–reptile dance.

Chase smoothed his hand down the horse's neck. "You're okay, girl. You're okay."

Lexi glanced at Duke. The dog had sent the snake cowering back to the forest. He sat on his hind feet, chest puffed out, eyes alert on the trees in front of him. If the last few minutes hadn't been so intense, Lexi would have laughed at the canine mayor of Four Cross Ranch kicking someone out of his town.

Chase wrapped his hand around Lexi's calf. "Can you take your feet out of the stirrups? Let's get you down on solid ground."

The second she tried to move her left leg, pain slammed into her knee. "Hold up," she gritted through her teeth.

Alarm shot through Chase's features. "What's wrong? Are you hurt?"

"I wrenched my knee."

With deft movements, Chase lowered the stirrup so she could ease her foot from its hold. "Is your other foot out?"

She nodded.

He wrapped his arm around Lexi's waist and slowly guided her off the saddle. It was not one of Lexi's more graceful moments in life, but Chase didn't seem to care.

In fact, Lexi noticed that Chase seemed to be in his own world. Sweat lined his shirt, and his face remained locked with intensity.

Mildred's shoulders twitched, and she huffed out a neigh, appearing to shake off the same stress Chase and Lexi were trying to recover from.

"I think from now on, I'm going to call her Millie," Lexi said, her voice shaky despite trying to lighten the mood. "She's too strong to be a Mildred."

With a fierce look behind his eyes, he gently grasped her hands and rubbed his thumbs across the tops. "Are you okay? What hurts?"

"Just my knee," she said quietly.

One of his arms slid around Lexi's shoulders

and pulled her to him; the other one wrapped around her waist. "I'm sorry, Lexi. I'm so sorry."

She clung to him and tried to get her breath under control. Part of her wanted to stay in the cocoon of everything that was Chase Cross, his strong arms, earthy smell and everything that made her feel protected. But another part of her knew his reaction felt a little off.

Something had shifted in Chase. He went from hero in a harrowing situation to someone being consumed by an overwhelming concern. While the sentiment felt good on the surface, she couldn't pinpoint what was happening. It was as if he was drenched in worry for her.

"Chase," she said gently. She pulled back from him, gripping his strong forearms for balance. "Chase, I'm okay."

He ran a hand over his mouth, but kept the other one available for her to use for balance. "I thought…" He shook his head. "Something really bad could have happened to you."

The picture that hung in the great room at the lodge of Laura skiing down one of her last black diamond runs came to Lexi's mind.

And when Lexi realized what was happening, her heart broke.

He was scared for her. Chase didn't want anything to harm Lexi.

She wouldn't allow anything to harm him as well. She had to let him know that everything turned out fine.

"Hey." She pointed to her knee. "I just need to walk this off. It's okay."

She didn't know if it was really okay. She just hoped so for his sake.

"And…" Lexi swallowed and lightened her tone. "You were right about Millie. Gentle strength. She *is* the most protective animal on the ranch. No way was she going to let that mean snake get anywhere near me."

Chase grabbed the back of his neck and looked around, as if replaying the incident in his head. Though he wasn't looking at Lexi, he gave a small nod.

"Plus—" Lexi ran her thumb over his arm "—Duke came to save me."

His attention turned to his dog.

Lexi said in a playful tone, "I don't want to cause any strife between you and your dog, but I think he likes me more than he likes you."

Chase turned his head to look down at her. He studied her face and sighed. "That's probably true."

"Chase. I'm all right. Promise."

Hunter arrived driving a small ATV. After he studied the scene, he said, "I think I missed all the fun."

"Lexi's hurt," Chase said.

"I'm not hurt." She shifted her glare from Chase to Hunter. When Chase's back was to her, she bugged out her eyes at Hunter, willing him to size up the unspoken pieces of the incident. Surely Hunter knew that Chase needed to believe Lexi was okay.

Walking over to Millie, Hunter pulled a few pieces of apple out of his pocket. He held them out for the horse, who gobbled them out of his hand. "Was it a snake?" he asked them while studying Millie.

Chase walked to the edge of the tree line. "Yes. But I didn't get a chance to see what kind."

"She just remembers being bit." Hunter stroked his hand down Millie's head, placating the horse even further. "I'm sorry, girl. That wasn't much fun the last time, was it? You didn't want Lexi to experience that, did you?"

While the men were distracted, Lexi stretched out her knee. She bit back the moan, but couldn't help the wince on her face.

Hunter's eyes shot to hers.

She held out her hand and shook her head, imploring him not to tell Chase. "I'm fine," she whispered as she put weight onto the knee to show him how fine she was. Only she wasn't fine. Her knee screamed at her. But she knew if she walked a little bit, it would find its bearings.

Chase bent to Duke, giving his loyal dog body rubs and praises for his valiant effort to scare the snake away.

Meanwhile, Lexi hobbled to the other side of Millie, trying to hide her limp from Chase. A few steps later, and she was right. Her knee ironed out the kinks, and she only felt a little soreness. Instead of screaming at her, her knee seemed to be gently admonishing her on the perils of horseback riding.

But she was tough. She could take it. And Chase wouldn't need to know. He didn't need that kind of pressure after losing his wife.

Hunter adjusted the stirrups on Millie's saddle. "I'll take Mildred and round up Harvey. He's probably at his favorite watering hole. You can ride the ATV back to the lodge." With a wave, he trotted across the prairie with Duke at his side.

Lexi had almost forgotten about Harvey.

Once she and Chase were settled in the ATV, she asked, "Why did you send Harvey away?"

Chase turned the vehicle around and pointed it to the lodge. "He gets a little aggressive sometimes under stress. I knew if he saw the snake or if I needed to calm Millie down, he wasn't going to be any help."

"Battleworthy," she said. "True to his name." And to his owner.

Before Chase hit the gas pedal, he leaned his weight into his folded arms over the steering wheel and looked at her with an apology in his eyes. "I think I ruined our outing. For sure I ruined our dinner. Harvey ran off with our food in his saddlebags."

"You didn't ruin anything." She offered him a small smile and shifted her attention to the acreage in front of them. "I've loved every second of getting to know your land, your dreams."

Chase took her hand in his. She wasn't sure if it was his hand trembling or hers, but the connection seemed to calm her adrenaline down.

"Can I ask you a question?" he said in a low voice while staring at their joined hands.

"Yes."

"Is this land, these plans—" he released her and ran his hand through his hair, a stark look of vulnerability in his eyes "—are they worthy of you giving up marrying for love?"

If he was going to risk asking the question, she would risk answering it honestly. She took his hand back.

"Growing up, I think I always knew that my mom was a difficult person to get along with." She sighed a long and heavy breath full of years of frustration, misunderstanding and confusion. "But there's nothing like the moment when you realize that your mother is just a selfish person. It's hard to reconcile that."

Chase used his thumb to rub lines from her wrist to each of her knuckles, and his eyes remained focused on her hand.

"But my dad raised me different. I think he knew he'd have to balance her out." She shook her head, remembering her father's constant attempts to cover up her mother's actions. "But I was wired like him. We were two peas in a pod. I think he knew I'd be okay."

Chase shot his gaze to hers but said nothing.

"I always knew the trust existed. But when I found out my mother had handpicked a husband for me and set up my entire relationship to her advantage, something broke in me." Her voice cracked, and she whispered, "I knew I had to do something beautiful with that money. To make it mean something."

"Lexi—"

She pulled their hands to her and squeezed, her voice begging him to understand. "It has to mean something, Chase. It has to go toward something good."

His eyes sharpened. "That's why you're willing to forgo love and marry someone?"

"Yes," she whispered.

"Why me?" he asked gruffly, as if trying to contain emotion.

So low, she was barely able to hear her own voice, she said, "Because what you can do to help veterans here is truly beautiful."

He swallowed, his Adam's apple bobbing.

After a beat, he said, "You're an exceptional woman, Lexi Gardner." He lifted her hand and kissed the back of it, his lips lingering just a touch. "I don't think I could have survived if something had happened to you today."

For most people, that sentiment would have spoken of sweet affection. But with Chase's burdened tone and his tortured past, Lexi's heart beat with pangs of confusion.

The table had turned.

In the beginning, Chase didn't want her to

marry someone who didn't treasure her. But now, she didn't want him to marry her if he truly didn't want to get married again. Maybe his wounds from the death of his wife were imprinted too deeply. Maybe she was asking too much of him.

But he'd said yes, and she had to trust him. Clearly, if he had agreed to get married again, it was for function only, which is the way she wanted the deal.

So, it was time to forge forward.

She squeezed his hand, let it go and brightened her voice to transition them out of the jarring snake incident. "The good news is, nothing happened to me today. That leaves me to share my big find for the guest room at the lodge. Which, I might add, is just in time for the Forresters' arrival tomorrow, and as a sidenote, I worked it out so I could be available to welcome the family with you."

"Oh, good. Thank you for arranging to be here." He rubbed his hands together, playing along. "Okay. I can't wait to hear about your big find. But if you paid a penny more than fifty percent off whatever this item is, I'm going to be disappointed in you."

She blanched. "Chase Cross, that's just insulting. I'll have you know I got this particular item for three dollars."

"Which is…"

"A throw pillow that says 'Cowboy Rule Number One: Don't Jog with Your Spurs On." She giggled so hard, she barely got the words out.

On a groan, he said, "Lexi, that's terrible."

She laughed harder. "It's hilarious."

"It's terrible."

"Well, let's wait until tomorrow and let the Forresters be the judge."

As they drove to the lodge, it felt good to laugh with Chase. But Lexi was still worried about what the future would bring.

CHAPTER SIX

LEXI COULD NOT believe this was happening. She'd had to put out so many fires today with her accounting clients, she'd missed meeting the Forresters at the lodge. Chase said it went well, but she was still disappointed she wasn't there to meet the first military couple to visit Four Cross Hope.

Late afternoon, she had texted Chase to let him know she was finally on her way. He was busy with a heifer in labor and asked if she could sign for a fertilizer delivery. Signing a document seemed more up her alley than delivering a calf. But she couldn't have imagined how wrong the fertilizer delivery would go.

Wiping sweat off her forehead, she grimaced. She was pretty sure her makeup was melting off her face. And she felt positive that the rolls of long, soft curls of hair she'd worked so hard on had flattened to her head.

She looked at the Four Cross Ranch foreman, his weathered face flushed with color. "Frank, I think we've got the last box of fertilizer back on the loading dock."

"Yes, ma'am."

It's not like she dressed up to see Chase. All she did was pair a nice shirt with her best jeans. Though she now worried about sweating in the stretchy crepe jersey top. She didn't want to change because she thought the Swiss dots on the puff sleeves added a delicate touch. Something feminine to her usually uber-practical wardrobe. And so what if she put on makeup and spent time on her hair?

Wait.

What was she thinking? He was supposed to marry her. Not date her.

Then why—on a regular old Monday—did her heart flutter in ways she wished she could cut off at the knees?

She didn't need any feelings confusing her. If Chase wanted to marry her, it was for the money. Which was fine. Because that's what she proposed. Right?

"Lexi?" Chase stood at the bottom of the cement steps. A booted foot with faded jeans rested on the second step. One hand on the metal railing. Her gaze followed the sleeves of his starched long-sleeved navy shirt to find his freshly shaven, perplexed face.

"You look nice," she blurted, then covered her mouth in horror that she'd said the words out loud.

"Calving season's not always glamorous. I had to shower and change." He grinned. "You should have seen me half an hour ago. We for sure wouldn't have gotten along for ten minutes."

"And the clean shave?"

He scratched the side of his cheek. "I'm hoping for fifteen minutes, so I went fancy."

She laughed.

Behind her, Frank cleared his throat. She whirled around. "Frank. Thank you so much for your help. Again, I apologize for the mix-up."

Frank crossed his arms. "We still have a problem," he said, irritation in his tone. Chase looked at Frank, and Frank explained. "The fertilizer order got messed up." His eyes slid to Lexi.

"I know. I apologize. I—" she stammered "—I will fix this."

"By tomorrow morning?" Frank asked, his

tone insinuating that he clearly didn't think she could. "We hired extra hands to help us get the fertilizer in. If we don't stay on schedule, it will decrease our hay production. Time is not on our side."

She couldn't blame him for his frustration. She had no idea how to solve this. "No. I can't get a delivery tomorrow."

Chase looked at her. "Is this the—"

"Yes." She sighed and closed her eyes. A second later she found her courage and looked directly at him. "This is the cheaper fertilizer company you warned me about. The one you said was poorly run."

To his credit, his face remained relatively blank, but something worked behind his eyes. They stared each other down, Lexi bracing for the reprimand she knew was coming, Chase probably calculating just how quickly he could fire her and cancel their marriage agreement.

Instead, he surprised her with his calm demeanor. "How soon until the new order comes in?"

"Next week." She didn't know much about farming the land, but she knew if her decision to save on fertilizer caused problems with their hay production, they would have to supplement with feed for the cattle. An unexpected budget item.

He pulled his phone out of his back pocket and sent a text. While they waited, he looked at her and winked.

Lexi stood frozen, trying to ignore the butterflies in her belly. My, he was handsome.

But the wink was different. Some men winked so often that it was part of their vocabulary. But not Chase. She'd never seen him do this before, and the gesture was something personal between the two of them as if it were their secret language.

No. She was not going to be able to ignore the fluttering in her belly.

A soft ping alerted Chase to a response. He looked at the screen, nodded and shot off a second text. When he slid his phone back into his pocket, he said, "Thank you, Frank, for your help. The Hendersons have enough fertilizer to help us out the next few days. We won't miss a beat. I'll head out and bring it back up here."

"You want me to do it, boss?" Frank asked.

"No. You're already working on your day off." Chase looked out over the property. "You've got to pace yourself during calving season. Go grab yourself some grub from the chow hall before your next round to check on the cattle."

Once Frank said his goodbye, Lexi clasped her hands and looked at Chase. "I guess I botched your dinner."

Chase raised his eyebrows. "Why is that?"

"Well—" she shifted from one foot to the other "—you're going to have to get the fertilizer."

"Yes. Which has just become Phase One of your Official Four Cross Ranch Orientation." The side of his mouth hitched in a small grin, and he cocked his elbow and offered it to her.

She couldn't help the giggle that bubbled out of her. She eyed him, then tentatively hooked her arm through his. "Phase One, huh?"

"Yes, ma'am." He led them toward the parking lot.

"Even though I used the fertilizer company you warned me about?"

He stopped. The look on his face caught her off guard. His hazel eyes turned serious. Sincere. "I'm starting to understand, Lexi, that our disagreements about budget items aren't because you don't understand ranch life or that you want to argue for the sake of winning a debate. But because you really want what's best for our property."

"I want you to get what you want, Chase," she said quietly. "I want Four Cross Hope up and fully functional."

He studied her. "I know."

Once they started walking again, she asked, "Did my fertilizer mistake ruin our ten-minute streak of getting along?"

A muscle in his cheek twitched and a glint of humor hit his eyes. "Not at all. The ten minutes hasn't technically started yet."

A soft breeze crossed their path. She wasn't sure what was happening, but something was shifting ever so slightly with the two of them. "Well, that's good. Because after hauling all of that fertilizer, I think I smell like a barn."

"You smell like the outdoors," he said in a low voice, "with a touch of wildflower."

Her belly fluttered again, and she shook her head. "Yesterday went well. Today, you're complimenting me. I'm not sure how to act if we're actually going to get along."

"If it gets too awkward, I can strike up an argument to put us both at ease."

She chuckled. "Listen, I'm sorry I wasn't here to meet the Forresters."

"It's okay. They got settled in. You'll get to meet them later." He veered them toward the ranch company truck and opened the passenger door for her. "How did work go for you today?"

"I might have picked up my phone to make a call and instead of putting the phone number into the phone app, I tapped it into the calculator app."

Chase threw his head back and laughed. It was hearty and full. And for just a few seconds, she got caught in the beauty of it.

Flutters again. Maybe she just needed to stop looking at him altogether.

After opening the door for her, he walked around the truck, hopped in and secured his seat belt. He turned on the ignition and threw his arm around the back of the seat to look behind them, his fingers grazing her hair in the process. But he froze, his attention caught on something at Lexi's feet.

When she looked down, she gasped. She'd completely forgotten she'd shoved her jeans into her boots and pulled her socks over them and up to her knees. "I'm so embarrassed," she murmured. "I was trying not to get my jeans dusty when we were hauling in the delivery. I stretched my socks over them as far as they'd go." Not knowing if she'd have time to change, she'd tried to preserve her jeans, even if she had to sacrifice her favorite socks.

She reached down to her boots, but Chase stopped her hand.

"Do your socks have a message written on them?" he asked.

She grinned, pulled the boot off her foot and angled her calf so he could see.

He read the words out loud. "'You are courageous.'"

Quickly, she pulled her jeans out of her sock, yanked the boot back on and straightened her jeans over the boot. She repeated the process for the other foot, feeling ridiculous.

He placed a hand on her arm, a playful tone in his voice. "Do all your socks have messages on them?"

"Maybe."

A small smile ticked at the sides of his mouth as he threw the truck in Reverse. While backing out, he said, "I need to know what your other socks say."

She giggled. "Why?"

"I don't know." With humor in his voice, he turned onto the country road. "All of a sudden, finding out your sock secrets has become a priority in my life."

"We'll just have to see how it goes for you."

Eight flats of fertilizer later, Chase and Lexi returned to the ranch and drove down to the storage barn.

"How can I help?" Lexi asked, looking at the giant fertilizer bags. No way she could lift one of those on her own.

Chase hefted one of the bags over his shoulder. "You can tell me what yesterday's socks said."

She crossed her arms in feigned defense. "Nice try."

"I'll take care of this. Why don't you go down to the chow hall and grab some dinner. I'll be there shortly."

With a nod, she turned on her boot and headed across the ranch. When she arrived at the door to the chow hall, her phone buzzed with an incoming text. It was from Chase.

Nate Forrester called. Problem with the master suite toilet leaking at the lodge. I want to fix it while they're out to dinner. I'll finish up here, check out the problem at the lodge, then head to the chow hall.

She immediately texted him back.

No worries. I'll go look at the toilet.

Three dots showed on her phone, indicating he was replying, but she shoved her phone in her back pocket before he could send a response. She was already on her way. She could fix a toilet with the best of them.

The xeriscape plants on the porch of the lodge tied the building to the surrounding fields. Instead of looking out of place on the beautiful land, the wood-and-stone house appeared to grow from the valley itself, as if a haven. A secret shelter at the foot of the mountains.

After grabbing a plunger and a toolbox from the maintenance closet, Lexi headed to the problem.

In the bathroom, Lexi was assessing the situation when her phone pinged with an incoming text that she ignored. She pulled a wrench out of the red metal box and got to work.

Moments later, Chase entered the master suite and approached the en suite bathroom. "You're working on the toilet? I texted and told you I'd handle it." His surprised and almost exasperated tone threw her off guard.

She turned to him and used the back of her

wrist to edge a lock of hair off her forehead. "I can do it."

He stood in the door frame, hands splayed on his hips, face perplexed. "I figured you for a call-the-plumber type."

She arched an eyebrow at him.

"Never mind." He swiped a hand through the air as if to erase his statement. "Gardner Economics would never let you hire someone to solve something you already know how to do."

"Plus, these pipes are new. I just figured the problem would be simple to fix. All I had to do was turn the wrench a few times to tighten the joint."

He shook his head as if her answer wasn't good enough. "But why would you volunteer? This is not a pleasant job."

Taking a moment to gather her thoughts, she washed her hands and dried them. She turned to him, crossed her arms over her chest and leaned a hip into the sink counter. "Chase. This is your life. It's also about to be mine. I want to help."

His eyes softened, and the room fell silent for a few seconds. Finally, he took a breath and nodded. "Okay. I get it."

"You do?"

"Yes." He scrubbed a hand down his face. "But I'm still worried about something."

"What's that?"

"So far, Phase One of Four Cross Ranch Orientation has involved a lot of manual labor." A sparkle hit his eyes. "I've got to up my game."

She giggled and shook her head. "You're original, I'll give you that."

"Hand me the plunger and toolbox and then we'll head out for dinner at the chow hall."

They exited the room. Once they stowed the plunger and tools away, they left through the front door of the lodge.

It felt good to be by Chase's side, to work together with him. Show him a little of who she was.

But the closeness also gave her pause. Lexi could no longer ignore what she knew to be true.

Her heart was in serious trouble.

WALKING AWAY FROM the lodge, Chase didn't know what to think about the woman next to him.

Lexi took everything in stride. She seemed to be all in. Surprising him the most was that she laughed. It was a gorgeous laugh. To top it off, he didn't know what to do with those amusing socks. He just knew everything that had happened today had done nothing but intrigue him.

And he wasn't sure how he felt about that.

Her hair was different. Long, shiny, with curls at the end. It looked soft. She looked soft tonight. Feminine. Intriguing.

There was that word again.

As they crossed the field, the sun gave his land the last bit of light. She shoved her hands in her pockets.

"Where's your coat?" he asked.

"I think I left it in your truck."

He stopped midstride and yanked off his canvas barn jacket and turned to her. Annoyed, he said, "You can't go anywhere on this property without a jacket. We might be having an abnormally warm spring, but you never know when the wind is going to pick up. This land will do a lot, but there aren't trees to block that wind when it shows up."

Her pink nose scrunched. She looked cute. And cold. "Are you upset with me?"

He held out the coat for her to slip her arms into, then turned her to him. It dwarfed her. She still looked cute. "I'm not upset," he said, pulling together the sides of the coat just under the collar. "I'm just—"

He locked his eyes with hers.

Intrigued. He was just intrigued. Heading straight toward enthralled, and he wasn't sure he wanted to go there right now.

But the next thing he knew, he was pulling her to him, slowly. Her eyes grew round, but she drew closer, placed her hands on his forearms.

He was about an inch away from kissing her. He squeezed his eyes closed and gritted his teeth. "I'm just concerned about you, Lexi," he whispered. "I don't want you to catch cold."

"Nothing's going to happen to me, Chase," she said softly.

But she couldn't guarantee that.

"Chase," a man called from behind him.

He immediately released Lexi, and she swayed, then stepped back.

Hunter was right. Chase was an idiot. What was he thinking?

Turning, he saw Nate and Harper Forrester dressed in jeans, sweatshirts and jackets walking toward them. Then he was hit with something else. After just being on the ranch for the day, the couple appeared more relaxed. Nate's military gait was almost unnoticeable, and he held his wife's hand. Harper's face looked fresh, as if a few hours on the land had given her a little bit of peace.

Chase stared at the couple. This was it. This was what he'd dreamed of giving to military personnel and their families. He wanted to take Lexi's hand in his and somehow tell her what this moment meant to him. But he didn't dare pull her close again.

Nate greeted him with a handshake.

"We got your bathroom back in full working order," Chase said. "I apologize for the inconvenience."

Lexi cleared her throat next to him and he glanced down at her. She'd pulled her lips in and to her credit was not saying a word. But her eyes danced.

"Sorry." Chase ran a hand through his hair. "Nate. Harper. This is Lexi Gardner, and she's actually the one who got your bathroom back to normal."

Harper looked to Lexi, and they both laughed.

Lexi shook their hands in greeting, aiming a megawatt smile at them, and said, "I'm so glad you're here."

"I am, too," Harper said. "We've been roaming around exploring the property today and there's something really special about this place."

"Thank you. Like I said this morning, you are our first official military guests. We hope to expand not just to more people staying at the lodge, but we have land farther out where we'd like to build individual cabins and add more recreation and emotional support options for families."

For a second, he wondered when he'd hear from the contractor. Then he worried if he'd have the money to start the project. Pressure began to build in his chest. But when he glanced at the Forresters, those details faded away. Four Cross Ranch was helping people, just like he'd dreamed it would.

Lexi beamed. She seemed to be truly proud of his place, and there was nothing to do with that but file it away with the other things he was learning and liked about her.

Harper looked between Chase and Lexi. "How do you two know each other?"

"Oh, um…" He looked over at Lexi.

She only came up with, "Well, uh…"

They stared at each other, and he realized

they probably looked like two deer caught in the headlights.

The wind swirled around them. Why couldn't he say anything? Better—what was he supposed to say? Lexi bit her lip.

Then it hit him. He turned to the Forresters and said, "She's my fiancée." When he put his arm around her, she was stiffer than a new saddle.

Nothing surprised him more than the fact that those words didn't hurt him. Those words actually sounded natural.

Harper clapped her hands and squealed. "Oh, that's so wonderful. Congratulations!"

But Nate's brow furrowed. "You made your fiancée work on the toilet? I know we're the ones here to restore our marriage, but you might want to rethink some things as well."

The group's laughter filled the field, two cows in the next pasture over even chiming in with their cattle calls.

When the chuckles died down, Harper asked, "When is the wedding?"

Without missing a beat, Lexi said, "In three weeks."

Twenty-one days until her birthday, but who was counting.

Harper looked at her husband and smiled. "You know what I have to ask them, right?"

The man nodded sagely. "We learned the hard way. I think you should."

She turned to Lexi and asked, "Have you gotten your marriage license yet?"

Reality slammed into Chase's chest.

Looking as stunned as Chase felt, Lexi said, "Oh, um…no, not yet."

Harper stepped closer to Lexi and placed her hand on Lexi's arm. "You might want to get on that soon. We rushed our wedding because of a deployment and forgot that one tiny detail that actually makes you legally married."

"Oh," Lexi said. Chase had been married before but had completely forgotten. What if they'd made it to her birthday only to ruin the entire plan because they never went to the courthouse to get their marriage license?

"It all turned out okay." Harper turned her smiling face to her husband and softened her tone. "Everything all turned out okay in the end."

Chase stepped back. "Thank you for the advice," he said. "We'll take care of that this week." At his side, Lexi stood ramrod straight, but he kept talking. "For now, you two go on down to the lodge. Enjoy a fire in the fireplace. We have s'more ingredients laid out for you on the kitchen counter."

"We saw that earlier," Harper said. "Such a nice touch. You've gone to great lengths to make us feel so welcome. And I love the throw pillow in the master bedroom."

Throw pillow?

"The one about the spurs," she said, and then it hit him. Lexi's ridiculous three-dollar pillow. "It's super cute and hilarious."

A wide smile split across Lexi's face. It was almost as bright as the few stars that had come out to twinkle in the last few minutes.

After saying their farewells for the evening, Chase looked down at Lexi. "You're going to rub this in my face, aren't you."

She aimed her smile at him, and he decided he didn't care if she did. "I'm not going to rub it in your face," she said. "But I do think I'm going to ask for full dispensation over the throw pillows in our marriage and at the lodge."

He narrowed his eyes. "I'm going to regret this, aren't I."

Something serious crossed her face, then her features softened and she whispered, "I hope not."

He pulled in a long breath, then released it,

never taking his eyes from her. He hoped she never had any regrets with him either.

"Chase?" she asked, vulnerability reflecting in her eyes.

"Right here, Lexi."

"Are we really going to get our marriage license this week?"

After a beat, he answered, "Yes."

CHAPTER SEVEN

STANDING ON THE steps of the county court-house, the idea of getting a marriage license fell with a thud to the bottom of Chase's stomach. No more musings about the intriguing sides of Lexi Gardner. No more thoughts of growing old together on the ranch with someone whose company he enjoyed. No more wondering if they could really make this bizarre situation work.

No. Standing on the steps of the courthouse with the morning Wyoming sun beating down on him only brought back flashes of Lexi's terrified face as Mildred bucked her. And the fear that saturated every cell in Chase as he tried to figure out how to save her.

He just didn't know if he could make a life-long commitment to another woman. What if tragedy fell on Lexi the way it came to his wife?

He wiped his hands on his jeans. He'd worn his good pair for the occasion.

Lexi stepped closer and lowered her voice. "You okay?"

He glanced at her and found her eyes held the same anxiety he felt. "Yeah. You?"

"I'm fine," she said, her entire body stilted. Delicate stitched flowers lined the sleeves and neck of her flowing white shirt. Her jean skirt hit her at the knees. And what he now deemed as her fancy boots completed the ensemble. She wore her hair down today in soft curls. He didn't know if she did any of this for him, but she sure looked beautiful.

Stilted. And beautiful.

They stood side by side and stared at the tall glass doors of the courthouse.

"Are we both lying?" he asked without looking at her.

"Yes," she said.

Slowly, they turned their heads to each other and locked eyes. It only took two point five seconds for them to burst out laughing.

"I'm sorry." She giggled through the words and placed her hand on his arm. "I'm so nervous."

"I know." He chuckled. "I don't know why I thought this would be no big deal."

"Well…" She cleared her throat. "It isn't that big of a deal if we think of it logically. It's like you said. I have seventeen days until my birthday. If we get the marriage license now, it takes the pressure off both of us. We don't sign it until we're sure we want to get married. And—" her voice gentled "—if we decide that it isn't best to get married, we throw it away. No harm done."

"No harm done," he repeated, the depth of her brown eyes drawing him in.

But for some reason, Chase felt like there would be harm done. To which one of them, he didn't quite know.

What he did know was that over the last week, he had come to care for Lexi. Which is why he proposed they get their marriage license today. At the time, it had felt like a solid decision. Logical. Safe.

Staring at the doors of the courthouse, Chase felt anything but safe.

When the proposition to marry Lexi first came up, he was intent on her marrying someone because they treasured her. His problem now was that the more time they spent together, the more he found *himself* treasuring her. His feelings bounced between total enjoyment at being with her and the debilitating fear of ever losing her.

But worse. He couldn't reconcile considering marriage with the trust money that came with her. The closer they got to her birthday, the more he understood only a fraction of the stress Lexi had endured over this money.

He stood by their decision to get the marriage license today. Though a small gesture, it did put a dent in the pressure that continued to build to her birthday.

He took his Stetson off and placed it over his heart. "If we get married, Lexi, I promise you, it will be a sincere partnership. True friendship. I would honor you in every way that I could."

"I know, Chase," she said with quiet confidence. "It's who you are. It's why I picked you. Why I trust you."

Her trust in him almost leveled him every day. What she couldn't understand was that while she carried the burden of the trust, he carried the burden of being chosen by her. It was not something he'd ever share with her. She didn't need more weight to carry on her shoulders.

"All right," he said in all seriousness, "I just need to know one thing before we head inside."

She straightened her spine and took a deep breath. "Okay."

He narrowed his eyes, purposefully adding drama to the moment. "What do your socks say today?"

Lowering her chin just a touch, she looked up at him through her lashes and gave him a coy smile. "I'm not telling."

"What?" He feigned hurt. "We are about to get a document that could tie us together for the rest of our lives, and you can't tell me what your socks say? Today, of all days?"

Lexi laughed and shook her head. "I'll tell you on the way out of the courthouse."

He sighed a fake-exasperated sigh, truly glad that they were laughing together. With their decision feeling less burdensome, he held out his hand for her. When she put her palm in his, he led her up the stairs and to the county clerk's office.

To get a marriage license.

Because maybe they were getting married.

Or maybe they weren't.

HOLDING A MANILA envelope with an unsigned marriage license in his hand, and a whole bunch of questions in his heart, Chase walked to his truck with Lexi at his side. His phone buzzed from his back pocket. When he saw what was on the screen, he slowed his strides.

"Chase? Everything okay?" Lexi asked.

Looking up from his phone, he said, "It's Nate Forrester."

She cocked her head. "Why do you have a strange look on your face?"

He took off his hat and ran a hand through his hair. "This has been a good week for the Forresters. So good that they want to renew their vows and wondered if it was possible to do that while they're here."

Her face lit up and she grabbed his arm. Excitement rolled off her, and she bounced on her toes. "That's great news. This is exactly what you hoped the nonprofit could offer people. Rest, restoration, maybe a new beginning."

The contradictory weight of the text crashed down on him. It was such good news, but at the same time a big ask. "Lexi. They leave tomorrow. How am I going to pull this off for this evening knowing I'm needed at the ranch?" He'd checked the records last night and they still had a substantial number of heifers waiting to calve.

She mimed like she was rolling up her sleeves and shot a confident smile his way. "Then I've got my work cut out for me."

"You don't get it. It's too much. You're under deadline, too. I'm sure you have work today."

"You're the one that doesn't get it. It's too much for one person. But it's not too much for *us*." She nudged his side with her elbow. "Besides, I'll work after the reception. This won't be the first all-nighter I've pulled during tax season."

His entire body blanched. "Reception? I didn't even think of that. Do they need a reception, too?"

She threw her head back and laughed. "Chase, what were you going to do? Renew their vows on the porch tomorrow morning while they're packing their car?" She tugged on his arm. "This is special. And I know how to help pull this off."

They locked eyes, and he couldn't seem to stop staring. She held him captivated.

Gently, she leaned her weight into his side and asked, "Do you trust me?"

He'd never felt like he and Lexi made a good team before. But right now, with her pressed against him, hope filling her eyes, he'd sign over his best bull to her if she asked.

"All right." He put his arm through hers. "Lead the way."

EIGHT HOURS LATER, Chase found himself outside of the chow hall wrestling a necktie. He'd rather be out wrestling a cow, but he felt drawn to the Forresters' vow renewal. The more he thought about it today, the more he dreamed of plans for Four Cross Hope. What else could God do on his land for military families?

Standing next to him, Lexi asked, "Can I put you out of your misery and help you with that?"

"I basically left everything else to you today. You'd think the least I could do was dress myself."

She stepped toward him, and he offered her the mangled black fabric that hung around his neck. "It wasn't hard," she said. "Harper found a dress in town, and the pastor was available. The ranch cook easily made tonight's barbecue dinner for a slightly larger crowd. I just put a few things together for the reception. Today actually gave me some great ideas for the nonprofit."

"Does that mean we're going to be arguing about purchasing budgets soon?"

"Well—" she glanced from the tie to him "—we're due a good disagreement. This week has thrown me off."

He couldn't agree more.

The abysmal knot he'd created with the fabric gave her a hard time. The same way her delicate wildflower perfume wreaked havoc with his senses. Why did her hair seem glossier tonight? And why did he notice that her hair seemed glossier? Probably because of the Kelly green sweaterdress she was wearing.

Her first attempt at the tie failed.

He lowered his chin to look at her, bringing their faces dangerously close. "I don't think you're doing much better with my tie than I was," he murmured.

She blinked and shook her head. "Anything's better than the noose you created," she said, getting back on task.

Good. He should get back on task, too. He couldn't be thinking this way about her.

When she finished with the tie, she patted him twice on the chest. "When you walk in, you'll see that we split the room into two halves. The ceremony on the left with the awning and chairs, and the reception on the right with the tables. The Forresters asked us to sit in the front row, either side, for the ceremony."

He studied her face. "You look pretty tonight, Lexi," he said softly.

Okay. Apparently, he *was* going to think this way about her.

A light blush hit her cheeks. "You clean up real well yourself, cowboy."

He nodded, having no clue what to say. He might have put on a nice shirt and tie with his jeans and boots for the vow renewal, but he certainly didn't hold a candle to her glow tonight.

When he entered the chow hall, he couldn't believe the transformation. The room was usually completely utilitarian, full of unadorned tables and chairs to feed the staff on the ranch. Tonight, it was transformed with fabric-covered chairs, tablecloths, tiny candles, and flower arrangements. He'd have to ask Lexi where she got all of this stuff.

A few minutes later, with the Forresters' best friends who'd driven three hours from Denver, the ranch staff, the Stimpsons, a few families from town, Hunter, and Chase and Lexi looking on, pastor Beckett Gentry officiated Nate and Harper Forrester's recommitment to each other.

Chase never considered himself a fan of weddings. But this moment felt a little bit sweet and a whole lot significant. He knew the pressure that came with keeping a military marriage together. By the grace of God, his marriage with

Laura took hold. And by the grace of God, Nate and Harper seemed stronger than ever.

Which gave Chase an odd thought. Would God grant someone even more grace to hold a second marriage together?

But this kind of thinking would only lead him somewhere he didn't want to return to in his lifetime. Loving another woman.

Losing one spouse was enough. Lexi might not be the quiet adventurer that his wife was, but that didn't mean marriage to Lexi would come without risk. God only knew the number of days anyone had. He'd learned that the hard way. In the most ironic turn of events, instead of Chase losing his life while serving his country on deployment, his wife had died right here on a Wyoming mountain.

No. He might be getting married a second time, but he wouldn't be trusting God with his love for another woman again.

ONCE ON THE floor of the chow hall, all thoughts of Lexi went out the window. It was strictly survival mode. Helping with food service on the buffet line and keeping up with small talk was about all he could muster after the day he'd had in the pastures.

Lexi, on the other hand, worked the room as if she was the perfect hostess, gliding between tables and gifting people with easy laughter.

Chase cringed inwardly as he tried to charm the guests. He was never good with people. He was dependable. Consistent. He was the man to get the job done. But he was not a people person.

He glanced at Lexi, who effortlessly served their guests with a genuine smile and interest in their short conversations.

Something hit him in the chest.

She balanced him. Her strengths filled the gaps of his weaknesses. He rubbed the spot over his heart, but the tightness wouldn't go away.

Commotion from the kitchen broke him out of his thoughts.

Three people flanked a three-tier cake as they walked through the swinging kitchen door. Its simplicity gave it beauty. Cream-colored icing with delicate polka dots covered the layers, and a row of beaded icing that looked like a pearl necklace circled the base of each tier. Four tall, skinny gold candles stood at the top, their flames sparking and illuminating the servers' smiles as they carefully walked toward the Forresters' table.

How in the world Lexi pulled that cake off, he could not imagine.

Adrianna, the kitchen hand farthest from him, announced, "Four Cross Ranch would like to give a warm congratulations to Mr. and Mrs. Forrester on their happy occasion."

Everyone clapped their well-wishes. A few offered cheers and whistles.

Chase scanned the room and found Lexi a few feet from the couple. When he caught her gaze, he grinned. She nodded in kind, a sweet smile on her lips.

But she broke their connection, glanced in front of her, and a look of horror morphed across her face.

When Chase followed her line of sight, he watched helplessly as one of the servers carrying the cake caught her hip on the edge of a chair and thrust the cake off-balance. Almost as if in slow motion, the top layer slid, its weight dragging the rest of the cake off the plate like a tugboat.

Right into Nate Forrester's lap.

Collectively, everyone froze. Gasps popped throughout the room. Harper covered her mouth with both of her hands. Lexi stood stock-still, the color draining from her face.

But Chase took charge.

He approached the three cake servers, the one who got caught on the chair on the verge of tears. In a calm voice, he said, "Why don't the three of you head to the kitchen and grab supplies to help clean this up."

They nodded in unison and scurried away.

"Nate." Chase turned to the wife. "Harper. I'm sincerely sorry."

Slowly, Harper's hands drew down from her mouth and revealed a huge smile. She burst out laughing. "I'm not," she said, waving her hand in front of her face, her words almost unintelligible because of her cackling. "That was one of the funniest things I've ever seen."

A few guests allowed their shoulders to shake and looked sheepishly around at each other. Several others started chuckling.

Contagious, the humor spread through the room in waves of murmurs and laughter.

The pit in Chase's stomach loosened a little.

Nate appeared put-out. He tilted his head to the side and looked at his wife, shaking his head. "I'm so glad this is entertaining you."

"I've got to get a picture of you like this to send to your platoon," his wife replied. She cracked herself up with her own comment and laughed harder.

Barely noticeable, Nate's lips tipped at the end while he continued to shake his head.

Lexi's panicked gaze darted from person to person across the room.

One of the servers brought white utilitarian kitchen towels and a small trash can. "One of the towels is dry, and one is wet with water in case that helps," she murmured.

Lexi may kill him for what he was about to do, but Chase thought it was the right thing under the circumstances.

"Nate, again, I apologize. I'd like to help in any way I can. We'll arrange and pay for dry cleaning."

"That's not necessary," Nate said with a resigned shrug and good-natured smile. "It's just a little sugar, flour and eggs."

Chase couldn't read Lexi's face. But she snapped to the situation and stepped forward. "Harper, I'll have a special dessert delivery brought to the ranch as soon as possible. Could we invite everyone to the dance floor while we wait?"

Two guests murmured jokes of spilling your cake and eating it too while they headed for the open dance space. Nate and Harper excused themselves to get Nate cleaned up and into a new set of clothes while Chase pitched in to change the linens of the table and switch out Nate's chair.

Lexi excused herself and made a call.

Chase didn't know what she had up her sleeve.

He went to the kitchen to clean up, mingled with a few guests, then headed to the buffet tables and put two plates of food together for Lexi and himself. She had to be as starving as he was by now.

Twenty minutes later, Lexi backed into the swinging kitchen door with a giant smile of pride and satisfaction on her face. "One gorgeous German chocolate cake has just been delivered to the chow hall and is being cut as I stand here and breathe."

He shook his head at her. "You're going to have to explain how that happened, but first—" he nodded to the plates in his hands "—I'm headed out to the back deck. Come with me and we'll finally eat."

The large wooden porch held six sturdy metal chairs where they sat down to enjoy their food.

After Chase handed Lexi a plate, napkin and utensils, they ate in companionable silence.

Music floated through mounted speakers. A country singer crooned about love, and Chase looked at Lexi.

He wiped his fingers and his mouth with his napkin, stood and offered her a hand. "Dance with me."

Her mouth parted, soft surprise in her eyes.

"Come on," he said. "Fertilizer, plumbing repairs, unexpected event planning and cake disasters are a lot to ask of one woman over the course of a week. But maybe I can make it up to you with a dance."

The corner of her mouth lifted, and she nodded.

He held out his left hand for her to place hers and wrapped his other arm around her waist. She fit perfectly, and he didn't know how he felt about that. He had held another woman once who fit perfectly.

"Thank you for dinner," she said. "It was right up my alley with Gardner Economics because it was free."

Her tone told him she was trying to make a joke, but he stopped their movement and looked directly into her eyes. "Lexi. You're worth paying full price."

Surprise crossed her face, and she looked to the ground.

He didn't mean to make her uncomfortable. He didn't exactly know why he said what he did, except it continued to bother him that she seemed to consistently settle for less than she deserved.

"How in the world did you pull off that chocolate cake?" he asked as he shifted his feet for them to continue swaying.

"The baker in town, Alison Velasquez, is a client who lets me sample her yummy desserts. Lately, she's been testing her cakes. I knew she had two extras as of yesterday and called her. The first one was the disaster cake. The second one was the German chocolate cake. When she heard about the cause, she gave us a steep discount and free delivery herself."

His lips twitched. "And what is this in exchange for, oh President of the Gardner Economics Club?"

"Nothing, really. I found a tax exemption that saved her a lot of money this year. She said she was grateful."

He shook his head and locked gazes with her. "You're one of a kind, Lexi Gardner."

"Me? You're the one who dealt with the cake

disaster. I was in such a panic." She released her hold on his hand and clutched her chest. "You kept your head and dealt with the entire situation."

"I thought you'd be mad at me for offering free dry cleaning."

"Sometimes spending is about calculating the degree of need." She swallowed and set her hand back in his. "But it can also be about doing the right thing. You were good in that crisis, Chase. I froze, but you were the real hero."

"I don't see it that way. You've spent the entire day and night adjusting and helping the Forresters at every turn."

She shrugged. "It was all hands on deck."

He squeezed her waist and deadpanned. "I'm an army man, ma'am."

"Sorry," she said on a giggle. "Whatever the case, your nonprofit is about to really come alive, Chase. This week went so well with the Forresters."

He drew back from her and studied her face. "You really believe in what I'm doing here, don't you."

"I do," she said without hesitation. Without

qualifiers. Without scolding him about the budget issues. Her answer was honest at its core.

Somewhere in the evening, he'd gotten lost.

He thought he knew what tonight was going to be about. They'd host a small ceremony and reception and call it a night.

Instead, he saw Lexi's work ethic, quick humor and her unexpected beauty.

He and Lexi worked well together. As if they were a team. As if tonight was orchestrated for them to navigate.

Together. He and Lexi.

LEXI NEEDED TO guide them out of this moment because she felt a pull toward Chase that had nothing to do with an innocent dance or a marriage of convenience. She guided them back inside.

"I mentioned earlier that I have some ideas for the ranch."

He blinked, his brow drawing down. "Yes?"

"Well. When we visited Bright Horizons, Mrs. Harding told me she married off the last of her four daughters and didn't know what to do with the centerpieces because she didn't need them anymore. So I had already made arrangements to pick up those supplies before this vow renewal had even come up."

Chase looked down at her and cocked an eyebrow.

"They're perfect." Lexi walked over to one of the empty tables and pulled the clear, round vase toward them. "We can save all of these items for future events. The vases are classic. The smooth river rocks are a wonderful tie-in to the land around us. We fill the vases with the rocks and then use foliage, flowers, flags, beads, ribbons or whatever someone comes up with to decorate however we want. You can use anything, really, depending on the event theme. And it's all free."

"Where are you going with this?"

"Chase—" she put her hand on his arm "—the Forresters won't be the only couple who wants to renew their vows to each other. My understanding is that the chow hall isn't in use all the time. We could use it as a multipurpose area."

Understanding dawned on him, and his face took on a look of wonder.

"Or maybe we have birthday parties or holiday celebrations. Festivals and carnivals. We'll get a storage closet and keep all of this stuff."

She held her hand out to the chow hall. "And then I can bargain shop for more decor along the way. Maybe trade with local artisans for their work to use at events. The possibilities are endless, really. The event closet can grow with the nonprofit."

"You've outdone yourself," Chase said in a tone that made Lexi feel both giddy and proud.

But then she thought of her recent financial decision for the ranch that wasn't free, and tension tightened in her shoulders. Especially since she had yet to tell Chase. She tried to rub the pain out of the muscle.

"Hey," Chase said, concern lining his eyes. "You okay?"

"Well, I suppose I should just come clean." She huffed out a long breath. "I called the builder. The one you targeted to contract for the new cabins for the veterans."

Chase crossed his arms and nodded.

"Originally, we had him slated to start early next year, and I was checking to see when he needed the deposit. But he shared that he recently bought out his competitor, which means he has more manpower, which means—"

"He can start sooner."

"Yes."

Chase rubbed his chin, now slightly darkened with a five-o'clock shadow. "But we don't have the funds."

"Not exactly. We can come up with the deposit for him to start."

"But…"

"But paying him is contingent upon other things." Things like a solid yield from their crops of hay. Avoiding unexpected repairs on ranch property. And maybe a marriage that would open a trust fund.

He stayed completely still but narrowed his eyes. "What did you tell him?"

As if someone turned a crank on a machine, the muscles in her shoulders tightened one notch higher. Her dry mouth wouldn't let her say anything. There were two parts of her at war. The accountant in her yelled warnings, and her heart yelled back a reply to take her worries elsewhere.

"Lexi. What did you tell him?"

She slid her eyes to the side. "I told him to come on Monday to get the lay of the land and that I'd set up a meeting with you."

Three long beats later, Chase threw his head back and laughed.

"What's so funny?"

He leveled his eyes on her. "Since my accountant made a risky choice, is this a good time to tell my accountant that *I* did something *she* won't approve of?"

"Have at it."

"I booked rooms at the lodge for next week. A veteran's family of four. Everyone in need of rest and recuperation." He cringed almost apologetically. "They arrive in two days."

"We can get the rooms ready in two days." But that meant that he was going to pay their expenses so they wouldn't have to worry about the cost of their room, board and recreation. Lexi pictured numbers on an antique cash register spinning higher and higher.

If the ranch was not only going to absorb the cost, but not profit from those accommodations, this was a problem. Especially after booking the builder.

Once again, her heart yelled louder than the accountant in her. Chase was talking about real people, in need, without resources.

They would simply have to find another way to get additional funding.

Stress that felt like an ice pick now stabbed her shoulders.

Or.

Chase and Lexi would really get married, and these mounting financial obligations wouldn't be a problem.

Chase ran a hand over his face, uncertainty behind his eyes that now looked tired. She couldn't be sure, but he must be having similar thoughts to hers.

Carrying a piece of wedding cake, Hunter sauntered toward them. "Congratulations to the bride and groom," he said.

Her entire body locked tight, and Chase seemed to freeze in place. Chase told her he hadn't shared with anyone that they went to get their marriage license today. Neither had she.

Hunter's eyes darted between the two of them. "I meant the Forresters, seeing as how I'm eating a piece of their wedding cake. But is there something you two need to share?"

Chase cleared his throat and shifted his stance, a picture of discomfort. "No. Nothing. Nothing to share."

Without saying a word, Hunter shoveled cake into his mouth. His piercing eyes held Lexi's. Once he swallowed, he asked, "How are you feeling, Lexi? Any pain or soreness still lingering after the incident with Mildred and the snake?"

Hunter's question turned his brother into a statue. Chase's eyes glazed over with a hint of fear, and it looked like his breathing had shallowed.

"I'm fine. That seems forever ago," she said to Hunter, though she stared at Chase. "Perfectly fine."

"That's good to hear." Hunter sent a keen look at his brother, then crammed the other half of the piece of cake into his mouth. With a nod to both of them, he walked away.

Not for the first time, Lexi wondered what kind of woman would catch Hunter's heart.

When she turned to Chase, he was in the same pose.

"Chase." Lexi placed a hand on his arm and quieted her voice. "I really am fine. You know that. It happened days ago." She squeezed.

He looked down at her, something fierce warring behind his eyes. "I do," he said, his voice gruff. "But it could have been different."

It could have. It could have been different, like his wife.

She knew. Oh, how she knew. The day after the snake incident, she sat alone in the Four Cross lodge and stared at the picture of Laura. Lexi didn't know why she did it. Maybe she was looking for the woman in the picture to talk back to her. To tell her how to get Chase past his fear.

But that wasn't logical. If her reputation was accurate, Laura was fearless, not reckless. But not afraid to take risks others would not. She was the reason for all of his fears.

Lexi looked at Chase and said the most distracting thing she could think of to pull him out of his dark place. "I completely forgot to tell you what my socks say today."

One slow blink, then a spark in his eyes. "You're right. What do your socks say today?"

Her face heated, and she just knew she was blushing. She leaned her weight into his arm and whispered, "My socks are white with pink letters that say 'Bride.'"

His entire body jerked. He blinked again, this time as if he were perplexed. Or confused. Maybe angry? "Bride?"

She placed her hand on her collarbone and stepped back, mortification spreading through her. "I'm sorry. I thought—" she shook her head "—I thought it would be funny. Because we got the papers today for the marriage license. I mean, we aren't married until we sign them, but technically I'm the…" her voice trailed off along with her confidence "…bride."

"Sure." He paused, sounding unsure, then nodded. "Sure. Absolutely. Bride."

Now both her heart and her inner accountant were yelling at her. Along with her brain and ego. She'd made a misstep in sharing that information with him, especially after Hunter's question had reminded Chase of the horse incident. She had to redirect. Now.

"Um, why don't we go say hello to the Stimpsons?" she asked.

"Sure," he mumbled. "I have to talk to the foreman first. Go on without me, and I'll join you in a minute."

Before Lexi could answer, Chase bolted across the room. Her emotions deflated.

Chase had darted from her faster than one of his horses. Why did it feel like her groom was running away?

And why did she feel like she got married today without actually getting married?

They'd gone to the courthouse for a marriage license only to come back to the ranch for someone else's wedding and reception. Everything felt a little real.

Lexi knew she picked her favorite white shirt

to go to the courthouse because it made her feel pretty.

Also, because it was white.

Chase showing up with a clean shave, pressed jeans and a blue shirt that set off his eyes didn't help.

But tonight, he looked even more handsome.

As she watched Chase across the room, she prayed he would forget about her socks. Forget about Hunter's ill-timed reminder. Forget about the pain his wife's death caused him.

Because she had a problem.

If we get married, Lexi, I promise you, it would be a sincere partnership. True friendship. I would honor you in every way that I could.

What if she no longer wanted a nice partnership with Chase?

What if she wanted something real with the cowboy veteran?

He couldn't give that to her.

Not only that, she was starting to wonder if she shouldn't ask him to give her a platonic marriage.

She cared for him. She cared for him in a way that she didn't know if she should ask him to do something he said he would never do again.

Yes, she had a problem.

The only way to move forward was to do the one thing she promised him she would do, which was to help the nonprofit. She would spend the next two days getting ready for their new guests and hope her feelings leveled out.

CHAPTER EIGHT

CHASE STOOD ON the far side of his property with the weight of his body leaned into his forearms atop the brown wooden fence.

It didn't matter that he'd checked in a family of four earlier this week. Or that, even if the bid for building the cabins took his breath away, his time talking with the contractor gave him new vigor for the nonprofit. Today was different. Today, clouds dimmed the morning with a shadow of sorrow.

The smell of grass, manure and a hint of something that could only be described as Wyoming sat with him.

His hat hung low on his face. Maybe it'd hide the tears that streamed down his cheeks.

Once a year.

Once a year, he allowed himself to cry over his wife's death.

With his eyes locked on the Snowy Range,

he shook his head. Every day, Medicine Bow Peak dared to show its face to him. It seemed especially cruel today. It had taken Laura from him.

He'd never understood her sense of adventure. It seemed out of control. Unnecessary. The military had forced him to live a life full of risk. But he never took risks for fun.

Laura thrived on danger.

She'd been younger than him by eight years and chasing a dream to ski in the Olympics. They'd put off having kids for that reason. When he'd left for his last deployment, they both knew she'd never compete at the top level. They both knew he'd come home, and they'd finally start a family.

But the mountain took her.

Something Chase couldn't fathom God allowing. The Almighty could move mountains. But He couldn't move this one? He couldn't simply allow them to start their family?

Chase groaned something guttural. He knew God was trustworthy. Sometimes he just didn't understand exactly what he was trusting.

"At least you died doing something you loved, Laura," his raspy voice whispered to the mountain.

An eagle soared into his vision, but Chase didn't break his line of sight from the snowy peak.

He heard the heavy crunch of grass behind him. Knew who it would be without looking. Using his coat sleeve, he wiped away any remnants of his grief.

The smell of strong coffee hit him before his brother edged into view. Hunter handed him a cup and kept a second mug for himself.

The brothers stood in an identical pose, weight forward into the fence, cups between their hands. Steam rose from their drinks and disappeared into the air.

"Five years," Hunter said.

Chase grunted.

"That mountain move yet?"

"Excuse me?" Chase asked, not breaking his focus.

"You've been standing out here awhile in the same position. I figure you're waiting for that mountain to move."

"Maybe I am." He lifted the hot coffee and took a swig, ignoring the burn as it went down. "Maybe I am."

Without warning, Hunter said, "Your mother-in-law is here."

The coffee Chase just drank got stuck in his throat. He coughed, the hot liquid punishing him while he tried to swallow it down.

Hunter pounded Chase's back but remained facing forward.

When Chase's throat had mostly recovered, he clarified. "Laura's mother is here?"

"I left her at the lodge with some coffee. Told her I'd come get you."

When Chase was married, he wasn't in country long enough to be close with his mother-in-law. But on the occasions they were together, they had a playful banter he enjoyed. A mutual respect because of the woman in common who they loved.

He had no clue why she would show up unannounced.

"She have a reason?" he asked.

"No."

Even though he knew he should move, the mountain held his gaze. Somewhere deep inside, Chase wanted something from this mountain. Normally, he figured he just wanted answers from God. But this year was different. He just didn't understand what about it was different.

Hunter looked down at his boots and scuffed

a toe once on the ground. "I can cover for you if you want."

"No." Chase scrubbed a hand down his face and pulled off the fence. "I'll go."

But as he turned, something churned in his gut. He glanced back to the spot where he imagined he lost his wife.

What do you want from me? he internally asked the mountain. Maybe he was asking his wife. Maybe God.

Hunter walked to the lodge by Chase's side in silence. When they arrived, he asked, "Want me to go with you?"

Chase gave Hunter a hearty pat on the shoulder. "No. Thanks, though."

When Chase walked into the dining room, he spotted Barbara. Petite, strawberry blond hair and a pert nose, she looked just like her daughter. The years had been kind to Barbara, though he'd always thought Laura's death robbed her of her vitality. Impeccably dressed, as always, in slacks and a silk shirt, she sipped from a coffee mug, her head held high. But from where he stood, Chase could see the dark circles under her eyes.

When she spotted him, a smile broke over her face although the familiar sparkle in her eyes seemed dimmer. Laura used to have that same sparkle.

His boots felt cemented to the ground, but he forced himself to pick his feet up and move toward her.

She rose to greet him.

But after a few heavy steps, he heard his name called behind him. When he turned, he froze.

"Hi there."

His entire body locked tight.

Lexi.

Lexi, who wore her hair down today and smelled like wildflowers. Lexi, who had asked him to marry her.

Lexi, who didn't know Chase was meeting his mother-in-law.

She smiled expectantly at him.

Chase wanted to hop on a train with a one-way ticket out of Wyoming. He cleared his throat. *Keep it simple. Professional.* "Hi, Lexi. What brings you to Four Cross Ranch today?"

At his side, he felt Barbara's presence, but he didn't dare look at her. Maybe he could move Lexi along quickly.

Lexi glanced at Barbara, then back to him. From her large purse, she pulled out something wrapped in a grocery bag. "You mentioned that the family staying here needed diaper wipes."

Barbara held her hand out to Lexi. "I'm Barbara Hartwell."

Returning the greeting, Lexi introduced herself. "What brings you to the ranch today, Ms. Hartwell?"

"I'm Chase's mother-in-law," she said proudly. But her next words were more subdued. "Today is the fifth anniversary of my daughter's death. Chase's wife."

The color drained out of Lexi's face. "I'm so very sorry for your loss." She shook her head as if she was trying to shake away the pain of the moment. "I'm sorry to say that I never met Laura. But I've heard many wonderful things about her."

"She was a quiet soul, but a force to be reckoned with." Barbara looped her arm around Chase's and leaned in. "I was thrilled when she married Chase. He was the perfect match for her, and she was the perfect match for him."

Lexi's pallor turned ashen.

"I don't remember a time when you two argued." His mother-in-law looked up at him, her watery gaze reaching back five years. "You two were made for each other. That kind of match only comes once in a lifetime."

Chase didn't miss how Lexi took a step back, holding the grocery package to her chest as if it were a shield.

"How do you two know each other?" Barbara asked him.

The question zinged around the room on a boomerang of anxiety.

Lexi works for me. She pushes all my buttons. She asked me to marry her. She's the first person who forces me to consider that there might be more for me in this life. Chase stood frozen in the tension of Barbara's question and didn't like it one bit.

Lexi's eyes darted between Chase and Barbara. She cleared her throat, but her voice still croaked. "I'm an accountant and do some work for the ranch." She took another step back and started talking faster. "I can see you're busy, Chase. I'll just leave these here on the counter." Another step backward, this time she caught her hip on the edge of the island. When she righted, she said, "It was so nice to meet you, Ms. Hartwell. Again, I'm sorry for your loss."

Before Chase could figure out how to smooth over the situation, Lexi was gone, and Barbara stared up at him with questions in her eyes.

The problem was, Chase probably had the same questions. But he didn't have a clue how to answer them.

LEXI TORE THROUGH the lodge hallway praying that the tears would stay at bay.

That kind of match only comes once in a lifetime.

She hightailed it to her car.

That kind of match only comes once in a lifetime.

After turning the key to her ignition with more force than necessary, she hauled off the ranch property without looking back.

On the country roads, her hands shook. Her breath came unevenly. And her nose stung.

Soon her vision would blur, and it wouldn't be safe to drive.

She pulled over to a scenic overpass designated for sightseers. After parking, she looked across the rolling hills of prairie, all leading to the foothills of a mountain.

Staring at the mountain, tears began to leak out of her eyes.

"How could I have been so stupid?" she whispered to the white peak.

With no one to tell her she was wrong, she continued to heap judgment on herself. "He loved his wife. Of course he would never marry again. He and Laura never argued. They were perfect for each other. He still holds on to her through his mother-in-law."

Her face heated and the tears came faster. "He didn't dispute anything she said."

That kind of match only comes once in a lifetime.

It never came in Lexi's lifetime.

A sob rose in her throat, and she felt like it was choking her.

She could not take her eyes off the mountain. "Lord. How could I have gotten everything so wrong? How could I have picked so poorly? Three times now."

But she didn't think she picked poorly with Chase. His heart was just with another. How could she ask him to marry again when he didn't want that for himself?

A question rose from the depth of her soul. One she'd known was there, but one that she didn't have the courage to ask. With her heartache releasing into the quiet space of her car, she whispered, "Lord, what do You think of me?"

The tears finally slowed, and she drew in a deep breath. Popping open the glove compartment, she found a small packet of tissues. While she was drying her eyes, her phone buzzed in her pocket with a notification. When she pulled

it out, the text message from her lawyer rico-
cheted her emotions and added another ingre-
dient to the dread pooling in her stomach.

I'll be in town tomorrow. Do you have time to
meet?

She didn't want to think about what her lawyer might have to say to her. Why did he want
to meet her in person? To soften the blow that
she couldn't get out of the conditions of the
will? Or maybe he'd found a solution, and she
had to sign some papers to get Chase and herself out of this situation?

Nothing felt right.

She took one more look at the mountain,
drew in a long breath and texted back, What
time?

THE WARM SPRING sun beat down on Chase's
back as he pulled his clippers out of his back
pocket.

Fence repair. He hated fence repair.

It gave him too much time to think. And
today, he had way too many things fighting for
attention in his brain.

At least his mostly loyal dog Duke was with

him. Though he currently had no idea the exact whereabouts of the golden retriever.

The unexpected appearance of his former mother-in-law felt like he'd been thrown from a horse. Maybe experienced an unexpected infiltration on the battlefield. He hadn't talked to Lexi since yesterday. Her reply to his phone call had been a short text about work.

His worlds had collided, and he hadn't the faintest clue how to handle things.

Barbara Hartwell's perspective on his relationship with Laura was muddied in grief.

The temptation to make the deceased perfect in memory could be strong. Chase felt it with Laura. It was easier to remember the good. But Barbara's memory had thrown a veil of inaccuracy over her imperfect daughter. And her imperfect son-in-law. It hadn't been an appropriate time to say anything. Laura's mother was deeply grieving the five-year loss of her only daughter.

But the look on Lexi's face when she realized who Barbara was to Chase about did him in. He'd watched her shut down right in front of him.

He should want that, right? Even if he married her—when he married her—in eleven days, he couldn't risk having feelings for Lexi.

Or her having feelings for him. Barbara served as a reminder of what happened when he loved someone.

Devastating loss.

But when his phone rang, he still hoped it was Lexi.

What he would say to her, he had no clue. All he knew was that he wanted to know if she was okay and what message her socks said today.

The phone lit up instead with Hunter's name, and before he answered, he looked up at their family's land. He wasn't in the mood to talk to his brother.

He stabbed the screen to take the call and asked gruffly, "What do you want?"

"Still in that chipper mood I left you in this morning?"

"You banished me to fence repair."

"Mucking the stalls didn't seem to take the fire out of you last time. I had to up my game." After a pause, he added, "Clearly I'm going to have to come up with something else."

Chase rubbed his cheek with the back of his hand. "Is there something you need?"

"I had a question about Lexi."

Duke appeared out of nowhere, shaking his

excited body and rubbing up against Chase as if he knew Hunter had just mentioned Lexi's name.

He leaned down and rubbed his dog's back. "What about Lexi?"

"I was just thinking." A prop plane flew overhead, and Chase followed it across the sky while his brother talked. "If you don't care about her, which you claim you don't, then what's the big deal in marrying her? What difference does it make?"

"Hunter—"

"But if you do care about her, which after what I saw at the reception it seems that you might, then why wouldn't you just marry her now?"

Chase shook his head, already tired of the short phone call. Why was his brother bringing this up now? "Hunter—"

"Either way, you care about her or you don't, it feels like you should think about it."

Duke jumped up and tried to lick Chase in the face. Chase wondered if this was a planned stealth attack by both his brother and his dog.

He released a labored sigh into the phone. "You know how I feel about getting married again."

"Good. Then you won't care that her lawyer's in town talking to her at the diner."

CHASE'S TRUCK BARRELED down the highway. A bunch of wildflowers bound up with a red bandanna sat by his side, his Stetson firmly on his head.

It just felt like a time when a man needed his hat.

Duke hung his head out the passenger window, a look of determination on his golden retriever face that matched the storm stirring inside of Chase.

He had no clue why he brought his dog. Maybe as a last resort. If he found out Lexi had done something ridiculous, he'd throw Duke at her to give her his puppy-dog eyes.

He wiped a hand over his face.

What a dumb plan.

All Chase knew was that his stomach clamped something fierce at the news that Lexi was at the diner with her lawyer. What if she'd changed her mind? What if, after seeing Chase with his former mother-in-law, she'd decided to do something rash? Her lawyer could misguide her. She could go back to her ex or find a mail-order groom.

The second Chase hit the diner, threw open the door and caught sight of Lexi across the room, he understood something else.

The thought of any man—who wasn't him—with her, no matter who it was, bothered him greatly.

When did that happen?

Lexi's eyes locked with his, her beautiful browns full of surprise. His chest rose and fell with his breathing, and he stared at her for a moment.

Yes. The thought of any man with Lexi, no matter who it was, bothered him greatly.

He saw his brother and Sheila out of the corner of his eye but ignored them and beelined it for Lexi.

Once he arrived at her table, he still only had eyes for her.

"Hey," she breathed, a slight blush hitting her cheeks.

The man across the booth from her, the lawyer he presumed, shifted and cleared his throat.

But Chase didn't take his eyes off Lexi. "Hey," he said.

He set the flowers on the table next to her, and her mouth gaped.

Placing one hand on her chest, she used the other to pick up the arrangement. With a look of awe, she stared as if it were a pristine vase full of expensive flowers purchased from the florist. As opposed to what it was, wildflowers from his field gathered in a frenzy on his way to get to her.

In a low voice only for her, he used the words she'd previously said to him. "Everyone deserves fresh flowers."

She looked from the offering to him, her eyes covered in a sheen of tears. "Thank you," she whispered.

The man across from her thrust his hand into Chase's line of vision. "Bob Morton."

Chase clenched his teeth, took a breath and slowly turned to the man. He needed to get a read on the situation. "Chase Cross."

Bob cocked his head and studied him while pumping Chase's hand just a little too hard. "I assume you're related to the gentleman at the bar who said hello to us earlier."

"Hunter. He's my twin brother."

"Ah."

Chase edged his hip onto Lexi's side of the booth. "May I join you?"

She nodded, and he scooted in beside her. Bob's eyes darted from Lexi to him.

Chase looked down at the table and for the first time noticed a pile of stapled papers. The words "Prenuptial Agreement" showed boldly at the top of the first page. His stomach plummeted to his boots. He might already be too late.

Maybe it was time to go get his dog.

But if Lexi didn't want him here, she would have said so. Chase kept his tail rooted in the red vinyl booth and looked at Bob. He nodded to the plate in front of the man. "How do you like your chicken-fried steak? It's the best in the state."

Bob ran his fingertips over his round, balding head. The older gentleman looked fit and well put-together in his polo shirt and khaki pants. Chase even saw the kindness in the eyes behind the bifocals, but that didn't mean he was ready to trust him. "I'm sure it's fine," the man said. "It's not what I normally eat."

Not a surprise. This man had city slicker written all over him. Lexi wasn't from these parts, but somehow she blended well with country life. Her boots weren't as dirty as everyone's native to the area, but she wasn't a shiny new penny, either. Something deep in Chase's gut knew she belonged here, in this community.

He hoped Lexi knew it, too.

Chase laced his hands on the table and asked Bob, "Where are you from?"

"Denver."

"What are you doing in these parts?"

The man flashed a glance at Lexi as if asking for permission, and when she nodded, he said, "I'm an attorney and came to discuss matters of a private nature with Lexi."

"And what kind of advice are you giving Lexi?"

She curled her fingers around Chase's forearm. He didn't know if this was an act of support or a warning. He also didn't care because he wasn't going anywhere.

Bob leaned forward. "All due respect, I'm not sure that's any of your business, Mr. Cross."

Chase picked up the prenuptial agreement and thumbed through it. There seemed to be two copies. One with the name Vance Miller in the groom's space and the other with a blank for the name of presumably a different groom. He still didn't know this guy's angle. "Did you bring these with you today?"

"Yes," Bob said.

"Then it is my business. Because I'm Lexi's fiancé." He cocked his head. "Which is why I'm wondering, you filled in one of these incorrectly and left the name of the groom blank on the other of these documents."

Bob held up his hands in surrender. "I was just trying to walk Lexi through her options. I was just trying to help."

He turned to Lexi. "Options?"

"Mr. Morton came to tell me in person that the will is ironclad." She licked her lips. "There's no way around the required marriage clause. So we began discussing the alternatives."

"What alternatives?"

Looking away, she said, "Vance Miller."

"Well, you're not marrying your ex-fiancé." She said options. There must be more. "What else?"

"And a…" She struggled to get the words out and closed her eyes. "A neutral party who could match me with a safe option."

He kept his voice calm. "I thought I was your safe option."

She looked to him. "After yesterday," she said hesitantly, "I didn't know how you felt. I didn't know…"

Lexi dug her fingers deeper into Chase's arm and looked at him as if pleading him to understand.

He understood. He understood that she didn't see what she thought she saw.

He studied her face and found beauty, vulnerability and a bit of a challenge behind her eyes. He spoke to the lawyer, but didn't take his eyes from hers when he said quietly, "She doesn't need your help, Bob. Or your prenuptial agreement."

She blinked, then exhaled a breath. He could almost feel the tension release from her.

Bob placed his hands on the edge of the table and pushed himself to sit taller. "Are you saying you're going to marry her?"

Chase glared at the man. "I'm saying she's worth more than your offer to coordinate something between an ex-fiancé who conspired with her mother for the money, or a mail-order groom who could be anybody."

Bob leaned in. "You may not get this, but I'm on her side. My job is to protect her."

That may be, but Bob didn't understand that Chase also considered it his job to protect her.

Bob got up to make his exit and pointed to the papers. "If something changes in the next eleven days, just let me know." With one look toward Chase, then back to Lexi, he said, "You know how to get a hold of me."

Chase's stare followed the man as he passed Hunter. His brother wore what Chase presumed was a matching glare to his own. Bob walked out the front door, right past Duke, who barked furiously at him from the truck, and straight to his flashy car. Once he drove off, Chase looked at Lexi.

She glanced at the flowers, to the stapled papers, back to the flowers, then up to him. "I'm sorry," she whispered, then cast her gaze down to her worrying fingers.

He gently took her chin and tilted her head to look at him. "Why are you sorry?"

"Because I asked you to marry me and then talked to my lawyer about other people. None of this is conventional. And all of it is confusing. I have no idea what to do about any of it. Or why you're even here." She blew out a long breath. "But I'm so relieved to see you, I'm not sure any of it matters."

He nodded, holding her eyes in his.

"Seriously," she continued, her entire demeanor seeping vulnerability, "I don't know why you're here."

"I needed to know what your socks say today."

A short chuckle burst from her mouth. Good. He wanted her to smile.

"They say 'Brave' on them."

"Perfect," he said softly.

"Now. Why are you really here?"

"I'm glad I showed when I did." He nodded to her untouched plate of food. "Every time a plate of chicken-fried steak goes untouched, a cowboy loses his spurs."

"Is that so?" she asked, a giggle in her tone.

He pulled her plate in front of him and cut the steak in half. After leaning over the table to retrieve an extra set of silverware, he unrolled the utensils from their paper napkin and pointed the fork at her. "Dig in."

She stared at him warily, but ate a few bites of the mashed potatoes. Good. He wanted her to eat something and relax.

From across the room, Hunter waved at him on his way out the door. Chase lifted his chin in return. He glanced at Sheila, who stared at his brother with stars in her eyes. Chase was going to have to talk to Hunter about his intentions with the waitress.

For now, he had his hands full with the beautiful, confusing but definitely-worth-fighting-for Lexi Gardner.

"So." She chewed a bite and swallowed. "Are you going to tell me what you're doing here?"

Sheila strolled by their table and set a glass of

water in front of Chase. He nodded a thanks to her and took a sip. "I'd like to ask you the same."

"We have other possibilities." She wiped her mouth with her paper napkin and looked at him. "You don't have to marry me."

Thunder rolled through him, and he growled his next words. "You do not have to settle for those possibilities."

She placed her hand on his forearm again, this time gently. "Chase, this solves all our problems. I get married and have access to the trust, which means I can use it for the ranch. And you don't have to do something you promised you would never do again by marrying me."

Confusion hit him square in the chest, along with something painful, yet sweet. "You'd still use your money for the nonprofit?" he asked softly, almost to himself.

"Of course." She squeezed his arm. "I believe in Four Cross Hope, Chase. With everything in my being."

He cleared away the emotion crawling up his throat. He had to stay focused, even if the sweet smell of her shampoo was throwing him off in such close proximity.

"Maybe I don't want an out," he said a little angrier than he intended. He threw his napkin on the table and turned to her. "Maybe I want a shot."

Lexi's brown eyes grew three times in size. She looked as surprised as he felt hearing the words come out of his mouth.

But he wouldn't take them back. He meant them.

"You don't want to get married again." She sputtered her words. "A-and the things your mother-in-law said. Laura was perfect for you. I can't—"

"My former mother-in-law is a good woman. But she didn't know anything about my day-to-day relationship with her daughter. It wasn't always an easy road." He shook his head. His relationship with Laura was one filled with love, but it certainly was not without challenges.

Lexi blinked. Twice.

He turned toward her and ran an arm across the top of the booth behind her. "I have a good time with you when we're actually getting along. Do you have a good time with me?"

Slowly, she looked up at him, her glassy eyes full of emotions he wished he could decipher. "I have a good time with you," she whispered.

He nodded once. "Good. I think we make a good team. Do you think we make a good team?"

Her face flushed pink, and she licked her lips. "Yes. We make a good team."

At her answer, the spot over his heart squeezed. He rubbed the place, but realized the squeeze wasn't painful. It was something he didn't quite recognize. Looking into her beautiful eyes, he said, "I can't make promises, Lexi. But I can tell you that I want to spend the next eleven days figuring this out together. Will you do that with me?"

"Are you sure?"

He hated that she had to ask that question, but he understood why. She deserved clarity.

"You want to know what I'm doing here?" He picked up the prenuptial papers and looked at her. Without breaking eye contact, he ripped them in half. "That's what I'm doing here," he said.

"Oh," she murmured, staring at the torn papers.

He returned his arm to the back of the booth and angled back toward her. When he gently cupped the back of her head, she stared up at him. He leaned in and pressed his lips to her forehead. Pulling back, he asked, "Will you spend the next eleven days figuring this out with me?"

"Yes," she said in a voice so quiet that he barely heard her.

He pressed his lips to her forehead one more time, having no idea what would come of the next eleven days.

Before today, he didn't know if she might change her mind. Now he didn't know if she'd flip-flop again. And he didn't know if they should put money down on this contractor, thus committing her trust fund to the cause and them to marriage.

What he did know was that he was all in to figure out a way to get through this—with her by his side.

CHAPTER NINE

PRESSURE. ALL CHASE could feel was pressure. Calving season was in full swing with each ranch hand taking shifts. Lexi seemed to be staying afloat as Tax Day approached, but he knew she was burning the candle at both ends. The contractor wanted an answer about an early start date. The Four Cross Ranch bank account was holding the line, but barely. And Lexi's birthday was a week from tomorrow.

Standing in the lodge, Chase shook his head. A new soldier on leave had arrived this morning. A good thing. But another thing all the same. He didn't dare tell Lexi he was personally absorbing the costs. His savings could handle it. What couldn't handle it was his schedule.

He could feel the exhaustion in his bones.

His phone rang, and when he looked at the screen, he wanted to ignore it. But if Hunter needed him on the ranch, he needed to know.

"Hunter," he answered. "Everything okay with that heifer?"

"She's fine. She won't calve again, but we got her stabilized."

Chase closed his eyes and exhaled. It had been a long morning. "Okay."

"You on property?" Hunter asked.

"Just got back from the bank and I'm at the lodge waiting on Lexi."

"You guys married yet?"

He walked to the front of the house and looked for Lexi out the window. He shook his head. His brother knew the answer. "You worried we got married and I didn't ask you to be the best man?"

"I'm worried you're about to mess up the best thing that's come your way in a long time. I don't understand why you're waiting a week."

"Hunter, Lexi's wrapping up tax season, and I'm just trying to survive calving season. Neither of us wants to fall asleep while we're taking our vows."

"You're hedging."

After a long exhale, Chase looked at the ground and lowered his voice. "I'm giving her every chance she needs to make sure this is what she wants to do."

"You're still hedging."

He squeezed his eyes closed, as if he could guard himself from the truth. "What am I supposed to do here? Marry a woman I'm not in love with so I can use her money to make all my dreams come true?"

"I can think of about three things wrong with that question."

Lexi drove up in her old car and slowly pulled herself out of the driver's seat. She looked as tired as he felt. As she grabbed something from the back seat, Chase decided to disregard his brother's last comment. "I've got to go. I'll head to the barn when I'm done."

He hung up before Hunter could say anything else annoying.

Chase opened the front door of the lodge just as Lexi made it to the top of the stairs holding two large grocery sacks. She stopped and her ponytail swayed behind her head. Jeans, a sweatshirt underneath an open coat, tennis shoes, no makeup, dark circles under her brown eyes—and this woman was still beautiful.

He cleared his throat. "Let me take your bags."

"I've got it. If I let go, I might drop them."

He approached her anyway, wrapped his

hands around the bottom of the bags and withdrew them from her. Before he got caught in the wildflowers of her scent, he headed into the lodge and set the groceries down on the counter.

They worked in companionable silence putting the food and drinks away for the new guest.

Opening the fridge, she stowed the milk on the inside of the door. "How many hours of sleep did you get last night?"

"A few." He put the last of the cans of food in the pantry.

"My schedule only gets like this once a year. Sometimes quarterly taxes can pick up the pace a little, but it's nothing like April." She drew her arms over her head and stretched out long. "What about you? Is this what life is always like for you?"

"There's nothing like calving season."

She put her arms down and shook them out. "I'm sorry to drop and run, but I've got to see a few clients today to finalize their returns."

"You going to finish on time?"

She smiled. "I always finish on time." She might be trying to look cocky, but she only looked cute to him.

Pulling the keys out of her pocket, she said,

"Oh, and fair warning. I'll sleep right through the day after Tax Day. It's a ritual and a necessity."

"Do you need me to bring you food?"

She touched the place above her heart. "Oh, thank you. That's not necessary. I can take care of myself."

On the way out of the kitchen, she stopped at the island. She ran her fingers over the documents on the counter. "What are these?"

He shoved his hands in the front pockets of his jeans. What an idiot! He shouldn't have left those papers out for her to see. "I turned in new projections to the bank. They're going to get a new appraisal for the ranch."

Slowly, she turned to him. "And reconsider the loan," she said, her tone flat.

He studied her. Nodded. "They might."

After a huff, she closed her eyes and talked to him. "Are you pulling out of this, Chase? My birthday is in a week. I'm under a lot of pressure. I'm exhausted. And I don't have time to figure out if you're playing a game with me."

He took a step toward her, a hint of desperation creeping into his voice. "Lexi, I'm not playing a game." But he was in an impossible position.

Her eyes popped open. She scooped up the

papers and held them out to him. "Then what is this exactly?"

He quieted his voice. "I guess I—"

"You guess you what?" she demanded.

"I can't reconcile marrying you for money."

She looked stricken. No. She looked betrayed. Then resigned. "If you don't want to marry me, just tell me now."

"What?" Hunter was right. He was messing up everything. "That's not it."

"It's okay." She started walking toward the front door and opened it. When she turned around, they were face-to-face, a breath apart. "It's okay, Chase. If you don't want to marry me, I get it." She barked a sarcastic laugh. "I promise you that I get it. I just need you to tell me so I can plan otherwise."

He took her hand. "Don't plan otherwise, Lexi. We're doing this."

She swallowed, a cold look on her face, her chin out almost in defiance. "You can tell me. Is it Laura? You don't want to get married again because you lost Laura?"

Was it Laura? He shoved the thought away. "No."

"Just tell me."

What had he done? His stomach clenched

tightly. His chest tighter. He schooled his tone and searched her eyes. "I am telling you. You're going to finish tax season, sleep for a day, and then we're getting married."

A tear slipped down her left cheek, and she quickly rubbed it away with her palm. "Okay," she whispered. "Okay."

WITH ONE DAY until Tax Day and five days until Lexi's birthday, relentless knots churned in her stomach. Today, it seemed as though the discomfort was spreading, and it felt like acid coated her insides.

Externally, Wyoming temperatures hinted at warmer days. Internally, pressure from Chase and Lexi's situation had built over the last two and a half weeks and was taking a toll. The clear skies behind the striking Snowy Range couldn't compete with the volcano swirling inside of Lexi.

She pasted a fake smile on her face and rang the Stimpsons' doorbell. Mr. and Mrs. Stimpson were old-school. They wanted their tax return printed, signed and mailed. She just needed to get their signatures. But maybe a visit to the couple at Bright Horizons would also serve as a distraction.

A wreath decorated in wooden flowers greeted her with the words "April Showers Bring May Flowers" scrolled across the top. It shook when the elderly woman answered the door. Upon recognition of Lexi, her face lit up. "Lexi. So good to see you. How are you?"

Lexi tried to widen her smile. "Fine. Fine. I brought you flowers." She thrust the vase forward. Nothing could be done for Lexi. But maybe Mrs. Stimpson's day would brighten from the gentle scent of the calla lilies.

Mrs. Stimpson's brow drew down in concern. "Come in. George is in the back on a call and will come find us when he finishes. You look like you need some lemonade, dear." Apparently, Lexi wasn't fooling anyone.

With careful movements, Lexi shifted to the couch and waited while Mrs. Stimpson chatted about the latest news in the retirement community and prepared the refreshments.

"Apparently Sam Gutton finally asked his sweetheart Myrna Franklin to marry him. They both moved to Bright Horizons after their loved ones died. They've been neighbors for three years. Not one date. And then bam, he popped the question. I can't even imagine the whiplash they must be feeling, going from friends to engaged in no time flat."

"I can kind of imagine it," Lexi muttered to herself.

Mrs. Stimpson leaned her head through the door. "What, dear?"

"Nothing." She swallowed. "It does feel fast."

Very fast.

Mrs. Stimpson returned to the living room and set down a tray. Store-bought sugar cookies were arranged on a stack of paper napkins next to two glasses of lemonade. She perched nearby on the couch and angled her body toward Lexi. A crease ran down the middle of her pressed pants, and her perfectly manicured hands lay together in her lap. "Now. How is that young man of yours. Chase? What is he up to these days?"

"Oh, um." Lexi rubbed a tight spot under her rib. She was thankful she'd worn her looser yoga pants with a long sweater tunic today. Her sensitive stomach couldn't have handled a tight waistband. "Calving season has him pretty busy. One of his brothers didn't come home to help this year like they'd hoped, so they're a man down."

At least that's how Chase's texts explained the situation.

There had been only short texts from him the last two days. Quick check-ins. She wondered if their last conversation upset him as much as it upset her.

The older woman's eyes narrowed, but she said nothing.

The small bite Lexi took from one of the cookies tasted like sandpaper. She washed it down with a sip of lemonade that caused a wave of nausea to run through her. It seemed her nerves weren't going to leave her alone until her birthday passed.

She turned toward the older woman and crossed her ankles. "Mrs. Stimpson, do you mind if I ask you a question?"

"Lexi, every woman my age wishes someone would ask them a question. Especially if they, in turn, get to talk about themselves. Bonus points if they get to give unsolicited advice."

Lexi laughed, but a muscle spasmed in her side. She bit back her wince and asked the question that had been swirling in the middle of her volcano. "Is love supposed to be sacrificial? And if so, what does that look like? And if that's the case, how does anyone ever get what they want if they're all sacrificing things for the sake of love?"

The woman peered at her so long, Lexi began to fear she'd probe further. One simple question might shatter Lexi's hold on her total confusion about where God's love fit into the mess created by the trust.

But Mrs. Stimpson straightened her sweater set and sat back. "Louella said something to me once that stuck. My guess is it's the kind of thing she would have wished she'd passed on to her granddaughter."

Tears hit the back of Lexi's eyes. The burden of the next five days left her with a deep weariness she desperately wished she could share with her grandmother. "What did she say?" she whispered.

Mrs. Stimpson took Lexi's hand in hers and gentled her voice. "She said whatever we think is ours...probably wasn't ever ours to begin with. And that we have to let go of something to know if it was really meant for us."

A sheen of sweat broke out on Lexi's brow. "It's hard to hear that advice considering what happened to my grandmother. She let go of my mother, and my mother never came back to her."

"Yes. But all was not lost." A smile peeked

at the edge of Mrs. Stimpson's lips. "*You* came back to her."

"But only for six weeks. Then I lost her."

She nodded. "But I don't think you truly understand. What was meant for her was *you*. Those six weeks she had with you felt like a gift to Louella."

"She said that to you?"

"Many times."

A tear streamed down Lexi's cheek. It wouldn't douse the volcano, but it spread out, filling the cracks of the parched wound her mother had left in her.

No matter how the next five days played out, Lexi never wanted to forget what Mrs. Stimpson shared with her. Lexi was chosen. Maybe not by her mother. Or through a marriage. But she was beloved by a grandmother who needed Lexi just as much as Lexi needed her.

She said whatever we think is ours, probably wasn't ever ours to begin with. And that we have to let go of something to know if it was really meant for us.

Chase's handsome face came to mind. The love for his family. Their land. Struggling veterans. His vision for the future of Four Cross Hope.

"I'm falling for Chase Cross," Lexi whispered through a sad, watery smile.

"I thought that might be the case," Mrs. Stimpson said quietly.

"But I don't think he was meant for me." Something tore in Lexi's heart. "I might have been meant for him, but I don't think he was meant for me."

Question filled the lines of the wise woman's face. "Are you sure about that?"

"No." She pictured Chase's fierce fear after the incident with the snake. "But I can't ask him to *make* himself be meant for me. That's not fair to either of us."

With no more wisdom from Mrs. Stimpson, Lexi received signatures from both Stimpsons. After a kind goodbye and heartfelt hugs, she left Bright Horizons.

When she got in her car, she checked her cell phone. Two texts and one voicemail. Caller ID said the voicemail was from her lawyer. She listened to it first.

"Hi, Lexi. I just wanted to follow up with our meeting last week and let you know that I talked to my buddy who's a judge. He shut me down pretty fast. There's just no way around the wording of the will. You must be married by your thirty-fifth birthday to gain access to the trust. Otherwise, I'll be contacting your second cousin who, by the way, is still married as of today. I checked county courthouse records." A heavy sigh came through the recording. "I'm sorry. I know that's not the news you were hoping for. Keep me posted."

Nausea swept over her. This time worse than the last.

She'd known this would probably be her lawyer's answer.

But why was her car so hot? And how come her body felt like it had run to Yellowstone and back?

She turned the engine over and aimed the air vents at herself full speed. Just those movements seemed to make her winded.

When she scrolled through her phone, the texts she found stoked the fire in her volcano. The first was from her mother.

Your birthday's in five days. I've found us an option. He'll split the money three ways. Call me. You are running out of time.

The text spiked a pain in her side. Of course her mother was still angling for the money. What did she mean she'd found an option? Was she trying to partner Lexi with Vance again? Or this time was it a complete stranger?

Lexi would always miss her mother. Miss what could have been. Miss the relationship she wished it had been. But she could never trust her again.

And the more she thought about the money, the sicker she became to her stomach.

She read Chase's text next.

I know tomorrow's deadline day for you. I think I can get away for dinner tonight if you want me to bring takeout to your house. We need to talk.

Chase was a good guy. A solid man.

She placed her phone on the passenger seat, gripped the top of the steering wheel and pressed her forehead into the back of her hands. Her gut roiled and her body was wracked with shivers.

Lexi never wanted to be the reason behind the pain in Chase's eyes. She never wanted to be the cause of the debilitating fear she saw in him after she was almost thrown from Millie. And she couldn't ask him to be a different man. She wouldn't want him to be.

Is this what falling for someone felt like? Surely that wasn't what was happening. She'd promised him their marriage would be based on a logical decision. An exchange. But she had the feeling she wasn't going to be able to keep that promise.

"Maybe I've gotten everything wrong in the past," she whispered, "but I know what I need to do now."

She sat up, brushed the remnants of her tears off her hot cheeks and aimed her car toward her house. She'd finish her work tomorrow, bypass sleeping for a little longer, and then have a talk with Chase.

CHAPTER TEN

CHASE'S PHONE TAUNTED HIM.

Only three minutes had passed since the last time he checked. No texts. No calls. Nothing from Lexi.

The woman was supposed to be at the ranch forty-five minutes ago. He'd reached out to her repeatedly, but she never replied.

The sun hung low somewhere in the sky, not that Chase had paid any attention to it for weeks. Neither did the calving cows. Their babies came when they were good and ready and had zero regard for the time of day or night. Weariness was in the soil. It felt like no one was getting any sleep this year.

He took his hat off and wiped his forehead with the back of his arm.

Hunter sidled up to him. "You going to talk about it or just make the rest of us around you miserable?"

Chase grumbled, "You going to banish me to shoeing the horses?"

"I wouldn't take a job from the farrier." He turned to Chase and crossed his arms. "But I might send you to KP duty just to get you off the land. You're making the cows cranky."

"The cows are cranky because they just gave birth. I hear it's not an easy task."

Chase turned from his brother. He leaned his weight into his forearms on top of the split-rail fence and aimed his eyes at the back of the chow hall where Lexi should emerge any second.

Hunter mirrored his stance next to him, but said nothing. Which meant he wasn't leaving until Chase gave him something.

On a sigh, Chase finally said, "The bank called."

"Hmm," was all Hunter replied.

"In spite of the new numbers and projections I gave them earlier this week, they turned us down again." He had even thrown in details about possible donors, but without concrete evidence of procured future funding, the bank couldn't make the loan. Even if the manager went to high school with him and knew the Cross family's upstanding reputation.

The muscles in Chase's shoulders felt like

rocks. Heavy, sedentary stress tightened just a bit more each time he thought of the ranch, the trust and Lexi.

He was torn about sharing the bank's rejection with Lexi. He didn't want to put more pressure on the situation. Because he couldn't secure the loan, the need for money walked a tightrope stretched taut between Lexi and him.

"Three days until Lexi's birthday," Chase murmured.

Hunter grunted.

His twin wasn't going to bail him out of the conversation. Typical. The man would throw himself in front of a train for him. He was loyal, almost to a fault. Had sacrificed his late twenties to raise their siblings. And Chase never knew how to compete with a man of that honor.

"What made you leave the military and go home to take care of Cora and Ryder?" The question had been festering between the twins for over a decade.

Hunter shooed a fly away from his face and settled back into the fence. "It's what was needed to be done."

Chase turned to his brother and leaned against the wooden rail. "But you'd dreamed of being in the military your whole life. We both did."

Turning his head, Hunter looked at Chase. "The family needed me."

"It was a huge sacrifice," Chase said, his tone perplexed. He just stared at his brother. His volume rose. "Why aren't you angry at me for not leaving the military with you? Don't you have regrets?"

Hunter shook his head as if he couldn't believe the questions Chase was firing at him. He squared his body to him and said in a disbelieving tone, "Chase, you seem to think that sacrifices can only lead to hardship."

Chase's entire body jerked back at his brother's confusing comment.

"I'm not saying it was easy to come home—" Hunter looked over his shoulder at the land "—but it doesn't feel like a sacrifice anymore because too much good came from it. Especially now."

"What do you mean?"

"In spite of everything that's happened to her, Cora's finding her way. There's something good and solid about getting to see that up close." He threw a hand out. "And Ryder—"

"Ryder's a piece of work."

A smile hitched at the corner of Hunter's

mouth. "I'm not nearly as concerned about Ryder as I am about you."

"That's saying a lot."

Hunter nodded once. "How's Lexi feeling?"

"What do you mean?"

"Sheila told me Lexi went by the diner earlier today and didn't look good."

She wouldn't. Her birthday was in three days. Maybe she was as wound-up as Chase was, trying to figure out how their situation was going to end. Calving and tax seasons could not have come at a worse time. He and Lexi hadn't had near the time together he had hoped heading into this week.

He looked out over the land, his horse grazing in the distance.

Who was he kidding? The incident with Mildred had freaked him out. Chase was more skittish than the horse. That snake had bitten him with a healthy dose of reality.

Caring for another woman would cost him something, and he wasn't sure if he had the means to pay.

But he cared for Lexi. Deeply. There wasn't anything he could do about it.

He rubbed the spot on the left side of his

chest. The one that had plagued him constantly for weeks.

A car drove by in the distance, but it wasn't Lexi's heap. "She was supposed to come by for dinner—" he checked his phone for the twenty-third time this hour "—but she's late. Really late."

"Makes sense. Sheila said it looked like Lexi could barely move." Hunter scrubbed the stubble at his cheek. "Maybe she didn't make it here because she couldn't."

Chase could barely hear Hunter's last words as he ran to his truck.

CHASE HELD THE phone to his ear, simultaneously pounding on Lexi's door.

Her car was in her driveway but parked at a funny angle. He'd been standing at the door for three full minutes knocking. He was now putting his body weight into his fist to create a louder noise.

In the meantime, she wasn't answering her phone.

Fear.

Raw, unadulterated fear coursed through his veins.

He spun around and walked along the side of

her house, peering in the windows. All the curtains were drawn. Something she told him she did to cut down on energy costs as the weather turned warmer. Pure Lexi.

Pure Lexi.

That spot on his chest burned.

The back door was locked. As he stormed off the porch, he knocked over a potted plant. Spilling out of the dirt was a rock. But something didn't look quite right about it.

He crouched down and realized it was a hide-a-key rock. Relief hit him as he slid the key out and proceeded to open her back door.

"Lexi?" he called as he bounded through the kitchen. "Lexi, it's me. Chase. Are you here?"

A low moan came from the living room, and he rushed through the swinging door to the sound.

Styrofoam take-out boxes were strewn across her rug, the contents next to Lexi's dumped purse. And phone.

Curled in a ball on her denim couch, Lexi's body shook. Her eyes were squinted closed, and terrible pain struck through her pale face.

His heart lurched in his chest, pulling him to sit on the edge of the couch beside her pain-wracked body.

"Honey?" A layer of sweat covered her face. He moved to touch her forehead, but he could feel the heat coming off her even before the back of his hand made contact. "Honey, you're burning up."

When he placed his hand on her waist, she cried out. A dreadful sound that jolted him back.

He scanned her body, looking for any hint of injury. "What else hurts, honey?"

"Mmm." She swallowed but didn't open her eyes.

He gently shifted damp bangs off her forehead. "Can you talk to me?"

She licked her lips and whispered, "Nauseated."

Nausea. Fever. Painful to touch. She needed to get to a hospital.

"Honey, you need to see a doctor."

"No," she moaned. A sob broke through, causing a fierce wince, clearly so painful for her to endure that tears streamed down her face.

Her guttural sound broke something in him. The entire picture of her ripped his heart out of his chest.

"Come on, honey." Trying his best not to jostle her, he bent low at the knees and scooped her into his arms.

She constricted as if she could brace against the pain, then her head lolled against his chest. The heat from her body radiated against his like nothing he'd ever experienced.

Should he throw her into a cold bath? But what if something was wrong internally? Delaying medical treatment could be fatal.

The responsibility for her life robbed him of his next breath. Almost debilitated him.

She shifted in his arms and curled into him, shivers bucking her entire body. "Chase," she whispered against his neck, her voice croaking. "I'm s-sorry."

His legs found their footing and he strode to the front door, leaning down to unlock it and walk through.

When he got her situated in the front seat, he texted Hunter, Headed to hospital with Lexi, and pointed his car in the direction of help.

He held her hand. He wanted to squeeze it. To reassure her that everything was going to be okay.

But he didn't want to hurt her.

And he didn't know if everything was going to be okay.

And Lexi pitifully...painfully...murmured his

name the entire drive to the emergency room. Followed by the word *sorry*.

DEVASTATING HEAT.

Scorching pain in her side.

Chase.

Oh, no. Chase.

She was sorry. She was so sorry he had to see her like this. That he had to deal with her in this state.

His wife.

His heart.

Her Chase.

Blackness. Finally—a beautiful black that took away her pain.

But it also took away her Chase.

Because when she woke up in the recovery room, with machines beeping, effective pain medication and a nurse who reassured her that she was fortunate they caught the ruptured appendix when they did, there was no Chase to be found.

CHAPTER ELEVEN

CHASE LAY IN the only spot in the world where he knew he could breathe. Out on his land. In the wide-open spaces. But now, Laura's mountain was in plain view. With Laura's memory at the edge of his sanity. With Laura's death searing into him through Lexi's broken body.

Once he'd heard Lexi had made it out of surgery all right, he'd bolted from the hospital.

Sleep was not his friend, followed by a frenzied day on the ranch tracking down two calves, the veteran leaving the lodge, rounding up cattle from a fence break, and one breech-birth calf delivery Chase had handled himself. All while picturing Lexi's pained, pale face coupled with the words the doctor described of an excruciating surgery to clean up her ruptured appendix.

He'd known he should go see her. He'd called himself all kinds of names throughout the day, the word *coward* on repeat in his head.

The fear of losing Lexi froze him with a white heat he'd never known. The hospital walls had suffocated him the night before. He couldn't go back.

By the end of the day, in an almost unhinged daze, he had saddled up Harvey and rode through his land. As acres and acres passed beneath him, he hoped the horse's hooves could pound out the pain in his chest. Could pound out the fear that refused to leave his bloodstream even though he knew intellectually that Lexi was okay. Could pound out the reality that he couldn't fathom that he almost lost someone else that he loved.

Because he loved Lexi. In the most terrifying, complete way. He loved Lexi.

He loved Alexis Jane Gardner, and he had no idea if he could handle loving her.

Which was what he was thinking about when on the unseasonably warm April night, he finally fell into a fitful sleep in the grass by his favorite part of the fence line, a direct line of sight to his mountain.

But that wasn't what he was thinking about when he felt a slobbery, scratchy tongue lick his cheek and smelled the unmistakable breath of a canine.

Chase gently shoved the whiskery face away from his and squinted with one eye open at his dog. "Duke."

His golden retriever's body shook with urgency.

"Your dog wants to know why you aren't at the hospital with Lexi," Hunter said, towering over Chase and blocking the early sun's rays.

"That's probably truer than you know," muttered Chase as he sat up, his bones groaning at him about being too old to sleep on the hard floor of the ranch lands.

Hunter's voice lowered with a tone he rarely used and only when he was upset with someone. "What are you doing out here, Chase?"

He cocked his legs and rested his elbows on his knees. A sigh came from deep in his chest. "I don't know."

Hunter looked toward the mountain, then back to Chase. "At some point, you're going to have to trust God with Laura. She wasn't ever yours to begin with. She was always His."

"And she died, Hunter." Chase tried to rein in his anger. He swiped at a bug on his arm. "What kind of a pep talk is this? Because I don't think you're very good at it."

"The kind where you get it straight in your head that Lexi isn't yours, either."

The words felt like a sucker punch.

His brother added, "And you're going to have to trust God with her whether you like it or not."

The second sucker punch packed more heat than the first one.

Chase scratched at the stubble on his face. "What if I can't?"

Duke barked his own rebuke at him as if he knew what the conversation was about.

"Tough," Hunter lectured. "You will. You'll do it every day because fear can't drive your decisions. You'll do it every day because there are no guarantees. And you'll do it every day because that's the choice we get. To trust God with the things that were His to begin with."

Chase eyed his dog. Then his brother. "That's not a fun set of truths, Hunter."

"Each day is in God's hands, whether we like it or not."

Chase roughed his fingers through his hair several times. He inhaled oxygen from his land. From his heritage.

"I love her," he said quietly to the ground.

"I know. But this problem's not a hard riddle to solve, Chase." Hunter crossed his arms. "Marry her."

Chase squinted up at his brother. "It's not that simple."

"Why not?"

"If I marry her now, she'll always question if it was about the money." He shook his head. "I can't do that to her. I can't let the woman I marry always wonder in the back of her mind if I did it for any reason other than that I treasure her and don't want to live the rest of my life without her. There should be no doubt in her mind. She deserves nothing less."

But her birthday loomed in front of them. In about seventeen hours, give or take a few minutes, she would turn thirty-five.

Hunter nodded, bent to slap him on the shoulder, looked in his eyes and said, "You'll figure it out." He extended a hand and helped Chase off the ground.

"That's it?" Chase laughed humorlessly. "You've spent the last month with so much advice about Lexi, I think you're out of your word allotment for the year. But now? Now that it's down to the wire, all you can say is that I'll figure it out?"

"And that you need to take a shower."

"Unbelievable."

With a grin, Hunter tipped his hat, said no more and sauntered back in the direction of the lodge.

Chase shook his head. He could not wait until some woman knocked Hunter off his feet. Couldn't happen to a better man.

Duke jumped several times and barked orders to Chase. He ran three steps in the direction of the lodge, then looked back and barked again. Three steps toward Chase, a bark. Then three steps toward the lodge.

Or maybe the parking lot.

It was as if his dog knew Chase was late getting to Lexi.

"I know, buddy." He rubbed his hands down his dog's excited body. "Don't worry. We're going to get her. She may not want me after the stunt I pulled leaving her, but we're going to try."

After an attempt at dusting off his hopelessly dirty jeans, Chase paused to look toward his mountain. Its strength could not be denied, but the white clouds at the summit made him think the peak was tucked into Heaven.

"What do you want from me?" he asked the

mountain. Maybe he was asking his wife. Definitely he was asking God.

"I want to trust You with Lexi, Lord," he whispered. "And I want to marry her."

A soft breeze swept over him, bringing a peace with its gentle touch. And the very distinct feeling that while he was staring at his mountain, somehow, someway, it had shifted a little. Created space. Given him room to breathe. And allowed him to leave his wife in the hands of the Lord. On the mountain. Where she belonged.

Which allowed him to leave to be by Lexi's side. At the hospital. Maybe for forever. Where he belonged.

LEXI'S BODY WOKE in stages.

Only her ears worked at first.

The beeps of a machine. Nearby rustling. And the low murmurs of voices.

Next, she could smell. Something metallic. A heavy cleaning product. A woman's perfume.

Prying her eyes open proved to be a bigger feat than she thought it would be. She could open them for a second, the room would focus, then blur, then she'd close them again.

Once again. But this time, the face of a woman in her view.

Did she call her mom?

No. She didn't. But she had asked the nurse to call her mom.

Because Chase had left her side.

The beeping machine next to her bed told her that thinking about Chase leaving her did not sit well. Her heartbeat had quickened. Probably because it was too broken to beat regularly when it thought about the cowboy. But she had to convince her heart this was for the best.

She couldn't ask Chase to be someone he was not. She couldn't ask him to love her. She never should have approached him to begin with.

So now, she'd have to marry someone else. Was there time for that?

Chase would be free to live in the memory of his wife, without the fear of losing someone else. Lexi would ask her lawyer for help contacting the neutral party to match her with someone. She would still put her half of the trust money toward Four Cross Hope, and Chase would get everything he wanted in life.

Because that's what love did.

She opened her eyes again. This time for longer.

Her mother held her hand.

When Lexi opened her mouth, it felt unpleasant. She ran her tongue over the back of her teeth. Did someone give her sawdust to chew? "Thirsty," she barely croaked out.

Her mom picked up a cup and pointed its straw toward her mouth. "Just take sips at first. Your body has been through a lot."

Lexi did as she was told. The cool water slid down her sore throat. She coughed, and her mom placed a hand behind her shoulders to move her forward. But pain shot through her side, and she winced at the movement.

"Sorry," her mother murmured. "The nurse wanted to know when you woke up. I'll go get her."

When her mother left to grab a nurse, Lexi leaned back, discouraged that two sips of water made her feel like she'd ridden a bull.

Her mother returned with a middle-aged nurse whose beautiful black hair streaked with white matched perfectly with the wisdom behind her experienced eyes. "Good morning, sleeping beauty. I'm Julie, your nurse." She checked Lexi's vitals and tapped information into an iPad. "We didn't quite know when you would wake up. Do you remember anything that happened?"

"Someone told me I had surgery but was fine."

"A pretty nasty ruptured appendix. We're keeping you a few days to pump you with antibiotics, but you'll make a full recovery."

Lexi looked around the room trying to orient herself with her situation. The dry-erase board caught her eye. The date had to be wrong. "What day is it?"

The blood-pressure cuff around Lexi's arm tightened. Her stomach did the same when she saw her mother's expression. It was a terrible cross between concerned and conflicted.

The cuff ticked tighter.

The nurse laughed. "Don't worry. We all saw your birthday on your chart. You didn't miss it. It's tomorrow."

"Tomorrow?" She'd slept through an entire day? Lexi tried to push to sit up further, but her side protested. She grimaced. "Tomorrow?"

"Well," the nurse said to the IV bag, thumping the drip chamber, "technically, your birthday is in about twelve hours."

Dread coursed through her veins along with whatever the nurse was giving her. It was noon. On the eve of her birthday. There was no time to find a different husband.

Before her appendicitis, she thought she knew

what she wanted. But she also thought she had a few days to think about it. Let it settle.

Twelve hours?

A sharp rap sounded, followed immediately by someone opening the door. It was strange to recognize a person simply by the way they knocked on a door, but the efficiency of the rap, not asking if they could enter and the whip of the privacy curtain aside only confirmed what she already knew.

Vance stood just inside the room. "Lexi."

At least the man knew enough not to approach her.

"How did you…" Lexi didn't know what to say. Again, the sounds on her heart monitor sped up and alerted the room to how Lexi felt about her ex-fiancé's arrival.

Her mother stepped forward. "I called him, Lexi."

"Hey, sweetheart," he said.

His endearment made her stomach clench. Or maybe it was the aftermath of the surgery.

A breath rushed out of her mouth. The money. "Of course you contacted Vance," she whispered.

Her mother, dressed in a champagne-colored pantsuit, folded her hands in front of her.

"When the nurse called, she used your maiden name. I know you're not married. I know your birthday is tomorrow. And I know what's at stake. You don't want to lose all of that money."

Vance sat in front of her in a designer suit. Maybe he came from work.

Or maybe he thought today was their wedding day.

Vance lowered his voice. "Lex. Think about this. You know me. It's not just that I could help, but that we could be the family we always talked about becoming." His eyes pleaded with her to understand. "My parents are here. Just in case you say yes. We all want this."

"Um…" Lexi's brain couldn't catch up. Mortified, she covered her face with her hands, dragging the IV tube across her body in the process. "Vance," she said in an agonized tone.

Too many things were happening in the room. Every girl wanted her mom to take care of her when she was sick. It was probably why she'd told the nurse to call her. But the woman before her? The woman who schemed to get her married off and take money from the trust? The woman who'd barely talked to her for almost two years until recently when her thirty-fifth birthday was hanging over them?

She wasn't sure she wanted that version of Clara Gardner in the room.

Vance turned and squared off with her mother but continued to speak to Lexi, his voice louder and more firm than before. "I have no intention, however, of giving your mother a portion of the trust fund."

Lexi's heart monitor sounded like a fire station alarm. She looked at Julie. "Can you please turn that off?"

"Your pulse has gone to concerning levels three times in the last ten minutes. I think we need to keep you monitored, all things considered."

She had no idea.

Her mother stepped to the foot of her bed. "Lexi, this isn't what you think."

"After last time, what is she supposed to think?" Vance said, using a harsh tone she'd never heard from him before.

Her mother's body stood stiff, and Lexi's blood-pressure cuff tightened again.

Every neuron in Lexi's brain had been firing on all cylinders to try to keep up with the events in the room. But at Vance's words, it was as if they all came to a complete halt. She turned her head to him. "After what happened last time with *you*, what am I supposed to think?"

"You're supposed to think—" Vance snapped his mouth closed. Then said quietly, "That I'm marrying you tonight."

"You're marrying him tonight?" a new voice said from the door.

A voice new to some people in the room, but a voice that Lexi recognized unequivocally.

Chase stepped from behind the curtain. "The door was open," he murmured, his eyes never leaving Lexi's.

The ticking cuff released Lexi's arm with a hiss, and the blood-pressure machine beeped wildly.

She only had a few seconds to take in his pressed jeans, starched white shirt, and the flowers in his hand. The look in his eyes held such confusion and vulnerability, her heart squeezed painfully.

"Who are you?" her mother snapped.

Chase's eyes narrowed, and he took in everyone in the room. He looked at Lexi. "I'm her fiancé." Ignoring the collective gasp, he asked, "You doing okay?"

Her heart squeezed again, this time with longing. In spite of the scene Chase walked into, he wasn't concerned with anyone in the room but her. She wanted to block everyone else out and stay in the zone of his words. Just the two of them. But her heart couldn't take it. Her heart remembered who was in the room. Her heart remembered how messed up everything in her life had become and how it had all congregated in the last twenty minutes at the foot of her hospital bed.

Chase glanced behind him. With a perplexed look, he scooted farther into the room and made space for the next person to enter.

The older gentleman, also dressed in a suit, looked at everyone and stated, "Beckett Gentry at your service. Did someone call for a pastor?" He looked at Lexi, the lines in his face full of confusion.

"I didn't call for you, Pastor Gentry," she said, "but it's always good to see you."

"I did," Vance said, and everyone twisted their necks to look at him.

The preacher smiled kindly at her. "Normally, I get called into hospital rooms for somber reasons. But this time, I got called to perform a wedding." He looked at each man. "So, which one of you is the lucky groom?"

Lexi's monitor beeped wildly as if it couldn't take the stress anymore either.

"Okay," the nurse said in a tone that made it clear she was not to be messed with. "We have a patient, nurse, pastor, mother and two possible grooms in this room, which is four too many people. Everyone out."

"But you don't understand," her mother pleaded. "In less than twelve hours—"

"Everyone." Nurse Julie did not break eye contact with her mother. "Out."

After a few seconds of silence, the awkward shuffling began.

Her mother threw a glare at Chase, then eyed Vance. When she looked at Lexi, she said, "For what it's worth, I didn't understand exactly what I was walking into." She swallowed and took a breath. Her tone gentled and the features in her face softened. "I'm glad that the surgery went well and that you're doing better."

The heart monitor and blood-pressure machine would like to debate those words, but Lexi kept her mouth shut. No matter what, she needed to hear that her mother was concerned about her health. As opposed to being concerned about her marital status or trust fund.

"I'll be outside," her mother said before she left the room.

Vance sighed. He rubbed the back of her hand with his. "I'm sorry, Lex. I—"

"With all due respect," Nurse Julie said, "I didn't kick everyone out so you could stay and have a conversation with my patient. She needs rest. And she needs it now."

His shoulders dropped, and he released a long sigh. "I'll be in the waiting room."

In the waiting room. Waiting. To know if they'd get married or not. While she waited in her hospital room, wondering the same thing.

The pastor looked at Lexi and gave her a kind smile. "I'm going to step out. If you need a listening ear, I won't be far."

With everyone exiting, Lexi lost track of Chase. He must have left without saying goodbye.

Again.

She looked at her hands and shook her head. He was the only one she wanted to talk to. But he was also the only one who she shouldn't talk to. She knew where he stood, and she wasn't going to put pressure on him.

Except she heard murmuring on the other

side of the privacy curtain. And then Chase stepped around it, standing square to her.

Julie cleared her throat in a way that told Chase she was not pleased.

"One moment, ma'am," he said to the nurse.

He walked the flowers to Lexi's table and set them down. There must have been fifty white daisies in the stunning arrangement. He held Lexi's eyes in his. "Because everyone deserves fresh flowers."

"Chase, I—"

He ran his finger down her cheek. "I'm here if you need me," he whispered. "And I'm here even if you don't need me."

Chase walked out of her hospital room into the lion's den of another possible groom, a preacher, a pair of her ex-fiancé's parents, and her mother.

Lexi stayed in her room of solitude and impossible questions.

She wasn't sure which of them had it worse. She only knew that she wished he was with her.

CHAPTER TWELVE

ONE NAP, A doctor visit, six hours and seven denied requests to speak to her later, Lexi heard the knock at her door and cringed.

How anyone got rest while checked into a hospital, she didn't know, but her situation seemed to exacerbate the problem.

Nurse Julie threw the privacy curtain aside. "Dinnertime."

"Anything good?"

"Most of it looks okay, but if I were you, I'd hoard the graham crackers." She leaned in and shared as if she were spilling state secrets. "The maternity ward denies it, but they've been known to steal our box for their mommas in labor."

Lexi chuckled, then looked at her food and sobered. "I'm not sure I have an appetite."

"Well, we need you to eat, so we can check successful digestion off your list before we release you. But your situation out in the waiting room makes even my insides a little queasy, and I'm known for having an iron stomach." She took Lexi's cup and filled it with water. "Your fan club keeps growing out there."

Lexi started to tear the wrapper off a cracker but froze. "Who else could be out there?"

The nurse gave her a little smile. "Hunter Cross and the Stimpsons."

This stopped Lexi. She cocked her head. "Do you know everyone?"

"When you work in a small hospital, you get to know a lot of the families in neighboring counties." Julie grinned. "I hadn't had the pleasure of meeting you yet but have been told by three people to ask you for help on my taxes."

"I wonder why they're all here," Lexi said, trying again to pull the plastic apart on the wrapper.

"I'm not sure. But I get the feeling they're here for you." Julie leaned in, took the package from her and ripped it open with ease. "*Just* for you. When and if you're ready."

When and if she was ready.

Lexi put a cracker in her mouth but didn't taste it. She chewed mechanically and swallowed it down with a sip of water. The entire process felt laborious, but not because she'd been sick.

It seemed her body wasn't going to cooperate until she dealt with the crowd in the waiting room and all that came with them.

She took a fortifying breath and said, "Will you please ask Vance to come into the room?"

Nurse Julie had been in the middle of checking her IV, but stopped, moving only her eyes to Lexi. "Vance?"

"Yes, please."

The woman's eyes darted back to the numbers on the IV machine, and then she nodded. "Okay," she said. She turned and took three steps, but at the door, she angled back to Lexi. "But if you need anything—" she lowered her voice "—and I mean *anything*, you press the call button."

At the thought of having her personal bouncer just one room away, Lexi smiled. "Thank you."

With a whoosh of the door, Vance rushed to Lexi's side. His hair was disheveled, and he had removed his tie. "Sweetheart. Lex. How are you?"

And with the sound of the pet names Vance used to call Lexi, she knew what she had to do.

She pushed her tray to the side, stalling while

she mulled over her words. "Vance, thank you for coming."

His alert eyes sharpened. "Of course I came. How are you feeling?"

"I'm better." She offered him a gracious smile. "At least, I'll be better once we pass midnight."

"Right." He gave her a curt nod and paced at the side of her bed. "Pastor Gentry stayed. So he can perform the ceremony."

"Vance—"

"There's an elderly couple in the waiting room who say they're your friends. I figure we can use them as best man and maid of honor." He frowned. "Though, those two are married, so she'd be the matron of honor."

He was rambling. He always rambled when he was nervous.

"Vance—"

He put his hands out. "And I know things aren't well with your mother, but I think you'd regret it if she wasn't at your wedding. So I've been trying to build a bridge between us."

"Vance," she said with more force.

He clamped his mouth shut and stared at her, his eyes part guarded and part hopeful.

"I can't do this," she said softly.

Placing his hands on his hips, his shoulders

drooped, and he bowed his head to look at the ground. "Don't do this, Lex."

"Please come sit next to me." She pointed to the chair beside the bed. "I need to say a few things."

His position remained the same, and he shook his head at the floor. "Please don't do this, Lexi."

The room was so quiet, it was the first time today that she missed the sounds of the heart monitor. Anything to break up the tension.

Lexi gathered her thoughts as moments passed. But time now felt different to Lexi. With her impending birthday, time had been unkind, the unknown ticking its pressure through her life for months. Years.

But as she took a breath and released it, she knew she had found peace with her decision. Time was no longer scary to Lexi.

After Vance sat in the chair at the side of her bed, he took her hand in both of his and rubbed the top of it with his thumbs.

Gently, Lexi said, "I can't marry you, Vance."

He nodded and continued to stroke the top of her hand.

"Can you look at me, please?"

He obliged, but his face held pain, letting her know her request wasn't an easy one.

"I can't marry you because that's not fair to you." He took a breath to say something, but she continued. "I'm in love with someone else."

That stopped him cold. Recognition crossed his face. "The guy in the waiting room."

"But he's not in love with me," Lexi said. "So, it doesn't matter from that standpoint. Except that it's not fair to marry you when I love someone else."

After one final run of his thumbs across her hand, Vance released his hold on her. He sat back and studied her.

"Someone once told me that I deserved to marry a person who treasured me." Lexi stared at her bare left hand, then looked at her ex-fiancé. "And the same is true for you. You need to marry someone who treasures you, Vance."

"Maybe. But what are you going to do about the money?"

"I'm going to let it go."

She took in her first full breath in four weeks. Maybe in two years.

Something struggled behind his eyes. "How can you just let it go?"

Two days ago, she might have considered

marrying Vance so she could claim the trust money. But the closer she got to her birthday, the more she understood something with increasing clarity as the seconds ticked away. She took a breath. "Because it wasn't ever mine to begin with."

Frozen in the wake of her words, Vance stared at her.

"Now," Lexi said with a definitive tone, hoping to pull Vance out of his stupor, "will you please ask my mother to come in here?"

"I'm staying, Lex," he said, his voice firm as he stood. "I'm staying in the waiting room until midnight in case you change your mind."

"But you won't stay after midnight, Vance." She could feel the sad smile forming at her lips. She whispered, "And that should be more concerning to you than letting the money go."

Shaking his head, Vance left her room, giving Lexi only a few moments to recover from one tough conversation and prepare for the next.

She smoothed out the top blanket of her covers and heard her mother's high heels clap against the linoleum floor before she actually saw her mother's face.

But the confident sound of her shoes couldn't cover her mother's uncomfortable demeanor.

Clara Gardner stood at the end of the bed, fidgeting with her hands and looking everywhere but at her daughter.

"Mom?" Lexi called. "Everything okay?"

"I should be—" She swallowed. "I should be asking you that."

Lexi stayed quiet.

"At least—" her mom threw a hand in the direction of the lobby "—that's what a certain Mrs. Patricia Stimpson just said to me."

"Mrs. Stimpson?"

"Yes." Her mother looked like a child who had been scolded. "It seems Patricia knew Louella and had plenty to say to me."

"I think they were close," Lexi said quietly, not knowing how this conversation was going to go. Patricia Stimpson was never one to bridle her thoughts. She only guessed the woman had given her mother a piece of her mind. It almost made her pity her mother.

"Could I please—" Her mother closed her eyes and shook her head. "What I mean is, would it be okay if I came and sat next to you?"

"Yes." Lexi shifted in her bed to angle toward the chair that Vance had just occupied.

Once her mother sat, she clasped her hands

together and instead of looking at Lexi, she spoke to her lap. "We grew up poor."

Lexi remained quiet.

"I had no skills. No education. And the only way I knew how to get out of my situation was to marry someone who could provide for me. I realize that's not a popular thought in this day and age where women can do anything, but it's all I could wrap my brain around."

"And the trust?"

"Louella was your father's mother, and I had no right to that money. But when your father died, I was hurled back to my family roots. I didn't cope well." A sheen of tears hit her mother's eyes. "I know what I did was wrong. That trust has always been yours. I should have let it alone."

Lexi wasn't sure what the future would look like with her mother, but this conversation felt promising.

"Mom, you have to let go of the trust," she whispered.

"I know."

"No. You don't. I mean, you really have to let go of the trust. I'm not getting married tonight."

Abruptly, her mother stood, her chair screeching back a few inches. "What are you talking about?"

"I let Vance go," Lexi said in a calm voice.

Squinching her eyes closed, her mother shook her head quickly several times. "That's probably the right thing to do."

Confused, Lexi studied her mother. "Why the change of heart?"

"Let's just say that being estranged from your daughter for two years is a pain I can't put into words." She wiped a tear off her cheek. "But the second you get a call that your daughter's in surgery, it rights your world back to where it belonged in the first place."

"Mom," Lexi whispered, the lump in her throat almost painful. She wasn't quite sure what to think.

"And what about that other young man in the lobby?" her mother asked.

"What other young man?"

"The one with the twin."

Chase.

Lexi's heart flipped at the thought of the man with the twin.

"He doesn't love me, Mom." She picked up another package of crackers and mashed the contents into pieces. "I'm not going to marry someone who doesn't love me. I deserve more. And so does he."

Her mother hitched a hip out and her entire demeanor changed with full-on attitude and authority. "And just how do you know what he thinks?"

Lexi threw the annihilated cracker package on the dinner tray. "Because he told me."

"Really?" Her mom's entire body bristled. "Because that man asked me for your hand in marriage not an hour ago."

Lexi looked toward the door as if Chase was going to walk through at any minute. "What?" she whispered.

"Yes, ma'am." Her mother yanked her jacket down straight. "Now, what do you think about that?"

He asked her mother for her hand in marriage?

Of course he had. He was the most honorable man Lexi knew. If he was going to marry someone, arranged or otherwise, he would ask the parents for their daughter's hand in marriage.

If Lexi's heart was on the monitor right now, it would spike off the charts.

Only…

She still couldn't marry him.

He was doing it as a favor to her. Forcing himself to morph into something she needed for the trust.

Even if the money could accomplish great things for his nonprofit, marrying Lexi would sacrifice who Chase was. And she couldn't do that to the man she loved.

"Will you please send Hunter Cross into my room?"

Her mother's head reared back. "Hunter? Chase's twin?"

Once Lexi convinced her mother to send in the correct twin, she waited.

She was doing the right thing. She knew it. Right things didn't always feel good when you were doing them, so she ignored the way her heart hurt.

Hunter entered the room and stood a few feet from her bed. He crossed his arms over his vast chest, but said nothing.

Lexi looked out the window, watching the sun go down on the eve of her birthday. "I need you to do me a favor, Hunter."

He grunted.

"I need you to keep Chase out of my room until after midnight."

It was 11:45 p.m., and Chase walked the hospital corridor like a caged tiger.

If he didn't love Lexi so much, he'd charge into her room and tell her how outrageous she was for trying to keep him out. Using his own brother, no less. Chase was going to exchange serious words with him when this was all over.

In some twisted way, Chase was thankful the woman he loved had someone else on her side to protect her. Just not to protect her from *him*.

Hunter stood sentry outside of Lexi's door. Arms crossed, stone-faced and completely impervious to any threat Chase made.

But that was okay.

Hunter wasn't the leader of this platoon. He just didn't know it yet.

As frustrated as Chase was when Hunter put his foot down and wouldn't let him visit Lexi, her ridiculous request lined up nicely with his battle plan. He could wait. He would wait.

Until now.

The Stimpsons stood in front of him, Mr. Stimpson rubbing the back of his neck. "Son, I'm not sure we should do this."

"Oh, hush." Mrs. Stimpson swatted her husband on the arm. "We are totally doing this. All that's required of you is to stand out of sight."

A smile cracked across Mr. Stimpson's face, and he held his hand out to shake Chase's. "I was always a sucker for a good love story. We're rooting for you."

Chase glanced at the clock on the wall. "It's go-time, Mrs. Stimpson. You're up."

The elderly woman pinched her cheeks several times. "This gives some color to my face for dramatic effect." And with that, she scurried down the hall to Hunter.

Chase desperately wanted to watch Mrs. Stimpson wrap Hunter around her finger. Instead, he hightailed it around the square that made up the ward where Lexi's room was located.

Once Chase arrived at the opposite side of the floor, he edged toward the hallway entrance and heard Mrs. Stimpson. "Hunter, they were admitting him to the ER when I left. I don't know what happened. One minute Chase was helping me get coffee and the next he fell to the ground."

Chase heard Hunter's concerned grunt.

"Mr. Stimpson stayed with him and said to come get you." Mrs. Stimpson added in an out-of-breath voice, "So much blood."

Chase bit his fist, trying to get rid of the laughter that wanted to bubble out of his chest. She was giving an Academy Award–winning performance.

Hunter mumbled something to the woman, and they headed to the elevator.

When the elevator doors closed, Chase glanced at the clock in the hallway. Thirteen minutes until her birthday. He slipped into Lexi's room.

Once inside, he leaned a shoulder against the wall, crossed his arms and stared at the patient. The most beautiful patient he'd ever seen.

Lexi had the decency to look guilty.

"I didn't realize you were so close to my brother," Chase said.

"Apparently, not close enough."

"What'd you offer him in return?"

She slid her eyes to the side. "I was going to set up his small business account for the therapy dogs with a tax program to help him with his quarterly reports."

He raised an eyebrow. "Using Gardner Economics against me?"

"Something like that." Her attention fell to the digital clock on her wall. She knew time was running out just as well as he did.

He hated seeing her in a hospital gown. Absolutely hated it. But anything was better than her pale face and curled-up body he'd held in his arms two days ago.

But here, the smell of tension smothered the medicinal hospital scent. Chase felt like he could choke on it. He needed to guide them to a different place, but he wanted the stress behind her eyes to ease first.

"Your mother's not always a pleasant woman," he said of Clara Gardner.

With one glance at the clock, Lexi said, "My mom's not entirely pleased with me."

"Hunter offered to teach her to repair the fence at the back of the property."

A smile came with a quiet giggle from Lexi. Good. He had her laughing.

"She'd be a piece of work on that land," she said.

"Doesn't matter." He grinned. "She'd be preoccupied."

While the pressure had ruptured in the room, it still felt heavy. He lowered his voice. "How are you, honey?"

She swallowed and winced slightly, a reminder to Chase of the tube she'd had down her throat just two days ago during a longer-than-expected surgery to clean up the rampant infection from her burst appendix. "I'm okay," she said.

He splayed his hands on his hips, hanging them off his pressed jeans. Well. Pressed jeans twelve hours ago. After sitting in the waiting room and, alternately, pacing several thousand steps, they looked closer to his everyday pairs. Not exactly how he wanted to look on his wedding day.

And yet, somehow Lexi in her hospital gown was perfect. Her face still glowed with beauty, and her eyes told a story he didn't ever want to end.

But they needed to cover a few topics first.

"You want to tell me why you were so sick that we almost lost you, but you didn't share with anyone that you weren't feeling well?"

"I didn't—"

Unable to be far from her for any longer, he took three strides, sat on her bed and gently took her into his arms. He worried he was crushing her, but couldn't help himself. "You scared me to death," he whispered into her hair.

When he released her, she drew back and said, "I was just so out of sorts. I thought my birthday was making me sick. I didn't think anything was wrong."

"You scared me to death," he repeated.

"I know." She put her hand on his forearm. "I know. And I'm so sorry. That's what I want to say to you. I'm so sorry. You had to bring me to the hospital, and that was probably so hard on you."

"Let me get this straight." He bent lower so he could look her in the eyes and understand if he heard correctly. "*Your* appendix burst and *you're* apologizing to *me*? It seems like you've got this wrong."

"Maybe." She looked over his shoulder then back at him. "But the thing you got wrong, Chase, is that you actually considered my marriage proposal."

"What? What are you talking about?" This time he was the one who glanced at the clock. This conversation just took a turn he wasn't sure time would allow.

She shook her head. "Can you sit back a few feet? I think this would be easier if I could explain it to you without being in such close proximity."

He narrowed his eyes at her. "I'm fine where I am." He wasn't going to give her space. If he had anything to do with it, he wouldn't give her space for the next fifty years.

But the feeling coming off Lexi said she had other ideas. He stayed where he was and braced for her words.

She picked at a stray thread on her blanket, and her voice became small. "I'm releasing you from my proposal."

Something metal clamped onto his heart. He steeled his voice. "Why?"

"Because I can't ask you to do that for me."

"Why not?"

She swallowed and looked straight into his eyes, her brown ones pooling with tears. "Because," she whispered, "I accidentally fell in love with you."

The grip on his heart released, and he took a beat to let her words soak into his bones. She fell in love with him. He kept his voice calm. "Good."

"Good?"

"Yes. Good." He took a breath, the space over his heart filling with something foreign. Something warm. Something peaceful. For the first time in four weeks, he could fill his lungs to capacity. "Perfect, in fact."

Her beautiful eyes blinked repeatedly, confusion crossing her brow. "Good that I'm releasing you from my proposal?"

"Yes." He nodded. He hated how torn she looked, but all would become clear in just a few moments. He stood and pulled a small velvet box out of his pocket.

This morning, he wasn't sure if it was wise to take extra time to shop for and purchase a ring, but he took the risk. When he showed up and Vance was in her room, he thought he'd chosen wrong and that the extra time away from the hospital might have cost him Lexi. But hearing of her love for him and seeing her stare at the box, he knew he'd chosen correctly.

He knelt on one knee, ignoring the hard floor, and said, "Don't be angry with me, Lexi."

"Angry?" she squeaked.

His lips lifted in a small grin. "I didn't have time to find a coupon for this purchase. I hope that doesn't make you too angry to answer my question."

Her mouth gaped, but nothing came out.

When he opened the box, a beautiful platinum band displayed a square-cut diamond. A stunning, no-frills diamond, for a stunning, no-frills woman.

"Now that you've recanted your proposal," he said, putting his heart on the line, "maybe you can accept mine. Alexis Jane Gardner, will you marry me?"

She touched her fingertips to her lips. "Marry you?"

"Will you argue with me for the rest of our lives?"

She blinked.

"Will you teach our kids Gardner Economics?"

"You want kids?" she breathed, her question lined with hope.

He nodded.

"I didn't think I'd ever get to have kids," she said on a sob.

"Will you wear matching shirts with me like the Stimpsons when we grow old?"

"The Stimpsons?"

A tear drew down her cheek, and he gently thumbed it away. "They're out in the lobby right now in blue-and-white-checked button-downs."

A single laugh bubbled out of her. But then her face fell.

She wrapped her hands around his and the box he was still holding. "I can't marry you, Chase."

He studied her face. She loved him. He knew it. So that wasn't the problem. "Did you already marry Vance?" he asked. "Because if so, he does not look like a happy groom."

Her face broke in shock, and she barked out a laugh this time. "No. I did not marry Vance."

The heaviness of getting married had weighed on her far too long. And while he was again glad to lighten the mood, he still had to get to the root of the problem. He gentled his voice. "Then why can't you marry me, honey?"

"Chase, you don't want to get married again. As much as I love you, I can't ask you to be something you aren't."

He stood, edged his hip onto the side of the mattress and sat beside her on the bed. After placing the ring on her bedside table, he took her face in his hands and pressed his forehead against hers. "And what if I do love you? Am I allowed to change my mind and say I want to get married again? To you?"

Slowly, so slowly it was almost painful for Chase to wait, she pulled back and looked at him. Her eyes perused his face, searching. He waited, trying to remind himself to breathe.

"Why are you saying this now?" she asked.

"Someday," he said quietly, "I'll tell you a story about how God moved a mountain."

"But what changed?"

"I can't live my life looking for guarantees. At some point, I have to trust."

She looked down at her hands, then back to him. The most gorgeous smile broke across her face. "Yes. I will marry you."

He nodded, knowing the battle wasn't over, but so very happy that they'd gotten this far.

One glance told him he only had a few minutes remaining to make his point.

Before he put the ring on her finger, or kissed this beautiful woman, he said, "And there's one more thing."

Her eyes darted around the room, as if something or someone was going to jump out at her. And, in a sense, his next request might feel like it.

"I want you to marry me tonight. At 12:01 a.m."

"Chase, what are you talking about? You know—" she shook her head "—you know that tomorrow is my birthday. We have to get married before midnight to save the ranch. There's a pastor in the waiting room. Let's do it now. We say 'I do,' sign the papers and it's done. It would take two minutes, and everything is solved."

That thing in his heart squeezed. She was ridiculously generous. But her generosity might kill their marriage before it started.

"I won't marry you a minute before 12:01." He pulled the marriage license out of his back pocket, unfolded the paper and placed it on her hospital tray. He pounded a pen flush to the top of it and left his palm covering both pen and paper. "We aren't signing this until it's officially tomorrow."

She leaned back, her head turning from marriage license to him. Once more to the papers and then back to him. "I don't understand."

"Lexi, if we get married before midnight, you'll always wonder if I did it for the money."

"No. I won't. I'll…" When her voice trailed off, she looked at him, her face full of hurt. "Is that what you think of me?"

"No," he said in a tone that brooked no argument. "Not in any way. But we can't risk this. We can't risk that at some point in time, this money becomes a third wheel in our marriage. We have to know, both of us, without a doubt, that we got married because we love each other."

She looked toward the clock. To the paper. Back to him.

He left his palm on the marriage license and pen. "You once told me that you needed the price of gas to go down and a universal charger that crossed electronic brands."

She released something between a laugh and a sob. "How can you remember all of that?"

"I think I remember everything you've said to me since the moment we met," he whispered.

She leaned in and placed her hand on his cheek, pulling him to her and resting her forehead against his.

"I can't give any of that to you, honey. And I can't marry you for your money." He brushed a lock of hair from her cheek to behind her ear. "But I can give you something more important."

"What's that?"

"I can give you the knowledge that you were chosen—" he brushed his lips against hers "—just for who you are."

"Because you treasure me." Her voice trembled.

"Yes," he said. Relief filled his chest. She got it. She finally understood.

"But what about the ranch? We have an opportunity to do good things with that money."

"Lexi." He pulled back. "Do you trust me? Do you trust God? Because that's the choice we get. I can't solve everything financial right now. But I refuse to marry you if it has anything to do with that money."

Her head moved in small, quick shakes, and he shifted his hands away from her face. "But my second cousin."

"That's not up to us. The only thing that's up

to us right now is this. Will you marry me? At 12:01 a.m.? And not a minute sooner?"

"This is absurd," she whispered.

"I know, honey. I know that Gardner Economics does not understand this. But marrying me cannot be about an equation. It has to be about our love for each other."

He took her hand and pressed it over his on the license and pen, then he covered their hands with his free one. They turned to watch the clock, their heads pressed together.

11:59.

His breathing sped up to match hers. Their hearts somehow knew they were running down the aisle to each other. And it would only be a few seconds longer.

"I love you, Chase."

The clock struck midnight.

"Happy Birthday, Alexis." He pulled back and took her face in his hands. He touched his lips to hers, promising her everything he had to give her.

"Ahem."

Lexi ran her hands through Chase's hair while he continued to kiss her.

"I don't think they care we're in here," someone murmured.

"I don't think they even know we're in here," another voice said.

Someone coughed. "Most grooms kiss their brides after the wedding. Do you want me to perform this ceremony now, or should I come back?"

Chase couldn't help his smile. He brushed a final kiss to Lexi's forehead and pulled back. She peeked around him. "We're really getting married now?"

"Only if you want to," he said, feeling so much love for the woman in front of him, he hardly knew what to do with it all. "I have a crew of people ready to put on a midnight wedding in the chapel."

She grinned up at him, making him want to kiss her all over again. "Yes, please," she said.

Within thirty seconds, the room flooded with friends and family. Chase carefully resituated himself next to his fiancée on her hospital bed and watched the scurry of people.

"Where did everyone come from?" Lexi asked.

He wrapped an arm around her. "I might have made some calls."

"They showed for me at midnight?" she asked in disbelief.

He squeezed her shoulder. "This town doesn't look at you as just an integral part of Gardner Economics. You're one of their own."

She put her hand over his and studied each person in the room, a look of awe and wonder on her face.

Alison Velasquez entered with a two-tiered white cake. "White chocolate on the inside with vanilla frosting on the outside." She placed the cake on a small table in the corner of the room. "And we can't forget this." After digging into the pocket of her jacket, she pulled out a plastic bride and groom and gently pushed them into the top of the thick frosting.

"That bride needs a different kind of gown. A hospital gown," Lexi said on a smile.

"But you do have a veil," Alison said as she scooted around people to get to Lexi. "I sew on the side and had an extra that hasn't been purchased yet."

"Let me help with that." Lexi's mother took the shoulder-length, three-layer veil. She had a brush at the ready and worked through Lexi's hair, then attached the veil comb to the top of her daughter's head. When she pulled back to inspect her work, a sheen of tears lined her eyes. "Is it okay that I'm here?" she whispered.

Lexi took her mother's hand in hers. "I wouldn't want to get married without you present."

The florist flitted around the room, attaching red rose boutonnieres to the men and handing long-stemmed singles to the women. She pulled out a huge bouquet of cream-colored calla lilies, bound by a silky cream ribbon. "Fresh and new," she whispered when she handed them to Lexi.

Someone caught Lexi's eye, and Chase followed her line of sight.

Frank wedged himself into the corner of the room, a 35mm camera hung around his neck by a woven strap that belonged back in the seventies.

"What is your foreman doing?" she asked Chase quietly, though not quietly enough.

Frank looked at Lexi. "I know more than just cows and fertilizer."

She giggled.

"He's the photographer for the wedding. He took most of the pictures in the lodge." Including the shot of Laura skiing downhill. Chase filled with warmth. There was something beautiful about Frank being here for this moment, too.

"I brought you a present," Hunter announced from the door.

"I'm not sure I want anything from you," Chase said in all seriousness, though everyone in the room chuckled. This group had had a front row seat to Hunter standing guard at Lexi's door.

"You'll want this," his twin said.

Their sister, Cora, peeked her head into the room.

Chase stood with his mouth open. It had been too long since he'd seen her. Her hair had grown and now covered the scar he knew was there, and her eyes told of a maturity he'd never seen in his little sister.

He got off the bed and engulfed her in a hug. "I'm so glad you're here," he whispered into her hair, his voice thick.

"I wouldn't miss this for the world." She pulled back, but kept a grip on his arms. "I wish Mom and Dad could be here."

"Yeah," he said. The space in his heart where only his parents lived squeezed.

"But I have something that puts them in the room with us." She shoved her hand into her jeans pocket and pulled out their father's wedding band. She set the ring in his palm.

He could only stare at it. "I don't know what to say."

"There's nothing needed to say," she replied softly. Then she took her voice up a notch and said to the room, "Are we going to have a wedding or what? I told Gretel Heard I couldn't deliver her daughter's baby until my brother got married, and she wasn't too happy. Let's get this show on the road."

Everyone chuckled, but Chase knew better. She'd drop him faster than a hot pan off the stove if a patient needed her.

He glanced around the crowd, but didn't find the other face he was looking for.

Hunter clapped him on the shoulder. His twin said quietly, "Couldn't get a hold of him."

Chase nodded once. He wouldn't let Ryder's absence ruin his wedding day.

"Age before beauty," Mrs. Stimpson said as she pushed through everyone to get to the end of Lexi's hospital bed.

Hunter scowled at the elderly woman and her husband. "You two have a lot to answer for."

Mrs. Stimpson stuck her nose in the air. "I'll do no such thing. If the roles were reversed, Hunter Cross, I would have done the same for you."

"I take it there's a story behind that comment?" Lexi asked Chase.

"I'll tell you later." Chase took his place next to his bride. "Suffice it to say, the Stimpsons played a role in getting me into your room."

Lexi smiled at Mrs. Stimpson. "I can't believe you're both here so late."

"Are you kidding? This is the most excitement I've had since Louella hot-wired Henry Gunner's scooter and took a joy ride through Bright Horizons."

Lexi's mother's mouth gaped. She clutched at her necklace. "My mother-in-law stole someone's scooter?"

Mrs. Stimpson grinned. "Stick around, and I'll tell you more stories you won't believe."

Nurse Julie tromped into Lexi's room.

"I thought you were off tonight," Lexi said.

"I *am* off," she said, crossing her arms. "Because if I was *on*, I would have to care about visitor hours and visitor capacity. But as of right now, I'm attending the wedding of a new friend. A new friend who needs her rest and therefore needs this to be the shortest wedding in the history of wedding ceremonies."

Pastor Gentry nodded to Julie and cleared his throat. "All right. Could everyone please proceed to the chapel and take your places?"

And with Chase standing to the right of the stage, in the dim light of the small hospital chapel, he watched as Lexi's mother pushed Lexi's wheelchair. Her mother on one side and the IV stand on the other, with a smile so big he wondered if it hurt her, Lexi slowly made her way down the short aisle to him. She was radiant. And he couldn't believe he was going to get to marry this woman.

After exchanging *I do*s, rings and short vows, they toasted apple juice, ate cake and finally signed the wedding license.

At 12:37 a.m.

CHAPTER THIRTEEN

Sun streamed through the blinds of Lexi's hospital room, begging her to see what the new day would bring.

Her birthday. Her thirty-fifth birthday.

In all her years of knowing what this particular birthday meant, she never imagined she would wake up to the sight in front of her.

She couldn't take her eyes off her sleeping husband. Hair tousled. Stubble shadowing his strong jaw. Legs stretched out long and boots crossed at the ankles. Arms also crossed, but against his chest, somehow making his shoulders appear wider, able to carry whatever burden came their way.

With slow blinks, a yawn and a stretch of his arms over his head, Chase awoke. He focused his eyes on her. "How are you feeling this morning, honey?"

"Wonderful," she said softly.

He pushed out of his chair and sat next to her on the bed. He took her hands in his and brushed his lips against hers. Sweet. Gentle. "Good morning, beautiful." His voice was thick with sleep and affection.

Heat hit her face, and it took her a second to understand what she was feeling. Something bashful seemed to flitter across her nerves.

"Don't blush," he whispered in her ear as he slipped his arms around her. "I'm your husband now. I get to tell you how pretty you are as often as I want."

She laughed, part nervous, part practical. "I'm in a hospital gown with my arm hooked up to an IV. Not to sound critical, but I think your bar is a little low."

He pulled back and grinned. "We've got to bust you out of this joint. And soon."

"Amen to that."

Her ringtone sounded from the bedside table.

Chase pulled her phone off her charger and handed it to her. When she saw who was calling on the display, she blanched. "It's my lawyer."

"Better take that, honey." He nodded to her and held her eyes in his. "It'll be okay. You can tell him what happened, and we'll figure the rest out. In the meantime, I have a small wedding gift for you. But you can't peek while I'm getting it set up."

She furrowed her brows at her husband, but hit the screen to answer, turned the call to speaker, then laid the phone between them. "Hi, Mr. Morton."

Chase positioned himself at the foot of the bed and proceeded to pull the covers up over her feet, bunching them so high she couldn't see what he was doing.

"Lexi, I'm sorry to call so early." Mr. Morton's voice sounded through the phone speaker. "But the lawyer representing the trust contacted me first thing and wanted an update on your situation."

A squeeze of her foot from her husband fortified her. "Well, I have some good news, Mr. Morton, but it might not be what you think." She smiled, and looking straight into Chase's hazel eyes, she said, "I got married last night."

Chase grinned back at her and removed her socks.

Mr. Morton started to congratulate her, but she interrupted him, still smiling and staring into her husband's beautiful eyes. "We didn't get married before midnight, Mr. Morton."

While silence came from the other end of

the line, Chase turned, blocking her view from what he was doing. Mr. Morton finally said, "I don't understand."

"We got married after midnight. The trust fund will have to go to someone else."

More silence. With the hospital covers still blocking her view, Chase slipped a pair of socks onto her feet. Lexi sat up straight.

She hit Mute on the phone. "I want to see," she said to Chase urgently.

"Patience." He held on to the railing and made movements that looked like he was toeing off his boots. When Lexi tried to peek around the bed to see what he was doing, he held up his hand to signal her to stop.

She rolled her eyes playfully and unmuted the phone. "Mr. Morton, are you still there?"

"Hang on, Ms. Gardner."

"It's Mrs. Cross now, Mr. Morton." Chase's gaze heated, and she winked.

"Hang on, Mrs. Cross." Lexi could hear what sounded like papers shuffling in the background of the call but was distracted when Chase sat next to her on the bed.

"Scooch over," he muttered quietly.

When she made room for him, in one fell

swoop, he slung his legs parallel to hers on the bed and yanked the covers off her feet.

Thick white socks covered her feet, pink letters across her toes spelling the word "Wife." On Chase's feet were the matching set with dark blue letters that spelled the word "Husband."

She burst out laughing and wrapped her arms around his neck. "I can't believe you did this."

"Ms. Gard—Mrs. Cross?" her lawyer called from the phone.

Tamping down her giggles, Lexi answered, "Sorry, Mr. Morton. We're here."

"What time was it you got married?"

"It doesn't matter. It was after midnight."

"I understand. But what time was it? Exactly?"

Chase snagged the marriage license off the tray table and held it in front of them.

This conversation was trying its best to dampen her first day as a married woman. But she wouldn't let it. Her lawyer must have to document all the details to pass the information on and close his file. She could respect that. "Our marriage license says we were officially married at 12:37 a.m."

"What time zone?"

"Mountain," she replied.

More silence. Lexi shrugged at Chase. She had no idea why this was taking so long. Chase took her hand in his. He thumbed the new rings on her finger. During the ceremony, he'd added a thin band circled with tiny diamonds.

"Mrs. Cross, the trust clearly states you had to be married by 11:59 p.m.—"

"Yes, I know."

"—Pacific time."

This time the silence was on her end. Slowly, both Chase and Lexi lifted their gaze from their joined hands to each other.

"What did you just say?" she asked, not taking her eyes from Chase, his face filled with the same expression of confusion and disbelief that no doubt filled her own.

"You had to be married by 11:59 p.m. on the eve of your thirty-fifth birthday, Pacific time."

"Lexi…" Her name trailed off Chase's tongue.

She could feel herself blinking rapidly. She knew she should say something. But her brain couldn't register his words.

"You were married at 12:37 a.m. Mountain time, which was 11:37 p.m. Pacific time. You successfully fulfilled the stipulations of the trust."

Mr. Morton continued to ramble instructions to Lexi. Something about filing the license with the state and getting it to him as soon as possible. Something else about proper channels and granting her access to the account.

Lexi couldn't be entirely sure about any of those details because she was preoccupied with kissing Chase Cross. Her husband.

EPILOGUE

"DUKE!" CHASE WHISTLED across the field, hoping his dog would respond to him. In the last year, Duke had all but abandoned his loyalties to Chase and vowed his life to Lexi. But the way Duke had been circling his wife the last few weeks gave him pause.

What was wrong with his dog?

For that matter, what was wrong with his wife?

Punctual used to be her middle name. But now he was out looking for her because their impending family dinner would start soon, and she was nowhere to be found. Lately, she'd lost track of time. And seemed a little tired. He'd have to talk to her about her work schedule. Getting the nonprofit up and running while still working with a few accounting clients had taken its toll.

Lexi exited a trail coming from a cabin. No

doubt she was welcoming the latest army veteran and his wife. They came to Four Cross Ranch with both their car and relationship on fumes. He prayed the ranch could offer them refuge and hope.

Chase's wife caught sight of him and waved.

She walked toward him, his dog pasted to her side. When she got to him, she lifted on tiptoes and kissed him. She smelled of wildflowers, his land and a life full of love.

Duke bumped Chase's hand, almost as if to push him away.

"What is wrong with you, Duke?"

Lexi giggled. "Nothing's wrong with him. He's just protective."

"From me?" He looked at Duke and said, "That makes no sense."

"It might soon," Lexi muttered, looking at her dog, a smile on her lips.

"You've been a little tired lately, so I thought I'd bring you a pick-me-up before family dinner." He handed her the travel mug of coffee he had in tow. "With peppermint. Just how you like it."

She looked at the mug, her brow a touch furrowed. "Oh, thanks. I'll just wait for it to cool down some."

"How are the Hensons?" he asked of the latest veteran family as he took her hand in his to walk toward the parking lot.

"Settled in." She glanced back to Chase. "What's going on with Hunter? I saw him working on the back side of the property earlier today. Did you banish him to fence repair?"

"He's pouting." She raised her eyebrows, and he explained. "Sheila told him she's engaged to her high school boyfriend. Happened right under his nose. He's so miserable to be around, he sent himself out to work the fence."

"I hate that he's upset. I think he enjoyed her company, but he was never quite committed to her."

"I don't think he knows what he wants." Chase shook his head. His brother had been tight-lipped. "I told him he had to be on his best behavior tonight, though."

Walking their way off property to the parking lot, they closed the gate and left Duke on the opposite side to stay at the ranch while they dined. He paced back and forth, yelping at them every time he turned. Chase shook his head. Seriously. What was going on with his dog?

When they reached the parking lot, Lexi

shaded her eyes with her hand and looked around. "Where's my car?"

"Over here." Chase led her to the side of the lot and stood them in front of a silver Ford F-150 Lightning truck.

She stared at him. "I don't understand."

Grinning, he pulled the key fob out of his pocket, held it out for her to see and beeped the locks open.

Her eyes grew wide. "What did you do?"

"Don't be mad," he said, unable to contain his smile.

She put a hand over her mouth and shook her head. "What did you do?"

"I am a very patient man. I waited a long time for you to purchase a vehicle suitable for Wyoming winters and terrain." She opened her mouth to respond, but he held his hand up. "Before you say anything, do I need to mention how many times we've pulled you out of a ditch?"

She shook her head once. His wife was cute.

"A buddy of mine inherited this truck, among other things, when his dad died. He and his brothers all clocked military time. Some fared better than others. He sold the truck to me discounted in exchange for weeks at the ranch for his and his brothers' families. But I might have accidentally written him a check for the full amount anyway."

She threw her arms around him. "You are officially a master at Gardner Economics."

"I learned from the best." He opened the driver's-side door, and Lexi climbed into the seat. "I need my girl in a safe ride."

"For more reasons than you know." She beamed a smile at him.

He thought he had learned all of Lexi's smiles. Light of the morning smile. Glad to see him smile. Her mischievous smiles that always threw him off. But this one—he didn't recognize this smile. And yet his nerve endings buzzed at the sight of it.

Lexi shifted her weight so she could pull something out of her back pocket. "If we're doing random gifts now, you should open this." She handed him a small card. "I made it myself." She licked her lips. "I mean, I had help. But it's homemade."

Whatever was in this card made his wife's cheeks pink. He ripped the envelope open and saw the contents. His entire body froze.

"I also got you these." Her voice quivered,

and she placed a pair of socks in his hand. Across the toes in black letters read the word "Daddy."

With a picture of a sonogram in one hand and a pair of socks declaring his fatherhood in the other, he looked at his wife. His beautiful, beaming, pregnant-woman-who-his-dog-is-protecting wife.

Chase stepped flush to the truck, slid his hands around Lexi and buried his face in her hair.

"Thank you for the truck, Chase. Now your girls," she whispered, "or your girl and your boy, will have a safe ride."

He didn't want to squeeze her too hard, but they stayed embraced for as long as he could manage before they headed to the restaurant. The entire night Chase spent glued to his wife. He felt unsettled if he wasn't connected to her in some way. An arm around her chair, a hand playing with her hair, their fingers intertwined.

He and his dog were about to come to blows to see who got to be by Lexi's side for the next nine months.

Chase paid the bill, and they walked Hunter and Cora to the front of the restaurant.

"Happy for you, man." Hunter clapped Chase

on the shoulder, then lowered his voice. "I don't think I ever want my own, but you're happy. Lexi's happy. All of that is good."

Before Chase could address his brother's surprising comment, Hunter grinned and said, "Aren't you glad we didn't hire the old man accountant?"

Lexi sent Chase a questioning look. He squeezed her to his side. "I never considered hiring anyone other than you."

Cora approached and went up on tiptoe to kiss him on the cheek.

"Thanks for coming to dinner, Cora." Lexi leaned into his sister for a hug.

"I'm thrilled for you." She pulled back but didn't let go of Lexi's arms. "I'm going to be an aunt," she squealed.

Lexi laughed and rubbed her flat stomach. "I'm hoping you'll be one of the first to meet this little one. Would you feel comfortable helping with the delivery?"

"I'm always up for a delivery." Chase knew that was the truth. "But you'll have to come off that ranch for me to deliver your baby." Cora flicked her hand out in farewell, and Hunter walked her to her car.

A tired Lexi insisted Chase drive the new

truck home. Within three minutes, she'd fallen asleep.

With his sleeping wife, carrying his baby, they drove past his mountain and straight home. To Four Cross Ranch.

★ ★ ★ ★ ★

WESTERN

Rugged men looking for love...

Available Next Month

Redeeming The Maverick Christine Rimmer
The Right Cowboy Cheryl Harper

....

Fortune's Secret Marriage Jo McNally
Home To Her Cowboy Sasha Summers

....

LOVE INSPIRED

His Unexpected Grandchild Myra Johnson
His Neighbour's Secret Lillian Warner

Keep reading for an excerpt of a new title
from the Historical series,
THE KISS THAT MADE HER COUNTESS
by Laura Martin

Chapter One

❦

Northumberland, Midsummer's Eve, 1816

Not for the first time that evening Alice felt ridiculous. She glanced down at the borrowed dress, the hem splattered with mud, and the delicate shoes. If they ever made it to Lady Salisbury's ball she would trail dirt all over the ballroom floor.

'Come, Alice. We can't stop now,' Lydia called over her shoulder before vaulting over a wooden fence. Alice followed a little more slowly, wondering how she had been dragged into this madcap plan. 'We're almost there. I swear I can hear the music.'

With as much grace and elegance as she could muster, Alice climbed over the fence, closing her eyes in horror as the material of her dress snagged on a protruding nail. There was the sickening sound of ripping fabric as she lost her balance and the dress was tugged free.

'Lydia, wait,' Alice shouted, looking up to see her friend plunging head first through a hedge. She had no choice but to follow, grimacing as she spotted the ripped area near the hem of her dress. Hopefully she would be able to mend it and clean it before her cousin even noticed the dress was missing.

She paused before the hedge, wondering how Lydia had made her way through the dense foliage, and then a hand shot out and gripped her wrist. Lydia was giggling as Alice emerged, an expression of surprise on her face, and soon Alice was laughing too.

'Just think, in a few minutes we will be whirling across the ballroom in the arms of the most handsome bachelors in all of Northumberland,' Lydia said as she gripped Alice's hand. 'Maybe there will be a dashing duke or an eligible earl to sweep you off your feet.'

For a moment Alice closed her eyes and contemplated the possibilities. It was highly unlikely she would meet anyone at the ball that could save her from the impending match that made her heart sink every time she thought of her future.

'My last night of freedom,' she murmured.

Lydia scoffed. 'You make it sound as if you are on your way to the gallows.'

'That is exactly what it feels like.'

'Surely he is not that bad.'

Alice screwed up her face and gave a little shudder. 'I am well aware I have lived a sheltered life so have not come across the scoundrels and the criminals of this country, but Cousin Cecil is by far the worst person I have ever met.'

'Perhaps your parents will not make you marry him.'

'I doubt they will save me from that fate.' Tomorrow Alice's second cousin, Cecil Billington, was coming to stay for a week with the single purpose of finalising an agreement of marriage between him and Alice. As yet he had not proposed, but Alice was aware of the negotiations going on in the background with her father. She hadn't dared enquire as to the specifics; even just the idea of Cecil made her feel sick.

'Then, tonight will have to make up for the next forty years of putting up with Cecil.'

Lydia grabbed her by the hand and began pulling her over the grass again. The house was in view now, the terrace at the back lit up with dozens of lamps positioned at equal intervals along the stone balustrade. Music drifted out from the open doors, and there was the swell of voices as those escaping the heat of the ballroom strolled along the terrace.

'Someone will see us,' Alice said, feeling suddenly exposed. There was only about thirty feet separating them and the house now, but it was all open lawn, and by the time they reached the steps leading up to the terrace it would be a miracle if they made it even halfway unobserved.

'Then, let us act like we belong. We more than look the part. If we stroll serenely arm-in-arm, I wager no one will pay us any attention. We are just two invited guests having a wonderful time at the Midsummer's Eve ball.'

Alice considered for a moment and then nodded. 'You are right. If we try to creep in, it will be obvious immediately. The only way we have half a chance is by pretending we are meant to be here.'

Instantly she straightened her back and lifted her chin, trying to mimic the poise and confidence of Lady Salisbury, the hostess of the sumptuous masked ball. Sometimes Alice would catch a glimpse of the viscountess stepping out of her carriage or taking a stroll through the extensive grounds of Salisbury Hall. She looked regal in her posture and elegant in her movements, and Alice tried to copy how she held herself and how she walked.

'Wait,' Lydia called and slipped a mask into Alice's hand. It was delicate in design, only meant to fit over the upper part of the wearer's face. White in colour, it had an intricate silver pattern painted onto it, a collection of swirls and dots that glimmered in the moonlight. Alice put it on, securing the mask with the silver ribbon tied into a bow at the back of her head. She looked over to Lydia to see her friend had a similar mask now obscuring the top half of her face.

Lydia slipped her arm through Alice's, and together they strolled slowly across the lawn. Despite her urge to run, Alice knew this ruse would work best if they moved at a sedate pace. No one blinked as they ascended the stairs onto the terrace, and Alice heard her friend suppress a little squeal of excitement as they reached the doors to the ballroom.

Neither girl had ever been to a ball like this before. On occasion they would attend the dances at the local Assembly Rooms, but even those were few and far between. Once Alice had begged her parents to allow her and her sister to stay with some friends in Newcastle to enjoy the delights of the social calendar there, but worried about their daughters' reputations, her parents had refused.

'This is magical,' Alice whispered, pausing on the threshold to take everything in. The room was large and richly decorated. The walls were covered in the finest cream wallpaper. At set intervals there were large, gold-framed mirrors, positioned to reflect the guests on the dance floor and make the ballroom seem as if it were even bigger than it was. From the ceiling hung two magnificent chandeliers, each with at least a hundred candles burning bright and illuminating the room. In between the mirrors on the walls there were yet more candles, flickering and reflecting off the glass and making the whole ballroom shimmer and shine.

The assembled guests added to the vision of opulence, the men in finely tailored tailcoats with silk cravats and the women in beautiful dresses of silk and satin. The theme of this masked ball was the Midsummer celebrations, and many of the guests had dressed with a nod to this in mind. Some women had freshly picked flowers woven into their hair or pinned to their dresses as they normally would a brooch.

'I have never seen anything like this,' Lydia said, her mouth open in awe.

'Thank you,' Alice said, squeezing her friend's hand. 'For making me come tonight. You're right. I deserve one last night of happiness before a lifetime of being married to vile Cousin Cecil.'

Lydia leaned in close and held Alice's eye. 'Enjoy it to the utmost. Dance with every man that asks, sip sparkling wine like it is water, admire all the marvellous women in their beautiful dresses.'

'I will.'

For a moment Alice felt a little overwhelmed. This was not her world, not where she belonged, and she was aware she didn't know how to talk to these people. It felt as though someone might come and pluck her out of the crowd and announce *Alice James, you do not belong here.*

A young gentleman, no older than Alice and Lydia, approached, swallowing nervously. He smiled at them both, showing a line of crooked teeth, and then directed his focus on Lydia.

'I know we have not been introduced, but may I have the pleasure of the next dance?'

Alice watched as her friend blushed under her mask. Lydia was bold and confident on the outside, but sometimes she would stutter and stammer amongst people she did not know.

'I would be delighted,' Lydia said, giving Alice a backwards glance as her partner led her off to the edge of the dance floor to wait for the next dance to be called.

Suddenly alone Alice felt very exposed, and she shrank back, aghast when she brushed against a large pot filled with a leafy plant with brightly coloured flowers. It wobbled on its table, threatening to crash to the ground. She lunged, trying to steady it, and as her hands reached around the ceramic she had an awful vision of the container crashing to the floor and the whole ballroom turning to her in the silence that followed, realising she shouldn't be there.

'Steady,' a deep voice said right in her ear, making her jump and almost sending the pot flying again. An arm brushed past her waist, reaching quickly to stop the plant from toppling.

For a long moment Alice did not move, only turning when she was certain there was going to be no terrible accident with the plant in front of her. When she did finally turn she inhaled sharply. Standing right behind her, just the right distance away so as not to attract any disapproving stares, was the most handsome man she had ever laid eyes on. He wasn't wearing a mask, and Alice reasoned there was no point. Everyone in the room would know who he was just by looking at his eyes. They were blue, but not the same pale blue of her own eyes but bright and vibrant, piercing in their intensity. He had that attractive combination of blue eyes and dark hair that was uncommon in itself but that, added to the perfect proportions of the rest of his facial features, meant he was easily the most desirable man in the room.

'Thank you,' she said, her heart still pounding in her chest from the worry that she was about to cause a scene with the crashing décor. 'That could have been a disaster.'

Simon smiled blandly at the pretty young woman in front of him and turned to leave, not wanting to get caught up in conversation with someone he should probably know. There were hundreds of young ladies in Northumberland he'd been introduced to, and he could never remember their names. It was one of the tribulations of being an earl: everyone knew you, everyone recognised you, and most expected you to remember them.

His brother had been good at that sort of thing, remembering every face and name, making connections between members of the same families. When out on the estate or visiting the local village Robert would stop and talk to almost everyone he met, enquiring after the health of various ailing relatives or newborn babies. Robert had been loved by their tenants and staff in a way that was impossible to follow, especially when Simon had trouble remembering even a fraction of the names of the people he encountered in the local area.

As he turned he spotted his sister-in-law entering the ballroom. He had a lot of time and respect for Maria, the dowager countess, but right now he did not want to see her. Recently she had been urging him to marry and settle down, which was the furthest thing from what he had planned for his life. Tonight no doubt she would have a list of eligible young ladies lined up for him to dance with, all perfectly nice and decent young ladies, but there was no point in him seeking a connection with anyone, not now, not ever.

Not wanting to get caught by Maria and her list of accomplished young ladies, he hastily turned back to the woman in front of him.

'I don't think we've been introduced,' he said.

'Miss Alice James,' she said, bobbing into a little curtsy. She looked up at him expectantly, and he realised she was waiting for him to introduce himself.

'Lord Westcroft,' he said, seeing her eyes widen. Unless she was a consummate actress it would seem she hadn't known who he was. He didn't like to view himself as conceited, but generally most people *did* recognise him when he entered a room. It was one of the disadvantages of being an earl.

'A pleasure to meet you, my Lord.'

'The dancing is about to begin, Miss James. I wonder if I might have the pleasure of this dance?'

'You want to dance with me?' She sounded incredulous, and he had to suppress a smile at her honest reaction.

'If that is agreeable to you?'

She nodded, and he held out his arm to her, escorting

her to the dance floor just as the musicians played the first note of the music for a country dance.

He had been dancing all his life, and over the years been to hundreds of balls and danced countless dances. Before his brother had died he had quite enjoyed socialising, but everything had lost its shine after Robert's death. Miss James stood opposite him and beamed, looking around her in delight. She was young, but not so young that this could be her first ball, and he wondered if she approached everything with such irrepressible happiness.

The dance was fast-paced, and as it was their turn to progress down the line of other dancers, Miss James looked up at him and smiled with such unbridled joy that for a moment he froze. Thankfully he recovered before she noticed, and they continued the dance without him missing a step, but as they took their place at the end of the line he found he could not take his eyes off her. Even with her mask on he could see she was pretty. She had thick auburn hair that was pinned back in the current fashion, but a few strands had slipped loose and curled around her neck. Her eyes were a pale blue that shimmered in the candlelight, but the part of her he felt himself drawn to was her lips. She smiled all the time, her expression varying between a closed-lip, small smile of contentment to a wider smile of pleasure at various points throughout the dance. When she got a step wrong, she didn't flush with embarrassment as many young ladies would, but instead giggled at her own mistake. Simon realised he hadn't met anyone in a long time who was completely and utterly living in the moment and, in that moment, happy.

As the music finished he bowed to his partner and then surprised himself by offering her his arm.

'Shall we get some air, Miss James?'

She looked up at him, cheeks flushed from the exertion, and nodded.

'That would be most welcome.'

Simon saw his sister-in-law's eyes on him as he escorted Miss James from the dance floor to the edge of the ballroom, stopping to pick up two glasses of punch on the way. The ballroom was hot now, with the press of bodies, and it was a relief to step outside into the cool air.

'I think Midsummer might be my new favourite time of year,' Miss James said as they chose a spot by the stone balustrade. She leaned on it, looking out at the garden and the night sky beyond.

'What has it displaced?' Simon asked.

'I do love Christmas. There is something rather magical about crackling wood on the fire whilst it snows outside and you are all snug inside. But I will never forget this wonderful Midsummer night.'

'Forgive me, Miss James, but have we met before?'

'No.'

'You seem very certain.'

She smiled at him. There was no guile in her expression, and he realised that she had no expectation from him. Most young women he was introduced to looked at him as something to be conquered. Their ultimate aim was to impress him so they might have a chance at becoming his countess. It was tiresome and meant he had started to avoid situations where he was likely to be pushed into small talk with unmarried young women. Miss James had no calculating aspect to her; she was not trying to impress him. It was refreshing to talk to someone and realise they wanted nothing from you.

'I think I would remember, my Lord.'

'You are from Northumberland?'

'Yes, my family live only a few miles away.'

'Then, our paths must have crossed at a ball or a dinner party, surely.'

He saw her eyes widen and a look of panic on her face. He wondered for a moment if she might try to flee, but instead she fiddled with her glass and then took a great gulp of punch.

'I have a little confession,' she said, leaning in closer so only he could hear her words. 'This is my first ball.'

'Your first?'

'Yes.'

He looked at her closer, wondering if he had been wrong in assessing her age. He'd placed her at around twenty or twenty-one. Young still, but certainly old enough to have been out in society for a good few years. It was hard to tell with the mask covering her eyes, but he did not think he had got his estimation wrong.

'I have been to dances,' she said quickly. 'Just not to any balls like this.'

'How can that be, Miss James?'

She bit her lip and flicked him a nervous glance.

'If I tell you, you might have me escorted out.'

It was his turn to smile.

'I doubt it, Miss James. Unless you tell me you sneaked in with the sole purpose to sabotage Lady Salisbury's ball or steal her silverware.'

Miss James pressed her lips together and then leaned in even closer, her shoulders almost touching his.

'You are half-right,' she said, her voice low so only he could hear.

'You plan to steal Lady Salisbury's silverware.'

She flicked him an amused glance. 'No, I am no criminal, but I did sneak in.' As soon as she said the words, she clapped her hands over her mouth in horror. 'I can't believe I just told you that. It was the one thing I was meant to keep secret tonight, and it is the first thing I tell you.'

Simon felt a swell of mirth rise up inside him, and he realised for the first time in a long time he was having fun. Fun had seemed a foreign concept these last few years. In a short space of time he had lost his brother, inherited a title he had never wanted and been forced to confront the issue of his own mortality. He'd been forced into making monumental decisions over the last few weeks, everything serious and fraught with emotion.

'You sneaked in?'

She nodded, eyes wide with horror.

'Are you going to tell anyone?'

'I am not sure yet,' he said, suppressing a smile of his own.

'Lydia is going to be furious,' Miss James murmured.

'There are two of you?'

She closed her eyes and shook her head. 'I need to stop talking.'

'Please don't, Miss James. This is the most fun I've had for months.'

'Now you're mocking me.'

'Not at all.'

'You're an earl. This cannot be the most fun you've had. Your life must be full of luxury and entertainment.'

'I find it is mainly full of accounts and responsibilities,' he said. 'That is unfair and very... I am well aware of the privileged life I lead. It is full of luxury and extravagance, as you say, but not fun.'

'That is sad,' Alice said, and she touched him on the hand. It was a fleeting contact, but it made his skin tingle, and he looked up quickly. There was no guile in her eyes, and he realised the furthest thing from her mind was seduction—whether because she had a young man she fancied herself in love with or because their backgrounds were so far apart she knew there could never be anything between them.

'It is sad,' he said quietly. 'So tonight I charge you with lifting this grumpy man's spirits.'

'And in exchange you will not expose my deception.'

'We have a deal. Tell me, Miss James, how did you manage to sneak in without one of the dozens of footmen seeing you?'

She motioned out at the garden beyond the terrace. Only the terrace was lit, the grass and the formal garden beyond in darkness.

'We crept through the garden.'

He glanced down and laughed. 'I can see there was a little mud.'

'I was terrified when we arrived that I might have foliage in my hair. We had to squeeze through a hedge to get into the right part of the garden.'

'That is commitment to your cause. What made you so keen to come here tonight?'

She sighed and looked out into the darkness.

'I doubt you know the feeling of helplessness, of not being in control of your own future,' she said with a hint of melancholy. She was wrong in her assumption, but now was not the time to correct her. 'Soon I will not be able to choose anything more thrilling than what curtains to hang or what to serve for dinner.'

'You are to be married.'

The expression on her face told him she was not happy about the prospect.

She straightened and turned to face him. 'I am to marry my second cousin, vile Cecil.'

'Vile Cecil?'

'It is an apt description of him.'

'I already feel sorry for you. What makes him so vile?'

Miss James exhaled, puffing out her cheeks in a way that made him smile. He didn't know her exact background, but by the way she spoke and held herself he would guess she was from a family of the minor gentry. Perhaps a landowner father or even a vicar. She knew how to conduct herself but hadn't been subject to the scrutiny many of the women of the *ton* had to endure, so the odd shrug of the shoulders or theatrical sigh hadn't been trained out of her.

'Where to start? Imagine you are a young lady,' she said, and he adopted his most serious expression.

'I am imagining.'

'Good. You are introduced to a distant relative about fifteen years older than you,' she said and held up a finger. 'The age gap is not an issue you must understand. I am aware women are of higher value to society when they are young and beautiful and men when they are older and richer.'

'I did not think you would be such a cynic, Miss James.' Simon was surprised to find he was enjoying himself immensely. There was something freeing talking to this woman who was a total stranger and had no expectations of him at all.

'Is it cynical to observe the truth?' She pushed on. 'This distant relative is unfortunate-looking, with a lazy eye, yellowed teeth and rapidly thinning hair that he arranges in a way he hopes will hide the fact he hasn't much left. But you have been raised to appreciate no one can help how they look so you push aside all thoughts of their physical appearance.'

Simon pressed his lips together. Miss James had an amusing way of telling a story, and he urged her to continue. 'I am channelling those very thoughts,' he said.

'Good. Then he reaches out and with a sweaty palm lays a hand on your shoulder. A fleeting touch you could forgive, but the hand lingers far too long, and all the while his eyes do not move from your chest.'

'He is not sounding very enticing.'

'Then throughout the evening he makes his horrible opinions known on everything from how the poor should be punished for the awful situations they find themselves in to slavery to how it is God's plan for the lower levels of society to be decimated by illness that spreads more when people live in close conditions.'

'I am beginning to see why he is vile.'

'And he does all this whilst trying to squeeze your knee under the table.'

'Your parents are happy for you to marry him?'

Miss James sighed. 'Last year my sister...' She bit her lip again, drawing his gaze for a moment. 'I probably shouldn't tell you this.' Then she shrugged and continued. 'Yet our paths are never going to cross again.'

'What if I add in the extra layer of security by swearing I will never breathe a word of this to anyone.'

'You are a man of your word?'

'I never break an oath.'

'Last year my sister was caught up in a bit of a scandal. Rumours of late-night liaisons with a married gentleman. For a month she and I were forbidden to leave the house, and my parents thought we might even have to leave Bamburgh and move elsewhere. Thankfully a friend of my father's stepped in and proposed marriage to my sister to save her and the rest of our family from scandal.'

'Did it work?'

'Yes, although there are still a few people who cross the street to avoid my mother and me if we are out shopping. My sister is happy as mistress of her own home, living down in Devon, and she has a baby on the way. All things for a short while we thought she might never have.'

'This has pushed your parents to make an unwise match for you?'

'I think they are panicked. They are aware the taint of scandal can linger for a long time, and they keep reminding me I am already one and twenty. There are no local unmarried young men of the right social class so they decided they would arrange the only match that was assured.'

'Could you not refuse?'

Miss James laughed, but there was no bitterness in her tone, just pure amusement.

'We live in very different worlds, my Lord. I have no money of my own, no income, no way of supporting myself. I cannot even boast of a very good education so I doubt anyone would employ me as a governess. My value comes in marrying someone who can support me and any future children and remove that burden from my parents.'

'Vile Cecil is wealthy?'

'Moderately so. Enough to satisfy my parents. He is eager to be married and comes tomorrow to stay to discuss our engagement.'

'He has not asked you yet?'

'No, but that part is a mere formality.' She closed her eyes. 'So you see, this is my one last chance to dance at a ball with whoever I choose, to get a little tipsy with punch and to take ill-advised strolls along the terrace with mysterious gentlemen.'

'Then, we must ensure you have the best night of your life.'